RETURN
TO THE
FIELD

RETURN
TO THE
FIELD

Alexander Fullerton

G.K. Hall & Co. • Chivers Press
Thorndike, Maine USA   Bath, England

This Large Print edition is published by G.K. Hall & Co., USA and by Chivers Press, England.

Published in 1998 in the U.S. by arrangement with John Johnson Limited.

Published in 1998 in the U.K. by arrangement with Little, Brown and Company.

U.S. Softcover   0-7838-0205-6 (Paperback Series Edition)
U.K. Hardcover   0-7540-1177-1 (Windsor Large Print)
U.K. Softcover   0-7540-2128-9 (Paragon Large Print)

The text of this Large Print edition is unabridged.
Other aspects of the book may vary from the original edition.

Set in 16 pt. Plantin by Juanita Macdonald.

Printed in the United States on permanent paper.

British Library Cataloguing in Publication Data available

Library of Congress Cataloging in Publication Data

Fullerton, Alexander, 1924–
     Return to the field / Alexander Fullerton.
          p.   cm.
     ISBN 0-7838-0205-6 (lg. print : sc. : alk. paper)
     1. World War, 1939–1945 — France — Fiction.   2. Large
type books. [1. France — History — German occupation,
1940–1945 — Fiction.]   I. Title.
[PR6056.U435R48   1998]
823′.914—dc21   98-18673

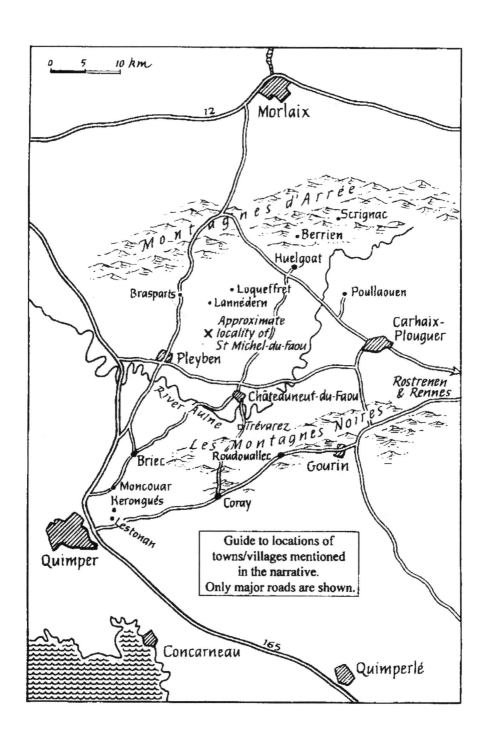

0   5   10 km

12

Morlaix

Montagnes d'Arrée

•Scrignac

•Berrien

Huelgoat

Brasparts•   •Luqueffret   •Poullaouen

•Lannédern

X Approximate
locality of)
St Michel-du-faou

La Pleyben

River Aulne

Châteauneuf-du-Faou

Carhaix-
Plouguer

Rostrenen
& Rennes

•Trévarez

Les Montagnes Noires

Briec   Roudouallec

Gourin

Moncouar
Keronguès•
•Lestonan   Coray

Quimper

Guide to locations of
towns/villages mentioned
in the narrative.
Only major roads are shown.

Concarneau   165

Quimperlé

Chapter 1

The black-painted Lysander loomed over her, blacker still against the moon and bigger-looking than she'd expected, or remembered from her training days. A plane with one cockpit for the pilot and another behind him for his passenger (or passengers; it would hold two easily enough, even three in emergencies) sounded small — and it was, comparatively speaking — but in this moonlight and from ground level it had a high and bulky look. High-winged, with massive-looking struts; big spats on its wheels, and painted bat-black to reduce visibility when on clandestine missions such as tonight's.

It was very cold. Grass still sodden, puddles on the tarmac. Smell of petrol. Marilyn put an arm around her shoulders, squeezed her: 'Have you back with us in two shakes, Rosie.'

'You bet.'

'Rosie.' Hands grasping her arms, and suddenly face to face: 'God, how *many* times one's said it —'

'With me, three now. Third time lucky *again*, huh?'

Same breathlessness, though. You said that sort of thing but still had the same queasy, tensed-up feeling. While the other thing she felt, in her

7

shapeless old coat and looking up at Marilyn's tall elegance, was shabby. It was by design, of course, the norm, befitting not only the general state of things where she was going — German-occupied France — but also the character she'd be playing. From the moment of take-off she'd cease to be Rosie Ewing, aged twenty-five, née Rosalie de Bosque — French father deceased, English mother still bitching away in Buckinghamshire — and become Suzanne Tanguy, former student nurse, French to the marrow of her bones. Pulling herself up the fixed aluminium ladder on this side — the machine's port side — and climbing in . . . The dampness on her cheek from that hug and kiss had come from Marilyn, for God's sake. A tear, or tears — first ever, and why *this* time? She was settling in, locating the safety harness as well as her luggage which they'd already put in — one tatty old suitcase on the shelf and the heavier but equally scruffy one down by her feet. She'd taken the pistol out of that one, transferred it to a pocket in her overcoat; it was a Llama, 9-millimetre, Spanish-made, with a Colt-type action. There were lots of them around in France, even in German hands, and 9-mm ammo was easy to come by. On her two previous missions she hadn't taken a gun at all, but last summer there'd been an agent code-named 'Romeo' with whom she'd gone out to a Lysander rendezvous in the vicinity of Rouen, the Boches had sprung a trap and there'd been a brief fire-fight in which 'Romeo' had been shot dead and she'd been taken prisoner. She'd resolved soon after that she'd be armed on any future deployment. There were pros and cons but on the whole she thought it was better to have the option.

Another innovation was that she was taking two cyanide capsules instead of only one, and had them in tiny pockets in the hem of the blouse she was wearing. Last time she'd sewn a single pocket into her bra. Marilyn, who'd brought the capsules down with her from London and handed them over half an hour ago in SOE's ivy-covered transit-house on this airfield, had understood the reasons for these changes, having read the transcripts of Rosie's de-briefing after her return last time. The de-briefing had been rigorous — had to be, of any agent who'd been in Gestapo hands and could have spilt beans that weren't for spilling. As she might well have done: another minute, and she'd have told the bastards anything they wanted to know.

One of the RAF ground-crew had come up the ladder to help her strap herself in, or to ensure she'd done so — which she had.

'All right, Miss?'

'Lovely, thanks.'

'Best of British, then. Take me 'at off to you, I'll tell you that. We all do.'

'Oh, go on with you. Thanks, anyway.'

He'd gone down, and seconds later the machine was moving, filling the night and her head with noise as it rolled forward. She saw Marilyn down there, as the plane's shadow left that group

— Marilyn with an arm raised in farewell, the other holding her fancy Wren hat on. The two behind her were the aircraftman who'd driven the Jeep and the WAAF girl who'd come out with them from the Cottage. Reek of high-octane stronger for a moment as the pilot turned across the wind. He'd assured her that although it was still 'on the breezy side' he'd do his best to give her a comfortable ride; he reckoned to be on the ground in France in one hour and forty minutes. The distance to their landing-field was 225 miles — 'as a strong crow might fly' — but he'd be detouring here and there to avoid 'flak-points' — meaning places where you'd be likely to be shot at. They'd be crossing the Channel at about 200 feet, to stay under the enemy's radar, but climbing to about 2000 to pass over the coast, somewhere to the east of Arromanches. When they were well inland, clear of flak-points and on course for their destination, he'd be coming down to treetop height.

He'd asked her, 'Done it before, have you?'

'Not this way.'

'Well. After this experience you'll never consider any *other* way.' They'd all laughed. Laughs came easily, at such times.

Only a few streamers of cloud up there now, fast-moving from the northwest. The course to the Angers district would be near-enough due south; the wind would help, she supposed. But he'd have taken that into account, obviously, and the answer to her lightning mental arithmetic was that she'd be on the ground by about one-thirty a.m. French time — Central European time, as they called it . . . The Lysander was slowing, almost stopping. On a very smooth runway now. Slewing round into the wind and the engine opening up again. What was that advice to the newly wedded virgin? Shut your eyes and think of England? Think of Ben, rather. Even though you were having to desert him now. Poor Ben . . . The machine was shaking and roaring like some creature in a fury, charging into a battering force of wind — with its tail up, already. Very short take-off and landing runs were a large part of the Lizzy's suitability for this kind of work, of course. Although landing strips had ideally to be 600 yards long and 400 wide, she remembered; she'd searched large areas of French countryside for such fields herself, in days gone by. *There,* now — off the ground even sooner than she'd expected, powering up with the moon's brightness somewhere behind her but already banking round while continuing to gain height. Suzanne Tanguy, on her way. Complete with a Mark III radio transceiver, half a million francs, the pistol, *two* suicide capsules, and a pounding heart . . . The money in fact wasn't for her own use, she'd be handing it over in Rennes to a courier from another *réseau. Réseau* meant network. While also in her pockets were — as well as a few Paris cinema and Métro tickets and some receipted bills — two crumpled, much-read letters, and a month-old clipping from a small-ads page in *Le*

Matin about a job for an assistant in a medical practice in Orange. Also a pack and a half-pack of Caporals, some French matches, and a lighter containing no fuel but with the initials D.M. engraved on it. D.M. for Daniel Miossec, to whom Suzanne Tanguy had allegedly been engaged and who'd been killed in an RAF attack on Brest a year ago. The job advertisement had been screwed up as if to throw away: you'd guess she might have applied for it and been turned down. The letters, of more recent dates, would be important as back-up proof of her identity and circumstances and of the job she *had* been offered. In fact she would have produced them in support of her application for the *Ausweis* entitling her to be travelling west from Paris. The *Ausweis* was in an envelope with her other papers, including food and clothing ration cards and a *Feuille Semestrelle* issued in Paris a couple of months earlier. It was the end of April now — April 1944, to be precise, April 26, a Wednesday — and what had begun to feel like spring seemed in the past few days to have relapsed into something more like winter.

Christ . . . Decidedly bouncy. Alternately dropping like something on a hangman's rope and bucketing up again. The thing was not to think about being sick: and to convince oneself it wasn't nearly as bad as it had been last time, when she'd landed from a motor gunboat in a little cockleshell of a dinghy, in black darkness and tumbling sea on a remote and rocky beach in Brittany. That *had* been worse, for sure.

Night air rushing — and damn cold. Moon-shine silver on the aircraft's metal skin. Thinking of Ben again, who'd been the navigator of that motor gunboat. Earlier this evening, on the way down from London to Tangmere, she'd dreamt about him. Partly she supposed out of this feeling that she was running out on him — the fact he didn't yet know she'd left, still had the bad news coming. But she'd dozed off in the big Humber and dreamt that her dead husband was trying to persuade her she'd been hallucinating, that it was Ben who'd been killed, not him. '*I'm* as fit as a flea, my lovely!' Johnny with his boyish good looks and chasing anything that wore skirts, and in that ghost-like evocation posturing slightly — well, typically — in his flying kit, the gear he'd been wearing when his Spitfire had plunged in flames into the Channel two and a half years ago. In the dream he'd clearly *wanted* Ben dead. Ben who was Australian and of whose existence he'd never known, on whom she herself had never set eyes until after Johnny had been killed — but with whom she'd have been spending this next week-end in London, only wouldn't now because she'd be back in France. While Ben was not only very much alive but should have every chance of re-maining so, thanks to having been wounded a few months ago, being consequently in a shore job now — at Portsmouth, where Rosie's flatmate would be ringing him tomorrow at lunchtime, telling him: 'Rosie asked me to give you her love and say please try not to worry but she can't make this weekend.' It was a form of words they'd agreed on; he'd know it meant she'd gone back into the field.

Hell. Bigger drop than ever. The sea's surface would be *less* than two hundred feet below the Lizzy, at this moment.

Good reason to direct one's thoughts elsewhere.

To her farewell briefing this morning, for instance, in the briefing flat in Portman Square. Such send-offs were normally conducted by 'F' Section's chief, Maurice Buckmaster, but he was away sick and a major by the name of Bob Hallowell had presided. Marilyn had come along with her, as she had on previous occasions. Hallowell routinely going over the details of Rosie's cover as Suzanne Tanguy and then touching on salient points in the rest of her written orders: she'd already committed them to memory, but he'd had a copy in a file resting on his knees. Comfortable armchairs, and coffee and biscuits on the table.

'What strikes me most forcibly, Rosie, is you're going to be very much on your own, with a hell of a lot to get done in what may be a very short space of time.'

Narrow brown eyes fixed on hers. Narrow, bony face, thinning hair. In his middle forties, she guessed, and probably not in the best of health. Asking her — in reference to a section he'd just skimmed — 'Another rather unusual thing — this stuff in Quimper's a rum business, isn't it?'

14

'The informer, you mean.'

'Given to us by our friends in St James'. One would hardly have expected such — generosity. Might they be getting some *quid pro quo?*'

By 'our friends in St James' ' he'd meant SIS, Secret Intelligence Service; who did not, in normal circumstances or in what passed for their right minds, cooperate much with SOE. SIS were gatherers of intelligence; their agents lay low, kept quiet, went to great efforts never to draw attention to themselves; whereas SOE organized weapons drops and sabotage operations, blew up railway lines and factories: in general, tended to queer SIS's pitch.

Rosie explained, 'I did a job for them, last time out. I think Colonel Buck may have twisted an arm or two, so — yes, you could call it a *quid pro quo.*'

'You must have rendered them sterling service.'

'I gather it's worked out quite well.'

'And *they* briefed you on this bit, I suppose . . .'

More a comment than a question. Turning the page, then stopping again. Frowning slightly, quoting: *'You will as soon as possible establish contact with local Maquis groups, through the good offices of Comte Jules de Seyssons . . .'* A slow nodding, then, as he scanned the next paragraph. 'Monsieur le Comte's to be our banker, I see. Useful fellow.'

'He's the king-pin,' she'd agreed. 'But you'll see other Maquis contacts mentioned too — Guy

Lannuzel at Châteauneuf-du-Faou, and a man called Jaillon further north. Village called Guerlesquin? My priority'll be to liaise with them and get some drops organized as soon as possible.'

'Drops' meaning parachute-drops of weaponry. Hallowell nodding . . . 'Drops to which we'll be giving priority. Yes. Then operation "Mincemeat". Then —'

'More drops, according to requirements, and training and planning for the Great Day.' Meaning, for action in support of the invasion. Which had to come some time this summer, surely. Spring, or summer. Some time between next week and the end of August, say. This was what Hallowell had meant about getting a lot done quickly — realization having only just dawned that the Maquis and the Resistance generally in that part of Brittany weren't anything like ready. Finistère wasn't Section 'F' territory — or *hadn't* been, until now.

'After "Mincemeat", the joint'll be fairly jumping, won't it.' Murmuring half to himself again as his eye ran down the headings and paras. Turning another page. 'Going over this as much as anything for my own info, Rosie. But you *are* going to have your work cut out, aren't you, one way and another. Single-handed — organizer, courier and pianist —'

'And District Nurse.' She added, 'I can now insert a very swift suppository, I'd have you know!'

She'd done five days' work in a Free French

hospital ward, French-staffed, at Camberley. Marilyn had giggled, Hallowell looked puzzled; she guessed he didn't know what a suppository was. Commenting as he shut the file, 'Cover's excellent, anyhow.' Then: 'Change of subject, Rosie. Do you have any qualms in your mind about "Hector"?'

She'd hesitated. Her immediate reaction was that 'Hector' should be head office's business, not hers. Except for maybe sixty seconds face to face on a remote landing-field in the small hours of the morning, she wasn't expecting to have anything to do with him.

She temporized: 'Should I have?'

Decisive shake of the narrow, balding head.

'No. We're simply — primarily — going through the motions. In pulling him out for debriefing, I mean. Also to scotch these rumours and uncertainties. For your private information — yours too, Marilyn, and in strict confidence — the source of the allegations against him is *highly* unreliable. To be precise, we happen to know the motive's nothing more than sexual jealousy. A Frenchman whom "Hector" himself recruited and whose girlfriend has recently — er — transferred her affections. To "Hector", d'you see. Unfortunately. One doesn't applaud or admire him for it — in fact he's been a damn fool, and he's in line to be told so in no uncertain terms. But that's effectively all there is against him, and he happens to have been doing a first-class job for a heck of a long time. Eh?'

Looking from Rosie to Marilyn, Marilyn gazing back at him with perhaps faint surprise, nothing more. Back to Rosie, then. All three well aware that sexual involvement by SOE agents with local French had always been unequivocally discouraged — for reasons that hardly needed spelling out, but 'Hector' 's present situation was a good example. Hallowell had shrugged. 'Always did have a bit of a roving eye. Doesn't make him a traitor, does it.'

'Is he an Englishman, or —'

'French father, Scottish mother. Educated mostly in Scotland. He was a flyer before he joined us. Right at the start — joined us, I mean — 1940. He'd crashed a light aircraft — after becoming an instructor of some kind. About 1939 — Civil Air Guard, wasn't it? Papa was pressuring him to join the family firm — engineering business, somewhere south of Paris. But he was having too good a time over here. Post-Varsity, this was. Anyway — did his back in, in the crash, couldn't ever have parachuted thereafter, and we nearly turned him down. But in other respects he was tailor-made . . .'

Why tell one all *that,* she wondered. All she'd asked about was his parental background — which as it happened was similar to her own. Except that her mother was English, not Scots. Rosie had been born in Nice, nearly 26 years ago; she'd been twelve when her father had died and her mother had brought her to England. As for 'Hector', though, all that mattered to her was that he'd be at the landing-field near Soucelles to-night. Herself disembarking, 'Hector' taking her place for the return trip. As always, the change-over would be made as fast as possible: ideally the Lysander wouldn't be on the ground for more than four minutes. Confirmation that the plane was coming had gone out this evening in the BBC's programme of *Message Personnels* — twice, in the 1700 and 2100 broadcasts — in the form of a statement to the effect that Bertrand had now left hospital. 'Hector' himself had set up the rendezvous, of course, with that code-phrase attached to it, as he'd done for arrivals and departures dozens of times before, picking the field and organizing the reception. He was to have rail tickets for her, return halves of those he'd have used himself in getting there, saving her from having to identify herself at the *guichet* at the small local station, Tiercé. From there she'd be travelling to Angers, thence to Le Mans where there'd be an item for her to pick up from the *consigne;* he'd be bringing her the ticket for that too. In fact she'd be going further west than Rennes — after making contact with this other *réseau*'s courier and handing over the half-million francs — but that was none of 'Hector' 's business.

Just as well. She wasn't happy with him knowing she'd be going as far as Rennes, even. Even if he'd been not 'Hector' but the Angel Gabriel she wouldn't have been happy with it. As a matter of principle, as much as anything, there was no damn reason he or anyone else *should* know. In

19

fact he probably was as sound as Hallowell said he was: but the allegations flying around head office were that the Gestapo knew all about him, who and what he was and his address in Paris — so how come he was still at large? — and also that amongst the many recent infiltrations of *réseaux* and arrests of agents, a significantly high proportion of those involved had flown into receptions which 'Hector' had organized. The implication was that they'd have been tailed to their ultimate destinations and used as stalking-horses to identify those with whom they then established contact.

It was possible, too. But as SOE's Air Movements Officer, 'Hector' must have arranged the reception of perhaps three-quarters of all incoming agents, so a high proportion of those subsequently arrested *would* have passed through his hands; he couldn't necessarily be held responsible for everything that happened to them afterwards. And another point in his favour was that he'd accepted the invitation to come back for de-briefing: it suggested a clear conscience. While in terms of her own present situation — this flight, and its reception having been set up by him — well, incoming agents had on some known occasions been met by reception committees of heavily armed Germans. When there'd been treachery by an informer, or radio interception, or — the most common thing — the radio ostensibly operated by an SOE 'pianist' but actually by a Boche impersonating that pianist. The 'radio game' or *funkspiel* had been played all too often, and many deaths had resulted. But this time, she thought, she was probably as safe as houses. If 'Hector' had been turned and was working for the enemy, his motive in accepting Baker Street's invitation would be to clear SOE minds of suspicion — so he could go back into the field and carry on — and/or to apprise himself of current operations or intentions. The last thing he'd want to do would be to foul his wicket tonight. For instance, she had an 'arrived safely' signal to transmit once she was clear and on her way; he'd know that, and he'd want her to send it.

The plane had its nose up, climbing. French coast ahead. Her own country: in a real sense, this *was* a home-coming. And she *was* Suzanne Tanguy, *had* been engaged to Daniel Miossec, and a young naval engineer of that name *had* been killed in a raid on Brest last year. Actually he'd been the fiancé of a daughter of a friend of Léonie de Mauvernay, who'd been an actress and was supposed to have been an even closer friend of Suzanne Tanguy's late mother. That old friendship accounted well enough for her having had Suzanne to live with her in her elegant small house close to the Bois de Vincennes, in Paris, after Daniel's death and her own nervous collapse, and then a few weeks ago writing to another, *very* special friend, Count Jules de Seyssons, telling him of Suzanne's misfortune and unhappiness and wondering whether he could suggest any place and manner in which a young

21

woman of her intelligence and nurse's training might find employment in country air, peace and quiet. It had been an obvious hint that Count Jules might take her on, at his Manoir de Scrignac on the edge of the Montagnes d'Arrées, where he bred racehorses. He had an invalid wife, so it might have seemed an appropriate billet for Mlle Tanguy with her albeit somewhat limited nursing skills. As it had turned out, he'd seen no way of fitting her into his own establishment, but he'd gone out of his way to persuade his doctor, Henri Peucat at St Michel-du-Faou, that *he* needed a general assistant in his practice. Peucat, a widower in his sixties and single-handed in a practice covering a wide area, apparently hadn't taken much persuading. The letters 'Suzanne' was carrying were one to Léonie de Mauvernay from the count, and one from Dr Peucat to herself, sent care of Mme de Mauvernay, offering her the job.

It had all been set up from scratch by Count Jules. The ball had started rolling when through a chain of Resistance contacts he'd got in touch with an SOE *réseau* in Nantes, whose organizer then met him somewhere or other where they'd discussed the possibility of having an 'F' Section agent assigned to his part of Finistère. The count had suggested that if the agent were female and could represent herself as having had medical or quasi-medical experience he'd provide her with a cover story that would be difficult to fault. After some hours of discussion, concentrating mainly on the objectives — and the count's motives in

22

putting such a plan forward in the first place — there'd been an exchange of signals with SOE in Baker Street, and a few days later they'd agreed to go along with it. Primarily because there was a good practical reason to — the need to have the Maquis armed, and quickly — but also because they had a suitable agent — Rosie — immediately available. There were complications within SOE involving Section 'RF' — which had been set up mainly to propitiate Charles de Gaulle in regard to British influence over French secret armies; 'RF' employed only French nationals as agents, and was supposed to have those western tracts of Brittany to itself. Objections must have been overcome; the count, éminence grise of local Resistance groups, therefore a key figure in de Gaulle's efforts to coordinate nationwide resistance under the banner of the newly created FFI — *Forces Francaises de l'Interieure* — wanted immediate action and was in a position to demand it. Then as soon as it was confirmed that an SOE girl agent was virtually ready for take-off he paid a business visit to Paris — racehorse business, which took him there quite frequently — visited Léonie de Mauvernay and dictated to her the letter she was to write to him, seeking a job in the country for her little protégé. It was she, Léonie de M., who had suggested the business of the fiancé who'd been killed in Brest, in fact borrowing the memory of the late Daniel Miossec from her friend's daughter. A nice embellishment had been Baker Street's idea of having a battered old lighter engraved with Miossec's initials.

Detail was enormously important. And a tangible object such as the lighter could be worth hours of hard and skilful lying.

The opening paragraph of Rosie's memorized orders read: *You will return to the field by Lysander from Tangmere to the vicinity of Soucelles in the Angers district, and will then go by train to Carhaix-Plouguer via Le Mans and Rennes. Rail tickets for those stages of your journey will be supplied to you by the returning agent 'Hector', who will also give you a consigne ticket to be exchanged at Le Mans for a parcel labelled MEDICAL EQUIPMENT — HANDLE WITH CARE, containing an 'S' phone for your own use.*

Consigne was what in England would be known as the Left Luggage office. The parcel would have been left there by 'Hector', presumably. An 'S' phone was a type of radio-telephone enabling an operator on the ground to talk to a low-flying aircraft overhead; it had obvious uses in connection with para-drops. She guessed this one would originally have been destined for use in some other *réseau*, probably one of those recently blown and closed down.

Of which there'd been a frighteningly large number, of late. Infiltrations of *réseaux* by informers — including French Gestapo agents — and arrests, disappearances. 'Hector' came to mind again: that question-mark against *his* name. But discoveries of arms caches, too; this partly ac-

24

counted for the current shortfall in weaponry available to the Resistance in Finistére, although another factor as far as the Maquis were concerned was the rapid increase in their own numbers: escapers from or evaders of forced labour in Germany, escaped POWs and hostages, *Résistants* on the run — and so on. Recruits were flooding in, encouraged by Allied successes in Italy, Russian victories in the East and rumours of imminent invasion. But the Maquis weren't much use sitting up there in the forests if they didn't have weapons in their hands, and know how to use them.

Rosie didn't like the Le Mans parcel business — having to show up and identify herself by producing the *consigne* receipt. She'd made the point at an earlier briefing session, but it had been set up by then and they hadn't wanted to change it. Might not have been able to, at short notice. 'Hector' might not have been contactable by then. Why couldn't he have left it at Rennes, she wondered?

Unless — seeing this suddenly — he wouldn't be coming from the Rennes direction?

She'd taken it for granted that he would be, because of the ticket business; but some other agent might be coming from there — a courier of his, for instance — meeting him at Le Mans, where he himself might be getting off the Paris express. Paris was his base, after all. It made more sense: his colleague giving him the return halves of the Rennes–Le Mans tickets, and 'Hector' bringing the 'S' phone from Paris, depositing it in the *consigne*. He obviously wouldn't want to take it all the way down to Tiercé.

The Lizzy had been flying straight and level for some time, she realized. France, down there. They'd have left Caen behind — off to the left. The pilot would be identifying rivers, lakes and forests: rivers and lakes silver, forests black. None of it would have meant anything to her even if she'd been able to look over — in the process getting her head blown off in the rush of bitingly cold air.

'Hector' might be OK, anyway.

Please God. As Air Movements Officer, with the detailed knowledge of *réseaux* and individual agents that he'd have amassed by this time — well, Hallowell must be absolutely certain that he was right, she thought. There'd be a *hell* of a lot at stake.

Next para then, as memorized:

At Rennes you will contact Elise Krilov ('Giselle') at or through the Café Trianon, deliver to her the parcel of 500,000 francs and request that she *acknowledge receipt in her next transmission.*

From Angers to Le Mans was about 95 kilometres, then to Rennes about 150. With two suitcases and the parcel, which she'd leave — parcel and one case — in the Rennes *consigne*. Better than hauling it all around the town, when there was every chance of being stopped and searched. The Café Trianon would doubtless be a cut-out, through which a message could be passed by telephone and 'Giselle' could then call back if she felt safe in doing so. All Rosie knew of her was that she was a courier and radio operator — as Rosie was too, in SOE and Resistance terminology a pianist — in a *réseau* rather macabrely codenamed 'Mortician', operating south and southeast of Rennes, which was on the dividing line between 'F' Section's territory and 'RF''s. The boundary ran north from Rennes to Mont St Michel on the coast.

The Lysander was losing height. Coming down to what the pilot had called treetop height, she supposed. Slightly *above* the treetops, one might hope . . .

Half an hour to go?

Visualizing the map, she guessed they'd pass about midway between Le Mans and Laval. The river Mayenne ran through Laval, and the Sarthe through Le Mans. Fifty kilometres apart, say. And halfway between them, flying south you'd be near enough on course for Angers, with the Soucelles field a dozen or fifteen miles on this northern side of it. And the Sarthe and the Mayenne converged there. She guessed that 'Hector' with his own flying experience might have picked a landing-ground in that locality primarily because incoming pilots would have the two rivers to lead them in.

Still losing height: and bumpily now, at that. Hadn't done this for a while, but the air-sickness was quick to make itself felt again. Steeling herself: mind over matter . . . Those rivers *would* be the answer — together with the further point that if he overflew the Soucelles area he'd soon find himself over the Loire — which he'd have to be blind not to see, especially with this moon on it.

End of *that* diversionary thought. Try another: why would a man like 'Hector' turn traitor?

It wouldn't be like breaking down under torture. She understood better than most how *that* could happen. How at a certain stage the pain took over — unless you were lucky enough to faint — to the extent that there was no thought left in your head other than to put an end to it by giving them whatever they wanted. But to go over to working for them was something else: you might agree to, in the course of being tortured, but then to go through with it, carry on doing it — that was very *much* something else.

Sending other agents to their deaths, for instance.

You'd use the cyanide, she thought. If you still had it and could get at it.

They usually offered money, to start with. And freedom, sometimes — or at least an ordinary prison instead of a concentration camp. In other words, a hope of staying alive. And of course cessation of pain and the fear of it, if there'd been torture. They also tried to convince you that you'd be joining the winning side. That was the motivation of many of the French who'd gone over to them.

She felt the plane tilt. Starboard wing lifting: altering course to the left. If he'd sighted the field, it had come sooner than she'd expected. Turning, banking with the port wing down, she was allowed a brief sight of moonlight reflected from some mirror-like surface — a lake, she guessed, or a widening of the river. Flooding, possibly. Gone now, lost, as the machine settled on this changed course: wings level, mercifully steady again, and the engine-note falling. Losing speed, that would mean, therefore height too, probably: she could feel it now, losing height quite fast. Could hardly have been at treetop level, after all . . . It would have been nice to have had some kind of intercom so the pilot could tell one what was happening, but these Special Duties Lysanders had no equipment that could be done without — no guns, armour or radio, for instance, all unnecessary weight removed in order to maximize speed and range.

Tilting left again. A long, seemingly endless turn. Circling?

Could mean he'd spotted the field. Or he reckoned he was close to it, and searching. Normal procedure when they did find it was to fly over it once, see the recognition signal which one of the reception team would be flashing from the apex of a narrow triangle of lights, the up-wind end of the proposed landing run, and if it was the correct signal, circle and come in again.

Imagining the reception party down there — somewhere — hearing the engine-noise and watching the sky. Remembering that time when the pick-up had been for 'Romeo'. There'd been a replacement for him coming in the same round-trip, so from the pilot's point of view it would have been the same as this — one body in, one out.

The machine had steadied for about half a minute, was now circling left again. Beginning to look bad, she thought. Can't find it: or the reception party's run into trouble. Must think he's over the landing-field or close to it: looking for a torch flashing the recognition letters at him. The letters that other time, she remembered, had been AK, and she'd done the flashing herself: the *Résistant* running the show had asked her to, since dotting and dashing was her special skill.

Christ. *Still* frigging around. Circling *right*-handed now; and the prospect in her mind of having to return to Tangmere. As much as was left of the night there in the Cottage, then a car back up to London — and hang around waiting for the next attempt.

Imagining the surprise in Ben's voice when he heard hers, though, over the telephone. That would be the *good* bit. With the weekend *on* again. He'd have been coming up to London anyway on Friday, for some interview or other — some news he'd said he'd have for her . . .

The pilot had throttled back. So — forget all that, *no* return . . . Flaps down, she guessed: feeling the machine dropping under her, and the cutting of power, louder roar of wind. Bracing herself for impact: and her right hand groping for the pistol, to be sure she could get at it quickly if she needed. In fact there was very little impact: a bit of a thump, then a bounce and a longish-seeming interval before the second jolt and then the drumming of the wheels. A reddish light flashed by on the starboard side; there'd have been one this side as well. The pilot was braking, slewing off-track and correcting again, mud and stuff flying and the rush of night scenery slowing very suddenly, then the machine juddering and slithering to a halt. Moonlit pasture all around, with a blackness of trees beyond it. She ducked for the case she'd had her feet on: to be ready to pass one case down, if there was anyone to pass it to. Otherwise throw it — the one with only clothes in it. There *was* a figure down there now, though: and another trotting up behind him. She called in French — nothing but French from this point on — 'Catch this?' and tossed the case down. Looking beyond them and all around: still only these two. No — a third, coming more slowly. Bent, and hobbling. She'd taken her hand off the pistol, heard the pilot shout, 'Out, please!' He was leaning round and over from his cockpit. 'Sorry took so long. Tell him he needs a new battery in his torch!' She was climbing down the fixed ladder, one-handed because of this other, heavier case. Turning then, to face a shortish, muscular-looking character who already had the case she'd thrown to him and was reaching for this one too, but she hung on to it. A shout from the pilot then: 'Passenger in *quick*, please!'

'Hector?'

31

'No.' A gruff voice: farmer, she guessed. Shouting up at the pilot in countrified French, 'No sight or sound. Better scram — eh?'

Rosie grasped a thick arm: 'Hector not here?'

'I said — *no* —'

'Don't know why or —'

'Nothing!'

Stubbled face by moonlight, wool hat pulled low enough to cover the tops of his ears: from the tone of voice one imagined his expression as indignant, as if he felt she was blaming him for 'Hector' 's absence. She turned back to the Lizzy, called up, 'No return passenger — hasn't shown up!'

'Sod *him*, then . . .'

He'd taxi back to about the point where he'd landed, so as to take off this way into the wind, over their heads. Moonlight flashed on his goggles as he leant over: 'Tell 'em stand clear, will you?'

A wave: she returned it. Throttle opening then, drowning her voice. Not that it mattered, the old man and the other one had seen the desirability of moving. Rosie meanwhile adjusting to the fact — as the noise built up again, marooning her in her own thoughts — that the circumstances were already entirely different from those which had been envisaged. No 'Hector', so no train tickets. Which on reflection — a few seconds, no more — mightn't be such a bad thing either. She hadn't really liked the train tickets dodge any more than she had the business of the parcel. And here and now what did make immediate and good sense

— as had been urged on the pilot a minute ago by this thickset character who, as the Lizzy came racketing towards them with its tail up, was yelling in the ear of his younger helper to see old Gaston got home safely — was to get the hell out, and quick.

Not by train, though. Not picking up any damn parcels, either.

Chapter 2

Dawn was in the sky behind her; the moon had gone down half an hour ago. The lanes were a mass of flooded potholes and the bicycle with her two suitcases on it was top-heavy, and had taken a bit of getting used to. She had the hang of it now, well enough. She had the lighter case in front of her, jammed on end into the pannier, and the one containing the Mark III transceiver and her pistol and the wad of cash was roped to the carrier behind. She hoped that if she was stopped during the day by patrols or at roadblocks they'd content themselves with a look into this easily accessible one, not make her struggle with the knots on the other. It might depend, of course, on whether or not it was a routine inspection — how hard they might be looking for a girl on a bike heading towards Rennes — which in turn might depend on the answers to various questions about 'Hector'. On the other hand they might only be in search of black-market produce — a duck or a pound of butter.

Jeannot — the man in the woollen hat — had transferred the pannier — *panier*, in French — from his wife's bicycle. She'd have paid them for it if she could have done so without giving away her own intentions, but as far as they knew it was only on loan to her, to be recovered with the bicycle itself in a few hours' time. Embarrassing, rather; they weren't well off, and effectively she was robbing them. It was to get the pannier that she'd gone with him to the house; he'd stashed this bike near the landing-field earlier in the day, so that she could have gone directly to the station. Mightn't have been such a good idea, she thought, looking back on it. All right in summer, to have killed a couple of hours snoozing in a ditch, but it would have been a dangerously long time to have had to hang around on a small country station. The bike had been provided by 'Hector' at some time in the past and had been used by other incoming agents who'd left it at the station for Jeannot or his wife to pick up later; and they were under the impression now that Rosie — or rather 'Zoé', as they knew her — was following the same procedure.

'Zoe' in English, but now in the French 'Zoé', with accent.

Jeannot had told her, 'First train that stops will be the milk train. Likely you'll be the only one boarding. But nobody'll fuss you.' Glancing at his wife — gypsy-dark and broomstick-thin . . . 'Nobody'd ever think she wasn't French — eh?'

'No, they would not. In fact —'

'I *am* French. You could call me Zoé, by the way.'

'Ah. Well . . .'

'A stranger in a place where you all know each other, though?'

35

'You'll need to see the station-master, to leave the bike with him. Mention my name — you're a friend, that's *it*.'

'Might there be Boches around?'

'Not at this hour.' A shrug. 'Not unless — you know, a flap on, or —'

'Right.'

Who was to say there *wouldn't* be a flap on?

Madame — Jeannot's wife, Rosie didn't know their surname and didn't need to — had given her a mug of coffee that was *ersatz* but better than most — ground barley, she'd guessed — and a hunk of bread with cheese. Another debt: but she'd insisted they could spare it. Adding then, '*He*'d have tucked in. Obviously won't come now — no point. But he'd expect us to take care of you.'

'Might need to take care of himself!'

Jeannot had mumbled it, his cheeks bulging. Rosie had asked him what he meant, and he'd shrugged, 'Could've run into trouble.' His wife had crossed herself. By 'trouble' he'd have been thinking of arrest, of course. They could have had no reason to suspect treachery, wouldn't have been doing this now if they'd had even a sniff of it. To Rosie they seemed extraordinarily matter-of-fact about it all. Their house was a *bar-restaurant-tabac;* they lived over the shop, and a former kitchen at the back was let as a workshop to someone who made and mended wheels for farm-carts. The restaurant part of the business specialized in rabbit stew, game pie and so forth;

Jeannot was a poacher and well known for miles around — not least to the local police, who turned blind eyes, had a free meal now and then, and if he'd been found prowling around in the middle of the night wouldn't have suspected him of anything other than snaring a few rabbits.

She was glad to have had the food and the warming drink. There were several things she needed to resolve, but the one clear essential was to get out of this district, *well* out, and preferably all the way to Rennes in time to contact 'Giselle' before curfew. She could have decided to take it more slowly and spend a night on the way — finding lodgings in one of the villages she'd be passing through, or sleeping rough, but nights in lodgings or hotels involved certain risks and it wasn't the best time of year for camping-out.

The distance was about a hundred and twenty kilometres. On the face of it, a marathon; but she'd done as much before, and recent bouts of pre-deployment training had left her fit enough. The weather didn't look like making it any easier, but at least she wouldn't bake inside her heavy clothes as she had last summer when she'd covered similar distances in the Rouen area.

Seventy-five miles — in about fifteen hours, say. Averaging 5 mph, therefore. Shouldn't be too bad, if she wasn't stopped at too many road-blocks. Touching wood — the table — while studying Jeannot's maps, a local one showing the narrow lanes between here and Tiercé and another that covered half Brittany, including the whole of her route to Rennes. She'd let them think it was the railway that interested her — the route she'd been supposed to have taken, south to Angers and then up to Le Mans, and west.

'There.' She'd put her finger on the map north-east of Rennes. '*There's* Fougères. Must be — what, fifty kilometres, from Rennes?'

'About that. No more, I'd guess.'

Jeannot had muttered, 'Not a bad little town, Fougères.'

Let not the right hand know . . .

Not even people like these. Exceptionally courageous people. In a population where most kept their heads down, wanting only to get by, and thousands worked actively for the Germans, *Résistants* like these formed a very small, outstandingly brave minority. But information could be wrung out of the bravest of the brave — out of Jeannot, for instance, while they held a knife to his wife's throat. Or vice versa. Here and now, they knew very well the risks they ran, and the penalties . . . About this night's events, meanwhile, all they could tell Rosie — Zoé, they'd called her once or twice — was that earlier in the evening they'd heard the BBC message they'd been waiting for, about Bertrand leaving hospital — 'Hector' having alerted Jeannot to it a week ago, at the same time giving him the recognition letters which he'd also been passing to London. He'd made a habit of this, apparently, since an earlier occasion when he'd only just made it to the landing-field, arriving on foot across country after the *gazo* in which he'd been travelling had run out of fuel. He'd almost killed himself getting there, and since then had made sure receptions could go ahead without him if they had to.

'If he'd had to go elsewhere — or run into trouble of some kind . . .'

'If he *had* — you'd expect to hear of it?'

'We'd hope to.' A nod. 'No guarantee we would, but —'

'And you'd clear out, at once?'

'Well, that's a problem.' He'd shrugged. 'The way we live — our life's here, nowhere else. All right, *I* could sneak off and join the Maquis, but whether this one here'd stand the rough living —'

'I'd make as good a Maquisarde as any of them!'

A shrug: 'Might have to. Not the first time we've discussed it, believe me. There's no easy answer though. Well — we'd hang on, that's the long and short of it. Trusting "Hector" to keep his trap shut.' Staring at his wife, wanting her agreement: she'd nodded, and told Rosie, 'He's a good man. If anyone could, *he* would.'

Meaning 'Hector' wouldn't crack under torture. And maybe she was right. She *and* Bob Hallowell.

It would have been pointless to have warned them, anyway. When there was nothing positive to say, nothing one *knew*. And Jeannot had just told her they'd sit tight anyway.

She'd checked the time, and he'd seen her doing it, pushed himself up from his chair. 'Yes —

39

want to be on your way, don't you?' Cramming in a last mouthful . . . 'You'll find the way, eh? Don't want me to come along?'

'I'll find it. Thank you very much. And I'll leave the bike in the care of the station-master.'

'Tell him it's my wife's. Hélène's, tell him.'

'You've both been very kind.' Shaking hands. 'Hélène . . .'

'Adieu, Zoé.'

Getting light — after a fashion. The village she was about to enter was called Champigné. Entering it as she was from the south she'd turn left at the crossroads presently, on to the road for a village called Lion d'Angers, about twelve kilometres away. Judging by Jeannot's map it ought to be a better road.

Women and girls on bicycles were commonplace on the French roads. With virtually all the men between eighteen and fifty away in POW camps or labour camps or munitions factories in Germany, women by and large had to fend for themselves and for their families — part of which meant foraging, cycling long distances sometimes to visit farms or black-market sources where this or that commodity might be obtainable. Families couldn't live on only the official rations. And in any case, with no petrol available, and only doctors and other special categories entitled to permits to own or drive *gazogénes* — cars, vans and lorries converted to run on either charcoal or bottled gas — bicycles were for most people the only way to get around. To and from work, for instance: even this early there'd be some on the roads.

Only the suitcases, Rosie thought, might make her conspicuous. But it was a reasonable hope that if they were looking for her at all they'd reckon on her travelling by rail. Might even have decided to stake out the Le Mans *consigne* — if they thought any agent in her or his right mind would walk into such a potential trap: let alone try to collect a parcel for which he/she didn't have the ticket . . . Other points were that 'Hector' shouldn't have been given her code-name — thus knowing it was a female agent arriving — and would surely never guess that a Section 'F' agent would be going anywhere west of Rennes.

Hence the idea of drawing Jeannot's and Hélène's attention to Fougères. The place-name had caught her eye on the map, that was all. But she did have a few things going for her, she thought. She might actually be in very little danger at all, on this journey. Apart from sheer bad luck — catching the wrong eye, looking scared, getting into some kind of accident . . . She was in Champigné now. In half-light: a cobbled street, old houses in need of repair. A few pedestrians, well wrapped up, an old woman who'd just emerged — standing there somehow blindly — might *be* blind, that was a light-coloured stick — but there were no other cyclists in sight at this moment.

A German truck — the sort they moved troops around in.

Pedalling on towards it. Accepting it as a familiar sight: nothing unusual or very interesting about it, to Suzanne Tanguy. Although the sight of it had shocked her — for a second. First sight of the enemy always did. It was facing this way; with some *Wehrmacht* unit's insignia on its wide front mudguards. And there were two other cyclists there now — coming this way, had been out of sight beyond the truck but were angling out to get around it. It was on this side of the crossroads — on its own right-hand side of the street, her left as she approached it — and there were two soldiers in the front, the driver in what looked like a forage-cap and the other in a helmet. Whether or not there were others in the canvas-hooded rear she'd only know by looking back after passing it. Which she would not do. She didn't even glance at the two in the front as she pedalled past on her own side of the road; just a few yards beyond it she had that left turn to make — and a *gazo* was overtaking her, simultaneously a heavyweight female cyclist coming wobbling out of the side road with an arm extended . . .

The *gazo* passed, Fatso wobbled out around the truck, and Rosie glanced back before she made her turn. OK . . .

And so much for Champigné. The next significant landmark would be about ten kilometres ahead: the rather strikingly named Le Lion d'Angers. She'd turn right there. Before it — about halfway — there'd be a turning to the left which she remembered from Jeannot's map

42

would lead back southward in the Tiercé and Angers direction.

She was sorry she'd had to deceive them about the pannier. The bicycle too, really. But the pannier had been Hélène's personal property; this bike, having been provided by 'Hector', was really SOE's.

Might send them a hundred francs, she thought. Anonymously — conscience money. Addressed to 'Hélène' in care of the *chef de gare* at Tiercé.

Might not, though. There'd be a post-mark on it, and the fewer clues one left, the better.

The right turn at this place — Le Lion d'Angers — wouldn't be at the first intersection, which was a right-angled turn on to the main road to the north, but a right fork just past that, on to another minor road. If there was a sign, it should be marked Segré.

No rain yet. Grey, fast-moving cloud from the north though, which might well be bringing some. It didn't feel as if there could be snow about, was definitely less cold than it had been in England.

Oh, Christ . . .

Road-block. She could see two lorries waiting, parked nose to tail, and a big *gazo* van half across the intersection with its rear doors open and a search in progress. Uniformed French police were doing the searching, but there was a *Wehrmacht* truck parked on the verge at the corner and *Feldgendarmerie* standing around nursing Schmeissers. There was also a small saloon car parked on the other side, with a tall man in civilian clothes leaning with his back against it, smoking a cigarette.

She slowed, and dismounted. Keeping the bike upright so that the weight of the case on the pillion wouldn't become obvious and excite curiosity. Rehearsing quickly, mentally: Suzanne Tanguy. Papers? Yes — here. The diversion story; *en route* from Paris, certainly, but also taking the opportunity of visiting my sister . . . Yes, the *Ausweis* was issued when I'd intended coming by train, but then when I saw the cost of it, for heaven's sake . . .

'*You!* Going which way?'

Pointing at her: a Frenchman, in plain clothes — wide-brimmed felt hat, grey raincoat. He'd strolled into the centre of the crossroads. Probably a colleague of the one beside the car. Similar type and clothing. Answering his question, she pointed too — towards that right fork beyond the main road intersection — and called as if she wasn't absolutely certain, 'Segré?'

'All right.' He beckoned to her to go on over. 'Come on.'

They'd be checking for black-market stuff, she guessed, wholesale quantities being trucked up that road to Laval and wherever else. Crossing the main road she glanced only briefly at the Frenchman, who was still watching her. French Gestapo, very likely: he had that look, and one had heard that in recent months a lot more had

44

been recruited. Many of them had criminal records: that had been the case right from the beginning. The very worst of them were Henri Lafont's lot, who operated out of 93 Rue Lauriston in Paris where they had torture chambers and Lafont had a steel-lined office for his own protection. But this one might not belong to Rue Lauriston; Lafont and his partner Pierre Bonny, a crooked former Paris cop, mainly targeted communists and *Résistants,* not black-marketeers, probably wouldn't waste their time on jobs like this one. Whatever it was . . . She was walking her bike across the road, having to pass within a few feet of the man in the hat, mounting carefully then when she got to the other side, aware of the bike's top-heaviness again as she did so. About half the weight in the case on the pillion was the transceiver's battery; the set itself weighed only about four and a half kilos. It was useless without a battery, of course — until or unless one had access to a main power supply. She was still half-ready for the shock of a shout recalling her: if he'd changed his mind, decided she *should* be searched. No shout came, though: by now he'd have forgotten her. She was conscious of feeling a bit self-satisfied as she rode on; having walked past him at a range of less than two metres, without apparently showing nervousness or anxiety, despite having this bag on the pillion containing one radio, half a million francs and a 9-mm pistol. Any one of which items would have been a certain passport to 'interrogation' and probably — if you survived long enough to get there — to the women's concentration camp at Ravensbrück.

L'Enfer des Femmes, they called it. The women's hell.

There was a light drizzle falling, by the time she reached Segré, riding straight through it and out the other side. Her road led roughly north-westward then. After about twenty kilometres there'd be a village called Pouance, then another ten or twelve kilometres would take her to Châteaubriant. By which time it would be about mid-morning.

Head down, legs pumping, eyes slitted against the drizzle . . . Might send the 'arrived safely' signal from Rennes tonight, she thought. Because they'd be waiting for it, that was all, and until they got it might link her silence with the 'Hector' business and guess she'd run into trouble of some kind. It would be better, anyway, to go on the air from Rennes than to break radio silence from anywhere further west before she had good reason to.

Thinking of Ben again: whether he *would* get himself back to sea when his knee was mended. He was counting on it: although he'd admitted, last time she'd visited him in the hospital at Haslar, that the doctors hadn't guaranteed it ever would be the knee it had been. But then again — as well to remember he'd got back to sea with one ear that still didn't work, after his previous smash-up in an action off the Dutch coast — winter of '41, before she'd known him. So maybe — if at some stage he found he could do without that stick — Ben being Ben . . .

A car swished past, spraying her. A grey Citroën: three men in civilian clothes in it. Almost certainly Gestapo; gray-painted Citroëns were their favoured means of transport. Nothing to do with her, though — it had vanished ahead, its horn blaring as it forced its way past other traffic.

The drizzle had become quite heavy; by the time she got to Pouance it was more like rain. This was a miserable little dump of a place, too. She'd been ready for a break, had had thoughts of stopping here, but now decided against it. In Châteaubriant there might well be a choice of cafés, not just one that looked ramshackle and in any case still had its shutters up.

Another hour's pedalling, therefore. To a cup of coffee, a cigarette or two and maybe half an hour with her feet up. Wooden-soled shoes weren't ideal for cycling: she'd learnt that six months ago, in Rouen. Still, it hadn't gone badly, so far. Ought to make Châteaubriant not much after ten o'clock; earlier on she'd reckoned on getting there around midday.

About the time June would be ringing Ben.

It would have been better if she could have told him herself. Although he'd known it would be this way; and there'd have been nothing to say that they hadn't already said to each other a dozen times.

Her calves and thighs ached. Face half-frozen,

hands too; her mittens had been soaked through hours ago. Unfortunately you couldn't equip yourself with gear of a type Suzanne Tanguy wouldn't have been able to get hold of.

She was in Châteaubriant nearer ten-thirty than ten, rode around until she found a café that was open, locked the bike to some railings and took both suitcases inside with her. A girl of about her own age, coming quickly from the nether regions, focused on them at once and spread her hands: 'We don't have rooms. Sorry. If that's what —'

'It isn't. Why would I want a room at this time of day?'

'I don't know. I thought — with baggage . . . But — excuse me, but you look half-drowned. As if you'd been in the river!'

She looked pregnant.

Rosie told her no, not in the river, just in rain; she'd come a long way, by bicycle, still had some way to go, didn't therefore have much time, only wanted a hot drink and something to eat — if there was anything available, at this time of day.

'Sausage — with bread?'

'That'd do.' If they ever had anything, they had bloody sausage. Fumbling wet-fingered for a cigarette. 'Fine. And coffee, eh?'

'That's easy.' She had a nice smile: and she *was* pregnant. Shaking her head . . . 'The *state* you're in . . . Look, there's no one here yet — like to come in the kitchen, where it's warm?'

Leaving Châteaubriant, she had a choice: stay

on this main road — the direct route to Rennes from Angers — or fork left after about three kilometres for Bain-de-Bretagne so as to come into Rennes eventually as if from Nantes. It was conceivable that they'd be watching the Angers road, Angers being roughly where she might have started from. If they'd been hoping to catch her at Le Mans, then realized she was a jump ahead of them? They weren't stupid, those people. Unpleasant to a high degree, but not stupid. After a couple of trains from Angers had come and gone, they'd have only to pick up a telephone to Rennes and arrange for a watch to be set on the Angers road. One car and perhaps two men would be enough. No need to stop all the traffic, they'd only have to concern themselves with girls on bikes with luggage. They'd reckon on having a reasonably good chance — why would she be on any *other* road?

Answer: because *she* wasn't stupid.

It would add about ten kilometres to her journey. But she had time in hand now, and the break in Châteaubriant had done her good. Not only the coffee and sausage and more or less thawing out, but that pregnant girl's kindness. Her husband was a *gendarme* stationed in Laval, she'd told Rosie, and this café was owned by his widowed mother. It was her first pregnancy; they hadn't been married long.

Anyway — it had been a relaxing interlude, and now she'd have to make up for it. Eleven-twenty: and the rain had thinned again to drizzle — stop-

49

ping now and then, tending to start again just when she began to think there might be a chance to dry out. The traffic after she'd turned off at the fork consisted mostly of farm lorries, carts and tractors, and the road was correspondingly foul. Thirty kilometres of it, roughly, to Bain-de-Bretagne, then about forty to Rennes. The last five or so of those, in the built-up area, might be slower going.

Get there about five, perhaps.

Her original intention, as from the briefing in London, had been to deposit the case with the radio in it in the *consigne* at the station — having taken 'Giselle' 's cash out of it first so as not to have to go back to it until she was ready to leave town. But she'd been planning on arrival and departure by rail, at that stage; now, there was no reason to go anywhere near the station. Very good reason to steer well clear of it, in fact. There were always military as well as plain-clothes police around — even *without* any special lookout they might be keeping now. Also, there was the bike — which she'd stick to, leaving Rennes. For better or for worse . . . She wasn't sure of the distance to Carhaix and beyond; although it could hardly be less than another hundred kilometres. More, probably — just to Carhaix . . . But if she could make another early start — finding some-where for the night — she was rather hoping 'Giselle' might solve that problem for her — on that basis, tomorrow might be another day like this one.

Grimacing into the drizzle, thinking *Lucky me* . . .

At the southern approach to Bain-de-Bretagne, almost immediately after she'd turned on to the main road, there was a road-block which they either hadn't closed yet or had just re-opened. The barriers, trestles and poles, were on both sides of the road, parallel to it, on the verges, and there were German soldiers standing around where an armoured vehicle was parked. Then as she got closer she saw two uniformed officers on *this* side, standing there talking and watching the passing traffic. High-fronted caps, peaks glistening wet, long-skirted coats overhanging their damn jackboots. She'd become conscious suddenly of a familiar hollow in her stomach. Fear: acute dislike, too; dislike heightened of course by the fear. Pedalling hard on the slight gradient, short, hard, panting breaths matching the piston-like action of her legs, and her face tight against the cold, in her own mental picture of how she might look to them as she passed — was *about* to pass them — the suitcase on the bike's pillion seemed — to her — about the size of the tall cylinder on a *gazo, must* attract their interest.

Challenging herself then: so what? Suzanne Tanguy: papers in order, on her way to this new job, could hardly be going there without a change of clothes, spare pair of shoes, a few personal effects, for God's sake . . . Open a case — are you joking? In this rain, get everything soaked?

For Christ's sake . . .

One of them was smoking a cigar. Not much of it left, hardly more than a stub. He was holding it clear of his mouth — a leather glove on that hand — and laughing at whatever the other was telling him. As relaxed as if they had some *right* to be here . . .

She was passing them — now.

Had passed.

No shouts, no order to stop. They might not even have noticed her. Pedalling on: brain still taut, nerves racked tight for quite a while before the tension gradually eased off.

Like the end of an attack of mental cramp. In sharp reaction finding herself almost laughing: telling Ben in that flood of relief *Oh, if you could've seen me then!*

He'd have been called to the telephone by now. Expecting her voice, hearing June's, knowing immediately what it meant. Maybe half an hour ago. He'd be off by himself somewhere, she guessed: reminding himself that he'd known the moment would come, and here it was, so —

So he'd come to terms with it, that was all. He had a gammy knee but his head was screwed on all right. *More* than 'all right': he had a hell of a lot going for him, had Ben Quarry . . . Shaking her head — shaking rain off so there'd be less to run down her neck — and turning her thoughts back to Rennes. A town plan she'd studied in London had given her an idea of the layout, of the main boulevards and where the river and the railway tracks ran, and so forth. She'd never set foot in the place, up till now, only passed through it in trains. Last time, she'd come from Paris and there'd been an SS officer — in civies, masquerading as someone he wasn't — behind her in the same carriage, believing that she was leading him to a Resistance cell which operated around one of the secret landing places, called 'pinpoints', used by the motor gunboats based on Dartmouth. The flotilla Ben had been in, at that time. But at Rennes, some men from another Resistance group had been supposed to board the train and take care of the German, and they hadn't: she'd been watching for them, and it had been a very bad moment when the train had pulled out and she'd realized they'd let her down.

As it happened, that westernmost of the gunboats' 'pinpoints' had been closed down now. She'd heard it only a few days ago, in the course of briefing. No details, nothing about what had happened to the people there — who'd been her friends, effectively saved her life . . . Anyway — the SS man in the train — where this tangential thought had started — she'd killed him. With a kitchen knife, in the lavatory at the end of the compartment, just minutes before the halt at Landerneau.

The only person she'd ever killed. She'd had some help with it, admittedly. *And* bad dreams, for some time after.

A *gazo* van passed close, sheeting muddy water over her and then over an elderly woman cyclist a few lengths ahead. The old bird was still shaking her fist after it, screaming imprecations, when a lorry did exactly the same thing.

She was in the outskirts of Rennes by four-fifteen. It was already getting dark. Dry though, by then, except for the muck coming up off the road. Thinking about routes into town and finding a café, and so on — as much as she'd memorized of it was based on a plan of the centre with the railway station as her starting-point — as it would have been — and the river, La Vilaine, trooping around to the north and northeast of it. So if you found the station and then turned north but stayed this side of the river you'd be near enough in the middle of the town. Find a café anywhere around there, then ring the Trianon and ask for 'Giselle'.

She was on the Rue de Nantes. No river yet, so keep going. Legs feeling as if they were full of lead. Head, too — muzzy . . . Having to force herself to concentrate: aware of being physically and mentally near-exhausted.

Better not even to *think* of doing much the same as this tomorrow . . .

Railway bridge, right ahead: the station would be somewhere along there to her right. Had to be: would have been to the left if she'd come in on the Angers road. So — under the bridge: and right, then. She was on the north side of the railway line now.

The only reason to find the station was of

course as a reference point. They'd have it staked out, for sure.

At least — if 'Hector' had been turned, they would.

Trouble was, you started thinking he *might* have been, and next minute it was part of your thinking that he *had*. Not necessarily so at all . . . Forking left here, away from the tracks. No option, no other way she could have gone. Quite soon after that, anyway, she was diverting back to the right again; then — well, *eventually* — pedalling into a square with a central garden and a very large edifice — surely the station building — U-shaped around the square's southern end. Place de la Gare, for sure. A fair bet there'd be a Café de la Gare too — maybe a hotel with a café under it. But — too close, not worth risking: instincts were worth a lot when you had nothing more solid to guide you, and hers told her that not only the station but its close surroundings should be avoided.

She rounded the Place and turned up an avenue leading north. What she needed was a café spacious enough to have a public telephone so placed that the staff and other customers at least didn't *have* to listen in. And preferably one that wasn't stiff with Germans. They had their own places — to which French people other than highly placed collaborators weren't admitted, and where there was a better variety of food and drink — but they came slumming too, quite often. To pick up girls, for one thing.

Then she'd found it: Café Dinard. A long front-age, and a rail outside to which bicycles could be chained, and some people coming out who looked ordinary, nondescript. Like herself — touch wood. Except she knew she'd be looking like nothing on earth, by now . . . Having tethered the bike, she took her cases off it and carried them inside with her, through double blackout screens into warmth and light, a reek of tobacco-smoke and garlic. Confirmation that she was looking like some sort of escaped convict came in an assort-ment of stares and double-takes. Ignoring them — looking around: seeing that there were a few unoccupied tables, also a telephone in an alcove at the far end of the bar.

She went over to it, carrying the cases, asked a young girl who was unloading a tray of beer glasses, *'Toilette?'*

'Through there — the door at the end.'

A black-haired woman further along the bar watched her go, and was still watching ten min-utes later when she emerged, feeling better and slightly cleaner. Madame then signalled to a waiter, whom she must have warned to be ready for this: one didn't maintain a *toilette* just for scruffy-looking girls to walk in off the street for a pee and then walk straight out again.

'If you please, Mam'selle?'

Grey-haired, stooped, pulling back a chair. At a table close to this one were two men in civilian clothes who might well have been SD, or Ge-stapo. Ordinary *Wehrmacht* officers wouldn't have been in civies, in an establishment like this; and they couldn't be *Abwehr* because since Rosie had last been in France the *Abwehr* — Military Intelligence — had been absorbed into the SD — *Sicherheitsdienst,* the SS secret police. They were Germans, anyway, in badly fitting dark suits, and they were taking an interest in Rosie. Maybe thinking she'd *wanted* to sit near them. Too late now, anyway: to have shifted, having noticed them, might have made matters worse. She nodded to the waiter: 'Thank you.' Putting her cases partly under this table but at her side where she'd be able to see them from the telephone.

Those two had resumed their conversation. It *was* German they were talking. She told the waiter, 'I'd like coffee, please.'

'And to eat?'

'Not at the moment. I may have a friend joining me.'

'Just one coffee.'

'Large one, please, with sugar.' It would be saccharine, but that was often referred to as sugar. Just as certain brown liquids were known as coffee. Why split hairs? She added, 'And a *jeton* for the telephone.'

'At the counter.'

She lit a cigarette first. Needing it: if she'd allowed herself to put her head down on her forearms on the table she could have fallen asleep within seconds. Leaning back, instead, inhaling smoke — devouring it — her eyes on the doorway where two priests were fumbling with umbrellas.

Must have been in here a long time, she thought, if they think it's still raining.

How one's mind worked. Dissecting everything — or trying to.

Get a *jeton*. Wait too long, might miss her. *Then* what? She got up, went to the counter. '*Jeton* for a local call, please. D'you have a telephone directory?'

'Not of recent date.' The proprietress, undoubtedly: she had that manner. Fifty-ish, hair coal-black, almost certainly dyed, small, sharp eyes, thick neck and shoulders. Sliding a telephone book across the counter, and scooping up Rosie's payment for the *jeton*. 'Still look as if you've been climbing mountains. Better than when you walked in, but still — that coat's wet through, eh?'

'Someone said earlier, as if I'd been in the river.'

A shrug of the heavy shoulders. 'If you'd told me you had, I wouldn't doubt it.'

The directory was greasy, stank of cigarette smoke and had numbers, names and doodles scrawled all over it. Rosie murmured, turning another page of T's, 'Truth is, I've come a long way, by bicycle. Going to a new job, stopping off here to see an old friend. And if she's not here after all that . . .'

She'd found it — Café Trianon — and was memorizing the number. Adding as if to herself, 'Ought to have my head seen to.' Imparting that much information in order to prepare the ground in case she needed to ask where she could get a bed for the night at reasonable cost. The waiter, she saw, had put her so-called coffee on the table. And one of the Germans was watching her, making no bones about it. She shut the book; Madame was moving along to serve another customer. She'd pack a hell of a punch, Rosie thought. The Café Trianon was in Rue St Sauveur; not that that told her anything.

'Yes — Café Trianon?'

A young girl's voice. For some reason she'd expected a man to answer.

'I'm anxious to get in touch with Élise Krilov. I was told I might find her there — or that someone would know where else —'

'Élise Krilov?'

'D'you know her?'

'Not — personally. I may know who you mean, though. Don't go, I'll enquire . . . Who are you, may I ask?'

'Old friend of hers. Zoé, tell her.'

She'd thought of bringing her coffee to the telephone with her, but had decided to leave it as a marker on the table. She was leaning with a shoulder against the wall and the suitcases in her field of view. Cigarette down to its last two centimetres . . . 'Hello, yes?'

'You're looking for Élise, I'm told.'

'Élise Krilov — yes. D'you know where —'

'Frankly, I don't. Although — well, tell me, is she expecting to hear from you?'

'Yes. Definitely.'

'And your name — you told my daughter —'

'Zoé.'

'Is that all the name you have?'

'All Élise would recognize. We're very old friends, but it's been a long time, she doesn't know my married name. We're — sort of cousins, really.'

'Is that so. Well, I hope you find her . . . Although — yes, that *is* a thought — I know one place she *might* be found — if she's in Rennes at all, that is —'

'Is there a telephone number?'

'If there is, I don't know it. But give me yours, where I could get back to you — my daughter can find out, it's on her way —'

'Extremely kind . . . I'm at —' she read the number from the faded printing in the centre of the dial. 'It's a café, the Dinard. You'd know it, I dare say. I only just got into town, though, and I don't know *my* way around —'

'Will you be there long?'

'In Rennes?'

'At the Café Dinard!'

'Sorry . . . Well — as long as necessary.'

'I'll do my best.'

'*Very* kind . . .'

She'd hung up.

It was a cut-out, as she'd expected. If 'Giselle' had any suspicions, she wouldn't ring back; if she had *serious* doubts, she'd get out of town.

Meanwhile it was Rosie, if anyone, who'd exposed herself to danger. If the Trianon telephone had been tapped — as it could have been — the next thing might be a squeal of tyres outside and men in black uniforms bursting in.

Not men. *Things*. Having met some in Rouen, at very close quarters, she was in a position to state that, categorically.

Telephone conversations were often eavesdropped on by operators who earned a bit extra on the side by acting as freelance informers — *mouchards*. Not that anyone would have got much of interest out of *that* call. Not unless the name Élise Krilov rang a bell somewhere: if she'd been arrested, for instance, and the word put out that a female SOE agent might be passing through and looking for her. Key words were what made telephone calls dangerous. As far as possible one avoided using phones at all — this was Baker Street's advice — but when you had to, there were words and names you tried not to use.

She was aware of the Germans' eyes on her as she returned to her table and sat down, pulled the coffee closer and stirred it before taking a sip to see if it was still drinkable. While she'd been at the telephone she'd seen the waiter bringing the Germans refills of what passed for beer; and they'd have to be here for some good reason, she thought. In their own canteens — *Locale*, they were called — they'd surely get German beer, not that swill.

One of them caught her eye, and smiled. She

looked away: then saw the waiter, and beckoned him.

'Mam'selle desires?'

'I'm expecting a telephone call. If someone — a woman — asks for Zoé, that's me.'

A nod . . . 'And while you wait for it — something to eat?'

'What is there?'

'The soup is good. There's also cheese.'

'Soup, then. With some bread, please.'

'Soup with bread.' Scribbling on his pad. 'No more coffee?'

'Garçon.'

The German who'd smirked at her: the waiter glanced round at him. 'One moment, Monsieur.'

'No, not one moment, *this* moment.' His French wasn't too bad. 'Bring the young lady some cheese as well, and put it on my bill.'

Rosie told the waiter, 'I want soup and bread only, and on *my* bill.'

'As Mam'selle wishes . . .'

The other German was chuckling. Muttering something like 'Bad luck, chum!' in German.

'You misunderstand me. As perhaps *you* do also, Mam'selle. I was hoping only for conversation, an opportunity to improve my French.'

The waiter stayed out of it. Rosie didn't blame him. She told the German coldly, 'I'm sorry. I'm very tired.'

'Yes — one can see —'

'Excuse me.' Turning away, fumbling a new cigarette out of the pack and lighting it quickly before he could display his gallantry *that* way. It was possible that he'd only wanted conversation. But who gave a damn what he wanted . . . She heard the other muttering angrily now — in his own foul language: but the thing was *not* to seem to want their good opinion, or curry favour. With nothing to hide, one *wouldn't*.

The waiter was back already. 'One soup . . .'

'Oh, that's fast service!'

'It's there in the tureen. Filling a bowl takes no time at all.' He transferred it and the greyish bread from his tray. 'It's good soup, I think you'll find. Ah —'

The telephone was jangling.

'Perhaps — ?'

'I'll see to it.'

She watched him cross the room to it; so did the Germans. He took the earpiece off its hook, listened for a moment, then turned towards her with a mournful expression and gestured negatively. Calling to the proprietress then: 'Madame?' There was an elderly man helping out there now, could have been either her husband or her father. The waiter had left the earpiece hanging, and had started over to meet a couple who'd just arrived; the place was full by this time, and the three of them were looking around to see where there might be room. He was looking at Rosie then — thoughtfully, stroking his chin.

Bringing them over.

'Mam'selle . . .'

The man was short and bald, in a shiny brown

suit, and the woman taller, grey-haired; the waiter was suggesting that they might share Rosie's table. And why not? She shrugged: 'Of course.' Then: 'I'm sorry, Madame, my baggage takes up so much space.'

'No inconvenience at all. Thank you . . .'

'Yes — thank you!'

He was bright pink — naturally pinkish to start with, brighter now presumably with embarrassment. For whatever reason . . . '*Very* kind. Who'd have expected it to be so crowded?' Rosie was thinking that the waiter had probably brought them to her as a kindness, a defence against the German — who no doubt would have persisted, had barely taken his eyes off her since that last approach. Still might, she thought. A hide like a rhinoceros — by the look of him. Also, being a member of the Master Race, polite to us lesser beings this evening — so far — only because he condescends to be.

Might not stay that way for long. She was mopping the last of her soup out of the bowl with the last of the bread — as Suzanne Tanguy would have.

Come on, Giselle, come on . . .

The cigarette tasted foul, when she relit it. She'd shifted her chair slightly — moving it out from the table, a slight disengagement from these newcomers, and at the same time turning it so as to face directly away from the Germans. Who did seem to have given up, now; although they'd ordered more beer.

Must have some purpose in hanging around, she thought again. Meeting friends here, perhaps. Or for 'friends', read 'tarts'.

'Was the soup to your liking, Mam'selle?'

'Very good, thank you.'

'Can I get you something else?'

'No — thank you. Except a bill, please. I have to wait for the telephone, but then —'

'Oh, stay as long as you like.'

His manner had become fatherly. Approving her aloofness to those creatures, no doubt. But he hadn't understood — and with the Germans listening she didn't explain — that she wanted to pay her bill because when the call came she might want to leave at once. She got a bill from him, anyway. And the phone did ring again, but it wasn't for her. She lit yet another cigarette. Thinking that a waiter, however good-hearted, would be in a difficult position in a situation of this kind, and he'd certainly done his best. But these others, who'd had soup and cheese, were just about finishing; and without having to look round, she knew the Germans were still there. She leant back — so that the woman was between her and them — exhaling smoke, gazing down through it at her suitcases. When these two left, that bastard *would* try again, she felt sure.

Looking up then — over to the doorway. Some customers had been leaving, and the last of them, a man, had hung back, holding the screen door open for someone else to enter first. A girl — who'd just appeared. Blinking at the light, and giving him a small smile of thanks. She was tall, perhaps in her late twenties, with dark hair and contrastingly pale skin, a figure like a mannequin's. She was wearing a loose-fitting coat, but that was one's clear impression. She'd stopped a few paces in from the door: looking around quickly, even urgently, narrowing her eyes to peer through the layers of smoke. Giving that up then, turning towards the bar, seeing Madame there gazing at her, and starting over towards her. Rosie at this point realizing — in shock, almost — that she knew her. At least — had seen her before. That long-legged stride — and her stance, *style* — unmistakable, now. She'd seen her on a beach: moonless night, an island called Guenioc — the pinpoint which had now closed down. She'd gone to her, touched her arm, wished her good luck, and the tall girl had murmured thanks but only briefly — curtly, even. *Needing* her solitude in that darkness, with the wash of the sea and pounding surf as background — in her first moments in France, or back in France, whichever . . . She — Rosie — had been on her way out, about to be rowed out to the gunboat from which that one had just landed.

Chapter 3

'Giselle — don't you know me? Your own precious cousin Zoé?'

Giving her the clue: she wouldn't have known they were supposed to be cousins or near-cousins, as Rosie had told Madame they were, earlier. The beach-girl had caught on, anyway . . . '*Zoé,* darling!'

A slightly oriental look. High cheekbones, and a slant to the eyes. She was examining Rosie too, meanwhile: both of them laughing — happy, even if meaningless laughter that rang true — reflecting old times, the fun they'd had together, plus a tinge of self-consciousness. In this line of work you did become something of an actress. The proprietress put in, 'Glad you found each other, anyway. One needs all one's friends — eh?'

'How right you are.' The tall girl nodded to her. 'And thank you, Madame.'

'You've been in before, of course.'

'Oh, yes. I know you too, Madame.'

'Come again. And that nice — companion. The artist — huh?'

Rosie had brought the cases over with her: she'd excused herself to the couple at her table, hadn't even glanced at the Germans. Not then, even less now, heading for the street door: but

67

conscious that they'd be watching.

'Giselle' had taken the lighter of the cases from her.

'Giselle —'

'Élise, or Lise.'

'I thought you'd phone me here.'

'Would have, but — problems . . . Here we go.' Pulling aside the blackout screen, adding as they went through, 'It's not much of a trek, you'll be glad to hear.'

To wherever she lived, presumably. Rosie told her, 'I have a bicycle here.' Letting the screen door clash shut behind her. 'Hang on, have to unchain it. Bikes vanish, don't they . . . Is there somewhere safe for it overnight, where we're going?'

'Of course. And the sooner we get there . . .'

Her French was that of a Parisienne *bien elevée*. Looking around in the three-quarter darkness while Rosie crouched, clumsy for a moment in finding the keyhole in the padlock. There was a moon behind the clouds, some filtered radiance. Empty, wet street, wet-black pavements, glistening granite-walled buildings. The whole of this town was granite. A group of old folk who'd helped each other across the road were debating whether to go in for a coffee: deciding against it, shuffling on. Élise asked her, stooping to pick up the other case, 'How did you know me?'

'We met on Guenioc. Remember? I was on my way out and you'd just landed?'

'Oh. *Oh* . . .' A pause . . . Then: 'You wished

68

me *bonne chance,* I remember.'

'But you were — preoccupied.'

'Well. Sniffing the wind — you know?'

'Yes. Indeed . . .' She'd got the chain off. Getting to her feet: 'Not far, you said?'

'A few hundred metres. I didn't see any patrols out, on my way here. What's *in* this one — bricks?'

'Guess.'

'Yes. Well . . . And *I'm* lumbered with it. Never mind . . . Listen — we can't afford to be stopped — I mean, especially in present circumstances. God knows, I hope he isn't, but Hector *might* be talking his head off. And he'd know about you, wouldn't he?'

'Hector?'

'Ah. You didn't know. I'd wondered . . . You do know who I mean, by "Hector"?'

'Air Movements —'

'Right. He was arrested, yesterday afternoon, in Le Mans. We only heard this morning, didn't know about your reception, you see, whether still to expect you, or —'

'Christ.'

'What I was starting to say — in case of — you know, emergency — field names and what we should know about each other. I'll kick off. My name you know — Élise Krilov. As it happens, it's my real name. I'm a portrait painter. I am, it's true. Well — after a fashion. I'm also working with this guy Noally. Alain Noally — heard of him?'

69

'He a painter too?'

'Sculptor. He's been doing it a long time, he's quite well known. Where I came into it is that we met in Paris three years ago — I was a student then. And — well, last year he sent for me. Needing — you know, someone to clean up for him. But I have time for my painting too. This will be your first meeting with him, won't it — I wasn't seeing much of him in those old days. In fact I was in awe of him. He's older — and quite famous, really . . . Anyway — when we wrote to each other I had a room at the Trianon — which you knew, of course, that's how you tracked me down — but since then I've moved in, I live with him. Where we're going now.'

'Live with him in the sense that —'

'In the same house. Live and work. You wouldn't know more than that.'

'All right . . . But when you arrived from England —'

'I arrived from Paris!'

'Of course.'

'As I said, he sent for me. D'you know I was having to work as a waitress then?'

'As well as painting.'

'As well as *trying* to paint.'

'I have a boyfriend who does that. Talks about it like that, anyway.'

'In England, a real one?'

'Oh, *very* real!'

'Don't tell me anything about him, then. What's your story as I *would* know it?'

70

A *gazo* passed. Pale, shaded lights barely a glimmer on the roadway: but there was another coming the other way now. She'd put a hand on Rosie's arm, steering her and the bike around a corner to the left. Narrow, empty street: both looking back to see that one's lights pass. The exchange of backgrounds was in case they were stopped and questioned: hauled in, put in separate rooms, questioned again. If you had the surface details right and they matched whatever was in your papers, and your story didn't conflict with the one they were getting in the next room, you *might* not be held for more prolonged and detailed interrogation leading eventually to Ravensbrück.

Although with Hector arrested . . . Well, if the arrest had been faked — which it might have been — they'd know everything *he* knew, at least.

Élise shouldn't have come to the café, Rosie thought.

'Zoé?'

'Suzanne. But just a minute.' She raised her voice a bit. 'At least it's not raining, like it did all day. Did where I was, anyway. And my God, the state of some roads . . .' Chattering, while two men on bicycles rode past rather slowly . . . Then: 'I'm Suzanne Tanguy. I've been in Paris, in the house of an old friend of my late mother's — that's where I was when I wrote to you — and now I'm on my way to take up a job as assistant to a doctor in his country practice — somewhere in Brittany is all you'd know — or assume. I was a student nurse, you see.'

71

'Perhaps that was when we met. Was it in Paris, your training?'

'Yes. Until they sent me to a hospital in Toulouse.'

'I was at the Sorbonne, you see. Let's agree we knew each other then. Until you departed for Toulouse, eh? I paint as *Lise* Krilov, by the way. Incidentally, the Krilov is because Papa is Russian. White Russian, of course, he detests the Bolsheviks. Which made him acceptable to the Nazis, of course — once Hitler had ratted on the Nazi-Soviet pact. You'd know this, I'd imagine.'

'But I don't need to have met your parents. Only to know *of* them. That your father's White Russian's about enough. Mother French?'

'Oh, yes.'

'They still around?'

'In Switzerland. I refused to go with them. For a painter, the only place to work is Paris.'

'Or Rennes?'

'Well — force of circumstances. You don't have to know it all inside-out, after all.'

'No. About me, though, what you might also know is I'd nearly finished the training course when my fiancé was killed in a bombing raid on Brest. He was a naval engineer. I had some sort of breakdown, and Mama's old friend took me in. And it's she who's found me this job I'm going to.'

'Hold on.'

A car — petrol-engined. In a hurry, shifting gear noisily as it swung into this road about fifty

72

metres away — coming this way and picking up speed. Going somewhere — touch wood — not patrolling, or searching for — *people like us* . . . Rosie was on the inner edge of the narrow pavement, her back against the stone house-frontage with the bike close up against her. Élise had sidestepped into a doorway, was more or less invisible: and the car coming so fast it was almost on top of them already — *still* picking up speed . . .

Gone. Petrol stink lingering in the cold, dark air.

'Weren't looking for *us*.'

'Let's hope no one is. Listen, though — did "Hector" set up your flight reception?'

'Yes. He should have been there, and wasn't. And the man who did meet me had no idea why. You heard of the arrest this morning, you say?'

'Resistance friends saw him arrested. They'd gone there to meet him in the station café — a meeting he'd requested — and it was outside the café that they grabbed him. One of them came to warn us before it was even daylight.'

'Couldn't they — he — have let you know yesterday by telephone?'

'Not sensibly. As far as they know, it's not immediately our concern. But also — as he explained — suppose the Boches had counted on someone doing exactly that, and put taps on the lines out of Le Mans?'

'Thought of that, did they? Because of the arrest being made so publicly. That's interesting. I wondered, myself — but for a different reason —'

'Suzanne — to the left, here. Let's save the rest of it till we're home. Nearly there — and I want Alain in on it, naturally.'

They were turning into a much busier road. She put a hand on Rosie's arm again: 'Have to cross here, then right at that corner, and — fifty metres, no more . . .'

Alain Noally shook his head at Élise — Lise, he called her — across a massive old fruitwood table. All three with cigarettes going: he'd had one stuck to his lower lip when he'd met them downstairs. He'd just reached over to light Rosie's and then Lise's. Growling as he slid back on to his chair, 'May have cooked our goose — you realize?'

'I've brought her. That was the urgent thing, wasn't it?'

Sending smoke pluming across the table. Shrugging slightly, glancing at Rosie as if for support. Rosie had gathered from earlier grumbling and Lise's brief explanations that he hadn't wanted her to go to the Café Dinard, had urged her to use the telephone, just tell her how to get here. Lise had tried once — she'd been on her own then, Noally not back from wherever it was he'd been — but the number had been engaged, and she hadn't persevered because she'd had doubts of it anyway, visions of the unknown 'Zoé' getting lost, wandering distractedly through the town, an easy mark for police or *Wehrmacht* patrols. Then he'd got back just as she was about to leave: he'd questioned her going but hadn't known enough about the situation to insist she stayed home and tried the phone again.

He was calming down now, but he'd obviously been kicking himself for *not* having stopped her.

Turning to Rosie now. A big man — seemingly all bone, no surplus flesh. A wide head of grey hair and a big nose, fringe of grey beard streaked with white. At least twice Lise's age: getting towards sixty, Rosie guessed. He'd been downstairs to meet them, looming huge in the doorway in the moment that Lise had got it open, grabbing the bike and urging her and Lise to come in quickly . . . '*Shut* it.' He'd obviously been waiting down there for some time. He'd dumped the bike somewhere and gone back to check the door was locked and bolted, then followed them upstairs. The ground floor was his working area, they had this middle floor for eating and daytime living — and the bathroom and his bedroom — while Lise had the upper part as her studio and sleeping quarters. She'd told Rosie that much while leading her up into this large, rather bare room with the magnificent table in the middle of it — where they were sitting now.

Noally asked her, 'Zoé's your code-name, what's the other?'

'Field name is Suzanne. Lise knows my background. We knew each other in Paris when I was a student nurse and she was — art student, right?'

'Where I first knew her, too.'

A private smile between the two of them. Rosie

wondered again about their relationship. It was guessable, she thought. Noally asked her, 'She's told you about "Hector" being arrested, I suppose?'

'Yes.' A lungful of smoke trickled out as she spoke. 'Arrested very publicly . . .' He'd started with some other question; she'd checked and nodded. 'Go on.'

'I was going to ask was your landing reception set up by him?'

Lise cut in, 'The answer's yes, and he should have been there but wasn't.'

'But he *would* have known who it was coming in?'

'That *an* agent was coming in. But there's more to it than that. The Lysander that brought me was supposed to be taking him back to England. Baker Street had invited him and he'd accepted.'

'*Had* he. . .'

'By the way — I've got your half-million francs in this bag.'

'I'm very glad to hear it. Thank you.'

Lise urged her, 'About "Hector", though — why was he to have been flown out?'

'Different question first — changing the subject back for just a moment —' Noally had his hands flat on the table, palms down, seemed to be studying their backs — 'the Café Dinard would have been full of people, eh?'

Rosie nodded. 'It was, by that time.'

'Boches amongst them?'

'There were some, certainly. One pair, anyway

76

— in plain clothes. One of them tried to engage me in conversation.'

'And?'

'And nothing. Chancing his arm, I suppose — no reason it should be more than that.'

Looking down again at his hands. A craftsman's hands: strong, blunt fingers. He shrugged, then. 'Not that it makes much difference. There are plenty of informers around, God knows. D'you know what is the Gestapo staff in Marseille?'

'No idea.'

'One thousand and fifty. Fifty Boches, the rest French.'

'Crikey.'

Lise stared at him: 'If that's true, it's an affront.'

'Of *course* it's an affront.' He was lighting a new cigarette. Eyes on her again. 'I *still* wish you hadn't gone there. The more I think about it. You *may* have blown us sky-high. This is fact, not just me beefing, we've got to face it. They've had him — what, one day. So if he's up to it, keeps his mouth shut —'

'We've been into this, Alain.'

'On our own we have, *she* hasn't. I'm saying — one more day, if we're lucky we'll have *that* long before the word goes out.' Pausing, looking at Rosie. 'What else would he know about you?'

'That I was coming to Rennes. He had to know that much because he was supposed to provide me with the return halves of railway tickets from — well, via Angers to Rennes. One of his own people must have been travelling from here to Le Mans, and I *think* "Hector" himself would have come directly to Le Mans from Paris, met this other person and then gone on down to Angers.'

A sigh; a gesture of vague helplessness.

'So there we are, Lise.'

'He might not tell them anything at all.'

'*Might* not — that's true. But it's safer to expect the worst: and if he holds out for another day he's done his duty, eh?'

The imperative — SOE's expectation of its agents — was to resist interrogation for forty-eight hours, time for other members of a *réseau* to go to ground. But they'd have to know of the arrest in the first place, obviously; and the Gestapo knowing all about the forty-eight-hour rule wouldn't normally make an arrest more publicly than they could help.

Rosie asked Noally, 'Do you know "Hector" personally?'

'No. We've had dealings with him — through Baker Street — but never met. Oh, I had a courier here for whom he arranged a lift to England. No direct contact with "Hector" though. It was a Frenchman I'd recruited and Baker Street agreed to accept for training. They set it up and gave us a contact address, that was all.' Nodding towards Lise: '*She* replaced that fellow and also my former pianist, but she didn't come by air.'

'I know she didn't.'

'Oh?'

'We met six months ago on a beach. In pitch

darkness, incidentally, and I still recognized her.'

'You did, eh. Yeah, well . . .'

His eyes were on Lise: his brown eyes and her greenish ones shifting a little as if tracing the contours of each others' faces. Rosie thought, *Sleeping on different floors, the hell they are . . .*

'So when she walked into that café —'

'It did take a moment, before I realized.' She changed the subject: 'About "Hector" — there are some who have the idea he's a *vendu*.'

Vendu meaning one who's sold out.

The smiles had faded. Lise echoed, 'Some who have the *idea* he is?'

She nodded. 'But I've also been told — yesterday morning, in London, although it feels more like a month ago — I was assured by a senior officer in Baker Street that he definitely is *not*. This man's known "Hector" a long time, also knows he seduced the girlfriend of the one who's denounced him. Despite which, since there *has* been this denunciation, they have to look into it. Hence the trip to London for de-briefing.'

'A trip he isn't going to make, now.'

'Maybe *decided* not to make.'

'It would hold water, wouldn't it,' Rosie agreed. 'Getting himself arrested instead — in front of witnesses he's asked to be there — to have us and Baker Street believe he would have gone if he could have?'

Lise stubbed out her cigarette. 'Air Movements Officer for the whole of "F" Section. Can't be a lot he *doesn't* know.'

Noally blew his cheeks out. 'If it's true, it's a disaster. And we certainly can't *count* on another twenty-four hours' grace. If they don't know it all already, we have to assume they damn soon will. The one obvious thing, meanwhile —' he was looking at Rosie — 'is to get you on your way as soon as possible.'

'First thing in the morning?' She saw his nod, and added, 'What time does curfew end?'

'Five o'clock. Breakfast at four, eh?'

'You're very kind.'

'Oh, my assistant here will see to it.' He'd winked at Lise. 'She'll give us some soup for a nightcap too, by and by. You've had something already, I imagine?'

'*Something,* yes . . . What'll you two do?'

'We'll sit tight. Nothing else we can do. Maybe keep our heads down for a while. Except for one job — the business I was seeing to this evening . . . But "Hector" doesn't know us — or *of* us, please God. The one thing that *might* drop us in it is Lise's appearance in that damn café.' He reached to pat her hand. 'You aren't exactly inconspicious, you know. This one knew you from a glimpse in the dark six months ago — huh? You're known around here, too. The bit of stuff I'm passing off as my assistant.' He nodded to Rosie. 'That's what they say. I'm tolerated because I'm an artist. But there's my little pigeon dashing in to meet her old buddy whom maybe they're watching because they know she arrived by Lysander the night before and they want to

80

know who her contacts are in this town — eh?'

They fascinated her. She was still thinking about them when she was on her way, leaving just after five a.m., taking the Rue de Fougères to start with — northeastward out of the town centre but then turning down right-handed to cross the river and work her way down south and westward to the Mantes road, the one she'd come in by yesterday. Pictures of them in her mind: of Noally as contained as he was physically impressive, often silent for long intervals and then swiftly, fluently, even savagely to the point. In love with Lise, obviously — as she was with him. Whether they had been before her arrival here as his pianist-cum-courier six months ago hadn't emerged or even been hinted at; Rosie thought it might have been so with him, at any rate. With her at that stage it might have been more — her word, *awe,* more than love, until she'd come here. Now, she was obsessed with him. He was old enough to be her father, but the difference in their ages might actually be part of the mutual attraction: and not only from his angle — grey-headed lecher obsessed with what he'd called his bit of stuff: half a dozen times in the course of the evening his enthralment by her on an entirely different level was so plain that she — Rosie — could have hugged him. Well — hugged them both. Lise intrigued her just as much: had done, she realized now, from that minute or two six months earlier when she'd been only a dark cut-

81

out, remote and uncommunicative on that surf-swept beach.

She'd mentioned her to Ben, in fact. It had been pillow-talk and she'd been trying to explain to him — also to herself, to some extent — the dichotomy of a compulsion to return to the field and a numbing fear of it: a state of mind which for her had been epitomized in the tall stranger's need for solitude, in those few minutes. She'd told Ben, 'That girl's *me* . . .'

Half a foot taller and different in just about every way, but — sisters under the skin. An extraordinary affinity, literally at first sight. Despite which she'd misled her — and Noally — into believing that she was heading for Fougères. Same impression that she'd left in the minds of the couple at Soucelles. Although she couldn't easily imagine either Lise or Noally cracking under torture, it was a simple fact that what people didn't know they couldn't divulge.

They'd have approved her caution, too. There was comfort in that thought. Recalling the scene last night, Noally leaning over the map, one blunt forefinger tracing the route to Fougères. His murmur: 'Won't take you long. If that's as far as you're going.' Not wanting any answer: dropping the subject, telling Lise, 'Better make her up a bed, if she's starting that early. I'm off to mine.' Pushing his chair back. 'See you both at cock-crow.'

'You *will* be up?'

'Of course. Think I'd miss breakfast?'

She'd let him think she believed the stuff about him and Lise sleeping on different floors; appreciating that he wouldn't want Baker Street to know he and Lise were anything but *chef de réseau* and pianist. Or embarrass *her* over it. They'd better not appear together at Baker Street, she thought, if they wanted to keep it dark. Anyone who wasn't blind or exceptionally dim could hardly have a doubt that they were in love and revelling in it.

She was on the Nantes road, the one she'd come in on, within about thirty minutes of leaving them, and would turn off westward a few miles south. It was going to be something like two hundred kilometres today, to St Michel-du-Faou. But no rain so far: mentally she crossed fingers that it might stay dry. The big thing anyway was having Rennes behind her now — more or less — with the cash delivered and no trail left anywhere. Except — possibly, but please God not — in the Café Dinard: remembering Noally's misgivings, which were the reason she was leaving town by this route instead of directly westward on the road for Carhaix.

Silly, really. First because there could hardly be a tail now, and second because if there was, a slight diversion like this would hardly guarantee throwing it off. Habit and training, was all: taking nothing for granted, and no risks that were avoidable. Plugging on — damp-skinned inside her clothes in cold dawn air and the lingering dark, telling herself grimly that she couldn't very well have done much better, this far. Having covered about half the total distance, and left no trail or clues anywhere that she knew of. Those were the facts — irrespective of how one might happen to feel, from moment to moment. Overall, it really was *not* so bad. Suzanne Tanguy, on her way to a job in the peace and quiet of the Breton country-side — with proof of it, and papers in good order . . .

Not as perfect as Alain Noally's and Lise's, admittedly. (Temporary mood of depression due to feeling lonely, having enjoyed being in their company, she realized, and missing them now.) But their papers were the real thing, their own genuine papers in their own real names. Lise's name was there for anyone to check on in the Sorbonne's class-lists — with no indication of a period of nearly a year which she'd spent in England. She'd fixed that, somehow. And Noally's showed that he'd worked from a studio in Pont Aven until 1940 when he'd moved to Paris, and later shifted back to his beloved Brittany — to Rennes, almost to where he'd started from. Nowhere in his documentation either was there any indication of time spent outside France.

Lise had asked Rosie last night — on the top floor, when they'd been preparing for bed — about the boyfriend she'd told her she had. 'You said he paints?'

'*You* said you didn't want to know about him.'

'So I did. Yes. Well . . .'

84

'Dead right, too. Far better *not.*'

Not to know, or spill beans unnecessarily. For one thing, personal background details could be used by a Boche radio-operator to convince SOE analysts in Baker Street that *he* was 'Zoe' — using her transceiver after she'd been caught. Knowing a name, a home address, date of birth, name of a husband or boyfriend.

'But it's good, is it? That's all I'm asking, really.' Lise had gestured downward, to the floor where Alain was doubtless cursing . . . 'The real thing — like I have? Don't tell him I said this, but —'

'You don't *have* to say it. I've got eyes . . .'

'I'll tell you anyway. It's so marvellous it scares me, it's *too* good. I don't mean scares me because we might come to grief — the obvious way, Gestapo, so forth — I mean how it might be when one day there's no war. I feel it's — like the air we breathe, the scene we're *real* in — you know?'

'I get what you mean.'

'You feel that too?'

'Well . . . He and I don't work together like you do. Obviously . . . But he's scared for me — and I am for him, when I let myself think about it. So — maybe not all *that* different . . . Anyway, what's to stop you hanging on to what you have — transfer intact to *any* different scene?'

It could be like that with herself and Ben, she thought. Scene 2, the same characters only stronger for what they've been through in Scene 1. She'd wondered, at times, about herself and Ben in a post-war world. If they both got to see it, anyway. That was the point at which you stopped worrying about it, knowing you might well *not*.

At which point Lise had cut in as instantly as if their thoughts had been overlapping.

'Could be I can't see us in another kind of life because we won't be?'

She'd startled her: by postulating what at some moments she'd feared herself. Shaking her head, though: 'Could be you're talking nonsense, Lise!' Smiling, to soften it. 'The Russian in you, I suppose.'

'You don't believe in Fate?'

'If you mean things happening to us that we can't control — if you want to call *that* "Fate" —'

'Don't you think Fate brought us together on that island?'

'Well — no. Not really. I'd say it was a dinghy.' She shook her head again, wincing at her own facetiousness. 'Something that *happened*, that's all.'

It was daylight, just after eight-thirty, when she turned west on to the road she could have been on right from the start. Having subjected herself to an extra ten or twelve kilometres, probably quite unnecessarily. But there'd been very little traffic and no hold-ups, the way she'd come, and one couldn't know that there wouldn't have been a block on this main road somewhere on the edge of Rennes. Fate, Lise might have said, could have played its part. And the last half-hour of pedalling up to this village — Montfort — had been a delight: daylight spreading and strengthening through a dawn mist over what had to be some of the most beautiful countryside in France.

The Rance, she thought that river might be, down in the valley. Summoning Noally's map to mind, reciting to herself the list of villages or small towns that lay ahead now: St Méen, Merdrignac, Loudéac, Mur-de-Bretagne, Rostrenen. Then Carhaix-Plouguer . . . A full day of it, and plenty of time for thought — even if 'thought' couldn't amount to much more than speculation, at this stage. Wondering now for instance as she left Montfort behind her what Baker Street would make of the news of 'Hector' 's arrest, which they'd be getting some time this evening. At this moment all they'd know was that he hadn't shown up at the landing-field; but tonight Lise would be tapping out a signal over her own signature as 'Giselle', starting with Rosie's pre-coded *'arrived safely and proceeding to designated area'* group and adding *Receipt of cash acknowledged. Hector arrested yesterday morning in Le Mans. Zoé consequently avoiding railways and not repeat not attempting to collect parcel.* Then she'd continue with whatever Noally would have given her to send. She'd have been transmitting tonight anyway, she'd said — not from their house, she had two transceivers in other so-called 'safe' locations.

Noally had recently sculpted a bust of a Boche

general, he'd mentioned over the hurried breakfast.

'Well, why not? I'm a sculptor and I have to make a living. We're not politicians, either of us, we're artists.' Nodding towards Lise: 'She'll paint any of them that asks. None have yet, but we've put little cards around.' He laughed. 'This fellow wanted a bust that'd make him look like a Caesar. I told him I'd make him look like he *is*, and nothing else. What else would anyone want, I asked him — and he was flattered to bits, would you believe it?' A shrug. 'Looks like an orangutan. But I tell you, Suzanne, it's good cover.'

'Must be . . .'

Lise had cut in: 'I'd like to paint *you*, Suzanne.'

'Yes.' Noally, with his mouth full, pointing at her: 'If you could get that mouth of hers —'

'It's the clue to the whole face, I agree.' Lise nodded. 'I'd give anything to have a mouth like that!'

'Nonsense.' Rosie was embarrassed. 'The last thing you need.'

'I'm a painter, my dear, I have an *eye* —'

'Two eyes, luckily.' Noally added, 'Beautiful eyes, at that. But your mouth, Suzanne — speaking as a *man*, don't bother about any other viewpoint —'

She smiled at Lise. 'Couldn't afford to be painted, anyway.'

'I'd do it for free, God's sake!'

'Well — that's different. Perhaps when this is all over —'

'We'll track you down through Baker Street.'

'What I'd *love* is a painting of the two of you together.'

'Might manage a snapshot. Come and visit us, bring your Kodak. Pont Aven is where we'd *hope* to be.'

'Lise.' Noally's hand had covered hers. 'Wasn't it you told *me* counting chickens is bad luck?'

Telling herself, *Mind on the job, now. And step on it, now it's light . . .*

Just short of nine: and the distance to St Michel-du-Faou roughly a hundred and forty kilometres. No chance of making it before dark, but to get there as early as possible *after* dark — by about seven, say, giving it ten hours — would mean averaging about 13 kilometres an hour. So aim at 15 kph — 9 mph, a fifty per cent improvement on yesterday.

She was working up to that already. Weather conditions were a lot better, and on occasion in the past she'd managed as much as 20 kph, so it should be easily achievable — especially with no stops, or only very short ones. Food needn't be a problem; she'd had a good breakfast, and Lise had provided her with a very large sausage sandwich and a half-bottle of water — which was jammed into the pannier along with the smaller of her cases.

Yesterday, of course, she'd started about two hours earlier, ignoring curfew. Jeannot hadn't even mentioned it. His wife had, but only in a passing reference to his poaching activities. She supposed that the chances of being stopped between Jeannot's house and Tiercé would have been minuscule, anyway. Whereas in an urban sprawl like Rennes, you'd be crazy to take any such risk — especially with a radio and a pistol in your luggage. On the subject of curfew, in fact, she supposed she'd taken a bit of a chance yesterday, even. Even taking her cue from Jeannot — who of course had been thinking only of that short distance to the station, where his friend the station-master would have put her under cover.

Curfew at St Michel-du-Faou shouldn't be anything to worry about. And if there was any really serious hold-up, she might find a night's lodging in Carhaix and push on in the morning. The hours of curfew varied from place to place and could be changed with instant effect by order from the local *Kommandantur*. After a sabotage attack, for instance, or a spate of them, they'd often clamp down. Shoot hostages too: that was routine. Twelve Frenchmen and/or Frenchwomen for one slain German, was the standard rate. Hostages could be people who'd broken curfew or infringed black-market regulations: or even who'd done nothing at all, if the number of offenders in custody ran low.

If she could keep *this* up she'd be OK. She was overtaking other cyclists: passing even a *gazo* that was puttering along in a cloud of its own smoke. A stink like old clothes smouldering on a bonfire. One woman cyclist had called to another, 'Got the devil up *her* tail — that one there?' Referring to Rosie, who'd left her standing. More shrill comments and mirth, fading behind her as she rode on.

Needing to push along, but also to blend into the scene, not attract *anyone*'s attention.

At St Méen — through which she rode sedately — it looked like market day. God only knew what they'd have to sell, or buy. There were some Boches in the streets too: grey-green uniforms, slung rifles, helmets. Bicycles everywhere — women and girls mostly, and one elderly man wobbling along. Children would be in school, of course. Speeding up as she rode out into green countryside again: aware that at about this point she'd be crossing from the *département* of Illes et Vilaine to that of Côtes du Nord; with Merdrignac about twelve kilometres ahead and then a longer stretch to Loudéac.

Thoughts running on, while she pedalled westward. About Noally and Lise for instance, their taking comfort from a belief that 'Hector' didn't know them or know *of* them. Could be misplaced confidence, she thought. If he *was* a traitor, there'd be arrests soon — not immediately, he'd want Baker Street to believe he'd resisted interrogation for some length of time; but after a few days or a week or two, maybe, there'd be arrests probably all over France, and some of those arrested would know things 'Hector' *didn't* know. One cat out of the bag leading to other cats, you might say.

She thought she'd be safe enough. Having the luck not to be joining any *réseau,* and the only people who knew of her existence having no idea where she was going.

And for the time being not having to transmit, either.

That could be a danger. 'Hector' knowing that a new agent — even *female* agent, if he'd had her code-name — would have been travelling as far as Rennes: then the Boche radio-direction finders picking up transmissions from some new pianist at work out there.

Slight incline here — the wrong way, up-hill, and lasting seemingly for ever. Having to put more weight and muscle into it, to maintain progress, and beginning to feel it — and to know that by the end of the day she'd be feeling it a damn sight more . . . A *gazo* van shaved past her dangerously close, then crowded in ahead of her to avoid an oncoming lorry — which had a sign above its owner's name on the cab reading *Au Service de l'Allemagne.*

Some service, she thought, for a Frenchman. There'd been a lot of those in the Rouen area, she remembered, but this was the first she'd seen on this trip.

Merdrignac . . . *Wehrmacht* transport parked in a field at the edge of the village. Or town, its inhabitants might call it. Troops were milling around in there, and *Feldgendarmerie* were keeping the traffic flowing past the rutted gateway. A convoy assembling, she supposed. She wondered if it occurred here routinely, whether it might be worth mentioning as a likely target for a daylight raid. She didn't slow, or show more interest than Suzanne Tanguy would have done. Through and out of Merdrignac, then. She thought she might be doing better than the 15 kph average that she was aiming at. But might lose time later, so no easing up.

At about this stage she promised herself that after Loudéac — another twenty-five kilometres, say — she'd allow herself a ten-minute stop, eat her sandwich, take a drink and have an alfresco pee. Then on to Carhaix with no further stop — touch wood. It would be about sixty-five kilometres from Loudéac to Carhaix — say seventy-five or eighty to St Michel-du-Faou.

Thrusting on: about an hour and a half, to Loudéac and the planned halt, and with the thought of food and even a brief rest becoming more attractive every minute. Long minutes, though, long kilometres — a long, long day . . .

Getting there, though. Head down, pedalling on. The only way she *would* get there . . . After a while — another hour, maybe — she gave herself a swig of water, while still on the move, and felt better for it. And finally, Loudéac *was* coming up: and she didn't have to wait until *after* she'd been through it, she realized: deciding this when she reckoned she had only a kilometre or two to go, on a long straight stretch of road with forest all along the right-hand side. As good a place as any: and some urgency now. But then seeing —

and within a minute or so coming up to, and passing — a black saloon car parked on the verge at a point where there was an entrance to the forest. If it hadn't been there that surely would have been as good a stopping place as she'd find — the trees for cover, easy access, and the bike would have been safe, close at hand. Then as she was passing this car she saw the two men who'd been pausing in their own journey apparently taking a compulsive interest in *her* — throwing themselves into their vehicle, doors slamming, engine firing, the car rolling forward to bump into the road . . .

Somewhere back there, behind her. She'd looked round to see it happening but had now passed, was pedalling on, not looking back — only maintaining her notional 15 kph, hoping to God they'd speed up and pass her. That they could not have been waiting for her. Nobody could have known she'd be on this road. Or recognized her, if they had known. They'd happened to be looking her way when they'd decided to resume their journey, that was all: and watching her prior to taking advantage of a lull in the traffic, a space of empty road behind her.

Should have passed by now.

For the moment, she'd forgotten her sandwich.

Men in civilian clothes driving petrol-engined cars did have a certain connotation — come to think of it. Odd that she hadn't registered this when she'd first seen them and their Citroën.

Preoccupied with her need for a pee . . .

They might have swung out and round to the left, back the other way?

Quick look back?

Instinct advised against it.

But wouldn't it be more natural? Suzanne Tanguy having nothing to hide, wondering in all innocence what was going on?

A *gazo* had just passed her. She eased her pedalling, glanced back over her left shoulder, saw the black car following about thirty metres behind. A couple of other vehicles had been forced into a queue behind it; that *gazo* had got by and another was coming now. Then a motorbike ridden by a Boche soldier sped past in a rush of noise like an angry scream. And yet another *Wehrmacht* convoy of heavy trucks coming this other way: she'd have seen it sooner if her eyes hadn't been so to speak in the back of her head; but nothing would get by for some time now, with that lot filling the other lane.

If they were what they seemed to be, you'd think they'd drive up abreast and hoot or signal at her to stop. Not just bloody follow. Why her, anyway? When there had to be about fifty thousand cyclists, most of them female, on the roads of France at this very moment?

Just amusing themselves?

They could, literally, get away with murder. If they were what she thought they were.

She wondered how Lise would have handled it. Or what Noally would advise. Noally's calm, wide-spaced eyes the colour of milk chocolate: he might have been telling her: *Get it over with. They want to play cat and mouse, show them the mouse doesn't scare that easy. Papers OK, everything OK, just don't let 'em scare you, eh?*

Her own thinking, of course, nothing whatsoever to do with Noally. He and Lise had only slipped into her mind because — well, *because* . . . All right — if she'd been joining a *réseau*, they'd be the kind she'd want to work with. In fact she thought of this afterwards, not there and then, there wasn't time. Also it happened that there was another forest entrance coming up — similar gateway, similar track leading into the trees . . . But on second or third thoughts she decided against it. She'd eased up a bit by then, and the car was so close behind that she could hear the sound of its engine in a high gear over other traffic noise including the regular *whoomph, whoomph, whoomph* of the heavy military trucks pounding by the other way. She'd changed her mind because she'd realized she'd be playing right into their hands if she'd stopped there.

Get into Loudéac . . .

Wherever there'd be people around. Not that any of them would lift a finger, whatever happened, but the presence of witnesses might deter the bastards.

Having slowed, she didn't speed up again. It could only be a very short distance into town now, and she didn't want to seem to be dithering. Although it was a fact she *had* been. Down to about half-speed now: it felt like dawdling. But you *would* ease up, coming into a town. She heard the change of gear then, and acceleration; the Citroën swept up, slowed as it came level, hung there for the space of a few seconds, the passenger's face a white smear in the wound-down window: startled by the sudden, noisy move she'd glanced that way — just once, quickly, and away again — at which moment there was another shift of gear and — extraordinarily — the passenger stuck his arm out, arm in a light-brown raincoat sleeve waving goodbye as the car shot on ahead.

Other vehicles were overtaking, then. The army convoy had all gone. This was already the outskirts of Loudéac. The forest had receded, there'd been a small lake — of which she'd been only vaguely aware before the Citroën had been alongside her — and now she was entering the built-up area: having in mind — still somewhat reeling mind — to do what she'd last thought of, stop in some populated place and eat her lunch, also get her thoughts together *and* look for a public *toilette* — rather than risk having those two resume their game on the other side of town, where again she wouldn't be able to stop for any purpose of that kind.

But with luck they'd be a long way ahead by the time she rode on. If they were continuing westward on the same road: and unless this *was* a cat-and-mouse game with herself as a serious target.

Then she saw the blocked road ahead. A slow filtration of vehicles through a temporary one-way

97

system, trucks and lorries being directed off to the right, at a junction there. French police and plain-clothes men checking papers — including those of cyclists.

Damn . . .

The black Citroën, waiting for her.

It was parked on the left, close up behind a canvas-topped, camouflage-painted half-tonner, which with another military vehicle ahead of it was blocking that side of the road.

Bicycles seemed to be getting through fairly easily. Two gendarmes were handling that part of it; it could have been that they knew most of the cyclists, the ones they were just waving through. One at this moment was having to show her papers, though.

A stranger would, of course. Especially one with luggage.

Plus the bloody Citroën . . .

Turn back, find a way round by side-roads?

Too late. You'd be seen, and then in *worse* trouble.

'Go on, child!'

Addressing *her*. Skinny old thing with whiskers on her face. Rosie shrugged, glancing round at her. 'No rush, is there?'

'May not be for *you*, young miss —'

'Come along, then! Don't want to be at it all day, do we?'

A gendarme shouting, beckoning . . .

And one of the men from the Citroën had been watching from the corner — beyond which they'd

98

no doubt be searching the freight-carrying vehicles. Until this moment, she hadn't seen him. But he'd seen *her.* Probably from the moment she'd come into sight. Just as well she hadn't tried to turn back. He was strolling over towards the gendarme who'd beckoned and called to her — and who as she wheeled her bike towards him spotted her suitcases and became noticeably more interested. His colleague was a few paces further up the road, returning an elderly woman's papers to her. 'Routine check, that's all. It's BOFs we're after.'

BOF standing — in French — for beef, eggs, cheese: BOFs therefore meaning black-marketeers. The woman had clawed her papers back: 'Sooner we all starved, wouldn't you!'

The other one was focusing on the case on Rosie's pillion. In a minute he'd be telling her to unrope it. She *knew* he would. At this moment, though, he only wanted her papers: his hand out in that familiar, demanding gesture.

'Papers!'

'All right. All right . . .'

Leaning the bike carefully against herself, to have hands free . . .

'Shouldn't bother with that one!'

A shout — from the Citroën man. She hadn't been sure that he was a Boche until she heard the thick accent. Raincoat hanging open, held back by his hands in the pockets of a suit too tight for him. Tight over his belly, anyway. Felt hat on the back of his head: thin dark hair, and a face of no distinction whatsoever. Gestapo, she thought, more likely than SD. Much the same type as the one who'd tortured her in Rouen. He was telling the gendarme jocularly, 'She's a Tour de France contender, that one. It's a fact — we paced her, she's a flyer!'

'Is that so . . .'

She had her papers out, told the policeman quietly as she handed them over, 'Pushing it along a bit because there's a job I've been offered, and if I'm late getting there —'

'Have to ride all the way back again.' The gendarme spat sideways, thrust the papers back at her after only a cursory inspection 'we've *our* job to do too, Mam'selle.'

'Of course.'

Leaving it at *that?*

But now the Boches. One was only a few metres ahead: she didn't have to look again to know it. Pushing her papers back inside her coat: avoiding the gendarme's eyes too now — fearful of showing anxiety, giving him an idea he mightn't otherwise have had: except that being right under that pair's pig-eyes —

He'd hawked again. Muttered, 'Good luck with the job.'

Instead of 'Open these cases, please . . .' Rosie met his kindly glance. 'Thanks —'

'Your turn, Grannie!'

The nearer Boche called as she started forward, 'Don't break your pretty neck, now!' The other one was joining him. Younger, but out of the same repulsive mould. Facetiously raising his hat — which seemed to amuse them both. But — as long as they were staying here . . . She wheeled her bike past them and across the intersection — as if she'd neither seen nor heard . . . Mounting carefully, then — *very* carefully: heart still racing, and a mind-boggling thought as she rode on — that she needn't have been here at all. Could have been with *him*. Now — this minute — in London — even maybe in bed . . . She whispered in her mind, *Ben, my darling, I must be raving mad . . .*

Chapter 4

She'd have been with him here and now, Ben Quarry reflected. There on the dance-floor even: he *might* have managed it, with her help. The band was playing 'Mood Indigo' — one of her favourites, they couldn't have sat listening and not danced. From this bar — it was circular, a sort of island; he was seeing most of the room over and between people the other side — he watched the slow-motion huddle of dancers amongst whom he and Rosie might have been clinging to each other at that moment. Would have been, if this was where she'd chosen to come after they'd got up and bathed, dressed, found a taxi. A few hours ago he'd have hurried to her flat after his interview in St James', they'd have gone straight to bed — the bloody knee would have been no impediment there — and he'd have kept his news to himself until after they'd floated back to earth.

Whereas in fact . . .

I could lay me down and die.

He could have been hearing her hum it: with her face against his jaw on the side with the ear that worked. And the leg that didn't: he'd have been leaning on her, a bit. And he'd have looked down, met that dreamy, happy look . . . Soft brown hair with coppery lights in it, wide-apart hazel eyes, and that 'eat-you-alive' mouth of hers. Not that conjuring up her image helped at all: it was more like masochism. Drowning the sorrow, meanwhile. He had two glasses of whisky in front of him and replacements kept coming, but it didn't seem to be having the effect it should have. Murmuring half aloud, 'Oh, Rosie . . .' Leaning with his forearms on the bar's glass-topped surface and his stick hooked on its edge, the dancers a slowly shifting kaleidoscopic *mélange* over there and the entwined gold stripes on the sleeves of his reefer jacket a brighter gold than the whisky. He wondered where Rosie might be now, what she'd be doing.

Time-difference of an hour and a half, of course.

'Hey, Aussie!'

Another Scotch. Courtesy of a US Air Force character name of O'Dwyer. There was another Yank in the group — or had been, they seemed to come and go, sometimes vanish and then re-appear after long absences — also some Poles and a Scotsman, a lieutenant who claimed to be a commando. Ben had dropped in at Shepherd's, with the intention of having a quiet drink on his own while getting his thinking into shape — to stop glooming over Rosie, and instead concentrate on the marvellous thought that when she finally got back he'd be right here in London to meet her — and marry her, this time no bloody argument — and some RAF who were among the missing now had for some reason included him in a round or two of drinks. That was where it had started. They'd decided to move on, he hadn't known where and it hadn't mattered all that much, they'd piled into taxis and ended up here, in one of his and Rosie's places.

He wondered where she was now — now, this very moment. If she'd gone over last night — no, Wednesday night, it would have been — probably by Lysander, which she'd told him would be her preference this time, but alternatively in a Hudson, or a Halifax or some such if they'd been parachuting her in — by now she could be anywhere at all. France was a big country and she could be in any part of it.

He nodded to O'Dwyer. 'Thanks.'

'My pleasure. You still crying in it?'

'Certainly not.'

'You sure look miserable.'

'How I *always* look.'

It wasn't true. He was a happy-looking man, most of the time. Rather large, with brown curly hair and blue eyes: 'wild-eyed' was an adjective Rosie tended to use. O'Dwyer was staring up at him — the Yank was about jockey-sized — as if questioning what he'd just said, about the look of misery being permanent. And the band had switched to 'You Always Hurt the One You Love'. Ben nodded towards the dancing. 'Hear that?'

'Inkspots.'

'Of *course* it's the bloody —'

'Hey, Aussie!' A hand on his shoulder: one of the Poles. 'Whatsa good get leave you don't enjoy it?'

'Good question.'

'*Damn* good question, Polski!'

'Aussie, whyn't you drink up?'

So it went on. He picked up a glass, took a sip, put it down again. Go down to Pompey tomorrow, he told himself. Pack gear, see them in the Haslar hospital on Monday, then back here. He'd had the offer of a bed or sofa in another man's digs in Fulham until he found a place of his own. The whole thing being that he'd got his old job back, would henceforth be working for an outfit in St James' called DDOD(I).

He'd had the call from her flat-mate yesterday at lunchtime, in the Coastal Force base at Portsmouth. Gosport, actually, across the water from Portsmouth-proper. And — all right, as he'd kept telling himself ever since, he'd known it would be coming some time: but for some reason hadn't doubted they'd have this weekend together. Rosie's flat-mate had been off to visit her mother in Somerset — so they'd have the flat — and Rosie had arranged to have leave from midday Friday to midday Monday. Then *wham,* this telephone call. There and then he'd hardly had time to take it in — except the way you'd take in being hit with a sledge-hammer. And he'd still had to come up to London, for the interview about the job up here: the beauty of which had been that since he couldn't be at sea, on account of the knee not being right yet, he'd at least be close to Rosie. *Would have* been. His move up here had been on the cards for a week or so, had needed only today's interview with his old boss to confirm it: and a lot of the pleasure as he'd foreseen it would have been imparting the glad tidings to Rosie this afternoon in bed.

Anyway — he'd got to Victoria soon after midday, dumped his gear in the Left Luggage and taken a taxi to the Nineties in Berkeley Street, where he'd lunched and then had only a few minutes' peg-legging walk down to St James' for the interview with this four-stripe naval captain known officially as Deputy Director Operations Division (Irregular) — and internally, in the department — as 'O'. It was a department of naval intelligence closely linked to SIS — hence its being housed in that building — and Ben had worked in it for a time, after being crocked-up in an MTB action a couple of years ago and then rated unfit for sea duty. All ancient history now, but he'd eventually got himself back to sea as a navigator in the 15th MGB flotilla which, based at Dartmouth and administered by this same DDOD(I), was used only for clandestine operations, running agents and munitions over to Brittany and bringing out shot-down flyers and other escapees.

Now, full circle. Back to the desk in St James' — at least until he was squarely on both feet again.

'Barman's looking to be paid, Aussie.'

'Right on . . .' Looking round at Rumpleburger

— or whatever he called himself. O'Dwyer and the Poles were back, too, the Yank with his nose already in the as-yet unpaid-for whisky. Ben put a handful of notes and silver on the bar, and the barman, an Irishman with a squint, began fingering out what was owing. Ben's father, who was in timber in Brisbane, sent him a cheque occasionally: hence his current affluence.

He told the barman, 'Have one yourself.'

'Thank ye, sir . . .'

'Here's to Poland!'

The Scotsman, holding up a glass. O'Dwyer asked him, 'What's wrong with America?'

'Don't know.' Looking down amiably at the little guy. 'Hard to put your finger on, exactly.'

'Let me tell *you*, then —'

'Ben — Ben *darling!*'

A woman's voice, behind them . . . Heads turning, eyes widening, exchanges ending in mid-sentence. She was looking only at Ben. He'd staggered on the turn, come up hard with his back against the curve of bar. She saw it and laughed: 'Whoops a-daisy!' She hadn't seen the stick, obviously thought he was stoned. She was tall, and exceptionally good looking. Dark glossy hair, creamy skin, wide dark eyes, fantastic body in a green dress he'd seen her in before. Actually she was in the MTC. Had been in the BVAC — British Volunteer Ambulance Corps — he remembered, but she'd transferred to the Mechanized Transport Corps because they got paid and 'Beevacs' didn't. Telling him, '*I* nearly fell down too — when I saw *you!* From over there . . .' A wave towards the tables beyond the dance-floor. '*Can* I believe my eyes?'

Huge dark ones: a man could drown in them. Ben *had* — experienced more or less total immersion — over a period of a few months, some while ago. Before he met Rosie, of course, and before this one — Joan — married Bob Stack — fellow Australian, until recently Ben's CO but currently on his way out to the Mediterranean, to command gunboat flotillas in the Adriatic. Bob and Joan were divorcing, as it happened. None of Ben's business, but she'd cheated on old Bob, really done the dirty on him, although she'd sworn blind in those earlier days that when she did marry she'd go straight.

Ben had thought the leopard *might* change her spots, too. At least he'd given her the benefit of the doubt. Wouldn't have taken a chance on it himself — although that had been her idea — which was partly why she'd grabbed at old Bob when he'd come blundering along.

The band was playing 'You Started Something'. She'd latched her hands over Ben's shoulders, and they'd kissed — after a fashion. Still holding on to him, then . . . 'On your own, Ben — as well as pie-eyed?'

'Neither.' Pointing left and right with his head. '*This* lot's pissed as bloody owls, but —'

The commando touched her arm, and pointed at the stick: 'Fellow's lame. Duff knee, or something.'

'*Ben!* Don't tell me you've done it *again?*'

Referring to the previous occasion: it had been just at the time she'd given up on him and corralled old Bob. He'd shrugged: 'Wasn't *my* idea . . .'

'Well, *honestly* . . . I'm sorry, I didn't see —'

'Doesn't matter. Have a drink —'

'No — you come and join us. Oh, please . . .' Half turning, beckoning to a slightly rotund Welsh Guards captain. 'Remember Billy?'

Billy Bartholomew — friend of Joan's brother Gareth, who was an earl, which made Joan *Lady* Stack. Billy was bleating yes, do join us, like it very much, old chap . . .

Looking pretty sick about it, actually.

'But why don't you join *us?*'

The commando's idea, this was. Supported enthusiastically by O'Dwyer and others. Joan told them, 'Awfully kind, but we're just about to eat.' Back to Ben: 'Lame or not, a few solids wouldn't do *you* any harm, my darling . . .'

In his house in St Michel-du-Faou, Henri Peucat tilted his chair back, reached to the sideboard for the cognac bottle. Motionless then with his hand wrapped round it and his brown spaniel's eyes on Rosie. Really very much like a spaniel's — brown and droopy, sad-looking. She quite liked him by this time — in a vague sort of way. She'd smelt brandy in the moment of the front door swinging open to her. An hour or so ago — roughly. Hour and a half maybe. She'd *got* here, was the thing — after two hard days and a short night in between . . . . Arrival she recalled as a glow of light — not in the hall but seeping from a room behind it — not all that bright but still dazzling from where she'd been, out in the street, while all she'd seen of Peucat had been the dark outline of a burly, slope-shouldered creature with that light from behind throwing a huge shadow across the pavement.

'Dr Peucat?'

'I can't deny it. How can I help you?'

'Suzanne Tanguy. You wrote offering me employment.'

'Well.' Peering out at her. 'So I did. So I did . . .'

He'd pronounced the 's' as 'sh'. She'd thought, *Marvellous. All this way and I'm stuck with a drunk* . . . He'd muttered something about not having expected her to arrive in the middle of the night — getting towards curfew, heaven's sake . . . Out on the pavement by then, with the door pushed almost shut behind him, looking up and down the dark street.

'Sorry.' Turning back to her. 'You'll be thinking I'm an old ditherer. And obviously you've come a long way, you must be exhausted . . . D'you have my letter with you, by any chance?'

'Yes. And other papers — I can certainly identify myself.'

'I'm sure. Needn't have asked . . . I think I'd dropped off, in there. You'd better come in — please —'

'What about the bike?'

'Oh Lord, yes. Garage at the side here. Should have thought. Falling asleep like that, leaves one a bit stupid. Probably am anyway. Here — I'll open up . . .'

It had been eight-thirty or so then, was getting on for ten now. She'd lost her way somehow in Carhaix-Plouguer, wasted time by starting out on the wrong road and having to go back and find the right one. She'd had about twenty kilometres to cover then, to Châteauneuf-du-Faou, where she'd asked for directions to St Michel and had been put on the road to a place called Plounévez-du-Faou where she was to turn left; and after a lot more hard pedalling she'd realized she was completely lost, in a maze of small, winding lanes, in pitch darkness and growing doubt as to whether St Michel-du-Faou even existed.

She'd simply found herself riding into it, eventually. Freewheeling downhill out of black, apparently abandoned countryside to some sort of road-junction with a tall building on high ground to the right and what had turned out to be a café-bar — there'd been light seeping under its doorway — on the corner in front of her where the road divided. She'd propped her bike against the wall and gone in, asked a man in dungarees who'd been reading a newspaper behind the bar whether this might be the village of St Michel-du-Faou and if so whether he could direct her to the house of a Dr Peucat.

He'd given her a long, hard stare. A well-fed

man in his middle forties, unshaven and balding, with a stomach that bulged the dungarees. Nodding — presumably having decided that she was harmless.

'Hundred metres, no more. There — Rue Saint Nicolas. At the bottom, church square's in front of you. Don't go into it, bear right — turning your back to the church, see *that* easy enough — and the doctor's house is on that corner. Corner of Place de l'Eglise and Rue des Champs Verts. Got it?'

'I think so. Thanks.'

'Someone ill?'

'Oh, no. I'm going to work for him.'

'Work for Henri Peucat?'

'I'm a nurse.'

'*Are* you, now. Well, listen, give him a message for me, will you? Tell him I've no damn customers except the kind I don't want, and now he's got you he might find time to drop in for a game of cards. Tell him that, will you?'

She'd given Peucat the message, and an account of the difficulty she'd had finding this village. She could have taken a much more direct route, he'd told her: a road from Châteauneuf that would have brought her in at the south end of the church square.

'Needn't have gone anywhere near Plounévez. I'll have to take you around a bit, acquaint you with the geography.'

'Or sketch it out for me, to start with? I'd like to get straight to work — now I *am* here.'

'Quite right. Anyway I've a map somewhere. But since I've been here forty years —'

'Long as that?'

Small-talk, for God's sake. She'd felt as if she could have lain down where she stood: like some animal in a field, sunk to her knees, then on down, rolled over and begun snoring . . . Peucat telling her — she wasn't sure now at which stage this had been — 'I'm sixty-one, and I came here when I'd just qualified. Then they had me doctoring in the Army — the first war, eh? Too old in 'thirty-nine, thank God. But apart from those war years I've been a lifelong fixture here.'

He wasn't anything like drunk, she'd realized. Just drank a bit. Vague in his manner, and perhaps a bit shy. She thought his teeth didn't fit too well — which from time to time gave an impression of slurred speech. He had a flat sort of face and a sallow complexion, a nose that might have been broken at some stage. His hair was still thick, with dark streaks in it but mostly grey.

He'd enquired rather diffidently when they came back in from the garage, in which he kept an old Ford *gazo,* whether she was expecting to live in the house with him. The question had surprised her: she'd asked him, 'Is there an alternative?'

'Yes. If you prefer it, you can room with my sister in Qinquis-Yven. That's about five kilometres away. She thinks you should . . . She lives alone, there's room enough.'

'Isn't there here?'

'Heavens, yes! My late wife and I brought up our children in this house, and now I'm the sole occupant . . . Look, you'd better stay here tonight, anyway. Whatever Marthe may say about it. Here, give me that suitcase.'

She'd let him take the lighter one, and followed him up the stairs. Thinking that if she'd had to move on elsewhere tonight she *might* have just lain down, given up the ghost . . . Hearing him mutter, 'Put you on the top floor. Well, not the top, that's attic — but this floor's where I sleep, you can be on your own, one up. Otherwise — tongues wag, don't they?'

'Won't they anyway?'

'Would if you moved in permanently, I dare say.'

'Is that your sister's reasoning?'

'It's the way she reasons, yes. Even though you are younger than my own daughters. And allow me to reassure you —'

'Could *you* put up with the wagging tongues?'

'Oh, certainly. Although there are times when my sister's doesn't so much wag, as lash . . . No, *my* reputation, such as it is —'

'It would be more convenient to live here. In view of the nature of my work — my *real* work, which obviously you know about.'

'It's a point I'd wondered about myself. Although you'd find ways to handle it — living at some distance from what's *supposed* to be your job, I mean —'

'Not easily. So — if it's all right with you?'

114

'It's settled. Consider yourself at home.'

It was a relief. She did want to get down to work at once, not waste time trundling from place to place. But — shades of Lise and Noally, she reflected. Separate floors. Actually, no similarity whatsoever . . . 'Attic's up there, you said?'

A short flight of very narrow stairs poking up into the narrowing roof-space: not much more than a fixed step-ladder. The doctor had grunted an affirmative, carrying that case into a bedroom, Rosie following with the other. It looked fine. Victorian, but — fine. Iron-framed bed, vast oak wardrobe, antique wash-stand. Peucat was saying, 'Have to fetch your own hot water from the kitchen. In that jug there. Not too much for you?'

'Certainly not. But — doctor, as I said — since we both know what I'm really here for —'

'Wouldn't we be idiots if we didn't?'

'Well — your name's all I know of *you* — apart from the fact that Count Jules brought you into this.'

'I'll tell you one other thing, then.' The spaniel's eyes blinking at her . . . 'Amongst my patients are a number who reside in the forests. *L'Armée des Ombres,* we call them — as you'd know, I suppose. But you might say that's a lot of what *I'm* here for, nowadays. In other words, we're on the same side — and what else do we need to know?'

She'd nodded. 'Do the Maquis come to you, or do you go to them?'

'They wouldn't come here. Except in very grave

115

emergency, perhaps. We have Boche soldiery right here in the village, heaven's sake. The way you came in, from Plounévez, a building on high ground as you came down to the corner? It looks bigger than it is, perched up there. That's now the offices of the local commandant. It was the *Mairie,* but his Worship now works — as much as he does, which is very little — from his house next-door here.'

'Right . . . Another question, though. I'm sorry, it's just — basic essentials, to set off on the right foot, so to speak — did you realize I'm a pianist?'

'You play a radio, you mean.' He nodded. 'One had assumed . . .'

'But don't worry, I've no intention of transmitting from this house.'

'You could — as far as I'm concerned —'

'They're too quick at detecting radio transmissions nowadays. Detection from long range, then they send the vans in. And men on foot then sometimes — detector sets on their backs. So — I won't. But I *will* keep watch to receive signals — and may I use the attic for that?'

'Of course.'

'Then I'd *definitely* like to live here.'

'And I'll enjoy having your company.' He smiled. 'Descending from the esoteric to the mundane — could you knock up our breakfasts, d'you think?'

'If you'd show me where things are.'

'I have a housekeeper — Melisse Loussouarn. A widow — Jacques Loussouarn was killed in 'forty, he was a gunner sergeant. She comes in every morning, cleans up a bit, goes off to cook luncheon at the priest's house — up the road here — and returns to make supper at six o'clock. Leaves it in the oven, usually, for when I want it. There's some for you now, incidentally — I had mine, earlier.'

She'd swallowed: at the thought of a hot meal . . .

'I *am* quite hungry.'

'You're also tired. Better come along down. Eat, then off to bed. Now you're here we don't want you cracking up.' He led the way again. 'Melisse Loussouarn's a good-hearted woman, you'll have no problems with her. My sister on the other hand — *means* well, but —'

'Will either of them know what I'm really here for?'

'No. I don't think they need to, either. You'll hide your radio?'

'Of course.'

'Don't misunderstand me. Nobody around here has any love for the Boches. *Nobody.* Least of all, either of those two.'

'Do they know you doctor the Maquis?'

'My sister perhaps suspects it. But from nothing that I've told her.'

Downstairs, before starting her meal she'd produced the letter he'd sent her, as proof of identity. Not that it *was* proof — she could have been an infiltrator, the real Suzanne Tanguy might have been behind bars with 'Hector' — but he'd ac-

117

cepted it as such. She thought perhaps he might not be as alert as he should be to the principle that no stranger should be taken at face value, ever: there were questions he could and should have asked, and hadn't. Asking her now, anyway, 'Were you in reality a student nurse?'

'Oh.' Mouth full . . . 'Well — in a way . . .'

'Where and when?'

Swallowing *delicious* rabbit, and mashed turnip . . . 'The truth, or the fiction?'

'Both, I'd better hear.'

She recited the fiction — Paris and Toulouse, and her breakdown after the fiancé's death — he'd heard that bit before, from Count Jules. Then, shrugging — 'The truth is I worked for five days in a hospital ward, just recently. In England, but it was staffed by French doctors and nurses, a ward reserved for de Gaulle's people.'

'So your nursing skills are — rudimentary?'

'I'm afraid so.'

'As long as we can pass it off. You should be seen doing *some* work for the practice — just simple tasks. Visiting patients who can't get here but only need their temperatures taken — or to have prescribed medicines brought to them, and so forth. I'll show you in the morning — my consulting room at the back there, they use the side door — certain days, certain hours. You can help with them sometimes, I dare say. The dispensary perhaps *not* . . .'

'I do agree!'

'It's the village as much as the Boches we need

to convince, after all. An aspect one should be aware of, incidentally — word gets round, the Boches have ears to the ground and pick up that word —'

'Yes. Of course . . .' She was scarcely awake, by this time, but felt she had to drag a few other thoughts together. Lighting a cigarette . . .

'Another thing is — I need to be able to get about. Visiting patients — that's perfect. But *any* reason to be out and about, including night-times — curfew hours, would they give me an *Ausweis* to cover that?'

'I can't see that they'd refuse. As my assistant — well, they *must* . . . I could see them tomorrow. Come along with me — let 'em see butter wouldn't melt in your mouth — eh?'

She'd nodded, breathing smoke. 'Think it'll work, do you? Passing myself off as a nurse, I mean?'

'There are nurses *and* nurses — believe me. And we needn't disguise the truth — Count Jules proposed I should take you on, after your mother's old friend wrote on your behalf — that's believable enough, for sure . . . You see, I have a big, busy practice here — and being no spring chicken . . .'

'Mightn't it be asked why you hadn't taken on a young doctor — who'd be *really* useful to you?'

'It would cost me a lot more, for one thing. I'm getting you dirt cheap — and I'm tight with money. Ask anyone around here, they all know it.'

'So it does — add up . . . I'll pay my way, incidentally. Domestically, food and —'

'Jules de Seyssons did have a word with me about it.'

'That's another thing — I must go and see him. Right away, if possible. Tomorrow, d'you think?'

'Day after. I'll take you, introduce you. Well, I'll telephone, but he's away at the moment — Paris — I think due back tomorrow. But you've reminded me — we discussed your imminent arrival, and he suggested you might start with a visit to Guy Lannuzel at Châteauneuf-du-Faou. There's urgent business to discuss, apparently. Might you do that tomorrow?'

She agreed — yes, she would. 'Urgent business' would mean a request for a paradrop, she guessed. Baker Street were standing by for such requests, had promised they'd be given maximum priority. But she also needed to see Lannuzel about 'Mincemeat', the Trevarez operation.

Another thought surfaced . . .

'Isn't Châteauneuf more or less on the way from here to Quimper?'

'To Quimper . . . Well — more or less, yes, you *could* go that way. The direct route is via Pleyben, you'd be taking a longer way round, that's all.' Peering at her: really, very much like an old dog's eyes . . . 'My dear, you're *very* tired. I think you should go on up . . . You've business in Quimper, have you?'

Nodding, as she inhaled. 'Yes.' It was business that didn't have to concern him, she thought.

She had other things in mind too — including sleep, as he'd rightly observed. And wondering about a bath: whether in any case she'd pass that up, have one in the morning. Thoughts tumbling over each other . . . For instance — maybe the doctor knew about the plans for 'Mincemeat', and maybe he didn't; there was clearly no need to discuss it with him now, anyway. Guy Lannuzel would be the key man in that, she supposed. Count Jules had put the idea forward, but Trevarez was in Lannuzel's area, *and* he was the man in touch with the Maquis in the Montagnes Noires. Peucat would definitely not know anything about the informer in Quimper. Even Count Jules might not. Didn't need to, either: it was SIS business, and Rosie's own, no one else's, she could handle that without bringing *anyone* else into it. Her head was spinning . . . She confirmed to Peucat — his question about having business in Quimper — 'It's just a contact I have to make.'

A nod, and a gesture, open-handed: 'Which obviously I needn't concern myself about.'

'The point is, as I do need to go on there — well, even if you were thinking of taking me to meet Guy Lannuzel —'

'I would, with pleasure, but my Saturday surgery's always the busiest of the week, as it happens.'

'Saturday. Of course . . .' She hadn't thought of that. Hoped Quimper *would* be OK. Well, touch wood . . . But she wanted to be on her own when she saw Lannuzel, anyway; she told Peucat, stubbing out her cigarette, 'I was going to say, I'd just as soon go by bike.'

Chapter 5

She'd slept heavily, as far as she knew dream-lessly, and woke thinking of Ben. She might have been having some dream with him in it, she supposed; but the recollection as she woke was of telling him a few weeks ago: 'My *last* excursion, anyway. I promise you.'

'*Can* you promise? I mean, you can *now* — and mean it — but if your Baker Street chums turn the pressure on again —'

'I'm giving you that undertaking now, Ben. I won't go back on it, I swear.'

She *would* stick to it, too. One way or the other. What Lise called 'Fate' might even guarantee it absolutely.

Might be unwise, she thought, to think too much about 'Fate' — in that sense, anyway. Especially with factors such as 'Hector' in the background. There were no guarantees against betrayal: no more than Ben had had against his ship being hit and blowing up.

She wondered how he was getting along. Whether he'd reconciled himself to it yet.

Bath, now. Even though it meant trespassing on the doctor's floor, and even if the water was lukewarm, as he'd warned it might be. Last night she hadn't had the strength.

Over breakfast — *ersatz* coffee, toast and some unidentifiable kind of jam — Peucat told her he'd tackle the local permit office on his own, and leave it to her to follow up next week. He was going to be busy in his consulting room most of the morning, but he'd fit it in; the Lannuzel call *was* urgent, he thought, and if she was going on from there to Quimper the sooner she got on her way the better.

'As a reason for visiting him — if I needed one — I could be getting some eggs, couldn't I?'

'That would be black market. What about an interest in hens, you're thinking of keeping a few here for our own use?'

'Subject to *that* being legal?'

'Of course. Just don't commit yourself. Last thing we need here is hens to look after. Guy's a charming fellow, but he's also a shrewd business man.'

In Quimper, she'd be visiting a dentist. Even if he didn't work on Saturdays, the surgery was in his house.

She'd finished her 'coffee' . . . 'Doctor — as well as the *Ausweis* to let me be out after curfew, d'you think I could get a permit to drive your *gazo?* And would you allow it?'

'I suppose — it might be useful. A patient to be removed to hospital and no ambulance available — if I were tied up elsewhere — one might present it that way . . .'

'And I could drive you sometimes — on your rounds?'

124

'*What* a kind thought!'

'And stop sometimes when there's a signal to be got out. Different places — and using the *gazo*'s battery, so I wouldn't have to tote mine round. Wouldn't be all that often, anyway.'

She'd done it that way during her last deployment, in the Rouen area. *Gazo* belonging to poor old 'Romeo'. Remembering when she'd got the news from Baker Street that he was to be brought home by Lysander: his huge relief, a surge of delight which she'd found infectious, so that the trip for all its dangers had felt almost like a holiday, although as it turned out it had been a prelude to his death.

Ben woke in an unknown bed. Darkish room but daylight showing through a gap in the curtains. Traffic-noise from out there. Opening his mouth, shutting it again: a taste like floor-polish.

Joan Stack?

He pushed an arm out to his left. Empty bed. He was on this other edge, more or less. Pain in his head — on the side of the ear that worked.

Oh, Christ. Rosie. Rosie gone . . .

Pushing himself up. A flat in Ebury Mews, he remembered. A feat of memory, incidentally, that was enough to prove he had *not* been drunk. Definitely had not. Could remember other things as well: arguing with her: or rather, her arguing with him . . .

This wasn't any *floor* he'd slept on. There'd been talk at some stage of sleeping on some floor.

At least, seemed to be alone in this bed. Checking that point again. And aware he *should* have been with Rosie.

Oh, Rosie. Rosie, darling . . .

It seemed impossible she'd actually — gone beyond recall . . . Chilling phrase, at that, God only knew where it had come from. Reaching with his right hand for a bedside light: he found it, switched it on.

Fair-sized room. Single bed with only himself in it, and the bedding noticeably — meaningfully — undisturbed. His watch had stopped. Looking around now, up on his elbows, seeing his uniform draped over the back of a chair and his halfboots standing tidily upright in the middle of the patterned carpet. Beyond them, at that end, a door was half open. No light beyond it. He pushed himself up into a sitting position, with a hand to the ache in his head. Feeling stupid, more than anything else: for not *quite* grasping yet where, what, how . . .

'Hello?'

Voice like a croak: his own, though, and it went unanswered. Looking at another door, a closed one. Brass fittings, and some sort of notice on it in a frame.

Hotel room?

He manoeuvred his gammy leg out of the bedclothes, slid himself out with all his weight on the good one. He was wearing underpants, he noticed, and one sock. His shirt and black tie were over the back of a chair beside a writing-table. It *was* a hotel room. Memory beginning to trickle back: even before he got close enough to the door to read the notice — which was headed *Grosvenor Hotel* and gave instructions regarding blackout regulations and air-raid precautions, the locations of hydrants and stirrup-pumps, routes to shelter in the basement, et cetera.

Grosvenor Hotel, Victoria. Because he'd stored his luggage in the Left Luggage on this station, on arrival from Newhaven yesterday; he'd gone there from Pompey to collect gear he'd left there and tried unsuccessfully to have sent along to him before. And Joan was using her brother's flat in Ebury Mews, which was close by and where she'd had the taxi take them. She'd been keen on his spending the night there with her. He remembered that. Also that Billy Big-Arse had been sent home hours before — soon after they'd finished supper. In any case he hadn't been enjoying the evening very much. When Ben had first met Joan, a bloody age ago, Billy had represented himself to him as her fiancé, and it was a fact that her brother Gareth, the earl, had been trying to persuade her to accept him. Billy had money, apprently: and Joan had been acquiring a bit of a reputation, in the circle in which they moved — or in Billy's case, floundered. It was surprising that he was still around, still taking punishment; and not in Italy where brother Gareth was — seeing that they were in the same regiment.

Extraordinary, though. Station hotels. Here now in this one solo, celibate — when he hadn't exactly been forced to it — and two years ago the Charing Cross Hotel, with Rosie. In every way as innocent and pure as the driven snow, nothing in any way premeditated or even thought of, but as it had turned out, far from celibate. On the night of the day they'd first met: she'd had a husband shot down and killed, and he'd had the news that he was getting back to sea. They'd met in the SOE building in Baker Street, where she'd been for an interview and SOE had turned her down — on grounds of being emotionally unstable, or some such — so she'd had *that* on her mind too; they'd gone out to have *a* drink together, had ended up having practically everything there was to drink in London, then blundering into the Charing Cross Hotel where there'd been only one single room available and he was *alleged* to have promised to sleep in the bath.

It was a memory he treasured, anyway. *Really* treasured. He thought Rosie did now, too.

There was a telephone beside this bed, he saw. He went to it, and rang down to the hall porter.

'I don't know what the room number is — but my name's Quarry —'

'Ah, the Australian gentleman. Room one-three-nine, sir. Like your bags sent up, I dare say?'

'You a mind-reader?'

'You left instructions with the night porter, sir, and he took the ticket round first thing. I didn't send 'em up before on account of the "Do Not Disturb" notice on your door . . . Will you be wanting breakfast?'

'Yes. Definitely. But what about paying Left Luggage?'

'You left ample funds, sir, if you remember. I'll send the bags up right away.'

Waiting for them to arrive — a page-boy brought them — he ran a bath. Then, lying back in the hot water, remembered more.

Joan's assumption that he and Rosie had broken up, for instance: because she wasn't with him and he'd been drinking on his own, she'd taken it for granted that Rosie'd chucked him.

'I wondered what you could possibly see in her, anyway!'

He'd countered with something like, 'Because the only time you ever saw her you were heavily involved with a shit by name of Furneaux.'

In Sussex — about six months ago. A country hotel that had weekend dances and where they weren't too particular about who shared rooms with whom. Furneaux, with whom she'd been disporting herself that night, was an MTB man. She'd protested, 'Mike's no shit, Ben. Rather a pet, actually. Not that there was ever anything *serious* —'

'Old Bob was entitled to take it seriously.'

'Well — *Bob* —'

'Good mate of mine and a hell of a nice guy.'

'Salt of the earth. Absolutely. Just happens to be *incredibly* dull. You're the man I should have married, Ben. You know that, don't you?'

'You'd have found *me* dull —'

'Oh, cast your mind back!'

'After a while, you would have. We weren't married, it couldn't have been more different.'

'Exciting, is what it was. You know it, too!'

'Suppose it was.' It *had* been. 'But I tell you — if I'd been Bob, the hell with divorce, I'd have bloody shot you.'

'When we were up in Suffolk — wasn't that a *lovely* time?'

'Did have our moments.'

'*Didn't* we. Ben, I'd have married you like a shot!'

In the bath — turning off the hot tap with his toes — the dialogue was playing like a record in his memory. Maybe improvising a little here and there: but this had been the shape and tenor of it . . . Challenging her, he remembered, with: 'Are we talking God's own truth tonight, Joan — no mincing words?'

'If you like.'

'Right. Well — listen . . . It was terrific. Not denying that for a moment. Bloody *marvellous*. But I didn't ever think about marriage. No — untrue — I did think about it, because you talked about it — but I didn't ever *contemplate* it — didn't pretend I had any ideas in that direction either — did I?'

'No, but —'

'Because I wouldn't have bet a penny on you sticking to the bloody rules. And what you've done to old Bob proves I was right. I'm going to marry Rosie — you'd better know that.'

'Except she doesn't seem to be around?'

'At the moment, not. Can't tell you where she is, either.'

'I bet you can't!'

Looking at her. The fact being he couldn't tell her because it was something one didn't talk about. *Nobody* was in SOE, if you asked one of them they wouldn't know what the letters stood for. He shook his head: 'In any case, Joan, honey —'

'I know what you're going to say. You wouldn't marry me, not if you were even more plastered than you are, you *sod* — you're in Portsmouth now, did you say?'

'At the moment. Won't be for much longer.'

'Where are they sending you?'

'Can't tell you. Sorry.'

'You were never mean to me before, Ben.'

'*Not* being mean. Damn it . . .'

'All right. No, you *aren't*. Actually that's the *last* thing I'd —'

'Not to you, anyway.'

'Still comes down to the fact I can't get in touch with you. If I wanted to ask you to my wedding, for instance?'

'To old Billy? Well — I suppose you *could* do worse.'

'How?'

'Oh. I don't know . . .'

'I'll give you all *my* numbers. So when you *do* see the light — or she gives you your marching orders . . .' She cocked an ear to the music —

they were playing 'Guilty'. 'Think you could dance?'

'With a stick?'

'Ben, I'm *so* sorry.'

'So am I. Frustrating.'

— *maybe I'm wrong* — *Loving you like I dooo* . . .

'I never enjoyed dancing with anyone *nearly* as much as with you, Ben.'

He thought of Furneaux again: the pair of them on that dance-floor in the place in Sussex, with a room booked for the night and old Bob thinking she was miles away. It had been sheer bad luck running into them, that far from Newhaven. Nothing serious, she'd just told him: so what *had* it been, just fun and games? Nodding to himself: exactly that. As it had been with him, too. She'd caught a waiter's eye, was holding the empty bottle up: singing under her breath: '— *then I'm guilty* — *Guilty of loving you* . . .' Eye to eye with him, then: 'That's a fact too, as it happens.'

He'd nodded to the waiter. Back to Joan. 'Listen. We had a *hell* of a lot of fun. It's also a fact you're about the loveliest-looking Sheila I ever set eyes on. Let alone — you know —'

'Yes. Oh, yes. Often think of it, matter of fact. Cigarette?'

'*Lovely* memories. Yes — thanks. But listen — you're beautiful, and so sexy there ought to be another word for it, and — fun, and — all of that. I was sort of gone on you, I admit it. But if we'd married I'd have finished up in old Bob's shoes.'

'You would *not*, Ben! That's the whole damn *point!*'

'Might've made three years instead of two, but —'

'Ben — however you thought then or think about it now, here's the truth. I was thinking about getting married and *wanting* to be married and it was all because of you. You had to be so bloody careful of yourself though, didn't you, little old Ben mustn't risk getting his bloody feelings hurt —'

'Here comes the wine.'

It took a long minute or two, getting it uncorked and poured.

'Thank you.' Sniffing at it, wrinkling her nose. 'Worse than the last one.'

'Same label. Different bathtub, maybe. Joan — there could be something in what you were saying then —'

'My absolute belief is if you'd asked me to marry you when we were up there — I say this in all sincerity, Ben — so there'd have been no Bob, no divorce, no what's her name . . .'

'Rosie, d'you mean?'

Rosie, who was back in France. He came out of the steamy bathroom, back into room 139 of this Grosvenor Hotel: remembering that he *had* got a bit mean with her at that point. And how it had come in waves — happy enough when he was letting her talk as if they were reunited lovers, less so when it was things as they actually were, such as the fact that he was going to marry Rosie.

But he'd felt sad, too, that she was hurt, and so sure — genuinely, it seemed — that he and she *would* have made it.

Then the taxi, he remembered, arriving at Ebury Mews. Her brother Gareth's flat, she'd brought him to; in Gareth's absence she had the use of it.

'Pay the man, will you, Ben?'

He'd had his wallet out, and she'd had her key in some door: he asked the driver, 'Victoria just round the corner — right?'

'Spitting distance, Guv.'

'Right. So take me there, will you. Joan —' looking round, seeing she had the door open and a light on inside — 'Joannie, look, I'll ring you — OK?'

She hadn't said a word. He'd thought of telling her he couldn't because of his knee, but that might have made the cabbie laugh.

Ring her now?

The thought of his wallet made him check it was still there, in the inside pocket of his reefer. As it was, of course. Spent a bloody fortune, last night . . . Anyway — first-class return warrant to Portsmouth, and a card — Joan's — on which she'd written the telephone numbers of the flat in Ebury Mews, cottage — her aunt's — at Rodmell in Sussex, and the MTC establishment in Brighton.

Ring her now?

Might send her a bunch of flowers. Chances were, she'd be a little sour: especially if he woke

her at this hour. Whatever hour it was . . . So —
breakfast first, then the bill including flowers —
hall porter'd handle that — then to Charing Cross
for the train to Portsmouth. And ring her last
thing before departure. Some such line as 'Lovely
seeing you, sorry I was a bit grogged-up, please
let's stay friends?'

Heading southeast from St Michel Rosie had
to pass through a hamlet called Loc-Guénolé,
then cross the Carhaix-Pleyben road, and after
another two kilometres she'd be in Châteauneuf-
du-Faou. Peucat had roughed out St Michel's
environs on the back of some medical form or
other, extending it on another sketch to guide her
to the Lannuzel poultry-farm, which was a kilometre or so east of Châteauneuf.

It was a pleasure to ride without all that weight
of luggage. Not to mention the transceiver, or the
pistol or vast sums of money . . .

She passed Loc-Guénolé almost without seeing
it. Also a few farm carts, a herd of half a dozen
Friesians driven by an old woman with a stick,
and a *gazo* lorry full of rubble. Not a single Boche
until she got to the main road, where she had to
dismount and wait while a whole convoy passed.
There were more of them about than ever, Peucat
had said; a lot of such movements, too. All coastal
regions were of course heavily garrisoned, especially around the U-boat bases; Brest was only
about sixty kilometres away, Lorient the same,
and Kernével — Doenitz's U-boat command and

135

communications HQ — was even closer, on the Lorient road to the east of Quimper.

She came into Châteauneuf-du-Faou from the north, and spent some minutes pedalling around. The Hotel Belle Vue, which Peucat had mentioned as the local Boche headquarters, was clearly identifiable by the swastika banner over its front entrance. She'd had a glimpse through trees of the same foul emblem decorating the former *Mairie* in St Michel. Then she was passing the Belle Vue when a Boche officer came out, hurrying towards a staff car that was waiting for him and calling back in German over his shoulder to some colleague in the hotel's entrance. A joke, perhaps: a smile lingering on his face as he turned back, glancing at Rosie as she went by, as if inviting her to share in his amusement. A soldier-driver had slid out of the car, pulling a rear door open with his left hand and saluting with the other; she rode on past it, remembering Peucat telling her over his map-drawing this morning that the commandant here was an easy-going man who tried to get on with the locals.

She thought, So *let* him try. Please God, the bastard wouldn't be here all that much longer. Invasion *had* to come this summer. Passing the church, which was impressive; she had a fair idea of the layout of the streets now. In case of future need . . . The staff car had continued straight on at the corner where she'd turned. There was a certain amount of other traffic, but not much, and it was virtually all agricultural: a *gazo* truck

136

loaded with manure, a tractor with a trailer . . .
In a shabby way, this was an attractive place, with
views out to lovely countryside, the valley of the
Aulne to the south of it with the river itself in
giant loops and beyond that the wooded slopes
of the *Montagnes Noires*.

Where Guy Lannuzel's Maquis groups hid out.
And between here and there, on the edge of the
Forêt de Laz, the Château Trevarez. At which
she thought she might do worse than take a look
before pushing on to Quimper.

Really lovely country, with a hint of spring in
the air making it feel and smell good too. Worth
coming back to when it was truly French again,
she thought. Bring Ben: show him the ruins of
Trevarez, tell him 'Look what *I* did!'

Well — I and a few others . . .

She came to the poultry-farm sooner than she'd
expected: a board with a painting of a fat red hen
on it, on a farm gate on her left, and a stone-built
cottage set back from the road, sheds dotted over
a field behind it. The track from the gate led to
a barn, and there were fields on both sides, some
of them recently ploughed. She dismounted, entered through a smaller gate at the side and
pushed her bike up a bricked path towards the
house. There was a *gazo* pickup truck parked at
the side of the barn — from which a man emerged
just as she happened to look that way again, past
a corner of the house. Long-legged, and limping
— a heavy enough limp for it to be noticeable
even at this distance — with some heavy load

balanced on his shoulder. That would be Lannuzel; Peucat had told her last night that he'd lost most of one foot in 1940 when he'd climbed out of a tank and trodden on a mine. In Peucat's opinion he'd been lucky, not only to survive the explosion itself but also to have been invalided while the going had so to speak still been good.

Dogs were barking somewhere up there. And the man had seen her, and stopped. Then called — having studied her for a moment, long-distance — 'Hold on a moment.' He went on to the truck — yelling at the dogs to shut up — dumped his burden, then came limping over to her.

Thin. A greyhound look about him. Lame greyhound. Dark hair greying at the temples, face dark with stubble. A young, lively face though; she'd have guessed his age as about thirty or thirty-two.

Rather a Ben type. Even to the limp . . .

'Help you?'

'Captain Lannuzel?'

'Guy Lannuzel. Rank's useless around here, stupid hens won't salute. How can I help you?'

'I'm here to help *you*. Count Jules suggested I should come. Suzanne Tanguy — working for Dr Peucat, as from today.'

Lifting his hands . . . 'Says it all, doesn't it?'

He had a slow, slightly lop-sided smile. Hadn't shaved for two or three days, she guessed. It was a strong face, under that camouflage; piercingly blue eyes, a firm handshake. Hard, dry hand.

138

'Come along in. Brigitte will give us coffee if we're lucky. You said "as of today" — meaning you've just arrived?'

'Last night. After two days on *this*.'

'So you can't have met Count Jules yet.'

'He's away. Back today, Dr Peucat thinks, but he'd left a message that I ought to see you right away.'

'Good of him.' A nod . . . 'Are you — English?'

'French.'

'That's what I thought — you sound it.'

'Well — since I *am* —'

'And proud of it?'

'As a matter of fact — intensely so.'

'Extraordinary, isn't it? Goes for me too, but — must be cracked, mustn't we . . . Park your bike there, if you like.'

Against the wall, between a window and the door which he now pulled open.

'Brigitte! We have a visitor!'

Gesturing to Rosie to go on in: into a warm odour of lamp-oil. Lannuzel called again, stooping through the doorway of a small front room, 'She's called Suzanne — the one we've been waiting for!'

'You can stop fretting now, then.' A girl came through, saw Rosie and put her hand out, smiling. 'You're very welcome, Suzanne.'

She was taller than Rosie: and by no means fat but large-boned, wide-hipped. About Rosie's own age. Brown hair tied back, blue eyes, features markedly similar to her husband's. Rosie said,

'Sorry to turn up without warning. Should have telephoned. Suzanne Tanguy, by the way: I'm a nurse, of sorts.'

'You've joined Dr Peucat. I know. That's to say, we knew you were expected — this brother of mine's been counting the hours . . . Please, sit down?'

'Brother?'

'Thought she was my wife, eh? But that's something I don't have. Brigitte has a husband though — still locked up, prisoner of war, in Germany.'

'So we believe. Not a word for months, however.' She added, 'My married name is Millau. My husband is — or was —' she crossed herself, swiftly and economically — 'a bomber pilot . . . Suzanne, would you like coffee?'

'I'd love some — if it's no trouble . . .'

'But listen.' Her brother cut in: 'If we should be interrupted, you might have called in to ask whether it's possible to buy eggs — which of course it is *not* —'

'And which I'd know. So the truth is I'm interested in acquiring a few laying hens. I came only to enquire about it — I'd need to build a pen for them, and heaven knows what else — so I've come to ask for advice, that's all.'

'Feeding them would be a problem, unless you grew your own corn as I do. And I doubt old Peucat's got room for that, has he? But OK, that's what we're discussing — now or any other time, should we need to explain ourselves.'

'Is that likely?'

'Oh, they sniff around. Neighbours, mostly. Never tell anyone *anything*, around here. Fine people, salt of the earth, but — you know . . .'

'I'll get coffee.'

'Bless you. And now, Suzanne.' He sat down, facing her across the table, having discarded a donkey-jacket. Tough-faced, muscular, the collar of a checked shirt visible above a sweater that had seen much better days. It was a rectangular table with four straight-backed chairs at it; two matching carvers flanked a fireplace heaped with ash. One picture only — the Virgin Mary with her infant in her arms. Lannuzel asked Rosie, 'How soon can we arrange for a *parachutage?*'

'*Arrange* for it — immediately. It should *happen* then within a few days. Or say a week. Depending on the weather, of course. But in London they're waiting for my signal, and they've promised immediate action. All I need is your shopping-list and map coordinates for the drop.'

'It's all ready for you. But — easy and quick as that, is it? Truly, no more than a week?'

'Is it a dropping zone that's been used before?'

'Yes. Not recently, but —'

'If it has been, and it's in the RAF's records, that'll save some time.'

'It must be, surely.'

'And have you done it before, you personally?'

'*Parachutages?* Sure. Several. But there again, not recently. Things have been bad for us — you know? Two of the three caches that we had were discovered — *and* hostages taken and shot —'

'Any idea how they were discovered? Infiltration?'

'One boy, they got hold of. He'd helped with an earlier drop. They beat him to death — he died in the gaol in Morlaix afterwards. They got both locations out of him, the other one he didn't know about. Poor kid . . . *Christ,* but they've a bill to settle when the time comes, uh?'

She nodded. 'On ropes from lamp-posts, and not too quickly.'

'We're of the same mind, then. But I was saying — those caches discovered, while at the same time Maquis numbers have trebled. From various causes — maybe you know —'

'Primarily because it's getting into people's skulls that the Boches aren't going to win.'

'Yes. That's about it. And that there's likely to be an invasion soon. That's my next question — *when?*'

Blue eyes blazing as if they had lights behind them . . .

'Invasion?' She shook her head. 'Can't tell. Don't know. But I think it has to be this summer. Could be next week, next month —'

'If it's next week we aren't going to be much damn use here!'

'So let's hope it won't be. All we can do is work as fast as we can. You'll have your drop, whatever you're asking for — within reason —'

'Brens, mortars, grenades, Stens, *arbalettes* — and listen, a dozen of the Stens with *silencieux?*'

Arbalette was the Maquis term for a bazooka.

She'd nodded: aware that they might not get every single item — Brens were in shorter supply than the far cheaper Stens, for instance — but if they didn't it wouldn't be her fault. She added, 'And rifles, presumably, and hand-guns. Explosive and detonators too. There'll be a lot of rail tracks to be blown up, when the time comes. I'd like to get together with you on that, sometime soon, make some outline plans for it. And what about training — would you accept weapons instructors if they were dropped to you?'

'We'd accept them, but we don't need them. There's a team of guys — well, my own sort, up there, and they can train the rest — when we have the weapons. You know I was a soldier — so were these. Good men, all of them. Only thing is, if there's anything new we *don't* know about —'

'I could help. I finished a refresher course only a few weeks ago.'

'You?'

Staring back at *his* stare . . . 'It surprises you?'

'You'd come into the mountains, teach us?'

'Well — how else?'

'I think I love you!'

On his feet, reaching to her across the table: Brigitte was in the doorway, edging in sideways with mugs on a tin tray. Her brother glancing round at her, holding both Rosie's hands in his: 'I've just fallen in love with this woman!'

'Well, don't overdo it.' Setting the tray down, she smiled at Rosie. Her face was weathered: you

143

could see she spent a lot of time outdoors. Nodding in her brother's direction: 'Goes a bit haywire, sometimes. Sometimes I think he might have been hit in the head as well as that foot. One day a piece of shrapnel may pop out of one ear and he'll come back to normal . . . Guy — sit *down?*'

'What I wanted to ask —' Rosie had lit a cigarette — 'was about to ask, just now — you said you've received paradrops before, but did you organize any of them yourself?'

'One, I did. Others I only helped with. Why, d'you think I might not be up to it?'

Getting up, shutting the door properly . . . Brigitte had left them again, having drunk her coffee scalding-hot. Lannuzel didn't want her to hear more than she had to. He'd told Rosie as the door was drifting more or less shut behind her, 'Safer that she shouldn't. I want to have her safe and fit for when her husband gets back to her. One of these days, please God.' Crossing himself, as she had. Rosie wondering whether they had parents alive; or what news *had* reached them of the husband. But there wasn't time for chitchat. From here to Quimper would be the best part of forty kilometres, she wanted to have a look at Trevarez *en route,* and to be back in St Michel before curfew. Didn't have much idea how long her business in Quimper was going to take, either.

Ring the dentist from here, maybe.

144

Lannuzel was back at the table; she answered his last question . . . 'No — of course I'm not doubting your competence. But very large resources go into every drop, and I'm expected to know how it'll be handled. The location, for a start — it's been used before, you said, but not lately: has the area around it been checked out recently?'

'For signs of Boche interest in it, you mean. Yes — the boys would know of anything like that. It's high ground, not overlooked from anywhere higher, accessible by way of a forest track so we can have transport right there. The transport's available and ready, too. The clearing's about a kilometre long and half as wide, thick forest all round. I have the coordinates written down, but I'll show you on the map as well. As to how it'll be handled — there'll be a reception team of sixty men — four groups of fifteen.'

'In the *Montagnes Noires*, all this?'

'Where else?'

'Will you have new caches ready — pits dug, or whatever — have it all out of sight before daylight?'

He nodded. 'Locations already picked. Better security, too, only a handful of us will be in on that part of it. We're very conscious of the urgency, Suzanne — that's why I've been pressing for it. And we could turn out four times as many men if we needed to.'

'That's something else. You're alert to the threat of infiltration, are you? Because — I'm sure

145

you're aware of this, but the more numerous your Maquis become —'

'The more careful we have to be. Yes. Vetting new arrivals is — rigorous. If there's doubt — well, they don't get by. A committee sees to it, I only advise when they ask me.'

'What happens?'

'Depends. When it comes to the worst — a hole in the ground. But you needn't concern yourself, Suzanne.'

'I'm sure not. It's your business. But it *is* a very real danger, isn't it. I know — a Boche infiltrated a *réseau* I was in, not long ago. And with the numbers you're dealing with — don't have to be Boches either, do they . . .' She took a pull at the stub of her cigarette, then squashed it out. 'Let's see what you're asking for. If I can get it coded in time, London will have it tonight. Or tomorrow — I've a full day ahead of me . . . Incidentally, there seems to be a lot of troop movements going on?'

'You've noticed, have you. Invasion fever, we're calling it.' He was on his feet: 'In other words, they've got the wind up . . . Sit tight, I'll get my notes.'

She'd glanced over his list, and checked the coordinates against his map. This lot wouldn't take long to encode: there was a set form for paradrop proposals and a code-letter combination for each type of weapon. He'd also listed supplies other than weaponry and ammunition,

146

items ranging from bandages to corned beef — which he'd put down in Maquis terminology as *singe*, or monkey.

She poised a pencil over a blank space at the foot of the ruled sheet of foolscap. 'We'll need a message for the BBC to send. How about "The first signs of spring are always welcome"?'

'I've often wondered who thought up that gibberish.'

'It takes a rare talent, let me tell you. You'll remember it though, will you, and listen for it — in case I break my neck, or something?'

'In case — yes. And in case I do I'll tell it to a few of them up there.'

'One other thing. No, two. The first is we don't have a code-name for you, and we may need one.'

'Well . . . Friends in the Army used to call me Guido. A long time ago, no one does now.'

'Guido. Fine.'

'Brigitte calls me that, sometimes. But between ourselves only.' A jerk of the head, towards the kitchen. 'What I was alluding to a few minutes ago, by the way — keeping her out of it, as far as possible — if you'd assist in that, I'd be grateful.'

'Of course.'

'This place is actually her husband's. Was his father's — a small-holding, it was my idea to go in for chickens. But it's theirs — I'm only caretaker, you might say, until he gets back, I want to hand it over in good working order — and his wife with it. If you get the point?'

'Sort of.' Staring at him for a moment. Then a shake of the head. 'Guy, listen. There's one matter you haven't raised. OK, so I haven't either, yet.'

His turn to look blank. She prompted, 'Château Trevarez?'

'Trevarez. *That* . . .' A shrug. 'Does it need to be raised? It was a suggestion from certain quarters, not from me — and in any case —'

'Are you against it?'

'Well — in a way, yes. I'd say the *parachutage* is what's most vital — and Trevarez, after all —'

'The *parachutage* you could say is in hand, now. There'll be others too — in the *Montagnes d'Arrées* for sure and perhaps elsewhere, and you can come back for more too — when you can handle it. The Trevarez project, though — obviously you haven't been told — we're going to hit the place, and we'd like help from some of your Maquis.'

'Count Jules know about this?'

'It was his idea. We've elaborated on it a little, that's all.'

'I'm amazed.' His eyes seemed to go duller, when the subject under discussion was of less interest or appeal to him. He shrugged, rubbing his unshaven jaw: the thumb pointing southward then: 'A few of *them* will be delighted, of course.'

'The groups you and the count have been restraining.'

'Yes. Our communist brethren. I've got more than he has, it's my problem more than his, but we see eye to eye on the subject. In a nutshell, those fellows want to be at it all the time — assassinate a Boche officer here or de-rail a locomotive there — with the result hostages get dragged out and shot, and the Boches are stirred up and make life more difficult for us, while what we *need* is time to get ourselves into shape for the time that's coming.' He opened his hands, palms upward: 'What does Trevarez have to do with *anything?* Upset a few U-boat sailors, spoil their holidays a little, and in return get a whole gang of innocent people shot?'

She nodded. 'I can answer that.'

Checking the time. Although this was as important as anything she'd be doing today. 'D'you have a telephone here?'

'Oh, yes. When it's working.'

'I'd like to make a call before I leave, if I may. Then how long'll it take me to get to Quimper?'

'On your bike?' He gave it a moment's thought . . . 'Two and a half hours, maybe.'

'I'll aim to do it in two, then. I'm a flyer. A Boche called me that yesterday. But — Trevarez, now. Actually there's a code-name for the operation — "Mincemeat" . . . I agree about cutting out pinprick actions, but this *won't* be anything of the sort — *not* simply to kill or inconvenience a few sailors. Although there are likely to be some in the château at pretty well any time, isn't that so? Submariners from Brest, Lorient, St Nazaire?'

'Brest and Lorient anyway. Yes, they come and go. We've thought of ambushing their transport, but it's always heavily escorted — armoured cars, so forth. But the fact is, Suzanne, their presence here does us no harm, they're no part of the garrison. The boys who want that place hit don't give a damn — they're communists, that's all, for their own political ambitions they want to be seen as taking the lead — and the *hell* with hostages. You know?'

'So we give them this Trevarez action, in return for their agreement to toe the line elsewhere — including joining the FFI.'

'You working for de Gaulle now?'

'Cooperating — we have a common aim, after all.'

'And have that lot *agreed* to this — line-toeing?'

'Count Jules believes they will. I'm surprised he hasn't discussed it with you. Anyway he must have known *I* would.'

'We haven't spoken in the past few weeks. He goes to Paris a lot, you know. But — Suzanne — it seems to me — well, it's still the same project, isn't it? One old château, a few Boche sailors shaken up — and afterwards, hostages murdered — to please the hotheads?'

She shook out two cigarettes and pushed one over to him. Leaning towards the match he struck then. 'May I fill in some strategic background for you?'

Gallic shrug: lighting his own Caporal, eyes blue slits above the flame . . . 'If you want to.'

'Don't assume this isn't relevant — because it damn well *is* . . . The U-boat war — it's far from over. The Royal Navy fought them to a standstill last spring, and they pulled out of the North Atlantic altogether — to the Azores, West Africa, Mediterranean, leaving the northern convoy routes alone for a while. But they're back at it now — with a new type of U-boat, new guided torpedoes — et cetera. And one thing vital to invasion prospects is to keep the convoys coming. Before, *and* after. Right?'

He nodded. 'So?'

'*So* — obviously the U-boats themselves, but also their command, communications, the whole administrative structure behind them, are now targets of great importance. Anything we can do to disrupt their operations is something we've *got* to do.'

'But not with pinpricks.'

'No. And unfortunately the bases themselves are too heavily protected for ground action to be a realistic option. As you were saying about their road transport.'

'Better targets for your air forces.'

'The bomb-proof submarine shelters make that largely ineffective too. Trevarez, on the other hand — well, you know it only as a leave-centre, rest and recreation for U-boat crews. On the face of it, a pinprick target. Although if one could knock off enough of them —'

'Break open the detention camp where hostages are held at the same time, maybe?'

'Well, *that's* a thought. Except they'd just take other hostages, wouldn't they . . . ? Anyway — did you know that once in a while the château is used as a weekend conference centre for the *Kriegsmarine*'s top brass?'

She saw momentary surprise: then recollection ... 'I'd forgotten. We did hear there'd been some such occasion. About a year ago.'

'It's a regular thing, now. Well — periodic. And our information is there'll be another one soon. Think of it — the naval staff all under one roof — and on your doorstep. The admiral commanding in the west here — name of Bachmann, he's the one who ordered the so-called "execution" of two Royal Marine canoeists about fifteen months ago — he *invariably* attends. Also —'

'How do you know this?'

'We do know — that's all. Take my word for it?'

'Very well.'

'I was saying — if we're lucky, Grand-Admiral Doenitz may favour us with his presence. He has only to nip up the road from Kernével: and those are *his* U-boat bases, all in spitting-distance — eh? But when he can't make it — off hobnobbing with Hitler, or whatever — he's represented by his chief of staff, Rear-Admiral Godt. Godt's his deputy, runs the U-boat force from day to day — another prime candidate for having his weekend spoilt . . . You with me, Guido?'

'Yes. Indeed . . .'

Fingers drumming softly: eyes bright again. Forehead creasing, then: 'One also sees snags, however. First, would your source alert us long enough in advance?'

152

'Yes.' She nodded quickly. 'That's essential. Several days' notice — and time meanwhile to work it out. It'll be a night thing, anyway.'

'Night thing . . .' He picked a shred of tobacco off his tongue. 'Yes, it would have to be. Beyond that, however — well, we'll put our heads together. And obviously we'll use the red brigade . . . But — any practical ideas? The château's surrounded by open park-land, for instance — perimeter fencing, and big iron gates with a guard on them — one might anticipate they'd reinforce that —'

'Yes. The guard's always reinforced, substantially. But nobody's asking you to assault the place, Guido. It'll be done from the air — RAF. That's one reason we *have* to have advance notice, to give them time to set it up. But — Pathfinders to light the place up — d'you know what I mean by Pathfinders?'

'Flare-dropping aircraft.'

'Right. Mosquitoes or Halifaxes. They come in low, illuminate the target for bombers right behind them.'

'So what d'you want of *us?*'

'Your men in ambush. Not too close — but all around, in the lanes and fields. It's for you to work out, you're the soldier. Might arrange to block the road approaches, at the last minute? There'll be panic — evacuation in all directions — wouldn't you expect?'

'Like cutting a cornfield. Catch the vermin as they scoot out.'

Nodding, stubbing out his cigarette-end. Low-voiced then, glancing up — keeping it quiet so Brigitte wouldn't hear . . . 'Better no shooting, maybe. When it starts, anyway, before they know we're there. Just throats to cut . . .'

Chapter 6

The château was a pretentious-looking structure of grey stone with conical-roofed towers at each corner and rectangular ones as well; the central façade with what was obviously the main entrance in it was recessed between two of those. Exceptionally tall chimneys looked as if they'd been added — or heightened, anyway — as afterthoughts: the general effect was more Germanic, she thought, than French. The RAF might improve it, in fact. She'd caught her first sight of chimneys and towers over treetops from some distance up the road coming south from Châteauneuf; then as instructed by Lannuzel she'd turned right at this road junction and almost immediately found herself passing the entrance gates.

Pedalling by slowly. No sign of any sentries or guards. But the gates were shut and chained, and there was a gatehouse; there'd doubtless be Boches inside it. Distance to the house from here about a kilometre: you'd hardly see it once all the trees were in full leaf. She rode on until she was out of sight of the gatehouse, then swerved in to the roadside and stopped with one foot on the grass bank — ready to push off and be pedalling on, minding her own business . . .

Only two roads to block, she thought. With farm vehicles, or whatever they could get hold of. Heavily laden farm carts, maybe. There'd be plenty of cover amongst these trees — other side of the road, the forest side, to her left as she stood now — and deeper inside the park were clumps of shrubs of some kind, might be rhododendrons. Cover inside there too, therefore. But they wouldn't want to be too close to the target. She imagined the bombers — or rather the Path-finders — as coming from the north, over Châteauneuf-du-Faou and picking up the looping pattern of the Aulne. As long as there was a moon . . .

Looking at the château again — about to move on, conscious of having no time to waste — but visualizing it as it might be on the night: flames bursting out of those very large windows, the roof erupting, towers collapsing and crashing through — and confusion, panic . . . Remembering Lan-nuzel's murmur of 'Throats to cut', and the glitter of excitement in his eyes. Although he'd given it more thought by the time she'd left; walking down to the gate together they'd agreed there'd have to be guns used, also maybe the bazookas he was asking for, to knock out whatever trans-port they might have. Not a bad idea, to immo-bilize them in there: not every bomb would hit the château itself.

Leave it to him, she thought. Pushing off now, getting going. This road would take her through the village of Laz — forest all the way, this stage of it — then after another ten kilometres or so to a larger place called Coray, where she'd turn right on to the road for Quimper — where she had a dental appointment now, for roughly two-thirty.

A woman had answered the phone, and Rosie had asked to speak to Michel Prigent personally. Lannuzel still there at the table, listening, his eyes fixed on her.

'If it's to make an appointment, Madame —'

'It is, but I also have an enquiry to make about a mutual friend. If he could spare me a few moments?'

'Who shall I say — ?'

'Just tell him Zoé. It's probably the only name he'll have been given by this friend.'

'Zoé. Very well . . .'

Slightly icy. Prigent's wife, she wondered? Then she heard voices in the background, and he came to the phone.

'Michel Prigent speaking. I did receive a message, Mam'selle, that you might be asking for an appointment. Are you actually in pain at this moment?'

'Well — off and on . . .'

'Have to see what we can do, then. Fortunate that I'm working this Saturday, I don't always . . . Do you know where I am in Quimper?'

'Yes, I do.' They'd shown her on a street-map, in St James'. 'And I'd hope to get there about two-thirty. The other thing, though — it's coincidental, but am I right in thinking that "Micky", as he likes to be called, may also be seeing you this afternoon?'

She'd used the code-name because telephone lines weren't secure; and the Germans would surely recognize the name le Guen. Prigent now following suit: 'Old Micky . . . Why, yes, here we are . . . It was he who recommended you to me, wasn't it? He and I were at school together — back in the Dark Ages. He probably told you? But yes, two forty-five. My wife made this appointment — the name's virtually illegible . . . I'll fit you in before him if I can: even if it means he'll have to wait a little.'

'I'll be there as close to two-thirty as I can.'

She'd hung up. Prigent would have rung 'Micky' then, told him he'd had a cancellation and would be glad to see him at that time if he could make it.

She wondered if Ben would have stayed up in London.

Probably not. She couldn't imagine him spending much time propping up bars on his own. He'd have had his mysterious interview and gone back down to Portsmouth, she guessed.

If you left a man on his own for — well, a year, say — or a few months — having refused to marry him — could you reasonably expect him to live like a monk? If he was as attractive and full of life as Ben was — and with a war on, all that?

Second question: would it matter?

Answer to the first one: yes and no.

And to the second: yes. But — as long as there was no serious involvement . . . Wouldn't applaud it, exactly, but — there *was* a war on. And one *had* declined to marry him. Because of the war, her job and his job — and having had one husband killed already . . .

Another 'but', though, in answer to that second question — it definitely would matter — a lot — if it was that Stack woman who got her claws in — if he was crazy enough to let *that* happen.

Most men would. She thought Ben wouldn't. She knew — because he'd had to admit it after she'd caught him out in some deliberate vagueness — that he and Joan Stack had been lovers — a couple of years ago, before she herself had known him. In fact she'd been married then, to Johnny: in whose fidelity one couldn't trust for more than ten minutes, once he was out of sight.

Her mother had been very keen on Johnny. And did *not* approve of Ben. Summed up her judgement, well enough. Rosie had introduced him to the old bitch when he'd had a few days' leave, just after Christmas, and they'd spent it at home in Buckinghamshire, not in her mother's small house but in the manor itself as guest of her uncle Bertie — who'd lived on one lung since being caught in German gas in 1918. Ben had got on well with him; had had something to celebrate, too — a DSC, the award of which had been announced only that week. Her mother *was* a bitch, though. Rosie hadn't realized it until after her father had died and they'd returned to live in

England. Before that either she'd been too young to notice, or Papa — whom she'd adored — had kept his wife in control.

Ben had been marvellous, anyway, putting up with her bad manners. *Was* marvellous . . . It was a weird thought, in present circumstances, that if things had gone as planned she'd have been with him now. Would have been for nearly twenty-four hours, by this time: with two nights and a day still to go. Originally the plan had been to meet at the flat around midday: she'd told him over the telephone last weekend, 'Don't be late', and his answer had been, 'Don't keep me waiting at the door!' In both their mind's had been the certainty that they'd be in bed within minutes of his getting there. Then on Monday, the last time they'd spoken, he'd said he couldn't make it until about mid-afternoon — because of some interview he was having.

Please God, keep that tarty Joan creature away from him?

He *liked* her — Rosie knew it — although at this stage in a reproving sort of way, for having done the dirty on his old mate.

It should be enough to keep him away from her, she thought. He was extremely loyal to his friends. As long as he didn't start feeling *sorry* for her. That could be fatal. Remembering another girl — name of Solange . . .

Oh, bloody *hell!* Roadblock ahead . . .

Nothing to be scared of, she told herself quickly. Nuisance-value maybe — in that any

serious delay might foul things up in Quimper —
if Prigent had 'Micky' there to meet her and he
couldn't wait. He worked as a clerk in the *Kommandantur*, obviously couldn't take unlimited
time off — even for dentistry.

Maybe he wouldn't be working on a Saturday.
Prigent might be summoning him from home.
But she thought the Germans in those places *did*
work six days a week.

She'd dismounted — as had half a dozen other
women cyclists ahead of her, all faced with the
problem of getting papers out while also wheeling
bicycles. Some might also have black-market
goods in their baskets, which they'd be trying to
hide. If you were caught black-marketing by
French police you might do a day or two in gaol,
but if Boches were involved or the gendarmes
were required to hand you over to them you could
find yourself being held as a hostage; then if there
was an assassination or sabotage — nothing you'd
had anything to do with or even knowledge of —
you could end up against a wall.

The only incriminating item Rosie had on her
was Lannuzel's shopping-list. And they'd only
find that if they searched her.

Which they would not. Papers being OK — no
reason to.

Touch wood. Take a fair amount of explaining,
that list.

How many times had she passed through
checks like this one, she wondered. Thirty times?
Fifty? Out of what had become virtually habit she

161

began taking longer, slower breaths, to slow her heartbeat.

Think of Ben.

He would *not* let himself get mixed up with that woman. Not only because of recent events — her cheating on Bob Stack — but also because she, Rosie, was here in France. She knew the thought of it made his skin crawl; especially after one of his former colleagues in the naval intelligence department had mentioned to him that the average life of an SOE pianist in the field was six weeks. That had *really* thrown him: despite her having pointed out that she'd already been in twice and come out twice, unscathed.

Almost unscathed. Ben knew all about the nightmares.

The women ahead of her were shuffling forward again, getting into line to file through where gendarmes and a grossly fat plain-clothes man — nationality uncertain — were checking papers.

Ben wouldn't let her down. Ever. Not in *any* circumstances.

Lise's voice, an echo in her brain: 'It's good, is it? The real thing — like I have?'

It was — and that was a marvellous thing to know. Not just hope — *know*.

'Papers?'

'Yes. Here.' Handing them over; then waiting patiently while the gendarme scanned them. He had no reason — thank God — to suspect they'd been forged in a grey stucco-fronted house on the Kingston by-pass.

In Quimper she found the Parc St Matthieu, then Rue Salonique, turned right into Rue de l'Argonne. Left then, and up to the next intersection: still seeing in her mind's eye a batch of the hideously familiar red-and-black posters, announcements of 'executions' carried out, pasted to the wall of a swastika-draped building back there.

Murderers. Sickening, sadistic anti-Christs. She could see a group of young ones on that next corner: louts in grey-green uniforms loafing on this weekend afternoon, gawping at passers-by. At *her* now, some of them, as she slanted around the corner into Rue de l'Yser. It led to a cemetery, but Prigent's house and surgery was about halfway along. She heard guffaws behind her — rich Teutonic humour, no doubt, out of those brutish minds.

Come-uppance coming soon, boys . . .

She dismounted, padlocked her bike to a gatepost, brushed herself off before she rang the bell. She was holding a handkerchief to her cheek when the door opened and a pink-faced girl in a white overall coat peered down at her.

'Yes, Madame?'

No wedding ring. *Not* Madame Prigent.

'I have an appointment. It's mademoiselle, actually.'

'I ask pardon, Mam'selle.' Careful smile: somewhat wooden-faced, in fact. Standing back to let her in, and pointing with her blonde head: 'Please . . .'

A narrow hall, and off it the usual kind of waiting-room: cheap furniture, a couple of framed diplomas, a window to the street and two other doors. The girl passed her, opened one of them and put her head in: 'The two-thirty appointment — Mam'selle Zoé?'

Two forty-nine now. From that inside room, a waft of some kind of antiseptic and a hissing of running water, and a male voice — just a few quiet words. The blonde backed out, shutting that door and crossing to the other one.

'If you please.' Holding it open. 'Monsieur Prigent hopes not to keep you waiting very long. But this is Monsieur le Guen.'

'Ah. Ah, well . . .'

Pushing himself up: from a hard chair, although there was a comfortable-looking sofa he could have been sitting on. 'Mam'selle Zoé, I presume!' Jocular: but it was forced; there was nervous tension in every movement. He was about fifty, with sparse grey hair, little grey moustache, narrow shoulders in a brown jacket that didn't fit. Maroon pullover, white shirt, frayed black tie. Rosie shook a cold, bony hand. 'I've been looking forward to meeting you.' Glancing at the girl again: 'Will Monsieur Prigent be joining us?'

'Not for the moment.' Slight surprise — as at a silly question. 'He has a patient . . .'

'I'll need to see him before I leave, that's all.'

'Of course.' Obviously she knew this had nothing to do with dentistry. Pointing. 'If you'd press that bell — it rings on my desk.'

'Right. Thank you.'

'Excuse me.'

She left them. More than a touch Germanic, Rosie thought. She sat down, on the sofa. 'Micky' seemed undecided for a moment, then pulled the chair further out and turned it more or less to face her. Keeping his distance: still with that tense, scared look. What she knew from her briefing in St James' — apart from the fact that his name was François le Guen and that he'd recently been recruited as a sub-agent by Michel Prigent — was that before the Occupation he'd taught German in some *lycée,* and that it was his knowledge of the language that had qualified him for his present job in the *Kommandantur.* Also that his wife had left him several years ago, that he had a son in a forced labour camp in Germany and a daughter who lived with him here in Quimper.

She took out her cigarettes. 'Smoke?'

'Thank you. If you can spare one.'

'Oh — I think so . . .'

'Well.' Searching for matches. 'One's ration doesn't go far. In fact —' he'd found them, was fumbling one out — 'if one can't afford the un-rationed variety —'

'Thank you.' He'd lit hers: she watched him putting the match to his own, managing it only with difficulty because of the visible trembling of his hands.

Scared of *her?* Or of life in general?

'Have you been told what I'm here to ask of you?'

165

'No. Prigent summoned me, that's all. And I told him — not on the telephone, I couldn't, that's one of the impossible things about it, on the telephone right there in the general office I can only say yes, I'll come if I can — meaning if my employers allow it. Well — Saturday, so — but I can't *argue* —'

'Of course you can't.' Shaking her head slowly, looking sympathetic, trying to stem the flow. 'Better if he called you at home, I'd have thought. I'm sorry, it was my fault this afternoon, turning up at such short notice.'

'That hadn't anything to do with it. And I wouldn't want him calling me at home — if he got my daughter on the line, next thing you know *she*'d be caught up in it . . . But I've tried to tell him — he's always too busy to listen — the fact is I simply want him to leave me *alone,* from now on. If they aren't suspicious already they soon will be, I have a *lot* of worries, and —'

'Micky —' It was a ridiculous name for him. Micky Mouse . . . Prigent's little joke? — 'I don't want to embarrass you — but if money's one of those worries —'

'It's not. He — Prigent — well, to a limited extent, he —'

'— takes care of it. All right. I *don't* want to embarrass you. I was only thinking that this *is* an extra job we're asking you to take on, so it might be no more than fair to — recognize that financially.'

'The problem is less money than — than —'

166

he was developing a slight impediment — 'than having anything to d-do with it at all. I'm sorry to say this, but — but I've had enough. *More* than enough. I'm — all right, I ad-admit it, I'm f-frightened. Not just for myself either, but for my daughter, they don't d-discriminate, you know, you know how they work, these swine —'

'I do know — yes. But please — listen . . . Nobody's making you do anything you don't want to do. Nobody could, could they . . . I'd *like* to persuade you to help us out, because if you won't — well, frankly, it'd be — a considerable blow . . . But — is there some positive reason to be frightened, suddenly? And does Michel Prigent know about it?'

'No, he doesn't. Only a few words I managed to get out just now when again he wouldn't listen. Fact is, I haven't spoken to him lately. Well, he hasn't needed me, obviously. That's partly why I suppose I'd been hoping I might be left alone now. Working with them as I do — under their noses —'

'I can imagine.' She'd cut in, stemming it again. 'It would call for a very steady nerve.'

'It may be my nerve's run out. *Worn* out.' He'd shivered. 'I can't pretend ever to have been — any kind of hero. But as a Frenchman — well, they more or less conscripted me, simply because I have a good command of their language. I used to teach it.'

'I knew that.'

'One isn't *proud* to be in their employ. Only —

a matter of survival. And then Prigent proposi-
tioned me, as it were in the name of France —'

'What you've been doing is *surely* in the interests of France!'

He seemed more relaxed now, she thought.
Blinking at her. A long pull at his cigarette . . .
Then, through smoke: 'Are you French?'

'What would you think?'

'I only wondered. Something Prigent said . . .
Anyway — you'd understand —'

'It's why I do what *I* do. Why I'm here.'

'One — lacks courage, I suppose.'

'The strongest nerves can wear thin, can't they.
And being worried for your daughter . . . Does
she know you're a *Résistant?*'

'Oh — she'd be astounded!'

'And proud?'

Gazing at her: a faint smile twitching, then.
'You flatter me. The extent of my — participa-
tion . . .'

'What does she do for a living?'

'Marie-Claude is a teacher — in the school
where I used to work. But her subjects are mathe-
matics and science — not *my* line at all.'

Rosie was looking round for an ashtray. He
scrambled up, fetched one from the window-sill.

'Thanks. Look — this favour I was going to
ask —'

'Better you didn't tell me. I truly don't *want* —'

'It's all right. I'd trust you with the secret, I
think — even if in the way you're thinking now
you might not trust yourself.'

'But why should you?'

'Instinct. As good a word for it as any. And it's my job — part of it, anyway. Don't you make *your* mind up about a person more or less instantly?' She saw the watchful, assessing look: assessing the degree of bullshit . . . She shook her head. 'I assure you, this would be simplicity itself. Also *very* important — far-reaching importance, it wouldn't be forgotten — you know?'

'What I know most clearly is I don't want to come here again. When he called today — Prigent, I'm talking about —'

'Don't you trust him?'

'No. Or like him. Tell you the truth, I never did.'

'But you agreed to work with him?'

'Well, one forgets, treats an old acquaintance as one would have *liked* the relationship to be.' A shrug. 'Pointless.'

'I see. But anyway — luckily — to provide the information I want, you wouldn't need to come here. Or anywhere else. Simply telephone him. And you could do it at night, rather than from your office. Is it an apartment you live in?'

'A small terraced house, in the Rue d'Etang.'

'If you'd do it — just this one favour — I think I could get you fifty thousand francs.' She saw the flicker of surprise and interest: went on as if she hadn't, 'What's more, the effort would be minimal. *And* your name would be on record afterwards — as I said. It's not a *little* thing, this — and all I'm asking for is one telephone call

'— less than a minute, perhaps ten seconds.'

'Some snooping first, presumably?'

'I have reason to believe it's information that passes routinely through your office.'

'The telephone call would be to Prigent?'

'Yes — but that'd be all — just that once.'

'Could I not speak to you directly?'

'Oh —' she shrugged — 'I'd sooner we worked through him, Micky. Only over the wire, after all, no actual contact?'

'Contact with *you* — yes. But — I'm sorry, no more involvement of *any* kind with Prigent.'

'It's a date, or dates, you'd be giving us. Literally a few seconds' work — for fifty thousand francs?'

'The money would of course be welcome. It would solve some problems. Things my daughter needs, in particular.' He paused, stubbing his cigarette out; it must have been burning his fingers, there was so little left of it. 'But it's not the crucial thing. I'll be honest with you — the crucial thing's not to wake in the night with one's heart going so fast and violently that — God, it's indescribable . . .' Leaning forward, forearms on his knees, hands clasped together, white-knuckled . . . 'Do you know what terror's like?'

She nodded. Bringing her pack of Gaullois out again. 'As a matter of fact, I do.'

'Well.' A shrug. 'But — you're young, strong —'

'A lot of us know what it's like. Thousands of

us — men and women of all ages and descriptions
. . . Here.'

'*Very* kind.'

'When the war's won, Micky — can't be more
than a year or so now, there *has* to be an invasion
soon — we'll come into our own, then. Stop being
frightened, start being — that word again —
proud . . . *Thousands* of us, including you and
me.' The match flared: she leant forward to his
cupped hands. Sitting back again then. 'What
we're working for. What you want too, I'm sure.
Especially as a man who *has* been working for the
Boches — which is how a lot of people — including Prigent maybe — might see it?'

He'd glanced at her momentarily, and nodded.
Taking the point, for sure. Placing the spent
match carefully in the glass dish on the sofa's arm,
then.

'Could I *not* telephone you directly?'

Expelling smoke . . . 'One problem is I'll be
spending most days and some nights out of the
house where I live. You might have someone
answering your call who not only knows nothing
about anything, but *mustn't,* either.'

'If I left a message to call me back? I'm *never*
out in the evenings. Well — no more than once
in a whole month, say. I'd ask for Zoé, and if
you weren't there I'd say please ask her to call
Micky. Nothing else, I wouldn't utter another
word.'

She shook her head. 'They wouldn't know anyone called Zoé, and I've no intention of burden-

ing you — or anyone else — with my real name. The object being — what you said — *not* to wake screaming in the night.'

'But you know *my* name?'

'As it happens. In the course of planning this operation —'

'From Prigent, you'd know it. And you say not me or anyone else, but you'd burden *him?*'

'What makes you think so? *I'll* be ringing *him* — probably every day at a set time — for any news he may have had from you.' She gestured: '*If* you're prepared to help.'

'Why couldn't you telephone directly to me?'

She thought about it. Having felt in the last minute or two that the ice was cracking: and very much aware that there was no way she'd manage *without* his help.

'You see —' speaking again before she could — 'I'm *not* going to telephone Prigent. I'm sorry, but that's all there is to it.'

Looking a bit pleased with himself. For having put his foot down so firmly, she supposed. Fine: *let* him feel good. She made herself sound hesitant: 'What if I called you and Marie-Claude answered? Or a cleaning woman — or —'

'I don't have one. Cleaning woman — good heavens, what next . . . But — I said, I'm very rarely out at night. If Marie-Claude did take your call I'd grab it from her, that's all.'

'What'll you tell her about this Zoé person who keeps telephoning? Some woman who's taken a shine to you?'

'I might let her assume — something of that nature.'

'But —' smiling at him — 'a girl you never see? Only receive curt telephone calls from?'

'Marie-Claude is not to know whom I may meet during the day. Or at weekends even. She has her own life, her own young friends, colleagues from the teaching profession —'

'I'd call you François, would I?'

'I suppose . . .'

'Or Monsieur le Guen?'

'François would seem more natural.'

'I suppose it would.' She nodded. 'All right.'

Settle for that, she thought. For the time being. If it upsets Prigent, too bad. 'Micky' was indispensable, whereas Prigent was a supernumerary, beyond this point. The truth of it was that if Micky had demanded twice that amount of money — it was the equivalent of about £250 — she'd have had to agree to it. Count Jules would provide it. He was banker, had accepted this arrangement in his talks with the Organizer from the Nantes *réseau*. It was a system SOE were applying wherever there was a well-heeled local on the team who'd agree to it, finding it advantageous usually from his own point of view, effectively transferring currency to a safer haven. It saved agents having to carry dangerously large sums of cash around more often than they had to. In the present case, Count Jules was to advance whatever funds were needed, and Baker Street would deposit the equivalent in sterling in his name in a London bank account.

She asked Micky, 'Shall I bring the money to your house?'

'Perhaps a lunchtime meeting. Either at the house or at a café. The Café Providence is one I often use. D'you know where that is?'

'There's a Parc de la Providence, isn't there?'

'Exactly!'

'Very well. I'll make my first call to you on Monday night. The money'll take a few days, perhaps even a week or so. And by that time I'll try to have a better way of keeping in touch than telephoning.'

'What other way might there be?'

'I'll let you know. But telephone operators have been known to listen in — haven't they?'

Staring at her: that queasy look again. He wasn't a difficult man to frighten. He'd moistened his lips: 'One should be — guarded, then.'

'*Very* guarded. Give me the number, anyway. And Monday night, I'll call . . . I'm so glad you're going to do this for us, François.'

'You make it so — logical. Inevitable, almost. When you walked in here — frankly, I had no intention —'

'I know — and I'm grateful for the change of heart. Others will be too — believe me, you won't regret it.' She crushed out her second cigarette not much more than half smoked. 'But now listen. Here's what we want . . .'

Chapter 7

She'd come into Quimper on the road from Coray — from the east — and would be taking the more direct route back to St Michel-du-Faou now, via Pleyben, but she still made a circuitous departure — eastward as if for Coray again but turning due north after a few kilometres into a country lane that crossed the Odet river and came out on the Briec road about five kilometres north of town, having covered about ten. With no reason to *expect* a tail, but every reason to ensure she didn't have one — or to know about it, if she did.

From here to Briec, say seven kilometres. Then about the same to Pleyben, and from there to St Michel another eight — via country lanes, that bit, and with darkness setting in. Thirty-five kilometres, say: should make it by six, Henri Peucat's supper time.

Encode Lannuzel's shopping-list then, and bung it off to London. Out into the sticks by *gazo,* maybe. Otherwise, early tomorrow.

'Micky' had left the surgery ahead of her. He'd been glad to hurry back to his duties, and when he was out of the way she'd been able to spend a few minutes in conclave with Michel Prigent — code-name for this operation, 'Cyprien'. He had to be near enough the same age as le Guen, but looked ten years younger. Dark — and sleek, well fed, barbered and manicured. Successful dentist to a 'T': but hard-eyed, she guessed ruthless. He made no attempt to disguise his contempt for his old school-friend.

'In a bit of a state, isn't he?'

She'd nodded. 'Seems to think his employers might have suspicions of him.'

'He has one advantage. Neither the Boches nor anyone else is likely to take him very seriously.'

'*I* take him seriously. He's indispensable, in this operation.'

'Trevarez. Yes — in that particular context, I suppose . . .'

'They've told you about it, then.'

'I told *them* about *him*.'

'Of course. Your old schoolmate, you recruited him . . . I'll be keeping in touch with him directly, by the way, won't have to trouble you again in this way.'

'It wouldn't trouble me in the least.'

'What I would be grateful for is if you'd keep an eye on him for us. And let me know if — well, if anything untoward —'

'Untoward?'

'You'd hear as soon as anyone, wouldn't you?'

'I'd hope to. But I'd guess he's as likely to throw his hand in as to fall foul of the Boches. Precisely why he's developed this aversion to working with me, or aversion to me personally, I don't know . . . Would I be right in guessing it's as a result of his persuasion that you're electing

176

to deal with him direct?'

'It makes sense, that's all. The information I need will come from him — touch wood — so why not?'

'Well . . .' A shrug of the heavy shoulders. 'How do I let you know — if I hear he's in trouble?'

'I'll call you if I have reason to think he might be. It would only be if there were a breakdown in communication between us. I'd be calling about my appointment; if you had no news of him, your receptionist might say you'll call me back.'

'But as I'd have no number at which to call you —'

'You couldn't — right. But you wouldn't need to. If you did have news for me, you'd have told your receptionist to bring you to the telephone there and then.'

'All right.' The smooth smile again. 'All right, Zoé.'

He didn't like her, she realized. Fair enough — she wasn't mad about *him*. Which he'd have sensed, of course — also perhaps anticipated, since relations between SIS and SOE were often not exactly warm. That plus his being cut out of her business with le Guen, whom he'd seen hitherto as *his* stooge.

Too bad. But another thing she didn't like was that he knew about Trevarez. It probably couldn't have been helped: he'd have had to have known about it in order to have produced le Guen in the first place — doubtless at the instigation of his bosses in St James'. Anyway, he could now be left out of it: while all le Guen had to do was keep his eyes open for an order to deploy a company of infantry to the environs of the Château de Trevarez, probably over a weekend, and pass on the date or dates of that deployment. He'd confirmed this afternoon that such orders — from General Dollman's 7th Army Headquarters — did pass through the *Kommandantur*'s general office, had to do so because troops required for any such purposes in the *Montagnes Noires* area would invariably be drawn from the Quimper garrison.

Le Guen had asked her, 'Some kind of Maquis action, is it?'

She'd shown surprise. 'What makes you think so?'

'Well — they say that those parts are crawling with them.'

'Why don't they do something about it, then?'

'Choose their time, I suppose. Perhaps they don't have the forces here they'd need. So much ground to cover — eh? Also they prefer to use French troops against Maquis, don't they — Milice or LVF?'

Milice were paramilitaries originating in the Petainist south, before the Boches marched in there as well; they'd spread all over, since. And LVF were *Légion Volontaires Français* — brackets *Contre le Boishevisme*, close brackets . . . What had done the trick with le Guen though, she thought in retrospect, had been that he'd found her sympathetic, the low-key touch of blackmail, how

178

much better he'd look in the long run if he had a record as a secret *Résistant* — and last but perhaps not least the little matter of fifty thousand francs.

She quite liked him — in a limited sort of way. Understood him and felt sorry for him, anyway. Imagining him as she guessed he'd have been at school with Prigent, for instance: physically rather feeble, probably getting knocked about a bit; hopeless at games, but a bit of a swot. All right, a bit of a drip. And you could imagine Prigent showing him the same contempt to which he'd reverted now. Recruiting him, jumping at the chance of having an agent right there in the *Kommandantur,* he'd have turned on the charm: old *copains* like ourselves should pull together, François old fellow . . .

Then resumption of bullying tactics. Prigent might be less clever than he thought he was, she suspected.

She was in St Michel soon after six, and Peucat opened the door to her. No scent of brandy. She'd asked him at breakfast, incidentally, how he seemed to have plenty when it was in such short supply — even cafés having certain days on which they couldn't sell it — and he'd told her that some patients preferred to pay in kind, and Timo Achard on the corner — the one who'd directed her to this house — was convinced he'd saved his wife's life a few years ago, thus felt a lifelong obligation to him.

'Exhausted again, Suzanne?'

'Slightly . . . Key of the garage, please?'

An armoured troop-carrier came rumbling from the left, up Rue des Champs Verts, its yellow headlights washing the nondescript house-fronts. Audibly slowing as it approached: but only to swing around this corner into the Place de l'Eglise. Peucat had come out on to the pavement and pushed the door shut behind him, to shut in the light from the hall. It had been dark for about half an hour and there was already a waning, flattened moon up there, in and out of cloud. It looked and felt like rain coming, with a moon so watery it could have been its own reflection in a puddle.

He had the garage door open. The racket of that vehicle fading southward . . . Rosie murmured as she wheeled her bike into the garage, 'Where'd those swine be off to, I wonder . . .'

'Not to church, for sure.'

'No . . .' Emerging . . . 'But they do, don't they. Always puzzled me. How *could* they believe in a God of love?'

'Or in a God that could love *them*.' Peucat paused, thinking about it . . . 'Well — if the truth's all in men's minds — as I suspect, at times — there's no limit, is there. You might have a patron saint of the concentration camps . . . Did you see my young friends at Châteauneuf?'

'Yes. That's all fine.'

'And Quimper?'

'That too. But there's something I'd like your

help with — I don't know if you have friends there?'

'Lots. Well — a few, anyway.'

Entering the house, now. Door shut: Peucat crouching to shoot the lower bolt. Sanctuary, of a kind — at least, it felt like it. She hung her coat up: a working girl, back from the day's hard grind. Turning to him, then: 'How was *your* day?'

'Satisfactory. As far as your *Ausweis* and driving permit are concerned, it looks like plain sailing. And we're expected to lunch at Scrignac tomorrow. Count Jules is back — I spoke with him. He's hoping to have Jaillon there in the afternoon, to talk business with you . . . Anyway let's have our supper now — and you can tell me what you want with my friends in Quimper, what *that's* about.'

'Yes. Right. I'll get it as soon as I've cleaned up a bit. Why don't you have your drink, meanwhile?'

Then homework, she thought — the Lannuzel shopping-list to encode. With a second one tomorrow, no doubt. Jaillon was Lannuzel's counterpart in the *Montagnes d'Arrées*.

She got the first one off the next morning, from a ridge on the edge of the Forêt St Ambroise. Peucat drove the converted Ford off the road into partial cover in a growth of still leafless beeches, Rosie connected the transceiver's leads to the *gazo*'s battery terminals, strung the seventy feet of thin aerial wire over low branches, and crouched amongst nettles to tap out her message. Peucat meanwhile leant against the car, smoking a pipe and keeping lookout. They'd been to the police together earlier, first thing after breakfast, to sign forms for her permit to drive the *gazo*. The gendarmerie was at the western end of the village, facing on to a cobbled market square, with a garage on one side of it and what seemed to be a rubbish-dump on the other, and it was open at that time on Sunday mornings. The young policeman on weekend duty — Peucat called him Gervais, and they were obviously on good terms — told her that by tomorrow noon, with luck, she'd be able to collect the permit from the *Kommandantur*, where it would be going first thing in the morning to be approved and rubber-stamped with the Nazi eagle and swastika. An *Ausweis* allowing her to be out after curfew might also have been issued by then. She should make sure of taking all her other papers with her, he warned.

'Do they talk French, there?'

'French employees do most of it. All it takes then is the Boche stamp on everything.'

Peucat had nodded. 'Probably rubber-stamp the employees too.'

The gendarme had glanced at him quickly, then at Rosie; the doctor had shrugged. 'Sorry. Better be off. Many thanks, Gervais. Your mother's well, I hope?'

He'd told her outside, 'He's one of us. A thoroughly good fellow. Any way he can help, he can be counted on.'

'Are there many like that?'

'More than you might expect.'

The cook/housekeeper, Melisse Loussouarn, was there when they got back to the house. She'd called in not to work, but to meet Rosie. *En route* to Mass, judging by her attire. She was a cheerful, pretty woman of about forty; it could only have been by her own choice, Rosie guessed, that she hadn't re-married. Except there weren't many men around, of course — only the very young or the old. Rosie assured her that she'd look after her own room, make the bed and so on, also mentioned that the rabbit stew and last night's fish pie had been delicious. And there were left-overs enough for tonight's supper. Mme Loussouarn's hand on her arm, then: had Suzanne yet encountered the sister of Monsieur le Docteur? She hadn't? Well . . . The brown eyes rolled . . . 'But to be fair, under her crust the old girl's not so bad. As long as one's a *little* careful . . .'

They'd set out in the *gazo* in mid-morning: up Rue St Nicolas and to the left around Timo Achard's bar, then immediately right, and from there bumbling along a narrow, twisting lane for about four kilometres to a village called Lannédern, where they turned right again on to a better road. The sky was clearing, with streaks of blue between patches of wind-driven grey cloud, but it had rained heavily in the night and the pot-holed lanes were still flooded. Rosie did her best to memorize every corner and landmark, while Peucat provided a running commentary on who lived here or there, whose farm that was, and so on. At a place called Loqueffret — only about three kilometres from Lannédern, but it had been slow going — might have been faster by bike, in fact — he waved his left hand northward: 'That fork would take us through the villages of Brennilis and Kerberou, and on to link with the main route up to Morlaix. I have patients in both those villages: and by Kerberou one's well into the *Montagnes d'Arrées*. As you can see . . .'

Dark heights, up there. Wilder and steeper country than the *Montagnes Noires*. Fine Maquis territory, obviously. They were still heading eastward at this stage: after about two more kilometres trundling through a hamlet which the doctor named as St Herbot, then grinding on slowly for about another five towards the larger rural centre of Huelgoat.

'Where I have a dozen or more patients. If time permits, on our way back we might stop so you can meet some of them. I have a rival there, but he's been in practice only a few years, and the country people are loyal for the most part. They don't chop and change . . . By the way, my sister —'

'Wants me to visit her, you said last evening.'

'She does, yes. I'll take you along, when there's an hour or two to spare. Incidentally, I was thinking that your own invented past — the fiancé who was killed in Brest?'

'Daniel Miossec.'

'It might appeal to her. She suffered a similarly

184

tragic loss. I never met the fellow; she and our mother were playing the cards close to their chests — as always . . . But he was a fisherman, had his own what d'you call it — trawler — up at Roscoff, several were wrecked in one dreadful storm, and he drowned. After which she could never give her affection to any other man.' He shrugged. 'You're thinking, *that* old classic!'

'No — why —'

'Look here, now. Up ahead here . . . That wilderness is what we call Mare aux Sangliers. We can drive on as we're going — straight through Huelgoat and up to Berrien, where this road joins the main one that comes up from Carhaix-Plouguer and continues northward to Morlaix — alternatively as we enter Huelgoat we can turn right, join that same road further south and follow it up between Mare aux Sangliers and the forest of St Ambroise. The road climbs there, into the hills — might be suitable for your purpose?'

'We've time to make the diversion, have we?'

'Not so much of a diversion, really . . .'

They found this place after about half an hour's slow climb in low gear — a fairly level section where the *gazo* could be driven off the road and Rosie would be in cover, out of sight of any passing traffic while Peucat could seem to be a motorist who'd just stopped for a smoke, or to admire the view; and within a few minutes she had it all set up. Red light glowing over the word 'send': power on, and ready to transmit. She shifted her position in the damp undergrowth, moved the set on to her lap — it weighed only five and a half pounds — and put on the headset — headphones — tight on her ears. Glancing round, with her fingers ready on the key, seeing over the tops of docks, nettles and brambles the *gazo*'s roof and above it a haze of smoke from the gazo's burner. To the left, Peucat's head and the jut of his pipe. All clear, therefore: starting with a fast ripple of morse identifying herself and seeking contact, then with the switch at 'receive', getting it — a 'go ahead' from the operator in Sevenoaks, Kent. Her own operator — Zoe's — with whom she'd connected directly through having her own individual crystals in the set. She'd inserted them before leaving St Michel this morning. This would have made the operator's day for her, Rosie guessed: knowing all about it because it was a job she'd done herself — at Sevenoaks, up to the time her husband Johnny had been killed and she'd been accepted by SOE for training as an agent. A whisper — her own — among the nettles: 'Good girl!' With the two-way switch back at 'send' and the morse key beginning its fast chatter, groups of letters and numbers which when decoded would be read in Baker Street as *First recipient code-name Guido repeat G-U-I-D-O requests paradrop soonest to previously used field co-ordinates as follows . . .*

Lannuzel's list of requirements, then. Followed by her own request for a spare Mark III transceiver and an 'S' phone to be included in the drop, the container to be marked with a Z for Zoe, and that the *message personnel* to be broadcast should be 'the first signs of spring are always welcome'. Then: *Operation Mincemeat in hand, date will be signalled when supplied by Micky,* and — finally — that a second paradrop request would probably be transmitted later today, and that she, Zoe, would be listening-out from midnight to 0100 tonight and alternate nights thereafter.

Finishing, she gave the Sevenoaks operator a chance to send anything she might have for her. But there was nothing. She switched off.

Gazo still there. No sounds of any other traffic: seemed they still had this hillside to themselves. Except perhaps for Maquis — whom one wouldn't expect to see but might well be seen by. She felt better for having got her first signal away. Sevenoaks now had the *Montagnes Noires* requirements, Baker Street would have the signal by dispatch rider within the hour, and the drop would be made even if she, Rosie, were to be arrested or shot dead between now and then. That was a good part of the reason she'd have liked to have got it away last night: a feeling she'd always had, when there was anything important to be sent — to get it away, have *that* much accomplished. The other side of the coin meanwhile was that the Boche long-range radio-detection experts might now be alert to the fact that a new pianist had started work somewhere in western Brittany. *New* pianist, unless they were able to identify her 'fist' — as an individual operator's morse-sending technique was called — from any tape-recording they might have on record from her previous performances. It was a possibility; and the worst possible consequence could be that if any such recording had been made during her last stint, the Rouen episode, they'd as likely as not be able to match this one to a photograph taken while she'd been in the hands of the Gestapo there. Which wouldn't be so hot.

Anyway — if they *had* picked any of it up, they'd have their ears cocked from now on for repeat performances. And they'd get one this evening, probably. After which, chances were they'd send out detector vans to get cross-bearings on subsequent transmissions from much closer range.

Might send vans out from Rennes, perhaps.

If they had any there. And if they *had* picked up that transmission.

If . . . She shrugged mentally, told herself *Just get on with it* . . . The odds were stacked against the visiting pianist, there was nothing new in that. You just had to keep it in mind, and be bloody careful. Such as — amongst other precautions — only being on the air a few minutes at a time. Which she had.

She called, 'Doctor — disconnect, please?'

'Of course.'

She unplugged the aerial wire, and moved through the trees parallel to the road, coiling it. It snagged here and there: being so thin — and black, difficult to see except close up. Returning to pick up the set, and then to the car, she had blood on one hand from a bramble scratch. Licking it off . . . Peucat asked her, completing his neat coil of the electric lead, 'Successful?'

'Should have been.' She eased the transceiver into the old valise — or Gladstone bag — which he'd found for her. The Mark III, measuring only ten inches by seven by five, easily fitted in at the bottom of the case, together with its bits and pieces — headphones, aerial and long leads, battery too when she had to have it with her. On top went a sheet of cardboard, then an assortment of bandages, cotton-wool and other medical bric-a-brac. She shovelled it all in, snapped the case shut and dumped it in on the back seat. No good hiding it: if you were stopped and they wanted to search, they'd search, and a bag that looked as if it might deliberately have been put out of sight would be the one they'd pick on.

Peucat had climbed in, was sitting with his hands on the wheel, ready to start off. Brown-spotted hands: and spaniel's eyes surveying her as she slid in and pulled the door shut.

'I want to tell you, Suzanne. I admire you tremendously.' He shrugged. 'For what that's worth — eh?'

She leant over, kissed his sallow, slightly bristly cheek.

'For what *that's* worth. Thank you.'

'As well my sister didn't see it.'

She'd asked him about his children — having meant to ever since he'd mentioned having some

— and he'd told her there were three daughters, all in distant areas of France, one son who'd died of TB as a medical student before the war, and another currently working in Paris.

'Calls himself a publisher. Some rag of a magazine I wouldn't wipe my boots on.'

'Pro-Nazi?'

A grimace: 'It's not my favourite subject, Suzanne.'

'I'm sorry.'

'It was the wrong one who died.' A glance sideways, then. 'Wicked thing to say, you're thinking?'

'No. But I'm truly sorry.'

He was going to Quimper for her next day — Monday — to visit some old friends by name of Berthomet. Paul Berthomet was a retired surgeon, in his middle seventies, and Peucat had thought of him immediately when she'd explained last night what she needed — a message-drop for François le Guen to use. That way, there'd be no need to use the telephone: when there was news of the troop deployment he'd push a note through or under these people's door, and they'd ring Peucat with a message about when some granddaughter's baby was due. Rosie hadn't mentioned le Guen's name and Peucat hadn't wanted to know it, but he'd said he was sure 'old Paul' would help.

Heading for Berrien now, after getting the signal off. Peucat telling her as the *gazo* lurched back

190

on to the road, 'About two kilometres. The views are spectacular — you'll see. We turn off to the right there, pass through a little place called Lestrézec — another two, roughly — and then to Scrignac about five.' He shifted gear again. 'Count Jules' ancestors knew what they were doing, when they built their manor. It's a beautiful house in the most magnificent position. Fine pastures too, for Jules' bloodstock. He's selling horses to Germans these days. How d'you like that?'

'Not much at all.'

'He could hardly refuse.' Glancing at her. 'Even if he wanted to. And why should he?'

'Well. I don't know . . .'

'He's a very astute fellow, believe me. He was a diplomat at one time, he's fluent in their language. Also has influence, and allows them to believe he wields it on their behalf. On the surface, that's almost true, in that he does his best to restrain the wilder elements of the Maquis from acts of sabotage and so forth.'

'Communist elements. Lannuzel was talking about it too.'

'It makes sense — as long as there's to be an invasion soon. Count Jules is no admirer of de Gaulle — he regards him as an upstart — but he's of one mind with him on his *attentiste* policy — to wait for the day, not waste lives and material to no purpose.' The doctor shrugged. 'I tell him he'll end up a staunch Gaullist, he pretends to be insulted.'

'Have you known each other long?'

'You might say so. I became the family's doctor because Jules' father hounded the fellow who *was* their doctor clear out of Brittany. He'd made advances to one of the girls — a sister of Jules — and the old boy took a whip to him. Then of course he had to look farther afield. Found me.'

'So Count Jules is quite young?'

'From where *I'm* sitting — yes. Fifty?'

'Oh . . . And has his wife been an invalid for long?'

'For some years. Chronic rheumatoid arthritis. She endures agonies.'

'Can you do much to help her?'

'Regrettably, very little. Except for pain-killers, for when it's at its worst. I can only prescribe them because Count Jules has connections in Paris and brings them back with him.'

'Is that what takes him there so often?'

'Who says he goes "so often"?'

'Guy Lannuzel mentioned it. He was explaining that he and Count Jules hadn't had a chance to discuss — well, one particular matter.'

'I see.' Peucat took a hand from the wheel, rubbed his jaw. Then: 'I'm about to indulge in idle gossip. But you might as well know. It's *almost* your business. In Paris there also resides the lady who found you your employment with me.'

'Léonie de Mauvernay.'

'Exactly. It's of very long standing.' He pointed ahead: 'Coming to Berrien now. We turn east here.'

The house was lovely; a sprawl of light-coloured stone and old timber, in a wonderful setting. Dramatic countryside, sheer and heavily wooded; the manor's own pasturage was probably the only level or near-level terrain for miles. The approach from the village of Scrignac was a dead-straight lane that seemed to lead nowhere else; a crumbly old wall about ten feet high ran along its verge for the best part of a kilometre, with a stable-yard entrance which they passed first, then stone pillars, iron gates standing open, a drive that circled three or four acres of parkland with oaks in it and the house standing well back — five or six hundred metres back, with an apron of gravelled forecourt.

Peucat muttered as he braked, drawing in close to a mounting-block, 'The seigneur himself. We've kept him waiting.' Rosie saw the count coming over to them: he'd been talking to an even taller character — who'd touched his cap and turned away up a spur of driveway that circled the far side of the house.

'Took your time, didn't you, Peucat?'

It was the passenger door he was opening, though. A big man: and strikingly good-looking, she thought. A face with humour as well as strength in it.

'Mam'selle Tanguy. Enchanted. My sympathy too — I know this old dare-devil, it's like travelling in a hearse, isn't it?'

'It was a very pleasant drive, Count.' Her smile

included the house as well as its owner. 'Even more pleasant to arrive. Much better late than never.'

'In any case you're welcome. Come along in.'

'If we *are* late, it's my fault. I persuaded the doctor to stop while I sent off a signal. Guy Lannuzel's requisition.'

'Ah. Quick work. And I've got Jean-Paul Jaillon coming after lunch, you should get another — requisition, if that's the word for it . . . Peucat — haven't I done you a good turn?'

The reference was to Rosie. Peucat looked at her too.

'As a matter of fact — yes, you have. She's delightful — as well as — what's the word . . . Purposeful?'

'What the doctor ordered, one might say.' Ushering her into a stone-flagged hall. 'I can see you've put new life in the old dog already. And you've been here only — what, two days?'

'Yes.'

'Not finding it too bad, I hope?'

'Not at all. The doctor's most hospitable. And I have made quite a good start. Some way to go yet, of course.'

'I'd be glad to hear something of your plans. To discuss *joint* plans, in fact, fairly soon . . . More immediate stuff we should try to get out of the way before Jaillon rolls up. Anyway I'll take you up to meet my wife first.' Another glance back. 'She's not good, Peucat. Really not at all. I brought her the stuff you wanted for her, and those white pills — ones she had before — do seem to help, but the new ones I haven't given her yet. I don't know the dosage, you see.'

'I'll attend to it. Don't worry.'

Sara de Seyssons was on a sofa in a boudoir adjoining her bedroom. Dark-haired, no grey in it, pale skin touched with rouge. A rather shapeless figure: dumpy, heavy-limbed in an exquisite, lace-trimmed negligée. A nice smile: round, brown eyes smiling too as Rosie crossed the room towards her — aware of her own shabbiness, in contrastingly elegant surroundings, and determinedly putting that out of mind as the chatter started.

She hadn't been downstairs, the countess told her, since the summer. She lived in this suite of rooms, here in the middle of the house, and her personal maid slept in a bedroom adjoining hers.

'So I'm well looked after. But I'm a fair weather woman, nowadays. I need warmth, the sunshine. Like a butterfly — that's a joke, eh, heaven knows what size wings I'd need! And what I'd do without Doctor Peucat — well, it's unimaginable . . . How *nice* to have you visit me. I know only a very little of what you're here for — enough not to make any demands on you in the way of nursing, eh?'

'Anything I *can* do — errands, or —'

'How kind you are. Sit down, please. I'd love to hear all about you — everything. One's so shut out of things, so — isolated . . . May we have a few minutes to ourselves, Jules? I could see Doctor Peucat later on?'

'Ten minutes.' He checked the time. 'Then we

must lunch, before Jaillon comes. Peucat can give you his full attention then — you won't want to be in on our deliberations with Jaillon, doctor, will you?'

'Certainly not.' He patted the countess's hand. 'I'll be up to see you later.'

Alone with Rosie, the countess wanted to hear all she could of the war's progress from the Allies' point of view, and then, to a large extent mixed with it, about Rosie herself. She couldn't talk about her work, so it became entirely personal — her childhood in France, her father having been a lawyer with a practice in Monte Carlo — and her husband Johnny being shot down and killed in 1941. Ben of course came into it from there on.

'Would you believe, I never met an Australian?'

'Well — you'd like this one . . .'

'I'm sure I would! My dear — when the Boches have been sent packing, will you bring him here to see me?'

'Yes. Yes, thank you, I'd love to.'

'*He'll* think it's a dreadful bore. But if he could stand it —'

'He'd love it. So would I.'

'Tell him you're bringing him to see the horses. He mightn't object to that so much. And Jules loves to show them off . . . Will you be married by then, perhaps?'

She hesitated. Then nodded. 'Perhaps. Yes, I hope so. Once the war's over — and if he's still keen —'

'But of *course* he will be!'

Faith in another woman's man. An idyll, the romantic certainty she might once have had for herself?

It might have been an arranged marriage, of course. In fact with a father who took horsewhips to men who made advances to his daughters — recalling Peucat's story — that didn't seem unlikely.

She thought, on her way down to lunch, that she might bring Ben here *en route* to visit Dr Peucat, then go on down to Pont Aven to have a riotous reunion with Lise and Noally.

Her daydreams. Antidotes to nightmares . . .

An elderly manservant served lunch, which consisted of braised venison followed by cheese. There was wine too, a local one out of a cask in the cellar and brought up in a carafe; it was delicious, but needing a clear head she drank only one glass. The butler withdrew when the cheese was on the table, and Count Jules changed the subject from horses and agriculture to paradrops and 'Mincemeat'.

'There's one thing I have to ask for, Count — in connection with "Mincemeat" . . .'

' "Mincemeat" . . .' Peucat looked surprised. 'None of my business, I'm sure, but —'

'You're right, it *is* none of your business.' Back to Rosie: 'Go on?'

'It's a question of money. Our informer — "Micky" — d'you know —'

'I know of the existence of an informer, that's all.'

'His code-name's "Micky". I met him yesterday, and I've had to promise him fifty thousand
francs. The agent who recruited him — not one
of my own people — well, he's messed things up,
rather, and Micky started off by telling me he
didn't want anything to do with us. And of course
we'd be sunk without him.'

'So this is a bribe.'

'You could call it that. I used other persuasion
too, but that's part of it. Anyway — they told me
in London you'd be financing all this. So although
I'm afraid it's rather a large amount, all in one
go —'

'I have that much in the safe. You can take it
with you. You'll tell them in London?'

'In my signal this evening. But on the finance
side generally —'

'Living and working expenses? Yes — as
agreed. I'll settle with the doctor here myself,
and keep accounts, give you a figure from time
to time . . . But tell me — this "Micky" of yours
— can we be sure he'll play straight with us
now?'

'I believe so.' She nodded. 'Dealing directly
with me, not through the agent I mentioned.'

'And did you discuss "Mincemeat" with Lannuzel?'

'Yes. He was surprised and not too keen, to
start with, but he's now enthusiastic. He hadn't
realized what an important target it was. He's
working out ways and means.'

'He's a very good man. A friend of mine was

198

his commanding officer at one stage, and thought highly of him.'

Peucat put in, 'His sister Brigitte has her head screwed on pretty well, too.'

'I must get him up here soon, anyway. That's a useful occupation he has, you know — eggs, poultry, day-old chicks, it takes him all over the place . . . Suzanne — apart from the money, is there anything else you need, that I might help with?'

'Only one thing right away. Whether I should raise this with you or with Jaillon I'm not sure — the question of whether any of the Maquis groups would like to have weaponry instructors dropped to them. Lannuzel said no — he has trained men there already, he told me.'

'I'll look into it.' The count nodded. 'But ask Jaillon too.'

He was showing her round the stables, when Jaillon arrived. Rosie had paused to fondle the velvet nose of the count's favourite brood mare; he told her, 'She's won a good few races, this one, in her time. Her sire came from Ireland — and my God, wasn't *he* something!'

'Germans buy your horses, I think the doctor said?'

'Some. But most buyers are French.'

'Still some who are rich enough, are there?'

'Fortunately, there are indeed.'

'Collaborators?'

'A number — yes.'

'Come *here*, do they?'

'Well, they have to. I've had a Boche field-marshal here quite recently — *and* certain politicians — at least one of whom please God will hang, one day. Yes — you name it . . .'

'Gestapo?'

'They don't advertise. That's to say they come dressed as civilians. But — yes, on occasion. And whatever they are, one knows that in many cases the money's stolen.' He looked back at her, at her face pressed against the mare's glossy neck. 'I'm sorry. I give straight answers to straight questions. It disturbs you — doesn't it?'

'Not you?'

'Well.' He'd turned away, to light a cigar. 'To allow oneself many scruples these days is a luxury one can hardly afford . . . Oh, at last — here's Jaillon.' He put his hand on her arm for a moment: 'The most important thing, Suzanne, is to remain *free*. And alive, of course. Behind bars, or dead, what use is one?'

Jaillon was brought to them by an extremely tall, thin man — the one Count Jules had been talking with when she and Peucat had arrived, she realized. His name was Vannier, and he was the gamekeeper. He'd been mentioned during lunch; as an active *Résistant* — as were all the estate workers, apparently, right down to stable-boys — and that he had a special value in that gamekeepers were licensed to be out and about at night, in curfew hours. With that and an intimate knowledge of every square metre of the surrounding countryside, he was the perfect link-man with all the Maquis for miles around. He didn't stay, having delivered Jaillon, but obviously knew who Rosie was — or what she was here for. He shook her hand very firmly: 'Great pleasure, Mam'selle.'

'For me too.'

Then Jaillon: 'Name's Jean-Paul, Mam'selle. Folks sometimes call me JPJ.'

Of average height, bald, built like a bull. A long time ago — the count had told her this too at lunch — he'd been an NCO in the Foreign Legion; and she knew that he was now an agricultural merchant and road-haulier, based at Guerlesquin which was about fifteen kilometres northeast of Scrignac. Rosie told him, 'We'll need a better name for you than that. A code-name — to use in radio messages especially.'

'Call me what you like.' A wink at Count Jules. 'I'll have been called it before, if it's rude enough!'

'Pluto?'

'Ah, that's a nice one.' He hung his tongue out, panted like a hound. Rosie had thought of it because she already had a Micky Mouse. Jaillon dropped the comedy act: 'But getting down to business now, Mam'selle — ?'

'Zoé.'

'Zoé. Code-name? Right, then . . . Zoé — M'sieur le Comte gave me to understand you'd organize a *parachutage* here within a matter of days — is that the case?'

'Yes. If you can give me your list.'

'Got it here. It's a long one, I must warn you. Been a long time without. Also —'

'Recruits flocking in, I suppose.'

'Say *that* again. It's a small army up there now. Makes for some problems, incidentally.' Glancing at the count: 'One or two I'd like to have your advice on, sir.'

'All right.'

Rosie cut in again: 'D'you have a location for this drop, and the Michelin coordinates?'

'All here.' Delving in an inner pocket. 'All here . . .'

In late afternoon she and Peucat drove back to Berrien, where instead of turning south he continued westward, through steeply undulating countryside towards one of the villages he'd mentioned earlier — a place called Kerberou. Halfway to it, though, they stopped so that she could get her second signal away to London; she'd encoded it before they'd started out.

Returning to the *gazo*, having given Baker Street Jaillon's shopping-list, the map coordinates and the *message personnel* — 'A darkening sky presages rain' — plus a request to transfer money to Count Jules' London bank account — she remembered Lannuzel's comment, 'Often wondered who thought up that gibberish' . . .

A more imaginative piece of gibberish locked in her memory was *Le chapeau de Napoleon, est-il toujours à Perros-Guirrec?* It would be broadcast at some time after the Allied landings, and would constitute an order to *Résistants* all over Brittany to come out fighting.

She wondered whether she'd still be here, by then. It was highly unlikely there'd be any invasion on the Brittany coast; so even given quick success elsewhere nothing much would change immediately. Except for stepping-up sabotage of railways, roads and communications, to at least hinder the passage of reinforcements to wherever battles *were* in progress. That would be the basis of plans to be worked out shortly with Count Jules and Lannuzel and no doubt others too.

'All right, Suzanne?'

'Fine. London's got plenty to be getting on with.'

She slung the valise over into the back as she got in beside him. It had le Guen's cash in it as well as the transceiver. And in her mind, further thoughts about the Boche radio-detection effort: that they'd now have intercepted a second signal from the same new pianist, on as near as damnit the same bearing. Wires would be humming, alerting security forces probably all over Brittany.

Or if they'd achieved a cross-bearing — they'd only have needed one detector van somewhere within say ten or twelve kilometres, getting a second bearing to intersect the long-range one — the danger would be a lot closer.

'Cigarette, doctor?'

'Just knocked out a pipe, thanks.'

She lit a Gaullois: with another unwelcome thought forcing its way in. 'Hector' — if he'd told them either voluntarily or under duress that a girl agent code-named 'Zoe' had been due to land at the Soucelles field and to travel as far as Rennes — if he'd known that code-name — and a new pianist had now started work somewhere west of Rennes . . . If they'd got even a rough fix on this second transmission — plus recognition of the pianist's fist, and *possibly* a photograph . . .

No reason to think he would have been given her code-name.

Exhaling a gush of smoke. She asked Peucat, 'How did you find your patient?'

'Sara de Seyssons . . .' He sighed, gestured helplessly. 'No appreciable change. More's the pity.'

'Is she as unhappy as she has every right to be?'

He set the *gazo* rolling.

'I can't answer that. All I can say is she's a woman who suffers a great deal of pain. I'd say her mind is fully occupied with her hopes of getting over it, getting to lead a normal life again. Getting *about* again. Suzanne, please forget that I ever mentioned that other matter.'

'All right. But was she ever — pretty, or attractive?'

'You mean you'd have expected him to have married a great beauty.'

'Well — *nice* as she is — and I do mean that —'

'Yes. What should I say . . . First of all — as you'll have heard before — beauty is in the beholder's eye. But also — she's a woman of integrity, courage, undoubtedly a certain charm —'

'Yes —'

'— and great wealth. An establishment like that one doesn't run on smoke, you know.'

'So he — Count Jules —'

'He's a product of his own age and background. *And,* she loves him. Listen — at Kerberou we'll turn south. It'll bring us down to Loqueffret — remember we came through there?'

Quinoualch, then Kerberou: left there, for Brennilis, Kerflaconnier, Loqueffret . . . Peucat drove in silence, Rosie relaxing, taking stock . . .

She had met all the main players now, and achieved her initial aims. In two days, for Pete's sake: it really wasn't bad. The two drops were laid on — subject to confirmation and dates from Baker Street — some degree of *rapport* established with Lannuzel, Count Jules and Jaillon, Lannuzel at work getting his team organized for the Trevarez operation, and le Guen set to pass the news out when he saw or heard it.

This evening, she'd wash her hair. Get a few other chores out of the way too maybe. Then of course set listening-watch in the attic at midnight. If Baker Street were really on the ball, they might even come up with some delivery dates.

Chapter 8

François le Guen woke sluggishly with Marie-Claude's voice urgent in his ears: 'Papa, wake up! At the front, front door — Germans, shouting and banging —'

'What?'

He'd been in a very deep sleep: having spent a couple of hours *not* sleeping, tossing and turning . . . Blinking at his daughter as she switched his bedside lamp on: 'What's time?'

'Ten past one!'

He was hearing it now. The bell didn't work, hadn't for a long time. Callers at one o'clock in the morning, though: Sunday night, this was, Monday morning. Recent events coming into focus: that girl yesterday — Saturday — at Prigent's surgery . . .

What Marie-Claude had just said: for 'Germans', at this time of night, read Gestapo, or SD.

Dreaming this?

Her hand on his shoulder, pulling at it. 'Please, Papa!'

'Jesus Christ . . .'

Muttering an apology then for the blasphemy: and getting control of himself — under his daughter's gaze, a major effort to wipe the fright out of his eyes. He knew how he'd look — would *have* looked — in those few seconds: unshaven, eyes like a scared rabbit's.

Hide it from *her,* of *all* people . . .

'They probably want something translated, or interpreted.'

Even to him, that had sounded stupid . . .

'At *this* hour?'

'Some wretched prisoner, perhaps.' Facing that truth, as part of the process of putting a front on this. 'It's the sort of time they choose, for such —'

'Papa, *whatever* —'

'Yes. All right.' Moving, reaching for his threadbare dressing-gown. 'You go back to bed, I'll see to it.'

They were still banging on the door and shouting, down there. In German — no chance of there being any mistake, they knew who he was, which house they'd come to.

'Open up! Le Guen! Open up!'

No mistake at all — except his own, in having anything to do with Prigent. He switched lights on from the head of the stairs, and started down — repeating over his shoulder to Marie-Claude to go back to her room. 'Lock the door. Go to bed. I'll come and see you when they've gone.'

That girl — if they'd caught *her?*

Unlikely. Prigent much *more* likely. But Prigent knew about the girl too, so she'd be in the same net. It would have started from the office anyway — precisely the danger he'd foreseen: Prigent's doing, and he'd rat on one quick as a flash if he found *himself* up against it.

'All right, all right . . .'

The bolts on the door then: top, bottom, then the chain, but it banged open that far, jarring the thing taut.

'How can I undo it if you keep pushing?'

'Let him open it, Kindermann!'

He knew that voice. The chain came off, finally. Stepping back, door swinging open . . . Knew the face too — and the man's name — Fischer, a lieutenant in the SD. They'd never spoken to each other, but he was in and out of the *Kommandantur* quite often.

The nightmare come to life. Incredible, but — reality. No waking up from *this* one.

But there had to be. Please God. Some kind of help, there had to be, some let-out. In his mind suddenly was that girl: as if *she* could save him . . .

'Think we enjoy standing on doorsteps, le Guen?'

'I was fast asleep. I'm sorry —'

'Bloody *should* be!'

He had three men with him — SS troopers, in uniform and armed with Schmeissers. Fischer himself in a new-looking grey suit. Crowding in: one of them kicked the door shut. Le Guen tried to address the *leutnant* again: 'I didn't hear a thing — until a moment ago —'

'This your sitting-room?'

It wasn't, it was the kitchen. He swivelled in its doorway: '*Is* there a room to sit in?'

'In here.' A small room, but it had double doors at the other end which opened into a tiny strip of garden; in summer when the doors were open it wasn't too bad. A little box of a room now. Fischer — average-sized, in fact a bit shorter than le Guen, but he somehow managed to take up a lot of space — followed him in and stood glancing around. Filling the doorway: jaw blue-black with one-a.m. shadow, pale eyes narrowed. He had rather full, unhealthily pink lips.

'Who else lives here?'

'Only my daughter, Marie-Claude. She's —'

'I remember. Your wife ran off with some salesman.'

'A motor engineer.'

'Used-car salesman, it says in your file. Not that anyone could give a damn . . .'

'May I ask the reason for this visit?'

'Is there a back door?'

'Yes — from the kitchen —'

'Check it and then stay there, Kindermann. Heller, stay at the front.' He pulled a chair round, and straddled it: again, knees and elbows sticking out, filling all the space on that side of the table. A nod to le Guen: 'You may sit.'

'Thank you, I prefer to stand.'

'Oh, do you. Piles, is it?'

The soldier who was still with them sniggered. He looked about sixteen. Fischer glanced at him, and gestured towards le Guen. 'Sit him down, Baier. We'll have a look in his mouth.'

'*What* —'

'Sit *down!*'

He did so — before the boy could put his hands on him.

'Now open wide.'

'I beg your pardon?'

'Your mouth — open it wide. If you don't, he'll force it open with a pistol barrel. You'd find that painful.'

'But what *for,* what *is* —'

'To see what dentistry you've had done recently — by that fellow who's called you over from your office several times now. What's the swine's name . . . ?'

'My dentist? Prigent. But what's —'

Fischer rose, threateningly. 'Open your damn mouth!'

The soldier had grabbed le Guen's sparse grey hair, forcing his head back.

'Hey, *please* —'

'Open!'

Le Guen opened his mouth. Internally, his head was spinning. Fischer came round the end of the table: stooping, grimacing with distaste as he peered into the gaping mouth . . . 'Who'd be a dentist, for God's sake. I've often wondered . . . All right, let go of him . . . I can't see anything that looks like new work in there, anyway. D'you want to tell me there has been?'

'No. No, because —'

'What did you go to the dentist for on Saturday?'

'I've had pain — *bad* pain —'

'You'll get a lot more soon, too. Are you admitting the dentist did nothing?'

'He examined me, in the hope of seeing what was wrong.'

'Couldn't pin it down, eh?'

'No.' He touched the side of his mouth: 'One here — a molar — he thought might be the trouble. But he could only have extracted it, which I didn't want — and he agreed, if after all it wasn't necessary.'

'Prigent's surgery's a rendezvous for spies — right?'

'No — not as far as —'

'You're a fool, le Guen. To think we wouldn't catch on to it.' He snapped a glance at the young trooper: 'Fetch his daughter.'

'No — *no* —'

'She'll be upstairs, in a bedroom —'

'Please, I *beg* you —'

'— if the door's locked and she won't come out, break it down.'

'Jawohl, Herr Leutnant!'

'What can my daughter have to do with this?'

'Precisely what I intend to find out. No — stay where you are . . . What's her name and occupation?'

'Marie-Claude. She's a teacher. *Completely* innocent —'

'Unlike daddy, huh?'

'*P*lease — leave her alone? She's just an innocent young girl, she has no one but me, her mother deserted us — as you know — I've spent all the time since then trying to sh-shield her from —'

'From what? From your own and Prigent's criminal activities?'

'No —'

'That was a confession, don't you realize?'

'Nothing *to* confess. I *swear* —'

'Really.' A nod . . . 'We'll see how it checks out when we get round to putting the screws on Prigent. What'll *he* tell us, d'you imagine?'

'Anything he said about me would be a lie!'

'Think he'd shop you, do you?'

'Papa! Are you all right?'

She was in the doorway — surprised and frightened . . .

'Sweetheart, don't worry about *me,* but tell this man the truth, whatever he wants to know just —'

'Why not get in first, shop *him?*'

Fischer suggested it casually, shrugging. Rising now, with his eyes on Marie-Claude. She'd put on the *robe-de-chambre* le Guen had given her for her last birthday. Pink, with a shine like satin: it had cost a lot of his own clothes coupons as well as a small fortune. She was very pale — paler than usual, even — with her fairish hair tied back and her blue eyes blinking. Like *mine* blink, her father thought.

'Sit down, *Fräulein.* Here.'

Fischer indicated the chair he'd used: standing behind it, pointing down at it, switching from German into clumsy, brutally loud French: 'Didn't you hear me? I said sit down!'

Her eyes hadn't left her father. Obeying now though, sitting . . . He could see her struggle against tears, the effort she was making. Swallowing, biting her lips . . . A mutter of 'Papa — what do they want with us?'

'It's a mistake. They have some notion that I'm a spy.' This was *his* effort, now — for *her* sake. Thin smile: 'Because I was at the dentist — that's all it takes, apparently.'

'And that's enough from you.' Fischer slid one haunch on to the edge of the table, steadying himself as he did it with a hand on the back of Marie-Claude's chair. 'Keep your mouth shut from here on — unless I tell you to open it.' He'd said it in German: returned now to his crude variety of French. 'Marie-Claude. Obviously you're aware of your father's involvement with this dentist?'

'Involvement? With Michel Prigent?'

'You go to him too, I suppose?'

'No, I don't, I go to Christophe Lemaître at Frugy. That's where we lived when I was little. But my father was at school with Michel Prigent and when he ran into him again he switched to him from Lemaître. I didn't want to, I stayed. Does that make him a spy?'

'Probably.'

'But that's senseless!'

'It may seem so to you, Marie-Claude. Indeed, your father has admitted he's tried to shield you — from his own activities, was the implication.' He glanced round: 'Le Guen, I'm prepared to accept that your daughter is probably unaware of the true nature of your relationship with Prigent. You, on the other hand, have a lot to tell us about it — and believe me, you *will*. We'll stick to you, therefore — for the time being, anyway.' Check-

213

ing the time. 'But not here, I think . . .'

'There's *nothing* I can tell you!'

'How often I've heard that . . . Anyway, you'd better put some clothes on. Baier — take him to his bedroom, see he gets a move on. Have a look round, while you're up there. Marie-Claude, stay here. When we've gone you can go back to bed. I'll be leaving one of my men here, that's all — mainly to ensure you don't go near the telephone. If it rings, leave it, *he*'ll answer it.'

He was to remember later with some degree of satisfaction that in the truck on its way through the deserted streets to SD headquarters his concern was more for Marie-Claude than for himself. Although he *was* sweating with fright: in cold night air, on the steel floor of the truck, handcuffed, bouncing as it crashed over railway lines and potholes. Fischer was in front beside the driver, Baier and Heller here in the back — Schmeissers on their knees, boots nudging his ribs.

Tell them whatever they want to know, he thought.

Whatever . . .

The truck braked, slewed to a rocking halt, and a boot toed him hard: '*Raus!*'

Out on to roadway, then stone steps with a swastika banner hanging limp and wet from the window above it. Through blackout screens into an empty stone hallway: unshaded overhead lights, Nazi posters on the walls. Fischer bawled

214

at someone to inform Sturmbannführer Braun that he'd brought the suspect le Guen for interrogation; there was the sound of a house-telephone being cranked in an adjoining room, and eventually a voice called 'Room fourteen, Herr Leutnant!'

It was at the back of the first floor. About four metres by five, blackout material covering one small window and in the centre a desk with an upholstered chair behind it and a hard, heavy-timbered one on this side. Straps on its arms hung loose: there were straps on the front legs too, he saw. There was also a directional light beamed at it from a stand close to the desk.

He felt sick, and was having to fight for breath: breathing more in short gasps than breaths, and conscious of a fast, seemingly erratic heartbeat.

Heart-attack imminent?

'Sit down!'

They pushed him down on to the chair. Baier — the kid — called towards the door by which they'd entered, 'Want him strapped in, Herr Leutnant?'

'Yes.' Boots were loud on the board flooring. 'Take the cuffs off one wrist.'

'It's not — necessary, sir —'

'What do *you* know about it?' A fist hit him behind the ear. 'Speak when you're spoken to!'

The ear throbbed now. Courtesy of Fischer, that had been. Nightmare, this *was*. The troopers, one either side, were tightening the straps on his wrists; the handcuffs dangled from the left one.

215

Fischer must have gone out again, and Baier with him; Heller stayed, leaning with his back against the green-painted wall.

The light beside the desk was dazzlingly bright. He could see the chair behind the desk clearly enough, but nothing to the left of it. He shut his eyes. What was likely to happen here was terrifying, but close behind that awareness was Marie-Claude alone in the house with that SS thug — Kindermann. From that, then, the thought of Saturday's girl telephoning and Kindermann taking the call. He thought she'd probably realize — at least suspect — hang up quickly and then stay clear.

Then what?

Must be about two o'clock, he guessed. Head forward, eyes shut — to avoid that light. Hearing his own voice telling that girl — the Saturday girl — 'I suppose one lacks courage.'

No supposition about it. Fact. One had grown up in the knowledge of it.

There were voices somewhere behind him — out in the passage, he guessed. They had the hollow, echoey sound of voices in an empty house. One was Fischer's: his tone suggested that the other was his superior. Sturmbannführer Braun, perhaps. It was a name one had heard mentioned once or twice in the office, but as far as he knew the Sturmbannführer had never shown his face there. Fischer must run his errands for him, le Guen supposed. Catching a few muttered words then — via the open doorway, the two of them pausing just outside and perhaps not realizing they'd be audible in here. Something about his having to be sent home first. *He*, third person — meaning himself, François le Guen? In which case, the word 'first' indicating that he might be sent home before *what?*

Fischer had replied, 'Yes — I suppose so, sir.'

'So go ahead. I'll get started.'

Boots thunderous on the boards. They liked noise. As if the more they made, the bigger or more important they seemed to themselves. Braun, suddenly in his field of view, wasn't all that big. He was thickset, though; his leather jacket bulged over the sweater he wore under it. Another one appeared on stage too now: taller, with a greyish, deeply lined face, thick greying hair. Sweater, no jacket, *Wehrmacht* uniform trousers, rubber-soled shoes. Braun's hair was yellow, plastered down — perhaps with water — and parted in the centre. His hands on the desk-top as he let himself down into the padded, round-backed chair looked inappropriately small, even feminine.

'All right.' A jerk of the tall one's head. 'Dismiss.' Dismissing Heller, Fischer's man, and taking his place against the wall on le Guen's right. There was an unpleasant look about him, although he was slightly less scruffy than Braun. An NCO, le Guen thought. It was his expression: a cold-blooded, hate-filled look. It was less unnerving to look at Braun — who had blond stubble on his cheeks and bloodshot eyes suggesting a late-night drinking session. The wet hair could have come from putting his head under a tap within recent minutes.

He'd opened a file.

'François le Guen. Clerk and translator in the *Kommandantur*. Also on the payroll of one Michel Prigent, who's an agent of British Intelligence.'

'*No*, sir!'

'What?'

Glancing up from the file: pink eyes like an angry bull's.

'I am *not* employed by Prigent.'

'He *is* an enemy agent, though — you confirm that, huh?'

He hesitated: beginning to shake his head — denying knowledge, not that fact or allegation . . . 'I had wondered. An agent of some kind — yes, but — no way of knowing. Except — I do know he's a Frenchman born and bred. We knew each other when we were children.'

'You've visited him several times lately and it wasn't for dentistry. Despite knowing he's an enemy agent — as you've admitted. You've known it for quite a while, huh?'

'No — only quite recently — and suspected it more than *knew* it. Now I *do* know, because —'

'— because you're employed by him — take orders from him — isn't that the truth?'

'No, sir! The *truth* is —'

'— that you dash round there every time he whistles!'

'He's been trying to persuade me to — well,

find things out for him, and I — I mean, working there, it's been — embarrassing, frightening — over the telephone in that office with people all listening — I mean I couldn't argue, they'd have made the assumption you're making now — erroneous assumption — if I may say so —'

'You jump to it when he snaps his fingers. *That* an erroneous assumption?'

'Well — yes. You see —'

'Why would he waste his time making calls to you — to the *Kommandantur,* at that, which obviously involves risk to himself — if you weren't making it worth his while to do so?'

'I suppose he thinks if he keeps pressure on me —'

'What kind of information is he asking you to get?'

'Whatever comes my way, I think. He said there'd be an invasion soon, and we'd come into our own, stop being frightened and start being — well, proud, he said.'

'Proud of what?'

'Of — being *Résistants,* I suppose.'

'So you're a *Résistant?*'

'No, I'm —'

'— lying, le Guen. You *must* know — and you're going to tell me — what he expected to get from you.' The small hands slapped down on the desk: 'D'you want to be taken down and whipped?'

He'd shut his eyes: moved his head from side to side . . .

219

The tall man pushed himself off the wall. 'Shall I —'

'Perhaps — but just wait a moment —'

'If I knew *anything*, I'd —'

'Sharpens the mind, le Guen, a good whipping. In the long run it might save us a lot of time.'

'But I can't tell you what I don't know!'

'I suppose you realize I can have you shot? Or do it myself, even, here and now — without needing anyone's permission? See here . . .'

There was a pistol — a Luger — in that small right hand, resting on the desk-top, aimed at his eyes . . . Le Guen blinking at it, at the small black hollow circle aimed and steady . . . A click then: Braun's small thumb had moved. 'That was the safety-catch. It's off now, I have only to squeeze the trigger. If I kill you here, now, there's nobody on God's earth will give a damn.' A shrug. 'Well, your daughter might shed tears, obviously, but —'

'I'll answer any question I'm capable of answering. Anything, *everything* —'

'But you said you know nothing!'

'Very little.' Shaking his head. '*Very* little. Truly, I swear —'

Braun clicked the safety-catch on and put the gun down.

'It'd be messy here. The orderlies wouldn't thank me. Better in the cellar. In the cellar we can do anything we like to you. Mulder there's an expert, he's broken much stronger men than you, believe me . . . Anyway, here's one thing you *must* know — what kind of information is Prigent expecting you to provide?'

'One thing only, that I know of. He's not *expecting* anything from me, though — I'd told him that I would *not* work for him!'

'*What* one thing only?'

'The names of informers.'

'Informers?'

'People who inform on *Résistants* or Maquis or — anything of that sort.'

'Have you given him names?'

'I don't know any. How should I? I told him first I didn't want to be involved, second it was unlikely in any case that I'd get to hear about such things. Exactly what I've been telling *you* — sir . . .'

'Wanted you to nose around for him, did he?'

'Yes. I told him I didn't have the nerve.'

'Was that your only reason for refusing his request?'

'Excuse, more than reason. I wanted no part in it. Frankly I'm not — well —'

'What else did he ask for?'

'Well — anything —'

'Wait!' Someone had knocked: came in without waiting for permission, pushed the door shut again. Fischer's voice: 'On the way, sir. No problems.'

'Good.' The bloodshot eyes came back to le Guen. 'What else — you were saying?'

'Anything I saw or heard. But I wasn't taking much notice, because as I've told you I had no intention —'

'Didn't he give you examples of the kind of material he'd find interesting?'

'No. He didn't.'

'You swore blind he'd never asked for anything in particular, but since then you've come up with his request for the names of informers. Perhaps your memory *does* need sharpening!'

'No — I'd forgotten that. That's all. I swear to you —'

'That bullshit about invasion coming soon. There'd have to be some reason for it, something he was leading up to. What would you *think* he'd want, in that context? Intelligence of troop movements or dispositions, fixed defences?'

'To identify informers — if information was being passed out about Resistance or Maquis preparations — *that* was the context.'

'You did know he was a British agent — right?'

'No. He could have been simply a *Résistant* — wouldn't they want to know things? Especially names of people who might have informed on them?'

'To whom d'you think he'd have passed such information if you'd given him any?'

'I suppose the Maquis — or other *Résistants.*'

'Was there ever any mention of radio communication? A radio link with London?'

'No. Why — is *that* —'

'Whom did you meet at the dental surgery apart from Prigent himself?'

'Nobody.' He felt himself shake: a shiver right through his body . . . 'Except a few patients. And

222

the receptionist, Prigent's assistant — a blonde girl, quite young.'

'Same one each time?'

'Yes.'

'Did she know you were there for purposes other than dentistry?'

'I don't know. I had no conversations with her — she's never said more to me than good afternoon, M. Prigent won't keep you waiting long — that sort of —'

'Did you occupy the dentist's chair?'

'Of course.'

'The blonde was excluded?'

'Yes. He'd say, I shan't need you, Gabrielle — and she'd —'

'Gabrielle.' He made a note. 'Who else was there?'

'When?'

'On your last visit, say. Day before yesterday, wasn't it?'

'Well.' Blinking: aware of Fischer somewhere behind him, near the door, and of the tall one watching maliciously from the side. He cleared his throat. 'I don't remember any others. May have been some, I suppose, there usually were. But who might have been sitting there on Saturday and who the time before —'

'Would it surprise you to know we've been keeping a watch on that house? Hasn't it occurred to you that we'd be bound to, knowing of Prigent's activities? Try again, now — who *else?*'

'As I said, there'd have been patients waiting.

One or two, usually . . . On Saturday, though —'
Screwing his eyes up, trying to remember . . . 'I
think there was one patient waiting when I arrived. A woman. Yes — I was booked to see him
ahead of her appointment, and Prigent was running late. I think she complained to the receptionist.'

'Describe her.'

'But — I couldn't, possibly!'

'Have you met other so-called patients who've
been there for purposes other than dental treatment?'

'No. Never.'

'How do you know?'

'Oh — how *would* I, indeed?'

'Has Prigent never introduced you to any other
person in his surgery — or in that house?'

Staring at him. Blinking . . . Then: 'No. He
has not.'

'So how would you explain the urgency of his
calls to you?'

'I don't think I quite — follow . . .'

'Take Saturday. At no notice at all he calls
you, you drop everything and run obediently
along. What this suggests to me is some other
person has turned up so he wants you there at
once. Otherwise — why the rush? And why
wouldn't he make an appointment the day before?'

'He'd had a cancellation, I think. I don't know
anything about any other patient, but since his
receptionist has to believe he's seeing me only as

a patient — well, as far as I *know* that's how it is . . .'

He watched Braun slide the pistol into a holster under his left arm, inside the leather jacket. One small hand went to his nose then, picking the left nostril with the tip of the thumb.

'We'll move to the next stage now. You'd better understand first that in view of your connection with Prigent — a known enemy agent, known to *you* as well as to us — if I allow you to walk out of here tonight you'll remain very much on probation, under our eyes.' Thumb against the forefinger, flicking away whatever he'd found in there. 'For keeping it to yourself — failing to report approaches from an enemy agent — I'd be justified in having you shot. Beyond question. Even though your refusal to work with him is a mitigating circumstance — *if* it's true . . . So. As it happens, I'm prepared to believe you on that point — and to give you a chance to redeem yourself by working for *us* now. Secretly, of course. You'll get in touch with Prigent and tell him all right, you've decided you *will* work with him. Names of informers, to kick off with — we'll give you a couple you can pass on. And whatever else he asks for . . . You'll tell us of every request he makes of you, and on occasion you'll give him the goods — tailor-made, provided by us. Perhaps some items he hasn't asked for, now and then. We'll pay you for your work — on top of your present wages, that'll be — and if you serve us well, earn our trust — who knows . . . But only you and the three of us in this room will know anything at all about it. You won't whisper it to any living soul. How does the proposition strike you?'

Blinking . . . Glancing at the tall one: then back to Braun. He nodded. 'All right. Yes.'

'Good. Wise, too . . . So you can go home now, and I can get to bed.' He glanced over le Guen's head: 'You'll take him, uh?'

A grunt, from behind there.

'Le Guen — if your friends and neighbours want to know, you've been interviewed and established your innocence. It was an indiscretion of your daughter's, not your own.'

'Marie-Claude's? What *kind* of —'

'Wait. You'll present yourself for work at the *Kommandantur* at the usual time. Tomorrow evening, from your home, telephone Prigent for an appointment — and take it from there. You'll submit verbal reports to Leutnant Fischer: he'll tell you when and where. Secrecy is vital — remember that. Prigent must believe you're acting out of patriotism and dislike of *us*. You were scared of the idea, but you've steeled yourself. He must not be allowed to suspect the truth even for a second; you'll tell no one, no one at all. Understand?'

'Not even my daughter?'

'Not even her.' Le Guen saw the quick glance he threw Fischer. Pointing at *him*, then: 'Take the straps off him, Mülder.' The tall man started towards him. Braun cleared his throat . . . 'The

226

fact is, you'll have no opportunity to tell your daughter. Brace yourself for this now. She'll come to no harm — you have my word for it — but she's in our custody, and will remain so.'

'*Custody?*'

'For the foreseeable future. I repeat, no harm will come to her. She's held as a hostage, with others.'

'Hostage — Marie-Claude . . . No — for God's *sake* —'

'An insurance policy on your loyalty to us — nothing else. Although regrettably hostages can be shot, in certain circumstances, she will not be. She'll be held at Kerongués with the rest of them — perfectly safe as long as you do just as you're told. So it's entirely —'

'It's *shocking!* I can't believe it! Look, there's no *reason* —'

'— up to you, you see. And don't breathe a word — because if Prigent did get to hear of it, and put two and two together — well, we might think *you'd* tipped him off, eh?'

'Look — I'd never have agreed —'

'Sooner qualify for a firing-squad? You *and* your daughter?'

Staring at each other . . .

'Please.' Shaking his head: eyes brimming. 'Please — I'd work better for you if you — let me have her back. Honestly, I *would*, I'd —'

'You'll work your brains out for us in any case. That's what the deal is. Unless you want to change your mind, refuse it?'

His hands were free now: the tall one straightening, moving away. Braun reached to turn down the lamp's beam.

'Insurance, le Guen. That's all it is.'

Chapter 9

At breakfast, Peucat proposed starting the day with calls on patients, around mid-morning dropping in on his sister, and on the way back seeing about Rosie's permits which by that time should be ready for her to collect. After lunch he'd be off to Quimper to see these old friends of his.

She'd nodded, yawning. It had been well after midnight when she'd turned in. Lucky in fact to have been able to knock off that early: Baker Street's signal about the drops had started coming in a few minutes after midnight. It had been only a short transmission and they'd had nothing else for her, so she'd been able to close down right away. Still having to decode the message, of course; it had told her that Guido's and Pluto's drops were to be made simultaneously this next Saturday at midnight Central European Time, recognition signals to be respectively ZG and ZP; also that a French weaponry instructor would be dropped with Pluto's consignment — Jaillon had asked for this, and that it should be a Frenchman if possible — and the spare Mark III transceiver and 'S' phone she'd asked for with Guido's.

Definitely must attend that drop, she thought. Get the gear before it did a Maquis-type disappearing trick.

Pouring herself more coffee, she asked Peucat, 'Before we go out, would you mind telephoning Count Jules and Guy Lannuzel for me? You'd want to ask after the countess, I imagine —'

'What else?'

'Tell them "Zoé asks me to say that the best day for a visit looks like Saturday — this coming one." Would you do that?'

'The *parachutages?*'

She nodded. 'They'll know what it means — and Count Jules'll pass it on to Jaillon. Oh, a bit more, though — you might add to the count "Jean-Paul's guest will be coming too".'

'Don't bother to explain, just write it down for me. But that's quick work, Suzanne!'

'Well. Has to be.'

'That much of a rush?'

The invasion, he was referring to, obliquely. She nodded, putting down her cup.

'We're into May now — d'you realize? Late spring, summer — they'll need good weather, won't they?'

'The Boches would be aware of that as well.'

'But not *precisely* when. Which month, even. Please God. And not *where*.'

'I'd bet on the Pas de Calais. Surely — the shortest crossing?'

'Maybe you're right.'

Before leaving the house she made a more thorough job of hiding her stuff in the attic. A feeling that maybe she hadn't taken enough trouble over it had worried her last night — visions of grey

Citroëns tearing into the village and halting with screaming tyres, fists pounding on Peucat's door, searchers bursting in . . . Anyway, she'd improved it now. There was a loose floorboard — several probably, but this was the one she'd been using — and the improvements were to push the transceiver and its bits and pieces, together with her pistol and le Guen's money, to arm's length, to be as far as possible out of sight in the musty-smelling under-floor space, then pile in litter collected from the eaves — remains of old birds' nests, bits of broken tiles, rotten battens — and after replacing the board to scatter muck and dust over it and into the cracks around it.

Spring had definitely though belatedly arrived. Clear blue sky, trees in fresh green leaf or bud . . . The village was contrastingly run-down, though: through lack of both money and materials, Peucat said, on their way on foot from one housebound patient to another. Then the phrase one heard so often: 'The Boches take everything . . .' People in the streets were also shabby — which made Rosie feel comfortably inconspicuous — and most looked underfed. Peucat commented on this too. 'We do a lot better than townsfolk, but for the poor it's tempting to sell their produce rather than eat it. So the black market flourishes, and they starve.' He pointed: 'L'Hôtel Grand Maison. The Boches billeted troops there at one time, but it's empty now. This is Rue d'Amoriques. Café de la Paix there —

never much of anything to be had . . . When we go to my sister, by the way — well, coming this way along Rue des Champs Verts — joins this one down there, see — past the gendarmerie where we were yesterday — might call in there on our way back later, incidentally — it's the left fork out of the market place. About five kilometres. We'll take the *gazo,* of course.'

'I'm glad to hear it.'

'A day off from your cycling. You'd need it, I dare say. Listen — I'll leave you with my sister when we get there. There's a patient I should visit in Lanvezennec — that'll give you about long enough.'

'Can you manage without my help?'

'Very droll this morning, Suzanne.'

'I must try to make myself useful, though. While you're in Quimper this afternoon, for instance — anything I could do?'

'Getting my records into order might be a good start. I'm no good at paperwork. Carried it all in my head — always have, but — so much now . . . And as for the accounts one's supposed to keep —'

'To visiting so-and-so, half a bottle of cognac?'

'Those I do *not* record. But sorting the paperwork would also familiarize you with names and ailments. That wouldn't be a bad thing at all.'

He'd telephoned Count Jules and Lannuzel, and given them the good news. By now it would be on its way up into the hills: the messengers, she guessed, would be Guy Lannuzel himself and the Scrignac gamekeeper, Vannier.

Marthe Peucat, whom they got to at about eleven-thirty, turned out to be a gaunt woman, stiff-backed, steely-eyed, with white hair, eyes like brown marbles and the same sallow complexion as her brother's. She had a slate-roofed cottage and half an acre of garden in which she grew vegetables and kept ducks on a pond; she showed Rosie around the outside before taking her in and giving her coffee and home-made biscuits.

The cottage comprised numerous small rooms with low ceilings and tiny windows. Ornaments on every surface. No fire in the grate: the kitchen was warm enough but in this sitting-room it was colder than outside.

'I told my brother that if you thought it preferable to live here, rather than in his bachelor establishment, I should be glad to have you. But you find it more convenient there with him?'

'Well — yes. It's most kind of you — I appreciate it — and this must be a lovely, tranquil place to live —'

'I like it, certainly. And I've lived here thirty years!'

'As long as that?'

'Since before you were born — eh?'

'Yes. Just. But as you said — working with your brother, it's much more convenient. I'd have to spend so much time cycling to and fro.'

'Good healthy exercise?'

'I do a lot of cycling anyway. Late at night, though — one can't hope to keep absolutely regular hours — and there's the curfew to think about. Also, any emergency calls come to him, naturally, and I don't believe you have a telephone?'

'That's all true. I don't — no. Wouldn't have any use for one. But people do talk, you know. A young girl like yourself, alone in that big house with a man who — well, admittedly he's getting on, but —'

'Your brother's a thoroughly decent man —' she'd been ready for this — 'and a most considerate employer. Beyond that, any suggestion from *anyone* —'

'I know.' She'd caught the point, and Rosie's look, which had indicated that *anyone* included herself, Marthe Peucat. 'You needn't tell me. I knew as soon as I set eyes on you — and in any case, as you say, my brother's an honourable man. Well — that goes without saying. The fact remains, men are men, and tongues do wag!'

'So let them!'

'It wouldn't upset you?'

'What matters is the truth, surely, not what malicious people choose to say to each other.'

'Well.' Surprise . . . 'I suppose it's — a point of view . . .'

'They can talk their ugly heads off!'

'You certainly know your own mind!'

Questions followed about her birthplace, childhood home and schooling, and her late father's business. Rosie gave truthful answers to all of it, except for not admitting that her mother was English and lived in Buckinghamshire. She had a fictional alternative to that. But then another abrupt change of subject — 'Tell me something else. If you wouldn't mind . . . How do you feel about the Resistance? Don't answer if you'd rather not —'

'I admire them enormously. Wish I had such courage.'

A gleam of approval . . .

'So. But are you always so forthright, Mam'selle?'

'Suzanne — please. Well, I suppose —'

'I should warn you — Suzanne — it could be dangerous, to be *too* outspoken. What if I'd been an informer — there are such creatures, you know?'

'I'd have been very surprised.'

'You would?'

'The sister of Henri Peucat?'

That went down well. She was smiling: not an obvious smile but a real one, showing in and around the eyes . . . 'I'm an inquisitive old woman, I'm afraid. So many questions — you'll think I'm rude!'

'Oh, no . . .'

'Haven't finished yet, either. Do you not have any — er — emotional attachments, Suzanne? No fiancé?'

'I did have —'

'Oh, but of *course* — I'm sorry, I remember now, Henri told me —'

She showed her the old cigarette-lighter with its engraved initials 'DM'. 'It doesn't work. Just a memento.' Fondling it, she'd allowed her eyes to become damp. All good practice . . . 'Apart from one photo, it's all I have that was his.'

The story of Marthe's young fisherman who'd been drowned off Roscoff came out then. Also mention of some of her brother's failings. Drink was one of them. But Henri was a good fellow at heart. Suzanne would find that as long as she made her own position and attitudes quite clear — as was so evidently her habit . . .

She told Peucat, on their way back into St Michel-du-Faou, 'She's not at all the dragon I expected. And she's extremely fond of you, doctor.'

'The fondness is mutual — broadly speaking. But she has a lively imagination and a bitter tongue. Believe me — I've had the rough end of it often enough! Didn't she question your living in the house with me?'

'It came up, yes. But — no worries now. Are we stopping at the gendarmerie?'

Even he was surprised that the papers were there, ready for collection. It was an indication of the doctor's repute locally — with the local Boches, even, apparently — that they'd signed and stamped both documents and returned them without wanting to see her or check her other papers.

She teased him about it. 'They must consider you one of the *Vertrauenmänner*, doctor.'

Trusted ones, that meant. Pro-Nazis.

'If you're calling me a skunk —'

'I wouldn't *dream* —'

A *Wehrmacht* motorcycle dispatch rider roared through Place de l'Eglise, past the Peucat residence and on up through Rue St Nicolas. They heard him shift gear as he rounded the next corner and shot up the short, steep hill to the *Kommandantur*. She commented as they reached the house and he unlocked its front door, 'There doesn't seem to be very many of them in or around this village.'

'Depends. Some days they're like ticks on a sow's belly. In you go . . .' He shut the door, re-locked it from inside. 'It's good that you got on well with Marthe.'

'I meant to tell you — she asked me how did I feel about the Resistance. Funny thing to ask a stranger?'

'How did you answer?'

'That I was all for it. It seemed to please her.'

'Oh, it would . . .'

'But you don't talk to her about what you do.'

'Why should I? Why would she want to know?'

'She wanted *my* views.'

'Well — she knows my *views,* all right!' He flipped his hat on to the coat-stand: by the quick glance round at her you could tell it was a skill that gave him pride. 'Now I'll show you where to unearth my patients' records. Keep you busy all afternoon — if not all week!'

'May I ask a tricky question?'

He stopped with his hand on the door that led to the back of the house, by-passing the kitchen.

'You may *ask*, of course.'

'If I slipped up — *really* slipped up, got arrested —'

'Suzanne, *please* —'

'If I did, it would almost certainly lead them here. They'd know you'd been housing me, you'd obviously be involved: so what would you do?'

'I don't know you're anything but what you appear to be — as Count Jules represented you to be. Which of course *he* only knew from the lady in Paris. She enquired on your behalf, he passed it on to me — that's all. I'd tell them you had no outside contacts that I know of . . . Whatever they were saying of you, I'd find hard to believe.'

'They'd find my radio. That alone — in *your* house — you know as well as I do — well, if I show you where I'm hiding it, would you get rid of it?'

'It won't happen, Suzanne. If it did — yes, I'd do that, and I'd take off.' A wave of the hand towards the mountains: 'I have friends out there, you know. Think about *yourself* — enough to keep you busy, eh?' His arm settled round her shoulders — guiding her through to his consulting room and office. 'I'll show you the drudgery that's in store for you. Then we'd better have a sandwich, and I'll be off.'

She worked all afternoon on his files and notes. At least the more recent ones weren't faded as well as scribbled in Chinese. He got back from

Quimper soon after six, and by that time she had the supper things ready. He'd enjoyed his visit to the Berthomets, he said; and as he'd expected, the old boy had jumped at the chance of making himself useful.

'At a certain age one can find oneself on the sidelines, willy-nilly. And for a man of his stamp — with things in the state they are today . . .' A shake of the greyish head. 'He'll be checking his door-mat every five minutes day and night!'

'And the address is twenty-one B Place Saint-Matthieu.'

'You have a good memory, Suzanne. With nothing written down.'

'Is the front door clearly distinguishable? No possibility someone in a rush might pick on number twenty-two A?'

'Quite distinct. Green paint on it. Those on both sides are white. The number's in white paint on the green.'

'Not too bad yourself, doctor.'

'Have to be on my toes, now you're here . . . What's the beautiful aroma?'

'Braised hare. Part of the hare Count Jules' gamekeeper gave you.'

'My mouth's already watering. A tiny apéritif first, perhaps . . .'

She waited until after supper before making her call to le Guen. It might be the only one she'd need to make, she hoped at least, until he had the Trevarez news for her. They'd have to meet then, obviously. Her intention now was to arrange to see him tomorrow or the day after, to give him his money and the letter-drop address.

The telephone was in the hall. She joggled for the operator, asked for le Guen's number in Quimper, and waited.

'That number is ringing . . .'

'*Already?*'

Peucat had told her it might take an hour . . . She heard the operator's loud sniff. 'Lines are less busy tonight. But your friend doesn't answer, I'll try again.'

Crank her handle again, she'd meant. Rosie heard her doing it. Wondering whether le Guen himself or his daughter might answer. He could be taking a bath, or —

'Yes?'

His voice, sharp and high.

'Micky?'

A fractional pause . . . 'I'm sorry, she's not here. You must be Zoé — it's only you who call my daughter "Micky" — am I right?'

Incomprehensible, in those first seconds. And his voice as strained as hell: as if someone had him by the throat. She was also conscious that the operator was quite likely to be listening. Almost certainly, seeing as the lines weren't busy . . .

'Zoé — yes.' Forcing her brain into a higher gear . . . 'But — you say she's — out, or —'

'Yes. Yes . . . But she told me you might call, and you'd arranged to meet her tomorrow at one o'clock — at the Café Providence? If you did

240

telephone I was to say how sorry —'

'Café Providence at one. Yes — that's right.'

'I thought so. But unfortunately —'

'I'll be there anyway. I have to be passing that way in any case. Oh, what a shame . . . She's not ill, I hope, in hospital or —'

'No. It's — her work, you know —'

'Some scholastic thing. Oh, well . . . You're all right I hope, M'sieur — on your own, I mean?'

'Yes. Oh yes — thank you —'

'I'll see her soon anyway, I hope . . . Goodnight, M'sieur.'

'Goodnight — er — Zoé.'

She heard him hang up, and did the same. Standing there for a few seconds in the dark hall: certain that he was *not* all right. Whether or not Marie-Claude was, he wasn't. Obviously scared of a telephone tap — which would be neither unusual nor surprising — but he also wanted badly enough to see her to have risked telling her where and when.

In a slightly obscure way, certainly. In the circumstances, probably the best he could have done. But it wouldn't have been obscure *enough*, by half, if any professional had either been listening in or received a transcript of it from the operator.

Back in the dining-room she told Peucat, 'I won't be doing much paperwork tomorrow, doctor. Have to be in Quimper by midday.'

She went by bike, through Pleyben and Briec,

starting out from St Michel at seven and cycling into Quimper just after twelve-thirty. It was a fine day with a breeze from the west and patches of high cloud. She had le Guen's money in two envelopes, one in each pocket of her overcoat; if she'd been stopped and searched she'd have said it was her employer's and that she was taking it to the pharmaceutical depot behind the hospital, that they'd warned him last week he'd have to pay off what he owed already before they'd let him have even another roll of sticking-plaster.

In fact she wasn't stopped. There was a road-block outside Pleyben, on the road west to Châteaulin, but traffic turning off southward for Briec and Quimper wasn't affected by it. By twelve-forty she was pedalling southwestward in a two-way stream of cyclists and *gazos* down Rue de Kerfeunteun towards the town centre — continuing too far, it turned out, turning right where she'd thought the road would bring her and finding she had to make another right turn northward: then, that the café was on this road — Rue de la Providence, on its corner with Rue de Locronan, some distance south of the gardens.

She rode on past it. It had the run-down look that everything else had. In summer with tables and umbrellas outside it would look a lot better, but there was only a stretch of uneven paving, a yellow-brick frontage and blue-painted double doors, one of which stood open.

Ideally, you'd find another café across the road and in sight of the one at which you were making the rendezvous, sit there toying with a beer or coffee while observing the comings and goings, noting especially any well-fed individuals with close-cropped heads who might also be taking an interest in it. In SOE training that was the recommended procedure. In this case her main interest was to see le Guen arrive: whether he did so alone or in company, and if the latter, *what* company. Especially if it separated from him at some discreet distance from the café.

Ten minutes to the hour. She cycled around the café's narrow northern end — a hairpin corner — and turned down Rue de Locronan. The café had one much smaller entrance on this side — at the top end, near the corner, a small door that was shut, probably not in use much.

Worth knowing that such an exit existed. If one should need it.

This was only a short road. Wider than the other, but terminating about fifty metres south — in the Place de Locronan, through which there was quite a lot of traffic in both directions. Amongst it at this moment one *Wehrmacht* half-ton truck: she watched it in case it was going to turn left, into a side-street connecting with Rue de la Providence, but it carried on southward — and good riddance . . . She waited until she could cross over, then took that side-road herself: left again into Rue Providence, and she was passing the café again, as before. Some girls who'd just arrived were putting chains on their bicycles: one looking up, laughing, a bright, happy face under

243

a mop of vividly red hair. The road was narrow at this point: she rode on up to where it widened and a few *gazos* were parked, and after another hundred metres or so she had the Parc de la Providence on her right — a wide expanse of grass and trees. Looking across it she could see a battery of anti-aircraft guns under camouflage near the far side, where the river ran. The river le Steir, she remembered from her studies in St James'. Smaller than the Odet — at this stage anyway. The camouflage over the guns was quite ineffective from this level; presumably would hide them from the air. Between here and there, people strolled; others relaxed on benches along a pathway parallel to the road.

Not a bad place for a rendezvous, perhaps.

Six minutes to twelve now. No military vehicles anywhere. Always a thing to look for — soldiers in trucks from which they could be whistled out to surround a building — such as a café . . .

None here, though. She rode to the top of the *parc,* dismounted, waited for a chance to wheel her bike across, then re-mounted and started back. Wondering if he'd show up at all. Once you knew something was wrong, *anything* could be: things that started going wrong tended to get worse. She'd thought last night of ringing Prigent in case he'd known anything about it; had decided not to partly for the obvious reason — the insecurity of telephones — but also because le Guen saw him as an enemy, needed to be assured that she was on *his* side.

244

Thirty metres from the café she stopped, crossed the road, took a spanner out of her saddle-bag and went through the motions of adjusting the height of the bike's saddle. Noon now: or a minute past . . . Watching southward: increasingly sure that the purpose of this meeting must be to tell her he was pulling out. Alternatively, he wasn't coming: might have been arrested, even. In which case, Prigent too — and anyone who'd been in contact with bloody Prigent . . . Shaking that out of her head, though: old Peucat's maxim was the best one: *It won't happen* . . . But an alternative she had considered — if le Guen backed out or fell out — might be to ask Lannuzel to have a watch kept on the château, for the arrival of troops and naval staff. In fact it would be the simplest way — using one's own people, no reliance on outsiders — but the snag was that it would almost certainly be too late and too slow, the word having to be passed to her, then by signal to London, and the RAF then asked to lay on the attack pretty well immediately. Their answer would most likely be a lemon, she guessed.

There. The man himself . . .

Hurrying in this direction, on this side of the road: coat flapping loose, porkpie hat down on his ears, gleam of white shirt-front and a splodge of what was probably a black tie . . . Pausing — on the kerb, looking left and then right: dropping a cigarette-end and putting his toe on it. Her spanner was back in the saddle-bag and she was fastening the strap by feel. Seeing him start across the road: doing the same herself now, wheeling the bike. The achievement of this reconnaissance being that she knew he'd come alone — no one either following or surveying. Not visibly . . .

Could be someone waiting inside the café, of course.

She was halfway to the corner when le Guen ducked into the blue doorway. She chained her bike to the railings: glancing around then while straightening her coat, brushing herself off.

All clear. *Seemingly* . . .

'Zoé!'

He'd been waiting just inside, looking nervously around: had noticeably jumped as he turned and saw her. She put her hand out to him: 'Micky — how *very* nice!'

'Oh —' licking thin, dry lips, '— for me, too . . .'

Black tie, all right. Same brown jacket and maroon pullover, too. He'd put a hand on her arm, guiding her towards a vacant table close to the doorway to the kitchen. Rather smelly — compounded, she thought, mainly of cabbage and whatever oil or fat they used. But the table was fairly well on its own, more so than others.

'Thank heavens you could come. I'm sorry for — the way I had to —'

'I'd have been here to meet Marie-Claude, of course.' A glance around, as if for a waiter or critically inspecting the decor . . . 'If anyone should enquire. Now to my surprise I've run into *you!*'

'Because after you'd said you'd be here anyway, I thought I might as well . . .'

'Yes. That'd make sense.' More quietly, then: 'What's happened, François, what's wrong?'

'Let's sit down. This all right for you?'

'Practically in the kitchen, but otherwise —'

'If it's *too* close to it —'

'No.' Reassuring him. '*I'd* have picked this one.' He looked distraught. Fumbling distractedly as he hung his coat up, and that awful hat; she kept her own coat on because of the money in its pockets. He looked even worse than he had on Saturday: her thought was *He* is *going to rat on me . . .* Then she caught his murmur — the drawn face close to hers for a moment — 'They've taken Marie-Claude as a hostage.'

'Oh, God — *François* —'

'To ensure my own — compliance. I've got to work for them — tell them whatever Prigent wants me to find out for him. It all came from him — those calls he kept making to me — and they know about him, that he's a British agent! So — I'm sorry, Zoé, but —'

'M'sieur, Madame —'

Little flat-chasted waitress: snub nose, freckles, curly light-brown hair . . . Recognizing le Guen: 'It's you, M'sieur. Haven't seen you just lately!'

'No — not lately . . .'

'Madame — today the soup is good, they're all enjoying it. There's also cheese.'

'I'll have soup. Bread with it. But we'll have a beer first, please — François, you'll have one?'

He'd sat down, at last. Looking from the waitress to her. 'I'm not sure . . .'

'*I* am. I'm parched. So you must keep me company.' She told the girl, 'Two beers, then two
soups with bread.' She waited until she'd gone,
and added, 'I'm paying, by the way.'

'No — I couldn't possibly allow —'

'And I've brought your money. Fifty thousand.
Now tell me, François — they've taken her hostage so you'll do what they tell you, they know
Prigent's an agent and you're to be a double
agent, informing on *him* . . . Right? When did it
all happen?'

'Sunday night.' He told her about the one a.m.
call, the questioning by Fischer and his accep-
tance that Marie-Claude knew nothing about
anything . . .

'But they still took her. I didn't know it until
they told me later, in the SD headquarters. Just
before he sent me home — a man named Braun,
a Sturmbannführer — *he* told me they'd taken
her.'

'Here's our beer.'

'Oh . . .'

Sitting back: shutting his eyes. Face pale-grey,
twitchy, and a shine of sweat on his forehead. If
there'd been a watcher, anyone with the least
interest in them, they couldn't have failed to see
that he was under enormous stress — or just ill
. . . Rosie saw the waitress noticing, the concern
in her eyes, and diverted her attention by offering
to pay — for the beer, or for the whole meal now

in advance; the girl told her it would all be on the one *addition,* later. She threw another look at le Guen, then back at Rosie, questioningly: Rosie shook her head, with a small, tight smile, implying *It's all right, I'm coping . . .*

'François? Smoke?'

'No — thank you, I just —'

She lit one for herself. Giving herself time to think: decide what the hell to say. What kind of hope to hold out: under what conditions he *might* still be persuaded to go through with it.

Hope of getting the girl out, was the only answer. Nothing else would do it. If he'd believe in that: if *she* could, even . . .

'François, listen. We'll get her back to you, somehow. I don't know exactly how, but — somehow.' She had vague thoughts of Peucat claiming Marie-Claude as his patient, using any influence he might have through the gendarmerie in St Michel, for instance, or of Count Jules pulling strings at some higher level. Neither of which, on second thoughts, could be contemplated — even if they'd have stood a chance. But — *something . . .* He hadn't yet had a chance to tell her he was pulling out, and her instinct was to steer him clear of this rather than wait until he came out with it.

She was aware, too, that he might well change his mind *again* the minute he was out of her sight. Also of the danger she herself was in, here and now. It was a risk anyway to be meeting in a public place; in the circumstances he'd just described it wasn't just a risk, it was idiocy. She wouldn't have been here, if she'd known.

But what else?

Glancing round: although the plain fact was you *wouldn't* see anyone taking notice. Boches were swine but they weren't simpletons.

'I mean it, François — we *will* get her out.' In the back of her mind, something Lannuzel had proposed . . . 'There's a man I must talk to, that's all . . . Aren't you going to drink your beer?'

'Oh yes . . .'

Shaking hand. A dribble down his chin as he put the glass down again. Mopping himself . . . Rosie wondering what else they'd asked him about, in connection with Prigent, and what else he might have told them. Among their more immediate interests, obviously, would be the identities of any of Prigent's associates or acquaintances, others using his surgery as a rendezvous. Le Guen had leant closer: 'He said — Braun did — she'd come to no harm. That she won't be among any hostages that might be shot, he meant. As long as I do as I'm told. I've *got* to — d'you understand?'

'Inform on Prigent. Yes.'

'But also —'

'Where are they holding her?'

'Where they hold all hostages — at Kerongués. Near there — near the village, I mean — but it's generally known as Kerongués. An old mill they — adapted.'

'And where is Kerongués?'

'About five kilometres east, on the road to Gourin. Like a concentration-camp, now. Wire fence perimeter, searchlights, machine-guns I dare say . . .' Grimacing: 'Imagine . . .'

'But if he said — what you just told me, that she'd come to no harm —'

'Yes, he *said* that, but —'

'Up to a point perhaps you can believe it. As long as they think they're getting value out of you — as they will be, if you're going to tell them whatever Prigent's after —'

'I *have* to!'

'I agree. You must. And without tipping him off, too. Prigent, I mean, don't risk it. Play straight with *them* — as far as you can. François, I'm terribly sorry this has happened. Also of course — well, I admit I have my own axe to grind, I want you there and still their trusted employee when this order comes in — the rein-forcement at — you know where . . . No, hold on — listen . . . What I meant about trusting them — I said, *Up to a point* — meaning as things are now, while they need you — but you've got to realize it won't last. They'll use you for a time, but they'll also be itching to arrest him — then it's over. And d'you think they'd release Marie-Claude to you then?'

'Yes, surely. Well — that's the *deal*, they —'

'I'd say she'll end up as a hostage like any other. I'm not saying this to make you feel worse than you do already, François —' she put her hand on his, on the table-top — 'only to face facts and do

251

what's best. We've *got* to get her out of it. Don't ask me how — I don't know — yet . . .'

Looking past him, at freckle-face coming with their soup.

'Hang on a moment . . .'

Guy Lannuzel would provide the answer — if there was one. He'd suggested something of the sort when she'd been telling him about the 'Mincemeat' plan. He'd argued that all it would achieve was get a lot of hostages dragged out and shot, then at a later stage he'd suggested avoiding this by breaking in and letting them all out. Before the action, presumably. At the time she'd wondered whether he was serious: concluding that it wouldn't help anyway, they'd only seize a few others and shoot them instead.

But she hadn't had this special axe to grind, then. They'd been talking about avoiding reprisals in general, not about extracting one individual.

Le Guen was receiving his bowl of steaming soup. She already had hers in front of her. Rabbit and turnip, she guessed, sniffing it. Grow long ears and start burrowing, any day now . . . Lannuzel, though: he'd made that suggestion very much off the cuff; faced with it as a serious proposition he might wish he'd kept his mouth shut.

See him this afternoon. Go that longer way round, then on back to St Michel-du-Faou, and make *this* trip again tomorrow. On a diet of rabbit soup, for Pete's sake . . .

The waitress had left them. Waft of some different cooking smell from in there as the door swung shut. Fish? Nobody had said anything about fish; she couldn't see any on other tables either.

'About Marie-Claude, François. There's a friend I'll talk to.'

'About getting her out?' A frown, and a dismissive gesture. 'It's not possible. You're trying to hearten me, but —'

'I believe it *is* possible. The friend I'm talking about —'

'Even if she escaped somehow, she couldn't then come home!'

'You're right. The answer's the Maquis.'

'Marie-Claude — camp out in some forest?' Gazing at her as if he thought she was raving mad. 'With thugs and —'

'No. It's the Boches who put it around that they're brigands and criminals. They're thoroughly good people, for the most part. Women among them too, now, she wouldn't be the only one. And she's young — and healthy, isn't she?' She put her spoon down; the soup was still too hot to drink. 'Alternatively she *might* be sheltered elsewhere.' Thinking of Sara de Seyssons, and that house big enough to hide a dozen Marie-Claudes in. 'Another thing, though — an invasion from England can't be long delayed. I doubt she'd be in the wilds for long. And meanwhile far less at risk than where she is now.'

Staring at her . . . 'They'd come straight to me — d'you realize?'

Spooning-up soup again, blowing on it . . . 'The Boches would, you mean, if she did escape.'

'Exactly.'

'Your SD friends. Yes. But this would have been my next suggestion.' Rosie nodded. 'Don't have a fit now — but why shouldn't you also disappear?'

'You're not — serious . . .'

'I assure you, I *am*. You and she together. Why not?'

'I suppose because I can't — imagine it . . .'

'To be with her, look after her — look after each other? Instead of leaving her to take her chances — and probably getting arrested yourself, eventually?'

'But —'

'Yes?'

'Well — how does one live? Food, shelter —'

'There are people who help. *Résistants* who organize collections, and so forth. Doctors give their services when required. Luckily, too, it's now the spring, and summer coming, life becomes much easier. François — here's a statistic. In the Bordeaux area alone, guess how many Maquis there are at this moment?'

'Heaven knows . . .'

'More than five thousand. That's a *fact*. Honestly — it's the one solution that takes care of everything. Don't you see? Incidentally, you could take fifty thousand francs with you, if you wanted — you'd be made *very* welcome!'

'It's still — make-believe . . .'

'It's how you see yourself — at the moment, what you *think* you *can't* do!'

'Pre-supposing that Marie-Claude could be got out of the camp — which would surely be *extremely* difficult —'

'Difficult, yes. But I think it can be done: I'll know for sure within a day or so. What *you* have to decide is whether you can measure up to it — effectively, François, how much you care for her.'

'I'd *die* for her!'

'But not endure a little anxiety, perhaps discomfort?'

A pause: gazing at her. 'You really mean this.'

'After the invasion — which won't be long coming — and when the Boches are on the run —'

'You made that point. I remember . . .'

'Think of your own position. You're working for the Germans. When they're beaten and we're picking up the pieces d'you want Prigent for instance pointing you out as having not only informed on him, but left your own daughter to take her chances?'

'But I have *not* —'

'You look like a collaborator, even now. You take their pay — don't you? All right, so you're going to help me — my people, as you've promised — and that would stand to your credit, we'd vouch for the fact you *had*. But where might Marie-Claude be by then? Besides, *could* you keep your promise to help us, with her in that place?'

'You know I couldn't.'

'So what's to your credit, when the time comes?'

'You're so certain such a time *is* coming . . .'

'Yes, I am. We all are. We know it.'

'And you're saying I'd be seen as a traitor, although the truth is I'm being blackmailed — with my own daughter's life —'

'That's the issue we're discussing, François. You don't have to give in to blackmail. Do this for us — as you've promised you would — and we'll look after you both. Everyone'll *know* which side you're on!'

'So now it's *your* blackmailing?'

'It's me asking for your help. Resistance and Maquis asking for your help. In return, as I say, we'd look after you. Hardly blackmail — fair exchange, *honourable* exchange . . .'

He was wiping his bowl out. Looking down into it, grim-faced.

'And as to poor Marie-Claude — you can't possibly be content to leave her in their hands?'

'Of course not *content* —'

'Well — imagine — when we get her out, and you're with us. Such a moment for her. All *your* life you'll know you did the right thing, and all *her* life —'

'Yes . . .'

Mopping her own bowl now. Glancing up, meeting his eyes again. 'Think about it? Meanwhile I'll talk to this man: and if he says yes, it can be done —'

'If it's really and truly *feasible* . . .'

He'd shut his eyes. Pale, long-fingered hands on the table each side of the empty bowl. A deep breath: eyes open and meeting hers then . . . 'If it's the way to safeguard Marie-Claude — as well as these other things — our whole future, the way you put it . . . And if he says he can do it —'

'If this man says he can, he *will.*'

'All right.'

'Meet me again tomorrow?'

'Tomorrow?'

'I'll have seen him by then. And there's no time to waste, is there. The order for the deployment might come this afternoon, for all we know. Let's hope it won't — be a bit *too* soon — but it could, couldn't it. And the thing would be — I *guess* — to get her out the same night, arrange a breakout simultaneously, and for you to be at some place to rendezvous with us. D'you have a bicycle, by the way?'

'Of course.'

'Cigarette, now?'

'I shouldn't. Smoking so much . . .'

'What the things are for, surely.'

'I still can't help feeling it's all — unreal . . .'

'The opposite. Reacting to things as they *are.* Same as — well, if you fall in the sea, you *swim* — uh? And as I say, if this man says it can be done —'

'Yes. Yes . . .' He was getting a match out. It flared, in his shaking fingers; lighting her cigarette, then his own. Bolt upright then, as if at attention, taking a long, deep drag: realizing, she hoped, that he really had no option, in his situation now . . . 'Listen. Let's meet tomorrow in the Parc de la Providence, on one of those benches. Might even stroll up there —'

'I must get back. Really . . .'

'Tomorrow at one, then. A bench say about halfway up. Let's hope it isn't raining . . . Listen — another thing altogether. I hope not to have to telephone you again. Telephones can be dangerous — especially now. Well, you know that — you handled it very well last night. But if I did have to — in some emergency — I'd say it's Zoé ringing to ask whether Marie-Claude's back yet. Are you supposed to keep it secret, that she's a hostage?'

'Yes. Braun said otherwise Prigent might guess what's going on.'

He would, wouldn't he . . . Anyway — you aren't telling this Zoé, the friend of Marie-Claude's who's on the phone, so all she'd know is Marie-Claude's still away — *somewhere*. Then whatever I needed to say we'd have to improvise, like you did last night. That was clever of you, by the way.'

A nod. 'I *must* go now —'

One more minute. Please — it's important.' She had her purse out, in preparation for paying the bill, but making use of it too as a reason to be looking downward, making the almost non-stop flow of talk less obvious — she hoped . . . 'François — for when you see the troop-deployment order, here's an address to memo-

258

rize. I won't write it down, just remember it — twenty-one B Place Saint-Matthieu. Not all that far from where you live — right? So — write on any old slip of paper, "The baby is due about —" and then the date, or dates. Fold the paper, go for a walk through Place Saint-Matthieu, put it through the letter-slot and walk on past. It's an ancient house divided into three. Green front door with the number twenty-one B on it in white. The doors each side are white, twenty-one B the only one that's green. Before you make the delivery, try to check you aren't being followed. Got it?'

'Place Saint-Matthieu twenty-one B.'

She nodded. 'Any time, day or night. The people who live there don't know who you are, your name or mine or what it's about, but they'll telephone the message to a number where I'll get it. No link back to you, you see — as long as you aren't followed.'

'Very well.'

'Believe me — it *won't* be forgotten.'

Nodding: getting ready to leave, looking round to check his coat was where he'd hung it.

'Until tomorrow, then.'

'Yes. And — thank you . . .'

A scared cat if there'd ever been one. But as far as it went — OK. Touch wood. *If* he meant it, and stuck to it — if it wasn't just that he was terrified, wanting only to get away from her. She thought of cementing their relationship with a farewell kiss, but it might have done more harm

than good. All right, she thought, tell that anec-
dotally — if you ever got a chance to tell any of
this — you'd raise a laugh or at least a smile; but
he could be scared of *that, she* was definitely
scared of *this* — all of it. They might well be
keeping him under surveillance, it would be almost surprising if they weren't, and this goldfish-
bowl of a café having been a haunt of his — well,
any of those glum-looking people sucking up their
soup . . .

An important thing was not to look or act
scared. Not to unknown watchers, and in this
present instance perhaps even more importantly
not to François le Guen. Who'd got his coat on,
was back at the table, hurriedly offering her his
hand. She leant back, to take it: 'François — if
you *have* to go . . . Oh, *hell*, nearly forgot — all
these francs — since I've actually got them here
— look, easier to do this outside —'

Chapter 10

He'd refused to take the money. She'd told him all right, she'd keep it safe for him. She'd have felt a lot better if he *had* taken it. Another worry that plagued her on her way back from Quimper was Michel Prigent: quite obviously she *ought* to warn London that he was blown, but there were also good reasons not to.

She was in Châteauneuf-du-Faou before six, and at Lannuzel's farm by ten past. She'd come about forty kilometres: with the prospect of another twelve from here to St Michel — some of it in the dark, at that — and then the whole thing to do again tomorrow. But the hardest work of all had been the hour she'd spent with le Guen. She wished he *had* taken the money. If he had, she'd have felt more sure of him. He was too naive to be dishonest: accepting payment would have imposed a sense of obligation on him.

Lannuzel's pickup wasn't where it had been last time. So he might not be here. If he wasn't, as she had to see him before she could get any further with le Guen and 'Mincemeat' she'd have to wait here for him, even if necessary sleep here. No great problem in that — she imagined — except that it would mean missing her hour's listening-watch tonight.

On the other hand, riding back in the dark wasn't much of a problem either, now she had her *Ausweis*.

'Hey — Suzanne!'

His voice came from behind her: she looked round, saw him coming from the farm gate. That long-strided limp of his. Donkey-jacket over his shoulder, open-necked blue shirt, blue trousers. She waved — relieved, glad to see him, and struck again by the similarity to Ben.

The dogs were giving tongue again, up there. They seemed to be kept shut up a lot. He'd told her they roamed free at night.

'Nice timing, Guido! Saw your truck wasn't there, I wasn't sure.'

'Truck's in the barn.' He jerked a thumb. 'I've been visiting a near neighbour, that's all — on a matter relating to *your* good news, as it happens. Saturday, eh?'

'Subject to confirmation. In other words the message you called gibberish?'

'The joys of spring, et cetera.'

'Something like that.'

He was beside her, now. 'Nice work, anyway.'

'They've been quick — as they said they would. But listen — all right with you if I join you, that night?'

'Perfectly all right.' He smiled down at her. '*Any* night.' She pretended not to have caught on; he took her arm, turning her towards the house again. Maybe the similarity to Ben went deeper than just appearances. 'Want to see how we handle it, do you?'

'Main reason is they'll be dropping some things I've asked for, and I'd like to be there to collect them. A radio-transceiver, and an "S" phone. Know what that is?'

'Sure.'

'For use on future drops. The container's supposed to have a "Z" for "Zoé" on it.'

'Easy, then. Glad to have you with us, too. Come in the afternoon or early evening, will you?'

'Fine.' They were almost at the house. 'By bike from here, or will there be other transport?'

'A lorry. *Gazo*. Was it just to ask me this, Suzanne, that you've dropped by?'

'No. There's a more important subject.' She leant her bike against the wall where she had last time. 'Important — also tricky. You may say impossible. How's Brigitte?'

'Blooming. Like me. May I say something rather personal?'

His eyes were on her face. Then a forefinger touching her lips. 'Your mouth fascinates me. I love to watch you while you're speaking.'

'I'll try to talk less, then.'

'Spoilsport. Any case it's not *only* your mouth . . . What I'm saying is — well —'

'Better *not* say it, Guido.'

'Don't tell me — a husband somewhere?'

'As good as. He will be — husband, I mean — when this is over.'

'Right now he's far away?'

She shook her head. 'Not to me, he isn't. I'm

telling you this seriously, Guido. I'm sorry — and flattered — but —'

'But bugger off.' Pausing near the door . . . 'OK. Although — if this lucky bastard lets you down — give me the nod?'

'He's no bastard, and he won't!'

'Unless he's a damn fool — which you'll say he isn't . . . Anyway — come on in.' Pushing the door open: 'Brigitte, look who's here!'

Brigitte didn't spend long with them: chatted with Rosie for a moment, then exchanged glances with her brother, shrugged, and murmured something about several hundred chicks in incubators needing to be seen to.

'Anyway — you have secrets to exchange — right?'

'Not secrets from you, I'd have thought. But it's — as I said, Guy, a bit — tricky.'

A smile from Brigitte: 'Then I *certainly* mustn't —'

'It's best she hears as little as possible, Suzanne.' He explained — by the look of him, wishing he didn't have to — 'Because — before she starts in on this again, having you as audience — actually I think I began to tell you when you were here before — this place is hers and her husband's. When he comes back, I'll move on and leave them to themselves — leaving him his wife in full working order, this is the point — *not* a fond memory, someone who *might* still be half alive in some prison or concentration-camp.'

'I'm quite ready to take my chances.' She'd come back from the door. 'No, Guy, it's all right, I won't "start in", as you call it. We've talked this over and over, Suzanne, my dear brother and I. He means for the best, but he's *extremely* obstinate, always has been.'

He nodded to Rosie. 'It's an infliction.'

'But how can you hope to keep her out of it? When she's living in the same house with you — obviously an active *Résistant?*'

'It's plain to everyone but him.' Brigitte shrugged. 'Look, are you sure you don't want any coffee, or tea?'

'No — thank you.'

'But d'you know, he actually thinks he could be arrested or shot or whatever — on one of these outings such as you're arranging for Saturday, eh? — and they either wouldn't come here at all or they'd believe me when I said I knew nothing about it!'

'Guy — it's a nice thought, but —'

'You tell him. I'll leave you to it. Come any time, though. Come when my idiot brother's *not* here.'

Lannuzel said as the door shut, 'I keep her out of it as far as I can, that's all. Obviously, you're both right, there's no way she can be isolated from it, exactly, but it gives her a better chance than if she was actively involved. No, wait, there's more — all my friends and co-*Résistants* know for sure she's truly *not* involved. They'd all swear to it — she *would* have a chance. And what I *want,* you see — suppose they caught us on Saturday — I could be shot or sent to Buchenvald, sure, but she could run this farm on her own — I've made sure of that — and pray God she'd be here when Paul gets back. OK — *if* he does, if he's still alive. I'm giving her — them — the best chance I can, that's all.'

'A very *slight* chance, isn't it. But — all right —'

'There's more. They lost a child. Don't tell her I told you this, but you might as well — understand it. Little girl eighteen months old. 1940 this was — near Lille. There was dive-bombing and machine-gunning of refugees. Paul had already been taken prisoner, she was on her own. So — I want her to have — you know, a life. Please God, with Paul, but —'

'You weren't ever married?'

'No. Not that that has anything to do with it . . . Suzanne — you don't want to be here all night, what's this you say is tricky?'

She nodded. 'Yes . . . Cigarette?'

'Thanks.'

Shaking out two Caporals . . . 'Remember you said — when we were talking about Trevarez — that a solution to the problem of reprisals against hostages might be to break into the detention-camp and let them out? And would it be the camp at Kerongués you were talking about?' He nodded. She leant towards the match: '*Would* it be possible?'

Lighting his own. 'Might be . . .' Breathing smoke . . . 'It *was* once thought of, I may tell you.

266

In fact I rather liked the idea: that's how it came to mind. But hardly worth doing if they're only going to grab another lot and shoot *them* — as I think you pointed out yourself, the other day?'

'It would be to get one individual out. Perhaps some others too, but only to confuse the issue.'

'So they can't identify the one you were really after.'

'Exactly. But primarily, to get *her* out.'

'A woman . . . You'd have some place for her to go then?'

'I'd thought the Maquis. Either your lot or in the *Montagnes d'Arrées*. She's a young school teacher — incidentally, might have her father with her.'

'You mean he's a hostage too, or —'

'No — he'd probably be joining us when we did it. An alternative, by the way, is Count Jules might let her hide out at Scrignac. I'll look into that — if you tell me you can do it. It *is* important, Guido. Her father's the informer who's going to tip me off when there's a date for the next naval staff conference at Trevarez. He has a job with the Boches in Quimper — they think he's *their* informer, and they've locked her up to keep him in line. That's how it is — he's not going to help unless I can guarantee her safety.'

'You can't. Who could?'

'All right — guarantee we'll get her out of that camp, say.'

'She'd be *safer* left in it.'

'After "Mincemeat"?'

267

Staring at her — puzzled. Then he'd caught on. 'Right. Perhaps not. We'd need to get her out *before* that.'

'On the same night, was what I thought. When with any luck they'll have their hands full.'

'Well — yes, that might not be bad . . .'

'Are you saying yes, you can do it?'

'I won't say it's *im*possible. If it's so — vital . . . As I said, we were planning a rescue of this kind, a while ago. Some of us were to dress in *Wehrmacht* uniforms — which we still have, of course. They were brought to us by Georgians — conscripts from Georgia, Soviet Union?'

'White Russians?'

Most so-called 'White' Russians in the Nazi ranks were poison. Thieves, drunkards, molesters. If anything, *worse* than Germans.

Lannuzel had shaken his head. 'These were forcibly recruited — dislike the Boches almost as much as we do. That's why they came over and the boys accepted them.'

'You wouldn't use them, though — would you?'

'No. Only the uniforms. I think if we did it I'd make it *my* job. Missing the action at Trevarez, of course . . . But just me and — three or four others. Anyway, that's detail.'

'The decision itself's important. If I can tell him we'll get his daughter out, he'll help us. At least, I *hope* . . . But if I can't —'

'He won't. Then no "Mincemeat".'

She nodded.

'Suppose you told him OK, we'll get the girl out — on the night — so you'll get your tip-off from him —'

'So I'd have reason to *hope* I would —'

'Then it might become impossible, for some reason?'

'No. I think we have to play straight with him. Word gets around, doesn't it. If we use people, then leave them in the lurch —'

'Yes.' A nod. 'You're quite right.'

'So do your utmost?'

'We'll — put our heads together.'

'Soon, though? Thing is, I'll be seeing him tomorrow . . . I suppose I could tell him you're working on it . . .'

Provisionally, he'd said, yes, she could. In fact she could tell him anything she liked, at this stage — and he'd try to give her a conclusive answer when she came on Saturday. He didn't command these fellows; they'd have as much say in it as he had, and they'd have to volunteer — having first satisfied themselves there'd be a fair chance of pulling it off without ending up dead or captured.

Cycling northward into growing dusk, she thought about where that left her, in the context of her meeting with le Guen tomorrow lunchtime.

She'd tell him yes. Not provisionally, but definitely. Instinct told her that if she didn't, she'd lose him: thus losing all hope of 'Mincemeat' too.

There were hardly any cyclists on the road at this hour. A few heavy goods or farm vehicles, some with no lights at all, others with small, dim ones, slits of weak light through blackout shields — and a *gazo* van or car occasionally. None of those in recent minutes, though, and no petrol-engined cars at all — none of the Master Race abroad tonight, it seemed. She was riding as close to the right-hand verge as she could; her bike had no lamp on it, only reflectors.

Fork coming up ahead. Immediately after it, she'd be crossing the main east-west road; but before that she'd have to cross the traffic — if there was any — on *this* one, in order to take that left fork.

Lights, along there . . .

Shaded headlights, and moving torches. A scattering of men in the road illuminated suddenly — uniforms, all *Wehrmacht* — then that torch-beam had left them, swept over a van's open doors. She thought tiredly *Here we go again . . .* Stopping with one foot down, looking back over her left shoulder and then ahead: she pushed off, rode across into the left fork, towards the lights and whatever was happening there. She might have held on, keeping to the right, but would surely have ended up the same way. Why would they put a block on only the *minor* road? Her papers were in order; anyway, there were nearly two hours to go before curfew at ten p.m., and one wouldn't have wanted to be caught trying to evade a road-check.

'Halt!'

A torch-beam shone straight at her, blindingly.

She stopped, and dismounted. A hand up to shield her eyes . . .

'*Kom! Venez!*'

She went forward slowly — a few metres, with the beam of light still on her. It shifted to the bike for a moment, then came back to her.

'Papers?'

She leant the machine against her hip, and eased the wad of documentation in its now somewhat tattered envelope out of the inside breast pocket of her coat. Holding it out towards him. This was an officer of some kind: high-fronted cap, rank insignia on the shoulders of his greatcoat. He'd taken the package and was holding the papers by one corner, his torch and the empty envelope in that same hand, flipping pages over with the other. Light gleamed on the barrel of a slung rifle — a soldier a few metres away, in the centre of the road. Others beyond him, and a military truck parked further along, close to the *gazo* van that was being searched.

'You're out late?'

'I'll be home well before curfew. There's an *Ausweis* there permitting night work anyway. I'm a nurse.'

'I am aware of it.' He gave the sheaf of papers another flip, exposing her *carte d'identité* with its passport-type photograph. Lighting it with the torch, then switching the beam to her — straight at her face. Gone, then: leaving her temporarily blinded . . . It was a moment before she saw that he was handing her papers back to her.

'I signed your *Ausweis* myself, yesterday morning.' His French accent wasn't too bad. 'I also take note that the original is a great deal more attractive than the photograph!'

Shrugging — as if she hadn't understood. Guy Lannuzel an hour ago — now this. She wasn't feeling in the least bit attractive: frayed and travel-worn, was the truth. Pushing the papers back into her coat. 'M'sieur . . .'

'Goodnight, Mam'selle!'

A heel-click, for God's sake — and he was lighting the way for her with his torch. Charm offensive? She mounted: loathing him, loathing all of them: wobbling a bit as she got going. Soldiers in the road and around the van turned to glance at her as she passed — astonishing herself in that same moment by recognizing their victim. A civilian — Frenchman — standing with his back against the German truck, arms up and hands linked behind his head, a look of shock on his unshaven but — as she remembered, from the only other time she'd seen it — rather genial, friendly face. The man from the corner bar in St Michel, the one who'd told her how to find the doctor's house. Name of — she got it: Timo Achard.

'On his own, you say.'

Peucat had waited supper for her. A pie mostly of cabbage, potato and cheese, with bits of sausage here and there. It was very good and there was plenty of it.

Rosie nodded. 'I'd guess it was his van. Greyish colour. There was no one else in sight — except Boches, of course.'

'His van is blue.'

'Could have been — in the dark and torchlight. Is he a *Résistant?*'

A shrug. 'Who'd know?'

'I'd have thought you might.'

'It's more likely he'd have been engaged in some black market, smuggling operation. I told you he could nearly always lay his hands on a bottle or two of cognac. Although if that was it one would have thought there'd be gendarmes present, not only Boches. As for *your* Boche, I think I know that one. An Oberleutnant — young, I suppose good-looking — to a female eye?'

'I was going to say, your friend Timo looked scared to death.'

'Could you be sure, in the dark?'

'Yes. They had torches shining on him. He and whatever was in the van were the focus of their attention. I don't think it was a road-block of the routine kind — I'd guess he was the target, I just happened to come along.'

Peucat looked worried. 'Timo's not one to scare easily. It would have to be — something quite bad.'

Like a man facing crucifixion, she thought: *that* bad. Except one's own imagination might have played some part. That dreadful impotence: nothing to do but pass on by, avert the eyes . . .

A little man on a Paris railway platform, she

273

remembered. Guillaume, they'd called him. She'd been passing within a few paces of him as they'd made the arrest — and she'd known he had plastic explosive in his briefcase. Two minutes earlier, he'd raised his hat to her.

He'd known what *he* was in for, all right.

She asked Peucat, 'Will you go round in the morning?'

'I think not.' A frown — as if he hadn't liked the question. Adding, 'If he's home, he's all right. If not, I'd wait until it's common knowledge he's in trouble — *then* go round, see Adèle.'

'But since you've heard about it from me, because in all innocence I happened to be there and saw it —'

'You're a stranger here, the odds were against your knowing him. Better they shouldn't have reason to believe you did. Connections with those in such situations should *always* be avoided, Suzanne — at least, when the connection isn't already known.'

She nodded, gazing at him, wondering where he'd got that precept from.

She changed the subject.

'Did you have a good day, in my absence?'

'A less energetic one than you seem to have had. Thank heaven. But — yes. No one died on me, at least.'

'That's something.'

'I was going to tell you — there's a document you have still to acquire — a *Carte de Travail*. I completed the application for you — next door here, it's the mayor who issues it. He's about as energetic as a five-toed sloth, but we should have it in a week or so.'

'I'll need a second valise to carry all these papers!'

'Reminds me. When you go on your trips — like today, Suzanne — don't you think you should take it with you, to give an impression of having work to do?'

'Maybe. Yes. Today was different, but — yes, if you'd tell me what I'm supposed to be doing — visiting which patients, and where, for instance. Incidentally, I have to go to Quimper again tomorrow.'

'*Again!* Good heavens . . . And I can't spare the *gazo,* I'm afraid. Otherwise I'd —'

'No, I wouldn't have expected . . . Anyway, that's not all — Saturday, I'll be going to the Lannuzels in the afternoon and I won't be back that night.'

Gazing at her: waiting for more. Then it clicked: 'Saturday, of course . . .'

She set radio-watch in the attic at twelve; nothing came in, and most of that cold hour she spent thinking about Prigent. She was very well aware of her duty to tell London he was blown and under SD or Gestapo surveillance, and that keeping the information to herself meant risking the lives of any other agents or *Résistants* who might be contacting him either in person or by telephone. His line or lines would quite likely be

275

tapped: her own call to him on Saturday even might have been recorded. Not that they'd get anything from *that* . . .

But — Christ, they *would* . . .

She'd given her name as Zoé — no surname — and Prigent had accepted this without question — and then she'd asked whether she was right in thinking that 'Micky' might also be turning up that afternoon. And since *then*, the same Zoé had rung le Guen on his home telephone — which was just as likely to be tapped — asking for and about the self-same 'Micky', who by that time had turned into a girl. To wit, into an alias for Marie-Claude, whereas in the Zoé-Prigent call he'd been male and the dentist's former school-mate — also known as François le Guen. The thickest of eavesdroppers would have realized that something stank — and that le Guen would have the answer to it, also to the identity of the Zoé woman. In fact if they'd monitored either one or both of those calls, old François was likely to be put through the wringer very shortly.

Wasn't likely to stand up to it too well either, she thought. Not if they really tried.

But maybe they hadn't tapped either le Guen's phone, or Prigent's as early as Saturday. Might only have got wise to the le Guen-Prigent connection when he'd obeyed Prigent's summons that afternoon. Otherwise would they have waited until Sunday night/Monday morning to grill him?

Might have. One knew damn-all of the background. Including how long they might have had suspicions of Prigent.

Anyway — leave that. If they had either of those calls recorded or in transcript — well, you'd get to hear about it. All you could do for the moment was pray they hadn't. And get on with it . . . Concentrating thoughts for the moment on Prigent and the risk to other agents or associates if one left him and SIS un-warned . . . Well — from his or their point of view it would be unforgiveable: *but,* one's own allegiance was to 'F' Section, SOE, one's brief included 'Mincemeat' — which in turn depended on le Guen remaining at large and cooperative — and if SIS were alerted to the present situation the odds were that Prigent would make a run for it, and that the SD would assume le Guen had tipped him off. They'd haul him back in, and in pursuit of the truth they'd almost certainly torture him to death.

In the course of it he'd tell them all he knew about 'Zoé'. Whose days would then be numbered. And 'Mincemeat' wouldn't get off the ground.

Sit tight? *Not* tell Baker Street?

Or not tell them until the night of 'Mincemeat', having on the face of it only then just learnt the truth? A retrospective version of events, if called for at a later stage, might be that she'd had no idea the SD had conscripted 'Micky' to work as a double agent. Hadn't known about Prigent either. She could have thought they'd arrested le Guen's daughter as a hostage like any other hostage: Marie-Claude for all Rosie knew might have stayed too long at a party and been caught out after curfew, or driven a *gazo* through a red stoplight. *Any* minor offence: one mightn't even have bothered to ask what. Then on 'Mincemeat' night old Micky, with his daughter restored to him, would have been moved to spill the beans.

It was unlikely, she thought — *hoping* she was still thinking straight, in the ice-cold attic — that le Guen would contradict that version: or even hear of it. He wasn't ever going to meet anyone from Baker Street, and Prigent's masters in St James' would have no incentive to seek him out. In the event, anyway, he and Marie-Claude would be safely under cover — with the Château de Trevarez flattened and at least some of those weekending brass-hats buried under it.

She woke with it still simmering in her brain. Ends justifying the means, was what it came down to. Also the fact that taking chances with other people's lives was a lot easier when you didn't know them.

Didn't know for certain they existed, even. That was even better.

Might well be frost out there, she thought. A bit late for one — third day of May, God's sake — but the light in the window had that steely look, and even with the bedclothes right up she wasn't all that warm.

Nose ice-cold.

Imagining — how one might feel if one heard later — even years later — that some other agent or *Résistant* had gone to his or her death in consequence of one's having deliberately withheld the warning about Prigent . . .

It was a truth which you carried with you always in the field that you could come to a sudden and very unpleasant end not necessarily through blunders of your own but through the carelessness or malfeasance of others. You could be playing your end strictly by the rules, quite unaware that events which would ultimately send you in chains to Ravensbrück were already shaping up elsewhere.

Semi-dozing, seeing this one like a piece of film. Prigent's surgery door on the Rue de l'Yser. A departing patient: featureless, anonymous. The blonde receptionist sees him out: there's an exchange of *au revoirs,* and the door closes. A car's engine starts — forty or so metres away, up at the cemetery end of the road. It's a grey Citroën, with two men in it: raincoats, soft hats, leather gloves. The car pulls out smoothly from the kerb and follows, maintaining a certain distance until Prigent's customer has gone out of sight around the corner. It speeds up then: to round the same corner, then overtake: and for the man gasping as he whirls round, freezing in a moment's shock then looking frantically for any way to escape, it's as stunning as an explosion — rocking halt of the grey car that's bounced on to the pavement ahead of him with its doors flying open and the two men ejecting: their shouts as they grab him . . .

'*In!*'

Flung in like something dead — which he will

be, soon. After intervals of pain, humiliation, horror.

She knew. Had been there, once. Was now out of the bed, snatching up her notebook and a pencil, pausing only for a glance out of the window — seeing there was no frost, despite the killing cold in this end of the house — then leaping back under the blankets so as not to freeze while drafting a signal as succinctly as she could make it. After a few crossings-out it ended up as *Micky reports Cyprien's cover blown. Strongly urge no action or warning to him before completion of Mincemeat, since Micky's contribution is vital and he would be held responsible and arrested if Cyprien evacuated. Suggest only action should be for contacts or communications with Cyprien to be suspended.*

Let them think *that* one out.

And probably decide not to alert Prigent's controllers in St James'. That would be safest: not trusting them any more than they — SIS — trusted Baker Street. She — Rosie — had established her own credentials in that quarter, but by and large there was little love lost between the two establishments. You could hardly have blamed them if they ignored an SOE request to sit on such information until further notice; Prigent after all was their man, just as she was SOE's girl. Could one imagine them not warning her if they heard *she* was in the Gestapo's sights?

Yes. If it suited them. If weightier considerations took priority. Yes, you could.

Anyway, she'd passed the buck — or would

280

have, once she'd got it away to Sevenoaks. The sooner the better. Have to take the Mark III along this morning, unfortunately.

Go via Châteauneuf-du-Faou, perhaps — stop somewhere quiet to get the signal off, then park the set *chez* Lannuzel and pick it up again on the way home?

A few extra kilometres' pedalling, as compared with taking the road through Pleyben. Better than lugging it all the way to Quimper, though — and then having it with her while making the R/V with le Guen. Which she wasn't much looking forward to, anyway. With every day that passed the risks *had* to increase. Whether they'd got on to Prigent through le Guen or on to le Guen via Prigent, that was the way it went: they were very much on to le Guen now, and every contact she had with him could be the one that led them to *her*.

In any case, those other possibilities: telephone taps, sharp eyes open for a girl agent using the code-name Zoé, and maybe linking this to the two radio transmissions that had been made in recent days and a third one to come this morning. After which, Zoé would be putting herself on public exhibition on a park bench in conversation with a man the SD might very well be watching.

Had to be chanced, anyway. Cowards died a thousand deaths, et cetera. Also, it seemed, lay around thinking up disaster scenarios when they could be getting up, getting dressed, encoding this signal — at the kitchen table, where it was warm, so OK, stoke the coal range first — then packing the valise with the Mark III and its battery at the bottom and medical odds and ends on top. Take half le Guen's money in it too, maybe. He might accept it, today — if he'd had second thoughts. He might have had. Otherwise, if one was stopped and had to account for it, it could be explained as Peucat's payment for the pharmaceuticals he was sending her there to collect.

He'd be up too, by the time she'd done all that. She'd make coffee for them both, then get on the road.

Bitterly cold, still. Wind from the east, of course, the still frozen East where the Russians were beating the bejasus out of the bloody Boches. Until a week ago they had been, anyway. But here the sun was lifting out of ground-level murk into a clear sky; the day would warm up, soon enough. Starting off, she was pedalling straight into that low, coppery blaze: at Peucat's suggestion, leaving St Michel eastward for Plounévez-du-Faou, thence southeastward to a wooded area near a village called Kérampresse. It turned out to have been good advice: a quiet, remote patch of country with good cover for herself and the bike and reasonably long views so you'd see anything that might be coming. She was on the air for only about three minutes — which wouldn't have given the long-range detectors much time to get on to her — and Sevenoaks had nothing for her. Unsurprising, as they'd had nothing last night either, but it could also be taken as an indication that Saturday night's drops were still on.

Guy Lannuzel wasn't at home, and Brigitte didn't expect him back before evening. She was in overalls, had emerged from one of the hen-runs in time to save Rosie from the dogs — Collie crosses, wolflike, ravenous-looking. Certainly, she said — leave anything she liked, for as long as she liked.

'You wouldn't want this to be found.'

'Oh.' A nod. 'All right.'

'Do you have a workshop? Where Guy mends things?'

'I'll show you . . .'

At the back of the barn where he kept his *gazo* and farm implements, a tool-bench and its surroundings were littered with bits of machinery and electrics. There was even an old car battery; she put the transceiver's with it. Then the set itself, a carburettor on top of it — and the other components separately — aerial wire in a drawer full of a jumble of flex, and the headphones in a chest with other junk. None of it would look as if anyone had tried to hide it.

'Thanks, Brigitte. Perfect.' Fastening the valise, which was a lot lighter now. 'I'll be back to relieve you of it some time this afternoon.'

Might stash her spare transceiver here when she had it, she thought — if Guy Lannuzel allowed it. The purpose of having a spare was as a replacement in case of irreparable breakdown or damage to this one, and to provide a degree of flexibility, so she could transmit from different locations without having to lug a set to and from the home base every time. You wouldn't transmit from this farm, only collect the set *en passant* and find some spot like this morning's, a few kilometres away. Or an empty house, ruined barn — whatever.

She rode back into Châteauneuf, and out of it southwestward on the road for Briec. Last time she'd detoured via Trevarez, which had made the trip quite a bit longer. Last time: that had been her first day here, Saturday. Today was Wednesday — and this morning only one week ago, she realized, she'd been in the flat in Portman Square — sipping real coffee and nibbling chocolate biscuits, talking about 'Hector'.

She told le Guen — on the park bench where he joined her just after one o'clock, having come dodging across from the river-bank side like a man avoiding shellfire — 'From now on I won't use the name "Zoé" on the telephone — *if* I have to ring you up again, which I hope I won't — in case your line's being tapped. I used "Zoé" elsewhere, you see, earlier on. It could ring a bell — and I'd sooner it didn't.'

'When you visited Prigent, you used it.'

He could be sharper than one realized or expected. She glanced at him, and nodded: offering him a Gaullois, which he accepted eagerly. Perhaps the SD hadn't started paying him for his work as an informer yet. She hadn't told him yet

284

about Kerongués — what she was going to tell him, perhaps with her fingers crossed . . . He sat huddled in his overcoat, although the day had warmed up considerably and she had hers folded on her knees. There were people straggling by in all directions, some just strolling, enjoying the spring sunshine; Rosie, watching them — idly, as one would — had as yet seen no one taking any interest in them. Although as likely as not you wouldn't: just as in the café yesterday. Here the main advantage was that if they'd had a tail on him she'd probably have seen it when he'd come dodging over as he had.

She explained — about not using the code-name 'Zoé' from now on, but having used it earlier — 'Wouldn't have meant anything to anyone, at that stage. But a lot's been going on, hasn't it? Your own visit to the SD for one thing, and my phone call to you on Monday. If they *are* monitoring your line.'

'You think they would be?'

'Might not. Might think with Marie-Claude locked up they've got you under their thumbs anyway. Any further contact with them yet?'

'Yes. Fischer — the lieutenant — came to the office this morning and took me aside, asked me had I been in touch with Prigent yet.'

'Have you?'

'I'm seeing him this evening after work. The same routine — dental appointment. He sounded friendly — although of course that means nothing —'

'He'll be friendly as long as he believes you're working for him. Just as *they* will. Was Fischer satisfied?'

'He's coming to the office again tomorrow.'

'And you'll make your first report then. Having seen Prigent tonight.'

He'd nodded. Leaking smoke . . . A clutch of nuns passing: eyes down, hands folded. Coming the other way — in total contrast, passing this bench now, a group of *Luftwaffe* men, swaggering, loud-voiced. She went on — le Guen had drawn his legs in to give them more room — 'François, listen — I have a report for *you*, about Keron-gués.'

Pale eyes on her, blinking into the sun . . . 'I — didn't like to ask.'

'Well, it's good, anyway. Affirmative. There *is* a way to get Marie-Claude out. They'd planned something like it before, apparently — and it *can* be done. Great news — huh?'

'It's —' gazing round, shaking his head — 'terrifying . . .'

'What — that we'll get her *out?*'

'The whole thing.' He muttered it again: 'The whole thing . . .' Sucking hard on his cigarette: 'Anyway — what do *I* do?'

'Just carry on. Then when you have the date and pass it to me — the way I told you, yesterday —'

'That's what I'm asking — what'll I have to do *then?*'

'The most likely thing is you'll drop your note

in at that address in the evening, isn't it. After work. But even if you do it at lunchtime — whichever — on the following day, meet me here at one o'clock. All right?'

'The day after I leave the note.'

'I'll get it that night at the latest, and — the following lunchtime, meet you here, tell you where to be and when. OK?'

'It may be.' Twitch of the head. 'It's still —' flicking ash away — 'you know —'

'Worrying, because it's outside your experience. Yes, I do know.' As *this* was outside hers, she thought: glancing calm-faced at passers-by. To be meeting him for the second day running — in public, broad daylight, when the SD were already breathing down his neck . . . She put a hand on his coat-sleeve: 'Listen — I don't want to prolong this longer than I have to — one or two other points, just quickly. If I had to use the phone to you from now on I'll call myself Béatrice. Hope I *won't* have to — obviously . . . Second, when we meet here the day after you've dropped the message, let's please make it only about one minute — or less. Maybe not even sit down, just walk and talk then separate. I'll just be telling you where to come at what time — that's all, save anything else for when you get there. And — last point, François — you realize, between now and then we won't be in touch at all. The next contact *you'll* initiate, with your note. Right?'

'Then — it'll be night-time.'

'Evening, rather than night. Still daylight, well ahead of curfew. Again, make certain you're not followed. You'll have about five kilometres to cover — to some place in the Kerongués area, obviously. We'll be waiting for you, and from there on —'

'*We?*'

'Yes, I and —'

'*You'll* be there?'

It seemed to have encouraged him no end; it surprised her that he hadn't assumed she would be anyway. She'd never doubted that she'd be needed — essentially by Marie-Claude, who'd no doubt be extremely frightened, would need to have things explained to her, *might* even have to be escorted to Scrignac — or elsewhere. Quite apart from Papa needing to have *his* hand held.

When he'd left her, she rummaged in her valise for the cheese sandwich she'd brought and had been rather yearning for. She wolfed it down while preparing for departure — putting her coat on unbuttoned, as the easiest way to carry it — fastening the valise and tying it back into the bike's pannier, then wheeling the bike into the road and getting going. Getting, thank God, *away* — into the comparative obscurity of streets crowded with other cyclists, and with the job not only done — this far, touch wood — but feeling that on two counts it looked less shaky than before. One was that although he'd declined to take any money here and now, he'd decided he *would* take it with him when he and his daughter went walkabout, and the other, that relief of his at hearing she'd be there on the night. The two things together seemed more or less to clinch it.

As long as he didn't have his mind changed for him by Messrs Fischer and Braun. Or forget this was his only hope.

Next stop, anyway — Lannuzel, for a positive decision on Kerongués — and to pick up the transceiver. And tomorrow, maybe — depending on that Kerongués outcome — to Scrignac, to let Count Jules know what was going on. Ring first — ask Peucat to — to check whether it would be convenient; ostensibly visiting his wife, of course, but he'd started all this, was entitled to be kept informed.

Might even do it by *gazo:* either with Peucat, or solo.

She wondered how le Guen would get on with Prigent this evening, how successfully he'd explain his new readiness to work with him. Then with the SD *leutnant:* he'd said, 'He's coming to the office again tomorrow . . .' One wouldn't know or hear a thing, until the message came from Berthomet. Not having unlimited faith in old François, the waiting wasn't going to be too easy.

Chapter 11

Ben stubbed out a Senior Service and reached down for his stick. 'About the lot, then.'

Hallowell nodded, shuffling the paperwork together. He was a major, and this was his office in 'F' Section SOE's building at 62–64 Baker Street; Ben had come by appointment to 'make his number' with him. DDOD(I) in St James' — where Ben was working now — controlled the clandestine operations of the 15th Motor Gunboat Flotilla, based at Dartmouth, and SOE relied on that flotilla for shipping agents and material into Brittany, and for bringing agents and secret mail out. Close liaison was obviously essential, and the SOE link was now to be largely Ben's responsibility.

Hallowell checked the time. 'Kept you longer than I should have. Asking too many questions, I'm afraid.'

Questions unrelated to SOE business too, some of them. About the circumstances of the action in which he'd been wounded, for instance. Ben had mentioned that if it hadn't been for the body-armour with which Coastal Forces were being issued nowadays he'd very likely have been dead. It was a fact — his armoured smock had stopped a lot of flying debris. Some disliked the armour on account of its weight — and you certainly wouldn't want to go overboard in it — but it was undoubtedly saving lives.

The soldier shook his hand: 'Looking forward to working with you, Ben. One other question, though — aren't you hiding your light under a bushel, rather?'

For a moment he didn't get it. Leaning on the stick, glancing down to where the man was looking — at his sleeve, the twin wavy gold stripes . . . He caught on: 'Hell. News travels fast around here, doesn't it?'

'That memo from your chief —' a nod towards the desk — 'has you down as a lieutenant-commander, that's all. Recent promotion, is it?'

'Could hardly be more so.' Ben explained, 'I've one reefer at Gieves now, having the half-stripe sewn on, and when I pick it up I'll leave 'em this one. Do it now, in fact. Thanks for the reminder.'

'My dear fellow.' He looked unwell, Ben thought. Haggard, hollow-eyed. Hence the desk-job maybe. Shaking his head: 'I'd think few of us would need reminding . . . May I be permitted one more personal observation?'

A grin . . . 'Many as you like.'

'Only that Marilyn Stuart tells me you're a close friend of one of our best people — who's just gone back into the field?'

'Rosie.'

'You're a lucky man.'

'You reckon?'

'Perhaps not in the immediate present — but

in the long run —'

'Yeah.' Blinking at him, but not really: telling himself it *was* the long run that counted . . . Then he changed the subject: 'Speaking of Marilyn — might she be around?'

'I'll find out.' Hallowell turned to the desk, picked up one of several telephones . . . 'Janet. Is Second Officer Stuart with us this morning?'

A pause . . . Then he brightened, glancing round at Ben . . . 'Good. Ask her if she'd spare a minute to see Lieutenant-Commander Quarry. He's here in my office — she knows him . . .'

Lieutenant-Commander, Ben thought, waiting. Not actually disliking the sound of it, but not used to it yet either. His new boss had told him on Monday when he'd reported for his first day's duty in that very hush-hush establishment that the job he'd be doing called for lieutenant-commander's rank, and the Admiralty had confirmed that he was about due for it in any case, by virtue of the fact he'd be celebrating his thirtieth birthday quite soon. Wherefore it had been decreed that as of that date — Monday May 1 — he was promoted to Acting Lieutenant-Commander, and should dress as such. Congratulations — et cetera.

It meant about an extra ten bob a day, he reckoned. Would also impress the old folks back home no end. Only damn shame was Rosie not being here to be impressed. Except she might not have been: might have just laughed . . .

Come to think of it, to have had her here with

him now — or even just not in France — he'd have willingly *dropped* a rank.

Hallowell said, 'Thank you, Janet', and put the phone down. He told Ben, 'She's tickled pink. Show you where we have her kennelled, shall I?'

He'd been down to Dartmouth yesterday, to see the flotilla, renew acquaintances among the gunboats' COs and others, and to call on DDOD(I)'s immediate subordinate, a commander RNR who planned the flotilla's secret missions from an office in the RN College — which had no cadets in it now, only Yanks. That was one change; another, he was told, was that further up-river were moored literally hundreds of landing-craft of all types. Preparation for the invasion, was the obvious conclusion. Anyway, he'd met a lot of old friends, and made some new ones. There were five motor gunboats in the flotilla at this time, including MGB 600 in which he'd been navigating officer for the best part of two years. He'd loved the job — the challenge of intricate navigation close in to that enemy-held coast, working only in the four-day moonless period of each month — and he'd only wangled himself a transfer to the Newhaven flotilla — with Bob Stack's help — in order to be closer to Rosie, who of course had been in London then.

And whom he'd first met in this very building in Baker Street, for God's sake: down there in the hall. She'd been rushing out, more or less in tears — she'd come to be interviewed as a candidate for the agents' training course, and some idiot had turned her down — and he'd been busting in, damn near *knocked* her down . . .

Hallowell had tapped on a door, then pushed it open. 'Here you are. We'll have a drink some time, eh?'

'I'd like that.'

'Ben!'

Marilyn: coming swiftly from her desk to meet him: taking his hand in both of hers. Tall, blonde, immaculate as ever . . . 'Congratulations on your promotion, Ben . . . Although you don't seem to have done anything about it yet?'

'Haven't had time. Didn't expect anyone here'd know about it anyway.' He pushed the door shut behind him. 'Only got told on Monday — and Tuesday was busy, then yesterday I was in Dartmouth — where some while ago I first set eyes on *you*, remember?'

He'd only seen her that time, not met her. She and Rosie had been standing at the rail of the 15th Flotilla's depot-ship, the ancient paddle-steamer *Westward Ho!*; she'd come down from London with Rosie, who'd been taking passage in MGB 600 from Dartmouth to the l'Ab-ervwrac'h pinpoint on the Brittany coast. Then he'd met her — Marilyn — properly here in London a few months ago, when he'd had leave from Newhaven and Rosie had introduced them one day when they'd met for lunch.

'As I remember it —' she'd pointed him towards a chair — 'I'd say most of the "setting of eyes" that afternoon was on Rosie.' She shook her head. 'No, thank you.'

He remembered — she didn't smoke.

'Don't let me stop you, though . . . Ben, I was so sorry to hear from Rosie you'd come to grief. Even though it doesn't seem to have laid you out for long!'

'I was lucky. Seems there are knee injuries *and* knee injuries. Also just run-of-the-mill surgeons and brilliant ones.'

'It'll be lovely to see something of you, anyway. An ill wind, in its way?'

He snapped his lighter off . . . 'Would be if *she* was around.'

'Well — she *will* be. Not for a while, obviously.'

'No. And I'm not griping.' He smiled. 'Just bloody miserable . . . But I knew it was coming, after all.'

'She hated having to leave without saying good-bye.'

'Lysander trip, was it?'

'Well . . .'

He shrugged. 'Silly question. Here's another, though, if —'

'All I can tell you, Ben, is she's working hard.'

'So you've heard from her already.'

'As I say, she's — working hard.'

'OK.' He nodded: having to accept that. His eyes on Marilyn's still, though. 'She's — quite something, isn't she?'

'Rosie? *Something?*' Slow headshake . . . 'Dickens of a lot more than *something,* Ben!'

'Might you ever have a chance — fill in a space in some message with "Ben sends his love"?'

She'd pushed the ashtray closer to him. Glancing at the same time — surreptitiously, but he saw it — at a clock. 'Names aren't a good idea. For various reasons.'

'Say "*you know who* sends his love"?'

'Well — might try . . .'

'But more important — when there's news of any kind — any at all that you're allowed to give me — seeing we're more or less colleagues now?'

'Any we *can* give you — if there ever *were* any —'

'Good *or* bad news — please?'

She'd frowned slightly. 'Let's not dwell on the possibility of there being bad news. *I* couldn't bear it — let alone inflict it on you. I'm *very* fond of her — believe me . . . Do you ever say prayers?'

A nod. 'On occasion.'

'That's the best answer, *I* think.' She looked directly at the clock, this time. 'Ben — nice as this is . . .'

'Nice for me, anyway.' He brought the stick into action: one hand on that, the other on her desk, pushing himself up. 'Happened to be here, thought while I had the chance.'

'I was hoping you might.'

'Oh, you knew —'

'She *will* be back, Ben — bright-eyed and —'

'— as ever. Yep. *Course* she will. Meanwhile you know where to get me — if ever there's anything . . .' He put his hand out: 'Marilyn —'

'Found anywhere to live, yet?'

'So happens I may have. In South Kensington, two rooms and the use of a tub. I'm due to inspect it this evening. I was going to say — how about a meal, some time?'

'Why — lovely idea. Not in the *very* near future, but —'

'If I promise I won't ask things you can't answer?'

Chapter 12

Saturday, May 6 . . . Lannuzel muttered, 'Here we go . . .' She'd only been here ten minutes: *parachutage* night, and her first visit here since Wednesday. He had an old wireless on the table, was fiddling with the knobs as the opening notes of Beethoven's Fifth broke through the jamming effort. The V-for-Victory beat faded with the announcer telling them in French, 'And now here are some personal messages . . .'

Twenty-five kilometres north of here, in the *Montagnes d'Arrées* Jean-Paul Jaillon — whom she'd seen at Scrignac on Thursday — would have his ear to this broadcast, too.

She'd left St Michel-du-Faou in mid-afternoon, having spent the morning in and around Peucat's busy surgery, wearing a threadbare white coat he'd found for her and chatting to patients in the waiting-room, up-dating their cards and generally making herself known. Had worked there yesterday too, mostly on paperwork; and now she was supposed to be visiting former patients in outlying areas with whom he'd lost touch; the last would be in the village of Landeleau, and so late — she'd have got herself lost at some stage — that she'd have accepted the old woman's invitation to spend the night.

The messages had started. First, a claim that certain varieties of rose did not have thorns. He'd asserted this twice. Now — 'From La Grande-Motte to Montpelier is a distance of nineteen kilometres. From La Grande-Motte to Montpelier is a distance of nineteen kilometres. The Little Owl hunts by moonlight, often in packs.' Lannuzel glancing round at her, rolling his eyes: he wasn't a *patient* man. Rosie thinking there'd be about half a moon tonight. Repetition in the background: '— often in packs.' It had been a few days short of full moon when she'd flown in. She lit a cigarette: had offered one to Lannuzel but he'd declined it with a brusque gesture: she'd thought OK, stuff *you.* The messages had suddenly become garbled, though: interference of some kind . . .

'Something something — *puis?*'

He muttered a curse: fiddling the knob, his teeth bared. Then the repetition came up loud and clear: 'A darkening sky presages rain.'

'Jaillon's!'

A thumb raised, then . . .

'The first signs of spring are always welcome. The first signs of spring —'

'*Right!*' Turning to her: '*That's* welcome! Your own immortal words, Suzanne! I'll have that cigarette now, if you're still feeling generous.' Raising his voice: 'Brigitte! Have to go out now!' Re-tuning: with the cigarette unlit in his mouth: settling on Jean Trenet's rendering of 'Que Rest-il de nos Amours?'. He nodded towards the fretwork-fronted wireless as Brigitte came in: 'Your heart-throb.'

'Going out?'

'I'll be half an hour. Shutting sheds and pens, anyone wants to know. I *will*, on my way back — so say about an hour.'

She asked Rosie when he'd gone, 'You went to Scrignac yesterday, you said?'

'Thursday. Henri Peucat lent me his *gazo*, I drove myself over there. Better than cycling, believe me. Well, especially in those hills!'

Friday, when she'd worked *chez* Peucat, his sister Marthe had arrived on the doorstep with dreadful news of the Achards, Timo and Adèle. Both were in Gestapo hands, it was thought either in Morlaix or St Brieuc. Marthe had been to their house and heard it from a neighbour who'd taken the children to their grandmother in Rennes and only just returned, had been tidying and shutting up the house — including the bar, presumably. The shock to Rosie, who'd never met Adèle but had actually witnessed Timo's arrest, had been compounded — and still was, although *he*'d pooh-pooh'd it — by concern for Henri Peucat: he and the Achards had after all been close friends for a long time, and there was the black-market Cognac connection too.

He'd assured her this morning over breakfast, 'That's *all* they'd have on me. And whatever they're holding him for, it wouldn't be *that*.'

But St Brieuc was bad news too; the Gestapo chief there, known as 'Shad', was notorious for his brutality.

Rosie hadn't told the Lannuzels about those arrests yet. Hadn't had time, for one thing, for another he mightn't even have known the Achards, and in any case tonight's *parachutage* was enough to concentrate on, for now.

Brigitte broke into her thoughts: 'How was our countess?'

'Sorry?'

'Sara de Seyssons — you were there on Thursday?'

'Oh — yes . . . Well — much the same. There are some new pills that are helping, but — you know.'

'Not much, eh? Poor Sara . . .'

Sara would have taken Marie-Claude le Guen into the household as a secretary and/or companion, at least for a trial period, but her husband had refused to hear of it. For the same reason that he hadn't wanted *her* there, had preferred to pass her along to Peucat. What it came down to was that he was determined to keep his nose clean in Boche eyes, remain in their view effectively *Vertrauen*. The manoir and its lands were to become a major Resistance base, once the balloon went up, and meanwhile he was determined not to arouse Boche suspicions of any kind or in any way at all. Under pressure from Sara then he'd agreed only that Marie-Claude and her father could use the place briefly as a staging-post — for an hour or two, being either collected there by Jaillon or taken on to Guerlesquin or thereabouts by the gamekeeper, Vannier: and on second thoughts, then, that they should use Vannier's cottage, not come to the manoir itself.

It would help, anyway. But he'd also expressed concern at the risks involved in the Kerongués plan, and surprise that Lannuzel was giving it his support.

Rosie had argued, 'But he was surprised to hear *you* were in favour of "Mincemeat".'

'There were aspects he didn't know about, I believe.'

'Any case —' she'd shrugged — 'he's keen on this now. Plans to take charge of it himself, in fact. He was hesitant when we talked on — oh, Tuesday — but yesterday I came back from Quimper by way of Châteauneuf, he'd been discussing it with his friends in the hills and they'd agreed on it.'

'He must have some plan I can't immediately envisage.'

'An idea of wearing *Wehrmacht* uniforms?'

'Oh. Those Georgians . . .'

'And he wants to borrow some transport from Jaillon. Some particular vehicle Jaillon has. He'll have been in touch with him by now. But from my angle, you see — if le Guen were to back out —'

'You'd have to drop "Mincemeat".' Count Jules had opened the door to the dining-room, waved her in ahead of him. 'Wouldn't exactly signal the end of the world — perhaps?'

'My brief's to set it up, that's all. And wasn't it your idea in the first place?'

'I put it forward — yes. It seemed worthwhile

— as you say. Especially the derivative benefits. Conciliating a major section of our Resistance colleagues — primarily in order to keep them with us, which at the present time is really quite essential both militarily and politically.'

It had sounded a bit pompous. She'd capped it more succinctly, 'With the added attraction — with luck — of killing Doenitz.'

'As you say. Killing him, and others . . . But my point is — should have been — that those were the considerations then, nothing madcap like this Kerongués idea.'

'So you'd drop it? Cancel "Mincemeat"?'

He'd frowned.

'If I said "yes" to that question?'

'I'd tell London, and ask for a decision.'

'I see.' Stroking his jaw . . . 'But you say Guy Lannuzel's in favour — to the extent of taking personal command. While from my own point of view the major factor — as I said, the Trevarez action as a general rallying point. Which is — well, *very* important.'

'So you agree: I can tell Guy?'

'If he's sure of what *he*'s doing . . .'

Lannuzel was back before six. The evenings were drawing out now, and it was still quite light. He told her — as if his sister wasn't in the room — 'All set. Next broadcast's at nine — right?' She'd nodded. 'Before that we'll have something to eat, and the lorry will be here at ten. Assuming we get the second broadcast, of course. Are drops ever cancelled at such short notice?'

'It has been known. Not often — but some emergency situation, or the aircraft suddenly not available.'

'Not *this* time, please!' He threw his donkey-jacket across a chair. Asking Brigitte then, 'You'll be off at — about eight-thirty, eh?'

'Yes.' She grimaced, at Rosie's querying glance. 'A hen-party, you might call it. Appropriate, eh? No distance, though, I go across the fields.' Nodding towards her brother: 'He'll be in the house when I leave. But I don't know he's going out, do I? And when I get back, if he's not here I'd only think *Oh, he's off with that slut again* — huh?'

'Not referring to me, I hope?'

'No.' She laughed. 'Definitely not. We do have a local slut, though, and she's part of the cast, so to speak, in this fantasy of his.' Looking at Guy again. 'He means well — but could anyone else believe it would fool the Gestapo?'

'It could.' He appealed to Rosie. 'Listen, now. If I'd set out to fool *her*. If I didn't want her to know I was involved in such things. Using her farm as a base for it too — there are people around here who'd confirm that she'd *strongly* disapprove. And I'm out a great deal on business — legitimate poultry business — how can she know what I'm doing from one hour to another? You can see that, can't you?'

She could. But she could also see Timo Achard. Might have anticipated — both she and Peucat might have — that having arrested him

304

those bastards would take his wife and put *her* through it too.

Nodding to Brigitte. 'Looking at it that way — maybe . . .'

The 'personal message' came in again soon after nine. Lannuzel looked relieved as he switched the set off. 'One hour to go. They'll all have heard it this time. Those trousers OK?'

She shrugged, looking down at them. They were Brigitte's working trousers: turned up at the ankles and belted in with string. She'd brought her own thick sweater, scarf and heavier shoes in the valise — which she'd be taking with her, in order to change back again when it was all over.

Guy had told her she wouldn't find the lorry very comfortable: even riding with him and its driver in the cab.

'Your bike'll go in the back, of course.'

'What's the story if we get stopped at a road-block, or by a patrol?'

'The way we go — very small lanes, then a forest track — well . . .'

'Not likely to meet a patrol, you mean.'

'But if we *were* stopped — out of curfew, all that —'

'As a chicken-farmer do you qualify for an *Ausweis,* to work in curfew hours?'

'No. But I'm well known around here, also I've good reason to be using by-ways and out late. It's called disposal of waste products.'

'Manure?'

'That's the nice word. Anyway, I wouldn't dream of using my own pickup for it. There's manure and manure, you know — and pig and chicken are both rather special. Borrowed lorry, therefore — I get to use it at night, no other time — owner's a pig-farmer, I help with his and he helps with mine. Local gendarmes know all about it — curfew or not, they're not worried.'

'Are we carrying pig tonight, or chicken?'

'Pig. It's more often pig. They produce more — you can imagine . . . Tonight's load goes to a farm near Roudouallec. Not a big load, enough for camouflage, that's all — surface dressing, you might say. Roudouallec happens to be where — well, never mind. I'm talking too much . . . Like some coffee?'

'Good idea. I'll do it.'

'I'll show you where.'

'That'll be a help.' She went through to the kitchen, and he followed; she told him, 'I saw Count Jules — day before yesterday. He's worried about the Kerongués plan, thinks it's dangerous.'

'Well — he's right. But —'

'He wonders if you're sure of what you're do-ing.' She'd filled the kettle, put it on the stove. 'It's not *insanely* risky, is it?'

'It's risky. But — put it this way — we'll have casualties around Trevarez that night — unless we're *very* lucky — and that risk's acceptable — for the reasons you explained. And without get-ting the girl out of Kerongués it can't be done, so it's — effectively, all one operation.'

'The Kerongués part though, *he* thinks is more so than the other. He has a great respect for you, incidentally.'

'He'll have more, when we've done it. Have to do it right, that's all. And there'll be a lot of satisfaction — good for Maquis morale, morale in general even. All over France, they'll hear about it.'

'It doesn't frighten you?'

'Here — want sweetener? Frighten me . . . Suzanne — if I said no, it doesn't, in the long run I'm lying. Also stupid. To be frightened or not frightened — what the hell. But here and now the *prospect* doesn't frighten me — if that's the question?'

'Yes. I suppose —'

'Doesn't mean I deny the risk. I said, we have to do it *right*.'

The lorry lurched in at the farm gate a few minutes before ten, and by the time it was turning in the yard they were out there, Lannuzel lifting Rosie's bike to pass it up. Two men on this rear side of the *gazo* burner were peeling a tarpaulin back — no light work, even with only a comparatively light scattering of muck on top of it. One of them leant over to take the bike from Lannuzel then, and slide it under the tarpaulin: two others had joined him and Rosie now, jumping down from the cab. Lannuzel calling, *'a va, les gars?'*

'Va bien, Guy . . .'

The driver, leaning out . . . Lannuzel introduced Rosie to them all: 'This one set it up for us.' A mutter, his head down close to hers: 'What should we call you?'

'Béatrice?'

Because 'Suzanne' would lead to Henri Peucat's nurse, and 'Zoé' could be on transcripts or recordings of at least one phone call. Lannuzel had told them: mutters of 'Béa' accompanied quick handshakes, then they were climbing back up — all four of them, leaving the passenger space in the cab for her and Lannuzel. Ducking down out of sight — going *under* the tarpaulin: three had anyway, the other was using a rake to spread the muck back over it. Maybe the nose would influence the eye: to a Boche peering over the tailboard for instance, trying not to breathe too deeply — the contents as seen by torchlight *should* seem to be random heaps of pigshit.

'Up with you — Béa.'

Into the middle of the seat: jammed against the driver, her left knee against the gear-lever. The driver offered her his hand: 'I'm Raoul.'

Mucky hand. She took hers out of it.

'And you raise pigs.'

'How'd you guess?'

Laughing, banging the wheel with his palms . . . Lannuzel meanwhile squeezing in, crowding her as he dragged the door shut.

'What's this?'

Solid object, in the right-hand pocket of her coat. She tugged at the cloth to free it, pull it up on her lap. 'Llama — nine-millimetre.'

'You don't say.' He'd managed to give her a bit more room. Speaking over her head to the driver then: 'OK, Raoul.'

'Yeah.' Shoving the gear-lever up into first . . . Lannuzel murmured, close to her ear, 'Must say, you're a *real* one.'

One didn't travel fast, by *gazo*. Not *this* kind, anyway. Engine-noise rather like that of some old motorboat: thumping, jolting, lurching on hard springs. The driver, she thought, must have loaded all that shit in: possibly by hand. Probably spent his whole life in this aroma.

What did his wife put behind her ears, she wondered?

If he had one. What a fate . . .

Knew his way, though — and without the aid of lights. Masked headlights had been burning when he'd arrived at the farm, but he'd switched them off then and left them off.

'Guy — mightn't it be better another time to send this lorry up in daylight, the rest of us going separately on bikes?'

'Not possible. Because — well, to take it up in the daytime and leave it several hours, that way we'd be drawing *more* attention to ourselves, not less.'

'Lot of eggs in one basket, I was thinking.'

If they were stopped by a patrol: either by ordinary bad luck or through information being laid. She'd been thinking that something like a hundred people had to know of this drop tonight.

Forest on the left now, and a slope of pasture on the right. The half-moon floated behind black treetops, lit the road only where the distance between it and the trees widened to fifty metres or more. On those light stretches one felt dangerously exposed: then a sense of relief, plunging back into darkness.

'Not much farther.'

The driver-pigman — name of Raoul — wore a wool cap and a chequered jacket, the kind they called a 'Canadian'. The Maquis tended to wear them too — so Peucat had told her when she'd asked him how they lived in the forests: having some notion of describing it to le Guen, forgetting for that moment that she wouldn't be seeing him again until it would be too late to matter — for him to change his mind.

Touch wood . . .

Forget him. Worrying about a change of mind on his part was only a way to lose sleep. Count Jules had pointed this out, on Thursday, when she'd confessed to having less than total confidence in his staying the course she'd set him on. The count had put his hands on her shoulders, lowered himself almost to her level and quoted, *'Les jeux sont faits: rien ne va plus, Suzanne!'*

In other words, she'd made her play, had now to wait and see how the dice rolled, meanwhile keep her nerve. He'd then kissed her lightly but lingeringly on the lips.

This one beside her, and then *him* . . . Despite knowing from Sara about Ben — she'd referred to him as 'Suzanne's fiancé' which effectively he *was*, even if he didn't know it. But Jules couldn't really have been trying it on, she thought. Although if she hadn't pulled away — as she had, with the thought in mind: *What about Léonie de Mauvernay?*

She'd asked him the question she'd put to Peucat. 'Tell me — if you would. It worries me, to think I could be a danger to you.'

'Danger?'

'If I were arrested —'

'Heaven forbid!'

'Well — yes. But if — say during the Kerongués action —'

'You don't surely intend to take part yourself?'

'Only to look after the girl.'

'But if her father's also on hand?'

'He's liable to be having hysterics too. No — I mean he's — the nervous type. I may bring them here, in fact — to your man's cottage. Anyway for the girl's sake I *should* be — around. What I'm asking, though, is *any* time if I were arrested — they'd find out I've been working for Doctor Peucat, and I suppose that you'd referred me to him. He'd tell them, I imagine — it's the truth, and other people know it, why not . . . So then maybe they come to you.'

'I'd also tell the truth. I was asked by Madame de Mauvernay to find a place for you — and I knew old Henri had thought of taking on a bit of help — eh?'

'They'd go to Madame de Mauvernay, then.'

'Well, they might.' He'd shrugged. 'But she might not be too easy to locate, you know, by that time.'

'Oh.' Gazing at him. 'You mean she'd have skipped?' The same shrug, again . . . 'You'd have tipped her off, and —'

'D'you think you *need* answers to all these questions, Suzanne?'

'No — certainly not. Sorry . . . Only wanted to know I wouldn't be dropping all the rest of you in the soup.'

'Stay out of the soup yourself — that's my advice.'

'And my ambition.'

It still was. Touch wood.

'Hold tight, Béa!'

Warning from the pig-man, as an opening showed in the forest ahead of them, on the left. He was watching it come, his fists and forearms like legs of mutton on the wheel as the lorry pounded into moonlight again . . . Dragging the wheel over then, turning into that gap: it was the beginning of a steepish climb, mostly in darkness again, with branches whipping the sides and the track winding as well as climbing. Splashes of moonlight occasionally, but never for more than a few seconds. Shifting gear: even slower then, grinding up the uneven, rutted track. Terrific vibration, in this gear . . .

Levelling out now: in a long curve to the left. The deep ruts would have been left by foresters' tractors, she supposed. There was to be one up here, Lannuzel had mentioned, tractor plus trailer, and some other vehicle as well — three separate loads for the three caches that had been prepared. She didn't want to know the locations: only that the stuff should all have disappeared from sight by the time the Boches came searching for it.

Probably would. Word seemed to get out when there'd been a drop. Not where, or who'd received it — necessarily — but a kind of whisper, not much more. A message written on villagers' faces, even — perhaps generated by reports of an aircraft having passed over at low altitude, or — potentially more of a give-away — having *circled* at low altitude.

It might be either one or two aircraft making the drops tonight. Most likely a Halifax, or Halifaxes. They'd been fairly extensive shopping-lists, she guessed more than one plane-load.

Lannuzel broke into her thoughts: 'Here we are now — Béa.' His arm round her shoulders tightened as Raoul wrenched the wheel over again — reaching at the same time to flick the lights on — up off the track and into a clearing. The lights were needed to avoid the few trees that had been left along that bank, and then some stacks of cut timber further in. Swinging hard right: lights off again as he braked and stopped. Gear into reverse: she'd moved her legs in time to avoid a cracked kneecap. Now he was backing up, with the wheel over the other way.

Stopped, and switching off. In a certain amount

of cover, and pointing back the way they'd come. Immediate stink of pig plus *gazo* burner . . . 'Do us, will it?'

'Do us nicely. Lads around somewhere, I suppose . . .'

Rosie muttered, 'This is *it?*'

He pointed. 'Through there — it's just a belt of trees left standing. Windbreak. Come on, I'll show you.'

Some 'lads' were around. Dark figures emerging from the trees — low-voiced as they met, shook hands. Rosie hung back, leaving him to handle it: these were his people, and this was their world, she was a stranger in it. They nearly all wore 'Canadians', wool hats or caps, Stens slung from their shoulders. The man talking to Lannuzel was telling him that the two other sections were already distributed around the wooded perimeter and that 'le Faisan' 's team were in position.

'Bit premature, Ollie?'

'Well — if it came early. Wouldn't want *that.* Waited this long, then fuck up?'

'Ollie' was what his name had sounded like. An almost English sound: short for Olivier, perhaps. Looking back — wondering if she was right to have left her valise in the lorry, and concluding she was, nobody'd pinch it. Didn't want to lug it around with her anyway. The tail-board was down, she saw, the team who'd come with them dragging the tarpaulin to the side, heaping the muck there. They'd spread it back over the load of munitions later, obviously.

'Béa . . .' Lannuzel reached to draw her up beside him. He had binoculars slung round his neck, she noticed: but no weapon. Telling Ollie and others, 'The visitor from afar who organized this for us. Name's Béa.'

Grins, warm handshakes: one of them told her he'd had a dog called Béa: finest nose on any hound he'd known. She laughed with them: Ollie murmuring, 'Tual likes dogs better than people, it's a compliment. Glad to welcome you, Béa — and thanks.'

She'd no idea how she'd come to pick the name Béatrice. It had come into her head when she'd been talking to le Guen the other day. Never known anyone of that name . . . She was walking beside Lannuzel into the tree-belt's darkness: moonlight was visible beyond it, beyond the striping of the trees' slim, evenly spaced trunks. Lannuzel had acquired a Sten, she saw — in the past half-minute one of the others must have provided it. This would be the western edge of the dropping zone, she realized. Ollie, leading, was a smaller man than Lannuzel, and like most of them, bearded. Slanting to the right, out of the trees — into moonlight and with an expanse of open, uneven ground in front of them. It was rougher than you'd land a plane on, but OK for *parachutage* purposes.

A short, heavy man who'd been sitting with his shoulder against a tree-stump heaved himself up and stuck his hand out: 'Quellec.'

'Ah, it's you, Jean. In this light you all look alike.'

'Not in the least, we don't!'

Lannuzel's short laugh . . . Then: 'Jean Quellec, Béa. Famous for arguing every bloody point. Béa set up this drop, Jean.'

'Delighted to shake her hand, then.'

She let him do so. 'Jean . . .'

Ollie explained, pointing, 'Two red-light markers each side. Saumon's down that end — five hundred metres from us — and the other side opposite these are Legrand and Blathier. Le Faisan's there at the top, of course.' To their right, his gesture indicated — at the narrowing southern end of a space about the size of three football fields end-on to each other. A single flash of white torchlight told them that le Faisan had spotted them too. Must have eyes more like an owl's than a pheasant's, she thought. It was a good big clearing — although not quite as big as Lannuzel had described it, that first day — and misty-silver in the moon's light, which at this juncture was filtering through high, thin cloud. Le Faisan at the top end would control the drop, flashing the recognition signal at the aircraft as it approached from the north; by that time this one who allegedly argued all the time would be showing a red light, as would another half a kilometre to the north on this side, and the two opposite them on the far side. Giving the pilot a marked rectangle and an aiming-point. The red lights — torches with red paper or cloth over them —

would be switched on when le Faisan began his flashing.

'It looks good, Guy.'

He grunted agreement. 'High ground, you notice, no one to look down on us. Except our pilot. With thirty men stationed in the woods we're not going to be taken by surprise, either.'

'It's *very* good.'

'Let's go visit le Faisan.' Glancing round: 'See you later, Ollie.' The rest had already vanished, melting into the trees.

Le Faisan had two men with him, who'd act as runners if he needed them. He was a tall man with a beaky nose: she'd thought his name might have been Faisant or le Faisant, but having seen the bird-like profile realized it was a nickname. He had a torch slung on a lanyard round his neck, and confirmed to Rosie that he'd been given the recognition letters by Lannuzel several days ago. ZG — initial letters for Zoé-Guido, as she'd realized — it was all the more obvious for the fact that Jaillon's were ZP, 'P' for Pluto.

'And a container marked with a "Z" —'

'We'll look out for it, don't worry.'

She and Lannuzel retired into the trees behind them, sat with their backs against the same beech trunk. The trees were mostly beeches but there were others too, and most of the leafage was well advanced.

'I was going to tell you, Guy — another thing I talked with Count Jules about on Thursday was coordinating sabotage of rail and road transport, when the invasion comes. Nothing that commits you to anything specific, but in general terms, how it *might* be coordinated — overall aims, et cetera. Best thing might be for the two of you to get together, before you bring any others into it — or Jaillon, even?'

'With you sitting in as umpire?'

'If you like. My job's only to support and assist. It's your business and his, I'm here to help any way I can, that's all.'

'Which is the diplomat — Suzanne, or Béa?'

'Oh, Suzanne. Béa's the one who dresses like a clown — baggy pants and —'

'Hear that?'

Listening . . .

'*Gazo* coming?'

'I'll go see. Tractor or the van or both. You OK here?'

'Go on . . .'

He'd gone. She took the 9-millimetre out of her coat pocket and rested it in her lap, checking first that the safety-catch was on. It was Spanish-made and except for the 9-mm calibre was very much like a Colt. And the reason she'd brought it with her — from England in the first place and also now, tonight — derived from her memory of that moment of disaster in Normandy last summer when poor old Romeo had had a gun in his hand and the Boches had naturally returned fire, shot him dead, whereas she having no weapon had remained alive: she'd wished there and then

318

she *had* had one, could thus have made them kill her too. She could tell herself retrospectively that she wouldn't have been alive now if she'd had one and used it, that in the long run therefore it was as well that she'd been unarmed; but she could also *very* easily put her mind back to how she'd felt then and what they'd done to her afterwards. Especially what they'd been on the point of doing.

In which case she *would* have been better dead. Ben or no Ben.

She blew into the barrel to dislodge any dust or fluff, eased the action fractionally to and fro, released the clip and withdrew it about halfway, shoved it back in. There were six rounds in the clip and one in the breech, and a spare clip of seven in the coat's left-hand pocket.

Don't worry, Ben. I'll be back. I swear . . .

Despite that kind of thinking, and the cyanide capsules, in her blouse, it wasn't a matter of *expecting* the worst: you had to assure yourself — assure Ben, in your thoughts, but *yourself*, in reality — that that kind of thinking was — well, theoretical. The blues in the night, or more consciously steeling yourself against the nightmare ever becoming real.

As old Peucat had said, *It won't happen, Suzanne . . .*

It had to the Achards, though.

Lannuzel was in sight now; limping back this way along the edge of the trees. Diverting and pausing to converse briefly with le Faisan . . . She

319

slid the pistol back into her pocket. Thicker cloud
was obscuring the moon; until this moment she
hadn't noticed. But the drop would be all right
— there was a lot more clear sky than cloud, and
— she checked the time — at least a quarter of
an hour to go yet.

'All right, Guy?'

'All here now.' Arriving, he put a hand on the
tree, let himself down beside her. 'Tractor *and*
the van. I've put your bike in the lorry's cab, time
being.'

'Hey. Listen . . .'

She *was* listening. It had been only the faintest
murmur ten seconds ago but was now clearly the
sound of aircraft.

Punctual enough, at that!

'I'm joining le Faisan.' Lannuzel: and he'd
gone. Aircraft noise closing from the north, the
note of it as well as its volume rising swiftly. Time
— four minutes past twelve. The Halifax would
be overhead she guessed in maybe half a minute:
having shed Jaillon's load up there northwest of
Scrignac. Or its mate having done that: doing it
at this moment, maybe.

Red points of light glowed. Le Faisan's white
light blinking: two longs, two shorts, then two
longs and one short. Starting again. Lannuzel was
standing beside le Faisan with binoculars up,
searching the northern sky: Rosie coming up to
join them — stumbling, from looking skyward
instead of where she was going. The plane's noise

was a solid roar and still rising, the red lights clear to see and le Faisan still at it — ZG, ZG, ZG . . . If she'd had an 'S' phone she'd have been conversing with the Halifax's pilot by this time.

'There! See it?'

Very loud and close: it would be at about five hundred feet, the usual height for a container-drop. She'd have asked the pilot what he had for them, and he'd be telling her, 'Twelve sacks of goodies, no bods.' Meaning twelve (or however many) containers, no humans dropping with them. No nylon parachutes therefore, only cotton ones — which were cheaper, and had a higher incidence of failure to open than nylon ones did. In any case containers came down a lot faster than bodies — you wouldn't want to be under one when it landed.

'Won't need to circle. He's right on line.' Lannuzel was lowering his glasses: le Faisan still flashing. Rosie saw the bomber suddenly: jet black, closer than she'd been ready for, thundering straight at them and then in the next few seconds in a blast of sound over the top, leaving its stream of spawn falling in a line slap down the middle. The flashing had ceased, red lights extinguished, the first of the containers already thudding into the ground and underbrush: thirty-plus pairs of eyes watching, marking . . .

'Whistle!'

Le Faisan blew it, as the racket overhead died into moonlit distance. Men were out in the open then, running: le Faisan's two helpers in the lead from this end, with him and Lannuzel behind them, Rosie on their heels. Maquisards from out of cover on both sides were already converging out there in the middle. One voice — Ollie's probably — shouting, 'Looks like eighteen!'

Eighteen containers. They'd all, including the one with her special items in it, have about the same mix of contents, so it wouldn't matter which went to which cache. The essential now was not to hang around here any longer than was necessary — not therefore to have to open it all up and sort it. Boche patrols *could* be homing in on this place. Containers were already being carried over to the transport: two men to each, and over the rough ground it wasn't easy going. Each container was six feet long, painted green and weighed — well, as if it might be packed with concrete. One 'chute hadn't opened fully and the container had embedded itself up to about half its length, had about five men working round it. Rosie telling herself it was bound to be hers, those delicate contents smashed. But it wasn't; hers was on its way to the transport before the 'Z' on it was spotted, and they'd got it to the lorry by the time she came trotting up. They'd left it on the tail end and gone back for another; Raoul offered to open it for her.

'Here we go . . .' Levering with the big screwdriver he'd been using, prising the thing open. Standing back, then: 'You know what you're looking for.'

'Thanks.'

'My pleasure, Béa.'

She was getting used to that name now, even quite liked it. Finding to her relief that they'd packed both the radio and the 'S' phone very well — bulky parcels of sacking bound with sticky tape, the bulk inside probably cotton-wool or sawdust. Having identified them, she decided to leave them wrapped with Lannuzel for transport back to his farm. Or maybe the 'S' phone to the cache: as long as she could get to it when she needed — which wouldn't be until the next drop. For the moment she put both packages in the lorry's cab with her valise — first extracting her bike, which would go under the tarpaulin after the containers were loaded.

Lannuzel arrived with a large group of Maquisards and the last two containers. They'd have searched carefully to make certain they'd got the whole lot, that there hadn't been say twenty, rather than eighteen. Le Faisan began counting the men off; Ollie took some with him to contact the two sections each of fifteen men who'd been stationed in the forest and could now be stood down.

'Back to camp then. See you Monday, Guy?'

'I expect so. Monday, yes. You did well tonight, you lads.'

Handshakes, farewells. She put her idea to him of caching the Mark III at his farm and the 'S' phone with the rest of the lorry's load — ten containers, the other two vehicles were getting four each — and he agreed. 'But we move *now*.'

323

Raising his voice: 'All loaded, is it?'

'Not covered yet.' The tractor's trailer had its four containers in it, but they were still piling timber on top. The lorry wasn't ready either — pigshit had yet to be spread. Rosie's bike was in there, though, and they'd got the tarpaulin over.

'One thing, Guido —'

'Uh?'

'The new Stens. Something I should show you. The container that had my things in it is open — might get one out of there?'

'Something about Stens you imagine we don't know?'

'It's possible you don't.' Challenging him — knowing her job and also not disinclined to take him down a peg or two. He could be patronizing, at times. She added, 'And I tell you, it's dangerous *not* to know.'

'All right.' Rubbing his head, impatiently watching the muck-spreading operation. 'You can show me when we get to — where we're going. I was thinking, we'll drop you *after* this lot's cached. Otherwise — three, four a.m., you want to be riding home early morning but not the middle of the night — uh?'

'But we arranged I'd go to Madame Sanson's. Her youngest child — I told you . . .'

'It's not necessary. She'll swear blind you were there, if she had to. It's better than actually going to her — this time of night, some neighbour thinking what a funny time to visit?'

It did make sense. After reports of low-flying

324

aircraft they might well be checking on any allegedly suspicious movements. She nodded. 'All
right.'

'Maurice — get your van away first. Remember
I need an inventory of all that stuff. Paul — same
from you — but you leave after us, please.'

'Give you five minutes — right?'

In the cab — letting the van get a head start —
for obvious reasons — she asked him, 'You said
"where we're going" — meaning Roudouallec?'

'Near there, yes.'

'All right. So this cache I will know, the other
two I don't have to, that's all. Only reminding
you — what one doesn't *need* to know?'

'Scared you'd give us away?'

'Someone might — and if it happened that I'd
been arrested —'

'I wouldn't suspect you, Béa.'

Raoul cut in, 'Damn well think *not.*' He had
the engine running. Repeating, scowling round at
Lannuzel, 'Damn well think *not!*'

'See, the impression we have of you?'

'Yes. Thank you — but I'll tell you something,
Raoul. Nobody — *nobody* — can be sure that
when those bastards get to work on them they
won't tell them everything they want to know.'

'Speaking from experience, you say that?'

'Yes. As it happens.'

'Christ.'

'Don't misunderstand me. We know people
have died with their mouths still shut. I'm saying
until it happens none of us can *know.*'

'Get going, Raoul?'

'Yeah. Why not.' Into gear, and revving, lurching forward. The waning half-moon was high now: the trees threw less shadow and even getting out on to the track he had no need of lights. Lannuzel asked her, 'What's this about the new Stens?'

Chapter 13

She'd explained to him that now Stens were being turned out in such vast numbers, being cheap and easy to make, some manufacturers weren't finishing them off properly, leaving burrs of metal in the barrels which could be dangerous if they weren't filed off. They'd found one in that unfinished state, needing attention before it was ever fired; there'd almost certainly be others; they'd all have to be checked and if necessary put right, in the course of the next day or two. This was in a barn, near Roudouallec, in which cattle had lived recently and doubtless would again very soon; Raoul had driven the lorry into it, the doors had been shut behind it and straw then forked aside to uncover timber flooring over a newly dug and cemented pit.

Seven a.m. now, and she was pedalling home to St Michel-du-Faou; there was a chill in the air and a pink flush fading in the eastern sky. She'd changed into her ordinary clothes in the barn, while the men had been at work sorting and stowing the various types of weapons, ammunition, explosives and other gear, and they'd had the lorry on the road again before six — leaving behind one man who lived and worked there — and stopping briefly then to drop Rosie and the bike off near Landeleau — to make for St Michel via Kérampresse and Plounévez-du-Faou.

Fifteen kilometres, roughly. Looking forward to breakfast, and to a few hours' sleep. Maybe even the luxury of a bath . . . Looking out for road-blocks meanwhile — which there might be, if the Boches had had word of the night's activities.

Road-blocks weren't likely in these country lanes, though. Patrols might be out, but even they would surely concentrate on the major routes.

She'd told Lannuzel about the Achards, when they'd been in the barn. He'd stared at her wordlessly: obviously knew Timo — or had known him. Then — eventually — 'I've had a good few glasses in that bar of his.' Gazing down at the men stacking weapons in the pit: adding quietly, 'Don't expect old Henri's too happy.'

'No. He's not.'

Glancing at her again: 'Achard wouldn't know anything about you, would he?'

'Only of my existence — as a nurse, working there. The day I arrived he directed me to the house, that's all.'

Plounévez was where there might be a road-block, she guessed, if there were any at all. Where this lane and several others crossed the north-south road between Châteauneuf and Loqueffret: it would be a fairly obvious place — or would be if this was the area of interest. It didn't have to be, the Halifax or Halifaxes would have flown over a lot of territory. And in any case she had her story ready, and her medical gear in the valise in front of her: she'd been visiting Mme Sanson, checking on the progress of her youngest child whom Peucat had visited about a week ago.

Ought to attend Mass, she thought. Not having done so last Sunday: and needing to conform, to be accepted as a regular member of the community. Peucat had in fact suggested it: last Sunday had been excusable, since she'd only just arrived, but two in a row might feed the gossips. *'And she wouldn't even cross the square to Mass . . .'*

Might leave it another week, all the same. She turned her thoughts to what she did have to do this morning — namely ask Peucat to ring Count Jules, ostensibly enquiring about his wife's health but in fact for news of Jaillon having received his *parachutage*. And tonight, keep listening watch — making up for the fact she hadn't last night. She'd listened on Friday, in case of any hitches in the paradrop arrangements — and on Thursday, which had been one of her regular, alternate listening-out nights, she'd received Baker Street's instruction *Advise immediately of any change in the Cyprien/Micky situation.* Obviously they were sitting on her report of Prigent being blown, but anxious to come clean on it *vis-à-vis* SIS as soon as possible.

It was a long haul up to the road at Plounévez. Struggling on, passing sombrely clad church-goers, on foot or in horse-carts, and a few cows being herded to or from milking; the thought recurred that at this rate, this much bicycling, she was going to end up with thighs like a weight-lifter's.

Which Ben might *not* like.

Well. Smiling to herself: thinking he'd *probably* put up with it . . .

It felt like a year, since she'd been with him.

There was no road-block at Plounévez; only church-goers, and a single gendarme who acknowledged her 'good morning' as she rode past him at the cross-roads. Four more kilometres then to St Michel, finally entering the village the way she'd arrived the first time, seven and a half days ago, freewheeling down to that corner with the former *Mairie* up to her right, Timo Achard's desolate-looking tavern right ahead of her as she braked and turned left into Rue St Nicolas. With a fleeting thought of the *leutnant* who'd been at the roadblock when they'd arrested Timo, and who'd claimed to have signed her permits: Rosie imagining him spotting her as she swept by, asking himself *Where might* she *have been all night?*

Home and dry though — almost. More by good luck than cleverness, admittedly. She was well aware that they could have nobbled her by this time, if they'd been more on the ball . . . But — forget it: assume the luck was holding and would last a while yet. For the time being, one *was* home and dry — and with a certain amount accomplished.

The garage door was open, she saw. So the doctor was up and about. She pushed her bike in beside his *gazo,* untied the valise from its pannier, went to the front door and knocked. Church-goers were on the move here too. An old man hobbling past in his Sunday-best raised his hat to her, and she smiled, murmured, 'Monsieur . . .' Wondering whether maybe she'd *better* attend Mass. And sleep this afternoon . . .

'Suzanne!'

'Doctor. All well with you?'

'With me — of course. But you — out all night —'

'The child's on the mend, you'll be glad to hear. Madame Sanson's youngest — remember? That's where I spent the night — so late getting there, I'd got lost —'

'It's all right.' She was inside and he'd shut the door. 'We're alone . . . Suzanne, you must be —'

'Yes, I am.' She mimed extreme fatigue. 'Also starving.'

'That's easily fixed, anyhow. Did it go well?'

'*Very* well. Guy's, anyway. D'you think you could give Count Jules a ring for me — well, not yet, but —'

'Of course. And I've news for *you,* my dear!'

Something he looked pleased about . . .

'Of the Achards?'

'No. Unfortunately . . . No — a telephone call last night from Paul Berthomet?'

It took a moment to sink in.

Last night . . .

Staring at him . . . 'Saying what?'

'Saying: "The baby is expected this weekend,

between the twelfth and the fourteenth." Hang on, I wrote it down, I'll get it.'

The twelfth would be Friday. Saturday night, therefore, the thirteenth, would be 'Mincemeat' night. And here and now — *now*, this morning — she sat down — collapsing, almost — on the oak seat beside the hat-stand, realizing she'd have to get to Quimper, more or less right away, to meet le Guen in the Parc de la Providence at one. She'd told him to meet there on the day after he dropped his message — which he must have done sometime yesterday. And before that, she'd have to see Lannuzel, to establish a place and time for le Guen to rendezvous with them on Saturday. With them, or with *her*. Sitting there in Peucat's rather gloomy hall, absorbing this — thighs and calves aching, brain also tired, finding it an effort to readjust . . .

Food — and a bath, if possible. Not a hope of any rest. Have to prepare a signal to Baker Street, of course: and stop *en route* to Châteauneuf to get it off to London.

'Here.' Peucat was back, offering her a slip of paper. 'It's as I said.'

She pushed herself up. 'Thing is — means I have to be in Quimper by one o'clock, and before that see Guy Lannuzel again. Need to phone him *now* in fact, tell him I'm coming — that he *must* be there, no matter what . . . Doctor, could you do that?'

'Easily. But you need sleep, Suzanne.'

'*Need*, can't *have*. What I will do is make some

breakfast. Have you had yours yet?'

'No —'

'All right, I'll get it. While — well, if you'd call Lannuzel now — this minute — please?'

A nod: 'And I'll take you — in the *gazo*, Châteauneuf first, then Quimper?'

'Oh!' She was startled: had had her mind on the bloody bike . . . 'D'you mean it?'

'Of course I mean it. You're in no fit state to drive — or bicycle, for that matter — so what alternative do we have?'

'I'll tell you one thing — you're an angel!'

He smiled, patted her arm. 'Tell Marthe?'

'I'll tell the world. Really. Oh, this is *marvellous!* But — Lannuzel — before he goes out or —'

'Just to say we're coming?'

'Leaving here as soon as we've had some breakfast. Because Brigitte's not well — I've brought you that news. It'll surprise him, of course, he'll realize it's something urgent.'

'She's *not* unwell?'

'Oh, no —'

'No. All right.'

'I'll start getting breakfast.'

In the kitchen, she thought about the signal she had now to draft and encode; whether to include anything about Prigent, suggest they might pass the warning to SIS now.

Or hang on until Saturday. Because if Prigent did a disappearing trick between now and then, and the SD assumed le Guen had tipped him off — well, it could still happen, the whole thing blown, the operation and all concerned in it. One-self by no means excluded.

Saturday the thirteenth, therefore. Preferably timing it so as to have Prigent warned no sooner than that evening, when le Guen would be already on his way.

She tapped out her message from the place she'd used before, the edge of woods near Kéram-presse: starting with *Parcels received intact, many thanks* — because Jaillon's drop had been successful, Count Jules had indicated — then telling them: *'Mincemeat' midnight Saturday thirteenth. Repeat, Mincemeat midnight May thirteenth. Suggest warning of personal danger should reach Cyprien same day, no earlier, otherwise there would be risk of operation being compromised.* She added that she intended listening out for incoming signals every night this week up to Friday May 12, then Sunday 14 and alternate nights thereafter; she finished with *Adieu,* and Sevenoaks acknowledged. That was that: she signed off, switched off. Waving then from the overgrown ditch in which she'd been crouching . . . 'All right!'

Peucat, at the roadside, waved his pipe — all clear. He'd disconnect the lead from the *gazo*'s battery now while she rolled up the aerial wire and packed it with the set and the headphones in the bottom of her valise. Medical gear went back in on top of it; she dumped the valise on the *gazo*'s back seat, in plain sight.

Sliding in beside him, pulling the door shut,

stifling a yawn. 'We make a good team, doctor.'

Lannuzel had spread his map on the table. Brigitte was showing the doctor her day-old chicks: at any rate they'd gone for a walk around the farm together. Lannuzel nodded, told Rosie, 'The immediate problem's getting the truck fixed by Saturday. I'll get on to Jaillon again.'

'What's special about this truck?'

'It's a military vehicle, former property of our own Army. Soldier-slang for it used to be a *bouc*.' *Bouc* meaning billy-goat. 'But with a bit of a touch-up you wouldn't know it from one of those small *Wehrmacht* things. JPJ's supposed to be having it done right now — paint-job including unit badges as currently seen in his district, and some other small changes.'

'Then what?'

'He's supposed to be sending it down to me. As I say, I'll chase him for it. It'll go in the barn there, time being. When the time comes — Saturday — I'll be its driver, le Faisan will be our *Oberleutnant*, and there'll be two other make-believe Boches in the back with room for the prisoner between them. Le Faisan's German is excellent, you see — better than mine. We'll be smartly uniformed, and armed with Schmeissers — which *work*, don't have knobs in their barrels . . . You know that business of the Stens amazes me?'

'Me too. Fact of life, that's all. But go on?'

'Well. Where to start . . . Le Faisan will take

335

the other two with him — here, to this village. Laz. You've been through there, I'm sure. It's to be our jump-off point.'

Rosie looked up at him, from the map: 'But not mine —'

'Of course not!' Sharpish: no sufferer of tired brains . . . 'The father has to come out from Quimper by bike, you told me —'

'What *I* was thinking. Sorry, I wasn't —'

'Let me finish this. I'll be moving the *bouc* to Laz — Thursday night, if Jaillon gets it here in time. Actually to a farm outside the village, the rendezvous also for those doing the Trevarez job. This way I have control of the whole thing, in its early stages — up to the last minute I could make changes if I had to. Anyway — around Trevarez we'll have a hundred men in position before the air attack comes in. Two separate forces, each with its own commander, and all from what we're calling the Red Brigade. The Commie element — and believe me, they're set to make the most of it. Smoke?'

'No, thank you.' She'd just put one out. 'What time do you foregather at Laz?'

'I and my team by ten o'clock — curfew time. The rest of them no later than that, probably earlier — as soon as it's dark. It'll be the last of the old moon, this weekend. The boys will arrive on foot, you see, singly or in groups, filtering down out of the forest quiet as foxes. It's a broken-down old farm but there's a good big barn they'll use. Deploying from there on foot too. Two kilometres to the château itself, but they've got to get settled into their positions, so I'll send them off at about eleven.'

'Leaving you and your team targeting Kerongués about midnight?'

'Yes. Taking what advantage we can of the air attack. As the crow flies we'll be twenty kilometres from it — no distance really, as regards sight and sound — and we'll arrive shortly before it starts. If they've any doubts of us they'll forget them when the sky lights up and the bombs start bursting — and we can use it too — "Come on, hurry it up, I want to get out of here!" '

'Is the plan simply to drive up and say you've come for the prisoner Marie-Claude le Guen?'

'More or less. She's wanted immediately for further interrogation, on the orders of *Sturmbann-führer* Braun. No time for formalities, it's urgent — so forth. They can get on the phone to SD headquarters for confirmation, le Faisan will tell them — as long as they do it quickly — but the line will have been crossed with another, they'll find. Le Faisan does the talking. He's capable of putting on a fine, commanding manner — as well as having good German. I'm to be a sergeant, by the way — watching his back, as it were. Any of them questions my accent, I tell them I'm White Russian. We'll have rehearsed our act by then, but it's near enough the same scheme we had before. I did mention . . .'

'Yes.' She lit a new cigarette. He was at the window, peering out. Turning back now, Rosie asked him, 'Where will I and le Guen be, while you're at Laz and then at Kerongués?'

He nodded, returning to the table. 'Here.' Forefinger touching the map just south of Kerongués. 'Lestonan — more hamlet than village, and you'll hole up on the farm on its southern fringe. Coming up from the main road, before the lane forks right to Kerongués or left to St Guénolé, it's on your right. A windbreak of poplars and a long stone barn with some of its roof missing, and the house behind it. I've picked it mainly because of your man wanting only a short ride out of Quimper. I'd have preferred to use a place at Moncouar — there.'

'*Would* be too far for him, you're right. But I see the point — that road, at Moncouar —'

'The river's another complication, of course. I'd thought of having you meet him down there then drive him up to Moncouar, but — an unnecessary complication, additional exposure, an extra risk we don't need.'

'Right.'

'Lestonan, therefore. You should be there I suggest before curfew. Make it the same for the girl's father — deadline curfew-hour, ten o'clock. The farmer's name is Perrot, Jacques Perrot — you have to know it in case you're questioned, but you won't see him, he'll have cleared out — gone to his brother's place for the night. You can use his kitchen — back door'll be unlocked . . . Look — you're going into Quimper now? You could divert a little and have a look at it — the

338

only farm there, right by that little fork.'

'Yes . . .'

'To get there now on your way to Quimper — turn left at Briec and fork left at Moncouar — over the river, and through Kerongués, you'll come to it on your left.'

She nodded. 'I'll sketch it for him. But on the night, how do I get there?'

'By *gazo*. Starting from here say eight-thirty. The *gazo* will be here ready for you long before that — it'll be stolen during the afternoon, in Scaër.'

'Christ . . .'

'Don't worry. We know where it is, and who owns it, and it won't be reported stolen until next day. It'll be ready for you here and fully fuelled, all you'll have to do is get in and drive it.'

'To that farm.'

'Yes. Park it in Perrot's yard — other side of the barn, that is — pointing out towards the lane, and leaving room for me to drive in and straight into the barn. You might have the barn doors open for us, in fact. But that's detail — there'll be a chance to talk again before Saturday, I hope?'

'Of course.'

'To go over it again, and any small changes. What I've been giving you is the plan as we've agreed it provisionally — with no date on it. Now we *have* a date — could be some new ideas'll come up, who knows . . . I'll outline the rest of it as it stands now, though . . . You get there —

339

to Lestonan — before ten, the girl's father arrives about the same time, you park your *gazo* and sit tight in a nice warm kitchen. We'll get to you with the girl soon after midnight. By a quarter past, say. I and the girl join you and her father in the *gazo*, I'll drive — oh, first of all I change out of the uniform, my own clothes will be in your *gazo* when you take it. But I'll drive —' his finger moved across the map — 'by way of only the smallest lanes, most of the way — I know them all, you see — and by this circular route — to — here, Lezèle. You'll have left your bike there, by the way — at Lezèle, yes. Perhaps on the way down here, Saturday afternoon — Henri Peucat might help out, with that. In Lezèle, anyway, it's the blacksmith's house we stop at. I leave the three of you there and take the *gazo* on to where I'll dump it — any luck, it'll be a week or so before it's found — and from there I hoof it back here, across-country.'

'And what about us?'

'From Lezèle, where you'll spend the rest of the night, the father and daughter will be collected early Sunday morning by one of Jaillon's lorry drivers. He'll take them to Scrignac, where I understand arrangements have been made — by you, uh?'

'Yes. The gamekeeper, Vannier.'

'Exactly.'

She nodded. 'It's good, I think. One thing — when you join me at Lestonan — the truck gets left there?'

'It goes into Perrot's barn, and the other three push off on foot. The truck will either be re-painted — demilitarized — there in that barn, or Jaillon will arrange to fetch it. He has one trans-porter that's really huge, you know. Any case — won't be *your* problem, eh?'

He'd left her no problems, she thought, as far as her own part in it was concerned. On the Sunday morning, for instance, after Jaillon's man picked up the le Guens she'd have only about twelve kilometres to cycle back to St Michel. Very much as she'd done this morning; might have been visiting in Huelgoat, where Peucat had a number of patients . . . Peucat at this moment in profile to her, at the *gazo*'s juddering wheel, while she alternately dozed and woke again, brain still tensed up anyway, refusing to let go. The state of the roads didn't help much either. It was great to be driven, all the same; great of old Henri beside her here with his yellowish, broken-nosed profile, patchy grey hair, soft old-dog's eyes sliding her way now and then, presumably to check whether she was asleep or not.

Lannuzel's plan did look good, she thought. Even the Kerongués part: the way Guy had de-scribed it, you could forget Count Jules' doubts.

See him again this week, maybe, explain it, reassure him.

She'd been dropping off, thoughts merging into a dream in which she was explaining it to him, up at Scrignac: half waking then, meeting

Peucat's glance, murmuring to *him*, 'It's a good plan.'

'Uh?'

'Oh.' A hand to her eyes. 'Talking in my sleep . . .'

'I'm glad it's good, anyway.'

It truly *was*, she thought. Simple — as Guy had said it would be, at some stage — intentionally so, and on the face of it easily achievable. More than adequate time-margins, for instance, and their route in the stolen *gazo* taking them well clear of the immediate Trevarez area. And the disappearing transport: that was first class, and — again — dead simple.

Barring accidents. Chance encounters, Acts of God . . .

Peucat glanced her way again. 'Hardly conducive to repose, I'm afraid.'

The jolting, he meant. You couldn't avoid all the potholes. She shrugged. 'You won't forget the turn at Moncouar, if I happen to have dropped off then?'

'I won't. And I'll wake you before we cross the river, if necessary. That's where the *Veldpolitzei* have hostages imprisoned, you know — close to Kerongués, just south of the bridge?'

'I did hear of it. But it's Lestonan —'

'Yes. Understood.'

'One thing, doctor — Henri, I should say —'

'Much better . . .'

'Might you have a patient at or near Huelgoat who'd back us up if I needed to have spent a night there — as Mme Sanson was prepared to?'

'Oh, I'm sure.' Empty pipe between his teeth — between the upper and lower set, that was. Sucking noises, at times, and dribble on his chin. No Prince Charming, that was for sure. He nodded, having made his mind up: 'One couple I'd be quite sure of. We could visit them some time, if you like.'

'*En route* to Scrignac? I ought to see Count Jules again fairly soon.'

'All right. I'll try for Tuesday. Suzanne — no, you want to sleep —'

'It's OK. Go on?'

'Well. When you asked me what I might do if you fell foul of our revolting lords and masters — does the question indicate that you feel yourself to be in such danger?'

Looking at him: frowning . . .

'Always is — danger, naturally.'

'But especially so? Whatever it is you're plotting for next Saturday, for instance?'

'I wouldn't say *especially* so. No.'

'I suppose it's really only a matter of degree.'

'There's also a difference — probably — between how one feels and how it really is. One can't know what's happening off-stage, as it were. But my only reason for mentioning it was the worry you could be drawn into it too, through association with me . . . D'you want to stop for a minute, to fill that pipe?'

'No. Good for me not to, for a while. Good for

you too — stinks, doesn't it?'

'Mind if *I* smoke?'

'My dear child . . .'

She lit a Gaullois. Thinking about that question — consciousness of danger. An honest answer might have been: *Yes, I'm conscious of it all the time.* Quite apart from anything that might develop during or after the Trevarez business.

But once that was out of the way: and if one was still at large . . .

She'd dropped off, and had then been jerked awake again. Cigarette still alight between the fingers of a slightly raised right hand, the side away from Peucat. He'd shot a glance at her as she'd woken, startled, then away again at the curve of road ahead, and into his rear mirror; there was a *gazo* van close on his tail, waiting to get by. Rosie leant back with her eyes shut, breathing the pungent smoke. Telling Ben in her rather jumpy mind: *It'll be all plain sailing after that, my darling, don't you worry . . .*

They turned off to the left at Moncouar, drove down to the bridge and over it into and through Kerongués; then another kilometre south to Lestonan. Just outside Kerongués she saw a signpost in French and German for the internment camp, but the camp itself wasn't in sight from the road and she had no reason to take any close interest in it. In fact one didn't want to be seen even glancing at it. At Lestonan, though, the Perrot farm was easy to recognize from Lannuzel's description, and when they were out on the main Coray–Quimper road Peucat pulled off into another farm entrance so Rosie could make a sketch-map for le Guen while he — Peucat — stuffed and lit his pipe.

On to Quimper, then. Entering from the east, over the river again and on westward, skirting the wooded Mount Frugy, then to the right towards the centre and Place Saint-Matthieu. Sunday traffic — in other words, not much of it. He parked on the other side of the square from the Berthomets' house.

'All right for you from here?'

Sound of a brass band and the tramp of marching feet: a kilometre away, maybe. She'd caught a snatch of it before, when they'd been passing to the south of the station. Boche feet, those would be, Boche boots slamming the roadway to the thudding of drums and some Teutonic dirge. This was a Sunday feature too: weekly parade of the bastards through the towns they fouled . . . She told Peucat, 'It's fine. Even a band to swing along with.'

'Ugh — *that* . . .'

'After I've seen this character I'll come back and wait in the car.'

'Won't come in? I'm sure they'd like it . . .'

'Better not. They've taken a risk already — thank them for me, please, but —'

He'd shrugged. 'Something like two o'clock, then?'

'Sooner — I hope. I'd guess one-thirty or

sooner. But I'll eat my sandwich then — and if you're long I dare say I'll snooze. 'Bye . . .'

Through Place de Locronan, then the road of the same name, into Rue de la Providence. The band's strains and the crash of boots and drums were somewhere off to her right and behind her, but getting closer, louder. Her skin crawled: as it tended to even when she heard their ugly language: this had a similar effect. Five minutes to one now: timing couldn't have been bettered. She had no doubt, on this occasion, that le Guen would show up: after all it was only yesterday he'd delivered his message *chez* Berthomet. And if he did turn up today, you could be fairly certain he'd go through with it on Saturday too.

Well — for his own sake, and his daughter's. As far as 'Mincemeat' was concerned he could disappear in a puff of smoke now and the attack would still go in. Beyond *that,* though, he'd still be out there, liable to be arrested and tortured — and to shop *her,* in the process. Highly desirable therefore to take him out of circulation.

Ghastly racket getting louder by the second. They'd have come west across the town centre and then turned north, coming this way up behind her now. Music definitely not the food of love: music as a blaring celebration of barbarism and brutality. She'd last had that thought in Rouen, she remembered. Music and stamping that shook the road, the buildings: and they'd like that, the bastards — like to see it, feel it, see the fear on people's faces.

What le Guen had described as lack of courage? Or simply nerves stretched permanently taut so that certain sounds or sights had virtually instant effect, brought the sweat out, shortened the breath? Remembering — seeing, virtually *feeling* — a pair of pliers, shiny-steel jaws, handles encased in rubber — in close-up, in the sweaty hand of a pig-faced officer of the *Geheime Staatspolitzei*.

She'd never told Ben about the pliers.

The café was open, she noticed — customers filtering in and out — those emerging gathering on the pavement and looking south — expectantly, doubtless to see the guard and band swagger past. Rosie pausing on the kerb, waiting for a gap in the stream of cyclists . . . Remembering as she crossed over and turned to her left on the park side of the road that she'd asked le Guen to make this a very brief meeting: meet, talk, separate . . .

With good reason, too. Third public exposure. And the park was full of people: some of them drawn to the roadside by the rising noise of the parade approaching, others drifting away from it. More of those, she was glad to see. She wished she had the courage to put her palms over her ears, make a show of shutting it out, shutting *them* out. In her own situation it would have been less courage than stupidity, but the urge was there and must have been legible in her expression: a tall, fierce-looking woman with a little girl in tow nodded to her, muttered, '*Salauds* . . .'

'Hideous, isn't it?'

The woman tapped her long nose, murmured: 'Soon we'll hear them *squeal* — like the animals they are!'

'Please God.'

'Yes. High time *He* took a hand in things.' She was trudging on — with the child at arms' lengths behind her and walking backward, gazing at Rosie as at a friend she didn't want to leave.

'Zoé?'

Le Guen — suddenly there, face to face.

She put her arms up to embrace him.

'François! Oh, *François!*' Glancing back over her shoulder, though — as the noise suddenly swelled — she saw the head of the column emerging from Rue Locronan and wheeling half-left, expanding into the road there where it widened: a huge red, white and black swastika, gleam of bayonets, drums, brass and boots louder every second. She turned back to le Guen, her hands on his shoulders and giving him her other cheek to kiss: then pointing with her head across the park: 'That way, shall we?"

'Yes — yes, very well . . .'

'All well with you, François?'

'You had the message, obviously.'

'Yes. And well done . . . Look, take this.' Impulsive again, seizing one of his hands in both of hers: 'Oh, François, it's so *lovely,* running into you like this!'

'But what —'

'We should look like lovers, François, not conspirators. Try to look less tense — put your arm round me —' she laughed — 'if you could bear to?'

'What is it?'

'Little map I just roughed out. In case my description's not good enough. Better burn it when you've got it in your head. It's where you should come on Saturday. D'you know where Lestonan is? All right, take my arm now, loosely — relax, look happy . . . *Do* you know it?'

'Lestonan . . .'

'Very close to Kerongués. You leave town on the route de Coray: about four kilometres, turn left into a small lane, and after about half a kilometre you'd come to a fork. Before you get that far, though, there's a farm on your right. I've sketched it: a line of poplars ends at the gate where you turn in, and there's a stone barn with a damaged roof. The house is beyond it. You'll see a *gazo* parked in the yard — I'll be there, and we'll have the place to ourselves. Be sure to get there before ten o'clock, curfew hour; it'll be a bit dark by then. I'll be there by about a quarter to the hour, in case you're early. If by any chance the *gazo*'s not there it'll only mean I've been delayed — don't panic, just wait. The kitchen door of the house will be open, by the way . . . All right?'

'Your map makes it plain, eh?'

'Wasn't what I've just told you plain?'

'I — suppose . . .'

'With the map as well, you *can't* go wrong . . .

Isn't that a horrible noise?'

'Yes. It is.'

The band was about level with them now. Gleaming instruments, crashing boots and drums, that disgusting emblem in the lead and a column of marching, helmeted troops behind. She clung to his arm: he looked ill, she thought. 'Not much longer now, François. Saturday before ten, remember — Lestonan. I'll have your money there, of course.'

'What about Marie-Claude, and —'

'We'll have about two hours to wait, in the farm kitchen. Soon after midnight the friend I've mentioned will arrive with Marie-Claude, we all get in the *gazo,* and — well, never mind *where,* don't worry about any of it, it's all arranged. All you have to do is be there before ten . . . Have you seen your SD friend recently — and Prigent?'

'Both. Not much to choose —'

'But nothing special?'

'No. Not really.'

'Well — a few more days, and you'll be clear of all of them. You've done *very* well — Marie-Claude'll be so proud of you, so happy!'

'It's going to be a long six days.'

'Then you'll have her safe and sound — and she'll have *you.*'

'God willing . . .'

'Just keep your nerve. We're so *nearly* there.' Her hands grasped his again. 'Au revoir, François.' Looking urgently into his white face, worried eyes with dark pouches under them: 'Remember this is to save your life — save *both* your lives!' She saw that go in like a bullet: he nodded, moistened his thin lips. 'Au revoir, Zoé . . .'

The band's noise had peaked, receding northward; there was a drift of people back towards the road. She'd be going back that way herself in a minute; but le Guen was heading straight across to where she supposed there'd be a foot-bridge over the river, and she waited — anxious lover looking after him with a hand half-up in readiness to respond quickly if he turned back to wave. He didn't, as it happened: but no one was following him, or as far as she could see taking any interest in either of them.

Chapter 14

She went to bed as soon as they got back, that Sunday, had a bath before supper (horse-meat, cold) and set listening-watch in the attic at midnight. Nothing came in, and she was more than ready for bed again after an hour of it.

Bomber Command, she supposed, hadn't been able to confirm the Trevarez attack yet. Tomorrow, perhaps, or Tuesday. They'd hardly back out; she thought, when they'd agreed it three weeks ago. Availability of aircraft might be the problem; they were over Germany in strength practically every night now, hitting targets of greater strategic importance than Kraut submariners' rest-homes.

Grand Admiral Doenitz had to be a strategic target though, surely.

Tomorrow, Monday, she'd spend playing nurse. Building cover was important, and there was nothing else for her to be doing at this stage. It was all in Lannuzel's court. His priorities as far as she knew them were to have the truck brought down from Guerlesquin, to confer with his Maquis friends — finalize plans, now they had a date — and arrange for a round-the-clock watch to be kept on comings and goings at Trevarez, the object being to know the size of the garrison

352

and reinforcements and whether there'd be U-boat sailors in residence and later if possible the ranks and identities of individuals attending the week-end conference.

If for instance next Sunday the BBC could announce the deaths of Doenitz, Bachmann and Godt . . . Imagining Ben hearing it, not guessing for a moment it was something *she'd* brought about. Smiling in the dark: happy with the prospect of several hours' sleep ahead of her, asking him in her imagination how many nicely brought-up girls ever had a chance of doing *that* — killing Nazi admirals?

Anyway — Monday, work with Peucat: Tuesday, to Scrignac, lunch with Count Jules — whom Peucat had telephoned and who'd invited them — and on Wednesday to Lannuzel again. Thursday might be another working day in the practice, and Friday as the last full day before action had better be kept free, in case of last-minute crises.

Tell Ben one day — deadpan, over a drink, or in a lull in conversation — *I once knocked off three admirals . . .*

She slept soundly and woke early, thinking of him and of the future. Foot of the rainbow: she wasn't even close to it yet but she could see it up there, would get to it eventually, climb it with him. Here and now, pray God his wonky knee kept him in that nice, safe job in Portsmouth until the whole damn thing was over. After all, he'd had his own command and won a medal — what else could an aspiring painter want?

Although there were no certainties. As well as anyone, she knew there weren't. They both knew it. As Lise had too — Lise's voice and question suddenly in memory: *Could be I can't see us in another kind of life because we won't be?*

It was a question she'd shied away from herself, once or twice. Lise really shouldn't have come out with it: one's private fears were best kept private . . . She was fully awake now: that was daylight outside the window. Time for practicalities — such as getting up, for instance . . . But also — delaying that a few more seconds — for having one's perspectives right: like envisaging the bombing of Château Trevarez as the next step towards getting home. Effectively, it would be. By Sunday morning, when she'd be pedalling back here from Lezèle, the whole of her initial brief would have been accomplished. She'd be able to settle down a bit then — concentrate on the nursing business for a while. At any rate until the expected furore over 'Mincemeat' had died down. Then resume the paradrops, perhaps of personnel as well as weaponry. And training, and organization — for instance expanding the present scope for joint action by Lannuzel's and Jaillon's forces by bringing in groups from adjacent areas too.

Then — invasion. Whenever: but probably quite soon. After that the task would be to prevent and disrupt movements of Boche troops towards the beachhead or beachheads. Disrupt everything. Blow up railway lines and roads, sabotage

354

the rolling-stock. Eventually, although it might take a little while, you'd have German withdrawal or surrender. And *then*, Ben darling . . .

But — before that, maybe — once the Free French came in, who'd need 'F' Section SOE? In this corner of France, anyway. That was a *lovely* thought. French paratroops dropping in strength and absorbing the Maquis in their own professional soldiering, the Boches on the run and people like oneself — and Lise and Noally, please God — surplus to requirements?

By the end of summer, say?

At Scrignac on the Tuesday Count Jules wasn't enthusiastic about Lannuzel's plan of action. In his view, he told her after she'd explained it to him, there was too much reliance on good luck.

'At least, on absence of *bad* luck. For instance — he'll be leaving the farm at Laz some time after eleven — because he's despatching the Trevarez force *at* eleven — right?'

'Yes . . .'

In his study, leaning over a Michelin map together, the count using a pencil as a pointer and his other arm tending to drape itself across her shoulders . . .

'How does he know what he might meet on the road? Here's Kerongués. He'll be using only the small lanes, you said. So — a route like this, perhaps. But he still has to pass through Moncouar. Probably coming through Landuda on the way there. It's a sizeable village, eh? Well — small lanes or not, throughout this area there are sure to be intensive anti-Maquis precautions. They know who's in those woods, don't you think they know damn well? They aren't going to trifle with the security of Grand Admiral Karl Doenitz, are they! Or even his deputy's — what's his name — ?'

'Admiral Godt.'

'Godt. Right. Or Bachmann. If I were responsible for security I'd have patrols out all over the place. Laz is damn close to Trevarez, too — I'd say *too* close. Guy Lannuzel wants the reins in his own hands as long as possible — understandably, perhaps — but to achieve it he's bringing a hundred Maquis almost into the open. If it was up to me I'd muster them in the forest — where they belong!'

'I think this farm's outside the village. Somewhere like this lane here — already on his route to Kerongués. He knows all the little by-ways.'

'I'm sure he does.' Tapping the map . . . 'But look — the Forêt de Laz here — enough of it to hide a thousand men in, let alone a hundred. And ground they all know well, by this time. The village itself, though — how does he know it won't be stiff with Boches?' Pointing again: 'Laz to Trevarez, about two kilometres — what's *that,* when it's one of the Führer's right-hand men for whose safety they're responsible?'

'Actually —' she moved sideways a little, to be less convenient an arm-rest — 'Doenitz may well not be there.'

'Never mind. He may be, and others certainly *will* be.' He shook his head. 'My dear — Guy is a professional soldier — I'm not. I'm not saying he's wrong and I know better — I'm sure I'd make an awful mess of it . . . But — you're seeing him tomorrow, you said?'

She nodded. She'd intended it anyway, but had had confirmation from Baker Street last night — Monday — that the RAF strike was on. Lannuzel was of course assuming it would be, but he still had to be told, and she had no intention of making any telephone calls about it.

'Tell him, if you would —' the count was folding his map — 'that if I were in his shoes I'd have that truck of Jaillon's waiting somewhere well to the west of Laz.' Opening the map partly again, poking a finger at it: 'Here, somewhere. Off the road, under cover. I'd have the Trevarez force gather in the forest, then let their own commanders get on with it while I made my own way on foot to join those three at the truck. It wouldn't matter then if Laz *was* full of Boches. I'd expect it, I'd expect the worst — which is very different from hoping for the best!'

'I'll tell him.'

'Give him my apologies for interfering. I'll look forward to having him explain to me why I'm completely wrong.'

'Wouldn't like to visit him yourself?'

'Unfortunately, I can't. I'm off on Thursday — Paris, again. It's unavoidable . . .'

She asked Peucat that afternoon on their way

357

down to Huelgoat — to visit the patients who'd give her an alibi for Saturday night — whether he'd known the count was planning another Paris visit, so soon after the last. Peucat expressed surprise: he hadn't known of it, Sara hadn't mentioned it either.

'A recent decision, then.' Rosie lit a cigarette. 'D'you think he prefers to be elsewhere, when things are happening?'

'How d'you mean?' They were passing through Berrien: would turn left in a minute. 'Your Saturday business, you mean?'

'Fact is, he's not too keen on it, in any case.'

'On the plan you told me in your sleep was so good?'

She nodded. 'He disagrees.'

'It's Guy Lannuzel's plan?'

'Yes.'

'Well — he knows his stuff. Saw a lot of action.'

'Count Jules is fully aware of it.'

'And you think he's putting distance between himself and — *your*selves . . . I know nothing about any of it, of course, but I can't see what disadvantage there'd be in his remaining at Scrignac. Conversely, how it would benefit him to be in Paris.'

'Except the obvious one?'

'Huh?'

Smiling: 'What usually takes him to Paris?'

Left turn coming up. Peucat shaking his head, lips pursed . . . Rosie thinking that if she was even half right, the solution might involve herself and

Mme de Mauvernay. If things went badly on Saturday and she herself came to grief, the trail of subsequent investigations would inevitably lead back to the former actress. In which context Jules had said last week, 'She might not be easy to locate, by that time.'

Because he'd have tipped her off and she'd be in hiding? If he'd decided that in present circumstances Suzanne Tanguy had become a bad risk?

On Wednesday she was at the Lannuzel place when Jaillon delivered the truck, or *bouc*. She was with Brigitte out in front of the house when the big pantechnicon van appeared, frontways at first — stopping with its nose at a slant in the gateway and displaying the inscription above the cab *Au Service d'Allemagne* — then backing out, turning in a series of elephantine lunges to and fro, finally re-entering backwards and grinding slowly up towards the farm's outbuildings. It backed up to the barn, stopped, and Jaillon climbed down. Lannuzel was coming by then, summoned by his sister.

Waving as he came limping up. 'Hey, Jean-Paul. Better late than never, huh?'

'Late? I'll tell you, you're getting bloody good service here!'

Tipping his cap back. You could imagine him as a Foreign Legion sergeant, Rosie thought. Tough as an old *bouc* himself. He came strutting over, touching his cap: 'Pluto at your service, Mam'selle Zoé. You'll have had my message of thanks for the *parachutage*, I hope?'

She nodded. 'Did they send all you asked for?'

'Near enough. Heard about the Stens, too. D'you have saboteurs in your English factories?'

'It's more like carelessness or greed. Churn 'em out faster, get more money.'

'And good men could kill themselves. But thanks for the warning.'

'Let's get it under cover, eh?' Lannuzel was pulling the barn doors open. 'I'll take this out . . .'

His *gazo* pickup. He didn't have to get it started; there was a slight incline and he had only to release the brake. He swung it round clear of the doors, and joined Jaillon at the transporter. 'No road-blocks, eh?'

A shrug. 'They all know me, anyhow.'

'Exactly. Shoot on sight, you'd think.'

Brigitte took Rosie indoors for some coffee. Murmuring, 'I'm not supposed to see this, anyway. It's something important you're doing, I gather. Trevarez — Kerongués?'

'If you know it all, Brigitte —'

'Heard those places mentioned, that's all. No — I only get bits and pieces . . .'

There'd been a resounding crash outside: Rosie went to the window, realized it must have been the transporter's tail-gate crashing down. They were off-loading chicken-coops now: the *bouc* would have been behind and under a load of them she supposed. She joined Brigitte in the kitchen: 'How's the poultry business?'

She told Lannuzel, when Jaillon had gone and

Brigitte was out on the farm somewhere, 'They'll probably hit Kernével at the same time as Trevarez. That was the idea a couple of weeks ago, anyway. No need to tell anyone because there's no ground action called for.'

'No. Good. Excellent, in fact . . .'

Kernével, the U-boat Command and Communications headquarters, was about twenty-five kilometres east of Quimper, near Rosporden. The attack would be in easy sight and sound of Kerongués, as would the one on Trevarez.

'But, Guy, I should tell you. I was with Count Jules yesterday, and I told him your intentions, roughly —'

'You did, eh?' Silent for a moment, staring at her. Then: 'Some reason you had to?'

She held the angry stare. 'I told you before, he had doubts about it. And he's the boss, more or less —'

'*Thinks* he is.'

'As far as I'm concerned, he is. If it hadn't been for him I wouldn't be here.' She added, 'And you wouldn't have had your *parachutage*.'

'All right.' He shrugged. 'And he has some beef now, has he?'

'He thinks you aren't taking into account the probable level of Boche security around Trevarez. Road-blocks and patrols, troops stationed in villages — et cetera.'

'Knows more of what goes on around here than I do, eh?'

'Well. He asked me to tell you —'

'Couldn't tell me himself?'

'He's off to Paris tomorrow — today I suppose he's busy. I did suggest that, as it happens.'

'When the invasion comes perhaps he'll remember he has an appointment on the moon!'

She shook her head. She'd thought more about it, since that chat with Peucat in the *gazo*, and remembered the rhetorical question the count had put to her that day in his stable-yard: *Behind bars or dead, what use is one?*

'Might be unfair, Guy. You and he know each other a lot better than I do, but my impression is that the invasion — being ready for it — is the one thing he has in his sights. He's a pragmatist, in fact. This is your job, your territory, he leaves it to you. No, he *does* — these were only suggestions. He asked me to tell you he'll look forward to hearing from you why he's dead wrong. He said, "Guy's the soldier, *I'm* not." '

'But he wanted it done, in the first place . . .'

'Yes. For reasons I explained to you. Now he's asked me to pass on these comments. *I'd* say he's only trying to be helpful.'

'Well. Perhaps. You put up a good case for him, anyway. Have you — been spending much time up there?'

'A lot less than I have here — as it happens. Are you suggesting anything, by that question?'

'Suggesting *nothing*, Suzanne.'

'Good. I don't want to be caught up in a lot of bickering. If men like you and Jules de Seyssons can't get on . . .'

Actually it was par for the course. Resistance leaders always bickered. By nature they were individualists — had to be. They were French, too. Lannuzel had shrugged: 'Gets my goat sometimes, this — absentee commander-in-chief. Anyway — as it happens, we've refined the plan a little — as I think I indicated we would. There's no change as far as you're concerned, but in other respects — for instance, there'll be Maquis observation of the routes to Kerongués to give warning of any road-blocks or patrols. Not that we'd expect any. Security around the château itself, yes, but they don't have the numbers to police the whole countryside. That's half the answer to our mutual friend Count Jules, incidentally.'

'One point he did make — instead of assembling your men on the farm at Laz, why not in the forest?'

'You want the answer to that?'

That brilliantly blue stare again. He wasn't in the least like Ben: she wondered how she could ever have thought he was. She shook her head. 'Not particularly. I've passed on what he said, that's all. If you resent it, tell *him*.'

'The farm is as remote as the one you'll be using. Also directly accessible from the forest. It has communications, too.'

'You mean a telephone?'

'What else? In that way it's ideal. Such a ruin of a place, you'd never expect to find a line connected. But if road-blocks are being set up, for instance, I'll hear about them before we start.

That make sense to you?'

'Of course it does.' She stubbed out her cigarette. Deciding not to risk reminding him that telephones were dangerous. 'And there we are. You say there's no change to my part in it — so that's all right — and I've seen the girl's father, meanwhile, he knows where to come. And I had a look at the place. So — if nothing goes wildly wrong between now and then, I don't need to see you again before Saturday — do I?'

Blinking at her. 'I suppose — not . . .'

'Fine.' She pushed herself up. 'If I don't see Brigitte on my way out, say goodbye to her for me?'

'There is one thing.' Pushing himself up: it was an awkward movement, on account of that foot. 'If you'd spare me another two minutes?'

'Of course.'

'It's quite important, actually. Here, I'll show you.'

The map was in a drawer of the table; he got it out and spread it. 'The question of our route in the *gazo* when we leave Perrot's farm. Incidentally, I'll be forcing the lock on his kitchen door, breaking it open — so if we were traced there it wouldn't have been with his knowledge or permission.'

'So I *don't* need to know his name.'

He looked surprised: then nodded. 'You're right. I hadn't thought of that . . . Anyway, see here. The route I'll take — as I showed you before — roughly like this. Using small lanes all the way

— crossing the Aulne here — to Lennon, over the main road here, Ty-Baise — and skirting to the west of your village. See?'

Through Quinquis-Yven, she noticed.

'Then on up this way — quite a wide circle, a good radius from where they'll all be falling over each other — all night, let's hope — and eventually, Lezèle. Where you'll have left your bike, eh?'

She nodded. 'That's arranged.'

'Good. But — if on the way north from Kerongués we had hold-ups — lengthy detours for instance if there were road-blocks — or patrols, or troop deployments — not likely but it's possible — if by the time we were in the area of St Michel and — oh, suppose it was getting light and there were patrols around, that kind of situation — it so happens there's a possible safe-house we might be able to make use of. At this little place, Quinquis-Yven.'

'Marthe Peucat, d'you mean?'

He lifted his hands . . . 'I was going to ask — had you met her. Obviously you would have sooner or later, but —'

'I'd no idea — of Marthe as —'

'No. And until now there's been no connection between me and her, in — this area. Socially, sure — she and Henri have known Brigitte since before she married. As I told you, this place belonged to her in-laws, the Millaus, and Henri was their doctor — brought Brigitte's husband into the world, all that. Socially therefore we know each other well — but as far as anything else is concerned, I only happen to be aware — second-hand, you might say —'

'Through Timo Achard?'

'That's clever of you.' He reached for his cigarettes. 'Although — well, I couldn't say — I don't *know* of any connection there either . . .'

Rosie was to say much later — *I felt sure there had been some such connection. Achard's part in whatever it was — I'd guess an escape line — would have been transport; when there'd been escapers, shot-down airmen or whatever, to be moved through the area. I first suspected it — saw it, almost — the day she came rushing into her brother's house with the news of the Achards being in Gestapo hands. She and Henri were both badly shocked — although he might have expected it you'd think, I'd seen Timo's arrest and told him — and if he'd known of that involvement — well, surely . . . Have to hand it to him, he'd taken that very coolly. Cautiously too — being so careful to stay away, rather than go round to see Adèle. In fact one was beginning to conclude that there was more to old Henri than met the eye. But there'd been another element too, the day Marthe brought the bad news — an element of secrecy, secrets he and his sister weren't sharing with me. I just felt it. You know, that atmosphere — the guarded way they looked at each other — almost trying not to . . . And come to think of it — I'd already begun to speculate about this — it seemed likely that Count Jules' girlfriend in Paris, Léonie de Mauvernay, had some deeper involvement than merely having written* a letter on behalf of Suzanne Tanguy. She'd have done that because Jules asked her to, but she'd have had to have been a Résistante *herself for him to have put her at that much risk in the first place. Perhaps she ran a safe-house too. Part of the grounds for thinking on these lines is what he said to me about her being able to vanish at short notice — having said it he'd realized he might be saying too much, and clammed up. And a more basic* element in this thinking — imaginative thinking, *you might call it* — is the old proverb *'Birds of a feather flock together'. As we all know, active* Résistants *are few and far between, a tiny proportion of the population as a whole, but when you get to know one* — well, close friends tend to be like-minded, don't they . . .

She'd accepted one of his Caporals; they were sitting again now, with the map still spread.

'You're saying we might stop at Marthe's instead of pushing on to Lezèle.'

'Yes — but only if we had to. For instance — if we'd run into trouble somewhere and one of us was hurt?'

'You want me to ask her whether in that kind of emergency we could knock on her door.'

'Exactly. You'd be as good as home — so we'd leave you there, and in the morning I'd take them on to Lezèle. Or if anyone had been hurt —'

'Henri could visit his sister. Marthe doesn't have a telephone, incidentally.'

'She's bound to have a neighbour who does. It

367

would be Marthe herself needing attention, of course.'

Rosie let smoke trickle out, drift across the map. She thought about it for a minute, making sure her instinctive reaction was the right one, then shook her head.

'I'm against it. Mainly because of the Achards. As a matter of principle, former colleagues of people in their situation are best left alone.'

'You think Marthe might be under surveillance.'

'Her house might be. It's an unnecessary risk from our point of view, and it also endangers her — *and* her brother. They don't arrest just one member of a household or family, Guido, they take everyone who's at all close to him or her.'

'Talking about Brigitte now?'

Shrugging: holding that angry stare again . . . 'Talking about the Peucats. But the same would apply here — certainly. Not that there's the least harm in your trying to shield Brigitte.'

'You're not willing to approach Marthe Peucat, anyway?'

'For the reason I've given you. Also because she doesn't know I'm anything but her brother's employee, and I'm averse to letting anyone know who doesn't have to. But, Guido — this is a good plan you have. I believe in it, I felt good about it when you described it on Sunday and I still do. Let's assume we *will* make it to Lezèle?'

368

Chapter 15

Peucat muttered to her at one point on the Saturday morning, in his consulting room, 'Better regard your job here as permanent. Wouldn't want to do without you.' It was the usual Saturday rush and she was organizing the patients and producing their case-histories as he needed them — case-histories all updated, at that; she'd done a lot in the past couple of days. But she was worrying a little about what time they'd get away — to Châteauneuf via Lezèle, with her bike in the back of his *gazo;* with a long night ahead of her, she didn't want to miss lunch. Even though Brigitte might be providing supper.

Roast chicken, maybe.

In the event, they were finished just before three p.m.; and by then she'd taken time out to make some cheese sandwiches. She had her valise packed ready, with le Guen's money and her pistol and spare clip of 9-millimetre in the bottom of it, other stuff filling the space above. Before breakfast this morning she'd also checked that the transceiver and its attachments were well hidden under the attic floorboard, and the board itself camouflaged with debris; her encyphering material she'd filed under 'R' for Rosie amongst the patients' records.

Preparation for a long absence?

Asking herself that question: having done those things instinctively, as natural precautions. Prescience? For some reason the thought took her mind to Lise.

They were on the road, eating the sandwiches, by three-fifteen. Four kilometres to Plounévez-du-Faou, and from there about seven to Lezèle. They'd stopped there on Tuesday on the way back from Scrignac via Huelgoat, for her to introduce herself to the blacksmith; he was going to fit a new section of rear mudguard to her bike while it was in his hands. He was small, wiry, and bearded: this afternoon he left a horse he was shoeing, came and lifted the bike out of the *gazo* for her. Bare-armed, muscles like knots in a rope . . . Nodding to Peucat: 'Getting about a lot these days, doctor?'

'Blame this young lady, Enoch. Supposed to be making life easier for me, in fact makes me work twice as hard!'

'That's young ladies for you, isn't it?' He winked at Rosie. Muttering on his way back into the forge, 'Early hours then, three of you?'

'Yes.'

'Use that door there. It'll be unlocked. In quick and quiet, eh?'

'No drunken singing, you mean?'

He laughed. She reminded him, 'The doctor doesn't know anything about it, you know.'

'Don't worry. But even if he did —'

'Yes. Safe as houses. But still —'

'Wise old bird, that one.'

Peucat got the *gazo* moving. 'Murmuring sweet nothings to farriers now?'

'Reminding him that all you know is I've left the bike to be fixed.'

'Ah. Thank you.' Then: 'I hope it isn't very dangerous, whatever you're doing tonight?'

'I hope not, too.'

A sigh. Yellowish-faced, and sad spaniel's eyes. How she'd remember him . . . She added quickly, 'It's not. But there's still no reason you should be caught up in it. Pity *you* don't have an old flame in Paris.'

That made him laugh. They didn't talk much after that, on the way south to Landeleau and from there west to Châteauneuf. Tonight's action did in fact entail considerable danger: she was also aware that the after-effects wouldn't be *in*-considerable. Remembering Bob Hallowell's comment in London three weeks ago: *After 'Mincemeat', joint'll be fairly jumping* . . .

They were at Lannuzel's place by five. Neither Guy nor Brigitte were in sight, although the pickup was outside the barn. Peucat didn't get out of the car, only told her as she reached into the back for her valise, 'See you at breakfast. I'll look forward to it.' In other words, he'd have his fingers crossed from now to then. She smiled into the concerned brown eyes: 'Don't worry if I'm late. I could be held up. Won't be if I can help it — I'd *like* to go to Mass.'

'We'll go together.'

371

'Lovely.' She stepped back, he released the brake and the *gazo* was chugging down towards the road: she put her hand up to wave after it, but turned at Lannuzel's shout behind her: 'What's *his* rush?'

She thought it was probably a dislike of fare-wells: in circumstances like these anyway. She felt the same: had even developed a certain *tendresse* for him — while remembering that only a fort-night ago her first impression had been of a slightly eccentric drunk. She looked back towards the gate again, but he'd gone: taking his soft heart and paternal feelings with him. She went on up to join Lannuzel.

'He has to get back. Saturday's a busy day for him, and we came by way of Lezèle.'

'At a snail's pace, no doubt?'

'Well.' She smiled. 'There's no smell of burning rubber. Is my *gazo* here yet?'

'In there.' Jerk of a thumb towards the barn. 'I was just checking it over. It's a Peugeot — in good order, won't let us down.' Looking at her valise: 'Want to leave that in it?'

'Sooner hang on to it, thanks. What news from the château?'

'Yes, I'll tell you.' They started slowly towards the house. 'We've had it under surveillance — as you know. You were here Wednesday, weren't you. Oh, yes — I'm afraid I was a bit — edgy.'

'No bones broken.'

'Good. I'm — relieved . . . Anyway — Thurs-day morning, two bus-loads of U-boat crew departed, and later in the day the same buses brought another lot. It's the way they usually change over apparently — change the bedding and clean up, I suppose, between one lot going and the other coming. But, they took the new lot away again yesterday morning — after just one night's stay, huh?'

'Sure it was the *same* lot?'

'As many as they ever have there, so it must have been. But — also yesterday — four armoured troop carriers, and a lorry with tentage. Sixty, maybe eighty men, under canvas in the grounds now, at the rear of the château — so it wasn't them the U-boat boys were making room for. Then in the afternoon — about this time — the brass began arriving. Four big Mercedes with swastikas flying, and about ten smaller staff cars. Not all at once, not together. There've been supplies arriving too — vans, *Kriegsmarine* commissary, one supposes.'

'Any clues as to who came in the Mercedes?'

'No. Unfortunately. Seems observation was difficult. So many vehicles parked around the front, the main entrance. Also I've stressed the need for maximum caution — not to risk being spotted, have them suspect we're taking interest.'

'Right.'

'But you wouldn't get anything much less than admirals travelling in big cars with flags on them, would you?'

'I wouldn't think so. Another thing is Doenitz probably wouldn't spend the weekend here, would he? One night maximum, I'd guess: might even just come for the evening, make a speech and push off again. Possibly to Kernével — *that*'d serve him right . . . Anything else?'

'What sticks in my mind is the short-stay U-boat leave party. Seems to me they must have known at least as soon as we did that there was to be a conference this weekend, so why send them in the first place?'

'If some staff officer in Brest *wasn't* told?'

She didn't at that stage see it as important. Someone had decided to remove the submariners: to give the admirals and their minions more elbow-room, sole use of all the château's facilities — bathrooms, hot water, whatever. Maybe it was a bigger conference this time than on previous occasions. The château was fairly large but not all that vast: in any case might well not have many bathrooms.

'Let's go in.' Lannuzel put a hand on her arm. 'I should have said, by the way — it's good to see you again. And I'm *very* sorry —'

'Forget it. More important things to think about, aren't there. For instance — if Doenitz *is* still to come, and arrives — he'll be quite noticeable, presumably — will you be told?'

'Yes. At least, if he comes before dark. Although — no, come to think of it, I'll be leaving here at seven — and the lads know it, later than that they won't call . . . I was going to tell you, though — another report I had was that some of the transport left the château last night after dark.

374

Not the big Mercs, some of the others. Whatever that tells us.'

'Drivers or other non-essential personnel given the weekend off, perhaps. The Mercedes are still there, are they?'

'Clearly visible.'

'When they arrived, were they escorted?'

'Motorcycle outriders, yes. Doenitz would have the same, obviously.'

'Not necessarily, would you think?'

Looking at her, then nodding. 'Small car, no escort, no brass hat even?'

'If he's alert to the fact he might be a target — and could accept the loss of dignity?'

It was all speculation: a toss-up, who was there and who wasn't. All you could say was that who-ever *was* would stand a good chance of being killed tonight, and one *hoped* Messrs Doenitz, Bachmann and Godt might be among them.

Brigitte provided a *ragoût* of boiled chicken and parsnip at about six. She was noticeably tense: watching her brother and the clock. It would be easier for her, Rosie thought, if she were allowed to know what was going on, instead of picking up scraps and having to guess at the rest of it. Knowing she'd be alone here all night, in at least partial ignorance of events, wouldn't exactly help.

Before they ate, Lannuzel took Rosie to see the stolen *gazo*. He'd fuelled it but was going to provide extra fuel as well, he said.

'You know how to fire it up?'

'Of course.'

'Because you'll be starting at eight, you say —'

'About then. Get there before dark — with luck.'

Sunset would be at about a quarter to nine. If she was stopped along the way her story would be that she'd visited a friend in Châteauneuf and from there was *en route* to see a family in Landuda where a child was running a high temperature. Or Peucat would have asked her to make this call. And from Landuda she'd be returning to St Michel by the direct route through Briec and Pleyben. Driving permit — yes, here. *Ausweis* freeing her from curfew regulations — here . . .

As long as they didn't check the driving permit against the *gazo*'s registration. If they did, she'd say a grateful and kindly patient had lent it to her: she'd done so much cycling recently on her trips around the far-flung practice, and her employer was using his own *gazo* this evening in the opposite direction. But her poor legs . . .

Touch them tenderly. Give the sod a quick glimpse of one — if he looked as if that might help.

Best of all, of course, just *not* get stopped. If Lannuzel was right in saying they didn't have enough troops to police the whole area thoroughly, there was a reasonably good chance one wouldn't be.

If. It was conceivable that Jules de Seyssons was right, Lannuzel quite wrong. Looking at him across the table, wondering about that: he met her thoughtful gaze, and she switched it smilingly to Brigitte: 'Best meal I've had since I arrived. Do you two get sick of chicken?'

'Not really. We go in for barter too, of course. Anyway, come again — whenever you like. I'm always here even if Guy's not.'

'Yes. Please come. I leave her alone too much, I know.' Lannuzel pushed his chair back. 'As now — once again.' Blue eyes on Rosie's. He wasn't in the *least* like Ben. She'd realized it when she'd been here on Wednesday, wondered how she could ever have thought he was. Missing Ben, clutching at a straw, deluding herself that she'd found some pale shadow of a substitute? Lannuzel leaned over, kissed her cheek: 'Good luck, Suzanne. See you later . . . Brigitte — I'll see *you* some time tomorrow morning. Not early — mid-forenoon, I'd guess.'

'Meanwhile you're with Diane?'

He shrugged. 'Your own guess — if you like. *I* would only have said I had an engagement. Huh?'

Brigitte told Rosie, 'Diane's the local tart.'

'The slut?'

'Of course — we spoke of her—'

'Family joke, that's all.' He spoke from the doorway of the staircase. 'Makes for a believable alibi, in any case.'

'Except if they checked they might find she'd spent the night with a Boche corporal.' She'd said that for her brother's benefit, speaking up so he'd hear. Murmuring to Rosie then: 'Is he telling the truth, tonight's going to be easy?'

'Well — yes . . . Matter of fact . . .' Honesty then made her qualify that: 'There's one bit I'm not mad about — but it's very much his own, and he and his friends are happy with it. Know more about it than I do, too . . . Otherwise — given reasonably good luck —'

'Given any luck at all —' he was back, shrugging on his donkey-jacket — 'it's a cinch. Believe me.' Stooping to kiss his sister for a second time. '*Trust* me.' Pointing, as he straightened: 'Midmorning, I'll walk in that door.'

She started out just before eight, in prettily fading light. Twenty kilometres, roughly, to Briec, but at some point before that she'd turn down to Landuda, then make a right-angle turn to Moncouar, and go sharp left there for Lestonan via Kerongués. A bit of a zigzag: perhaps forty kilometres altogether.

Brigitte looked older than her years, when they said goodbye. Rosie had warned her about the air attack at midnight, assured her that her brother wouldn't be anywhere near it: she'd suggested: 'Best turn in, block your ears.' But her eyes especially: needing more reassurance than Rosie felt she could give. Nothing like this was ever a 'cinch'. And Brigitte had already lost a child — in what must have been terrifying circumstances — had for all she knew lost her husband too, and had now to face the possibility of losing her doting brother.

Rosie chided herself: *And you sometimes imagine you have problems.* Westbound through Châteauneuf-du-Faou . . . Two gendarmes were strolling through the market-place, didn't even glance at the stolen *gazo* as it passed them. Then outside the Hotel Belle Vue with its swastika banner dangling limply in the still evening air a parked *Wehrmacht* truck had soldiers in it and others standing around, seemingly waiting to embark. She'd been following a horse and cart at a slow walking pace, was now stopped altogether for several minutes while another cart inched by, coming this way.

Pig, she thought, sniffing. Looking then for Raoul: but it wasn't him. She wound the window up, and lit a cigarette. Seeing more young soldiers coming: a file of them, edging around the cart and passing between it and the *gazo*'s bonnet to the pavement, pushing through the others who were crowding there — but sauntering, glancing around, each in turn having a good look at her. Forage-caps, not helmets: lads in their teens or at most early twenties out for a Saturday-evening jaunt.

Looking for Diane, perhaps.

Moving — at last . . . Around that thing, then passing the cart too: through the town and out of it southwestward. Eight-twenty: the low fireball of the sun was blinding, brilliant orange between horizontal layers of black cloud.

There weren't any major turnings off this road,

not in its early stages. After about three kilometres there was a ninety-degree bend to the right, and the road followed the course of the river then for about one kilometre. The light on the water was fantastic. Thinking of this sunset and its colours spread all over: of bombers being prepared and armed on some English airfield under the same lit sky, for instance: and at Newhaven, where before his smash-up Ben and his friends would have been waiting for it to fade. They let it get dark or darkish before they sailed, he'd explained to her, in case of being spotted by *Luftwaffe* reconnaissance as they put to sea; their aim was to arrive on 'the other side' undetected, ready to spring surprises.

Or to take their chances. From the little he'd told her about it, she thought it must have been touch and go whether he'd get his boat back at all: they'd sunk something or other, then been trapped by some other force.

Now, she thought, all he had to watch out for was that Joan creature.

She was coming up to the bridge where the road swung left across the Aulne. Rattling over it. Thinking ahead again: after about a couple of kilometres there was a crossroads, of sorts, an intersection with a minor road which was also the direct route between Pleyben and Coray. About eight kilometres short of Briec, that would be. Briec might be a likely place for a road-block.

Might turn down sooner. There were two or three smaller roads — lanes — that would bring

380

one down to Landuda without going into Briec at all. Edern, that village just before Briec was called. She could see it in her memory — although with the blaze of sunset right in her face now she couldn't see much *here* . . . One hand up, and squinting into it: slowing a bit. Black silhouette of a little church, just off to the right: that *was* the Pleyben-Coray road . . .

And something going on . . . Slowing even more. There was a small crowd on the roadside, around a *gazo* truck. Right on the bend, obscuring whatever might be beyond it. A few people turning this way — waving at her — wanting her to stop? Looking at them as if she didn't quite comprehend: then she was past them, telling herself she couldn't have helped anyway: certainly couldn't have stopped, become caught up in God only knew what. *Some nurse, you are, Mlle Tanguy* . . . Could have been someone sick or dying: Nurse Tanguy mutters, *'Tant pis'*, drives on by.

Well — not being a total idiot . . .

Sharp right-hand bend coming up. There was a turning to the left there as well, she remembered: in fact that way you'd hairpin back to Trevarez — via Laz.

She'd made the bend, round to the right. The sun was down: the sky burnt-orange, the cloud all dissipated or scattered on the wind. Slowing again — for seven meandering cows herded by two small, ragged boys. Emaciated — cattle and boys . . . Le Guen would be on his way by this time, she guessed. And in the Château de Tre-

381

varez the nobs would be at dinner. At the trough: last guzzle — for some of them, anyway. Le Guen *would* have set out, she thought: he had only six or seven kilometres to come, but he'd have been twitching with nerves all day and he wouldn't willingly have risked being caught out after curfew. Clear of the straggle of cows now, accelerating again: deliberating whether to take the next turn to the left — in roughly four kilometres. It would be a left turn with a right fork almost immediately after it, and it would save her having to pass through Edern, where several small roads impinged and there might be a road-block.

But there wouldn't be, surely. A kilometre further along, a similar block in Briec would cover the north-south road as well as this one.

But the north-south road mightn't interest them, since it didn't lead anywhere near Trevarez?

Make your silly mind up!

OK. Next turn left . . .

Car coming up behind, rather fast.

She slowed a bit, and eased in closer to the right. Slits of masked headlights growing and brightening in the Peugeot's rear-view mirror made the surroundings darker still. All the colour overhead had gone. The car behind was closing up fast enough to be petrol-engined. First car in either direction for several minutes, as it happened.

Come on, come on . . .

Hanging back there. Reminding her of those

Boche louts when she'd been getting towards Loudéac. It definitely had slowed.

Gendarmerie looking for a stolen *gazo*?

About a kilometre to go to the turn, she guessed. Wondering whether it would be wise to take it or better to carry on, if this thing was still behind her when she got there. Carrying on would mean chancing her luck in Edern, while turning left — well, you'd be leading them into a patch of country where you'd be better off without them.

Landuda, though. She did have an address to call at. *That* story'd stand up, all right. At least, if they didn't check on the *gazo*'s registration.

She saw the convoy then. The car behind her had dropped back a little, and on the left-hand side of the road — which for about a kilometre was virtually dead straight just here — there was a line of heavy *Wehrmacht* trucks parked on the verge. They weren't showing lights. Figures moved around them: the flare of a match or lighter lit a pale face under a helmet and another leaning close. Rosie counted the big trucks as she passed them: seven — eight — nine . . .

Nine. All behind her now, she had only the rear-view mirror to go by — seeing the car that had been behind her pulling over to that side, its seepage of headlight washing the sides of trucks as it bounced up on to the verge beside them. Its lights went out, then: and she was having to concentrate on the road ahead, in order not to miss the left-turn that had to be coming up — any moment now.

There . . .

And she was on her own: no traffic from either direction to see her make the turn: she took it carefully, unhurriedly: and then more or less at Peucat-pace through the lanes. Dusk deepening over lush, spring-scented countryside — and having it to herself. Relief was tinged by worry over that parked convoy, though. There could be about twenty men in each of those trucks, and there'd been nine of them — pointing towards Châteauneuf-du-Faou, apparently killing time, and joined then by a staff car from the direction of Châteauneuf.

Didn't *have* to mean a bloody thing.

A couple of hundred men, though: with Laz — what, about six kilometres from them, if they took that right fork?

At the Niver corner — a little church — she turned right. Still making for Landuda, but by what was probably a shorter route — via a hamlet called St Adrien. Photographic memory plus absorption of maps' details came in useful, at times like this. At St Adrien — there'd be no roadsign, at most you'd see a few cottages, farm buildings — she'd go straight over, turn left at the crossroads after that one. The alternative to passing through Landuda would have been to get on the Briec–Quimper road for a kilometre or so, turn off it again at Moncouar. But she thought that would be the worse risk of the two — which it might well have been, since Landuda when she

384

got to it turned out to be a ghost-village: nothing moving, not a glimmer of light anywhere. Ten or fifteen minutes past nine, she guessed — when she drove into it southward and out again westward, seeing no living soul and as far as she knew being seen by no one. She couldn't read her watch in the *gazo*'s dark cab, but that was what it had to be.

Near enough four kilometres from here to Moncouar.

Those trucks must be on some night exercise, she told herself. Waiting for the dark: and/or for the rendezvous with whoever had been in the car. An umpire controlling the exercise, perhaps. Nothing to do with Trevarez, or Kerongués.

Well — *obviously* nothing to do with Kerongués . . .

At Moncouar she turned sharp left in the southern end of the village, without touching the main road at all; she was heading south then, for the bridge between Gougastel and Kerongués. Distance to Lestonan about five kilometres: six, say, to the Perrot farm. Where le Guen *might* be already.

Scared stiff, no doubt. It was going to be a long, long evening, sitting with him in that kitchen, trying to calm his nerves. Roll on Lezèle, she thought: final handshake, good luck, François. Those had been heavy-going sessions that she'd had with him, and tonight wasn't likely to be much better.

That was Gougastel she'd pounded through.

Bridge just ahead now. Odd that they'd selected this point to bridge the Odet — just where it widened. Anywhere to the east of this you could practically have spat across it. There it was, anyway: she was braking, slowing, then grinding over: off the bridge then, she was in Kerongués. Marie-Claude within a few hundred metres of her. Passing the sign at that turn-off that led back towards the river and the prison camp, thinking of the shock the kid would have when Lannuzel and his friends had her brought out to them. Rosie had suggested this evening that he might let her know what was happening as soon as he safely could, so she wouldn't be left wondering for any longer than might be necessary whether she was being taken to be shot.

Now the Lestonan fork. Bearing left: with only about four hundred metres to go from here. She could already see the poplars ahead there on the left: and soon after, lower down, the ridge of the barn's roof against a few early stars. Nine twenty-five, she guessed. Braking sharply: that was the entrance, where the trees stopped. As she turned into it, she flicked the lights off — not keen to have Perrot's neighbours come investigating. She could see the corner of the barn easily enough without the lights — and the nearer end of the squat little house further back . . . Swinging the wheel over: around that corner into the yard and stopping, then reversing up close to the house but where the end of the barn cut off any view in from the road. Stink of cows, or slurry. Lannuzel would have plenty of room to drive in — in about three hours' time. Or two and a half, say. In, and straight into the barn.

She switched off.

No sounds, no movements — except for sound from the *gazo*'s burner. When it had cooled, she'd refuel — as requested. Fuel — charcoal — was in the boot, parcelled in an old tarpaulin.

There was no light showing from the house. Not that one would have expected any. Even if le Guen was in there. The odds were he'd be crouched in a corner with his teeth chattering. Thinking of that as a characteristic, not in a condemnatory sense. People had or acquired different levels of stress tolerance, that was all. She pulled her valise up close and opened it, delved into the bottom of it for her gun, and transferred it to the right-hand pocket of her coat. Feeling for the safety-catch with her thumb, sliding it off then on again. She left the valise where it was, for the moment, opened her door and got out, closed it soundlessly and started towards the other end of the house. The door at the roadside end was the one into the kitchen, Lannuzel had mentioned. She passed the nearer one without even trying it, therefore. There was cow-shit all over the yard, right up to the house wall: luckily the pats seemed to be mostly hard. When you trod in a soft one, she thought, you'd know it.

She was a couple of metres from the door when she heard a car coming. Cars plural, in fact, but at first she thought only one. She froze, close to the wall. The car was coming from the south, the main road, and swept past, travelling fast — or seemingly fast, in such a narrow lane: she saw the swift passing flare of its lights as the engine-note peaked and began to fall, but a second one was coming — close behind it and exactly the same. Petrol smell then as well as cow. She heard the noise fading northward, and could tell they'd taken the right fork — for Kerongués and the bridge, the way she'd come about two minutes earlier. She stayed where she was, listening — for any more that might be coming, or for those two returning: coming *here,* maybe, having realized they'd shot past? Nothing, though, only the deepening quiet. They might have gone over the bridge, or have turned off to the Kerongués prison: but petrol-engined cars travelling in company by night and at that kind of speed would almost certainly be Gestapo or SD.

But then again — why not? That *was* an internment camp. They obviously would visit it, from time to time. Just as the military did conduct night exercises, troop convoys did stop on roadsides, on occasion.

Deep breaths, Rosie. Slow the thing down . . .

The door *had* been forced — as promised. She pushed at it — gently, but the hinges were stiff and needed a solid shove. Left hand on the door, right one finding the gun in her pocket. She called softly into the house, 'François? François, it's me — Zoé . . .'

Gun out — at sudden movement —

Cat — or large rat. There'd been a thump, then a skittering sound. Nothing human. She could smell lamp-oil and feel the kitchen's warmth, but she was alone here, could feel that too, now.

Telephone . . .

Peucat jerked awake. He'd dozed off at his desk, where he'd begun a letter to one of his daughters. Had managed only three or four lines, he saw, before dropping off. An empty glass, and a three-quarters empty bottle: and heaven knew where the next might come from. Poor old Timo: and Adèle. God give them strength . . . He shuffled across the room and through to the hall, where the phone had just rung again.

'Peucat.'

'Call for you from Quimper. Hold on . . .'

'Yes? This time of night? Who's —'

'Henri — it's me . . .'

'Paul?'

Paul Berthomet. Peucat reached to a light-switch and checked the time: It was a few minutes to ten. Late enough, but it felt even later. He'd have thought his old friend would have been in bed by now — snuggled up to old Sylvie's not inconsiderable bulk . . .

One of them ill, he guessed. Or worse — Sylvie'd been living on borrowed time for years.

'Henri?'

'What's wrong, Paul?'

'Well — I've a fellow here — don't know him from Adam, just came banging on the door, but

I think — he *seems* to be straight, and he's given me certain evidence, not proof exactly but —'

'What are you talking about, Paul?'

'I'd better just put him on. Please — M'sieur . . .'

'Dr Peucat —'

'Yes?'

'Forgive this intrusion. My name's Prigent. I have a most urgent message for a young woman who may go by any name at all but to me used the pseudonym "Zoé". She won't be with you now, I know — unfortunately —'

'I don't know anyone called Zoé.'

'It was to you, at your number, she arranged for a message from a person by name of le Guen to be passed by M. Berthomet here — wouldn't that identify her to you?'

'What's this about?'

'Doctor — if you know how to contact her or any of her friends —'

'What friends?'

'Colleagues. I hoped there might be a telephone —'

'I've no idea — where, or of any telephone, or even what you're telling me!'

'Her colleagues then. Far as she's concerned, *I'll* try . . . But anyone associated with her or — this thing tonight. It's blown, doctor — all of it. Whatever they're doing — Trevarez or Kerongués, wherever — they're in a trap, *that's* what I'm telling you. I'm finished too — I'm on my way out: *en route* I'll *try,* but —'

'This is gibberish, to me. Whoever you are —'

'Michel Prigent. If you have any way of contacting them — call them off, tell them to clear out, quick. Le Guen — who dropped your message here? — he's in SD hands, whatever he knew, assume *they* know. So — up to you, doctor . . .'

A voice in the background — Paul's: 'If that's all now, M'sieur — I'll speak to him again.'

'Very well . . .'

'Henri?'

'Yes — Paul, you *believe* this, you say?'

'Whatever it is, *he* means it. All I want to say is — Henri, look after *yourself* now. Whatever else is going on — I beg you . . .'

'You needn't worry about me. But I must be quick now. Paul — thank you!'

Sylvie's voice from the background: 'Give him my love!'

'You heard that. Mine too, Henri. Good luck.'

The line went dead. Peucat made sure of it, then joggled the telephone rest. His eyes were watering; he wiped at them with his sleeve, muttering, 'Oh, please, please —'

'Yes, caller?'

He gave her the Millau number at Châteauneuf. 'As quickly as possible, please?'

'I'll try. Lines seem to be busy, all over. All of a sudden . . .'

'My call really is — very urgent —'

'All right, doctor.'

'Oh — you know who —'

'Naturally. Who *doesn't* know Dr Peucat of St Michel-du-Faou?'

'Well, I just had a call from a raving lunatic . . . Anyway — if you could be quick, please?'

'Well, don't hang up . . .'

Nightmare. Eyes screwed shut again. The name Prigent did ring a bell of sorts: there was a dentist in Quimper of that name . . .

'You're connected, doctor!'

'Thank you *very* much . . . Hello?'

'Henri — that you?'

'Brigitte — my dear girl. I suppose Guy's not with you?'

'No. Won't be back tonight either. But why, what — ?'

'Listen. Are you able to get in touch with him — or any of them?'

'No. Well — I know where they were going to . . . But — what's the time now? After ten? Anyway — has something gone wrong?'

'I had a call, a minute ago — a warning. Someone who used a different name for — you know, my assistant — he said it's blown, it's a trap, whatever they're doing they must pull out — *immediately,* or —'

'Mother of God . . .'

'Is there any way we could get a message to him?'

He heard a breath like a gasp. Then: 'If I go myself. The *only* way. I need a minute to *think* . . . No — Henri, I *will* go. At once, I'll —'

'Be careful? Take care, Brigitte — my *dear,* if *I* could do it —'

'You can't. *You* take care. Goodbye . . .'

He wondered whether the operator would have been listening. And whether there was anything else he could do. It seemed obvious there wasn't, though. All he could do was get his bag down: it was three-quarters packed already, always was.

Warn Marthe?

He decided against it. She had no connection with Guy Lannuzel or anyone else down there — or with Suzanne either. She'd be safer left *un*-warned, clearly uninvolved. Suzanne, though — her radio, somewhere in the attic . . .

Ten o'clock had passed. Still no François. Rosie was outside, refuelling the *gazo*. There was a shaving of moon up there now, giving enough light to work by. Enough for le Guen to find his way by, you'd have thought.

Or to be seen by, and stopped, and questioned. If he was stopped now he'd be infringing curfew, would stand to be arrested.

Or — funked it?

Suppose he didn't turn up at all? Facing this as a possibility, and putting one's mind to it calmly, logically . . . When Lannuzel and his team got here — with Marie-Claude, touch wood — it would be primarily *her* loss, absence of Papa. It would make things more difficult — if she was anything like her father — and then it would become the Scrignac gamekeeper's problem. No father to look after her, only this young, fright-ened girl to be found a refuge somewhere or other. Vannier would work it somehow: he knew them all, he'd take her to some group that already included women. Or — conceivably, Rosie thought — Sara de Seyssons might over-rule her husband's veto and take her in. Suggest this to Vannier, maybe: as a request directly from herself — Suzanne Tanguy — to Sara. The annoying thing, though — if le Guen *had* let one down — although she didn't see how he could have or would have, at any rate not of his own volition — was that this Kerongués end of the business had been set up solely for his benefit.

Needn't have bothered. As in fact Lannuzel had proposed. Use le Guen, then forget him — and his daughter. A proposal which she'd instantly rejected. Folding the tarpaulin back into the *gazo*'s boot, and pushing the lid down quietly: could slam it shut properly later, she thought, when getting the thing fired up, making a noise in any case. At say ten minutes to midnight. Open the barn doors then too. With le Guen here by that time — please God. There was a far bigger issue involved than just the problem of the girl being on her own: she hadn't yet squared up to it — to the total disaster she was foreseeing at this moment — *if* he wasn't coming.

A fox screamed, not more than fifty metres away. Eerie, nerve-tautening sound . . .

Time — the watch-face by moonlight — ten twenty-five. She went back to the kitchen door, picking her way over and around cowpats. Pausing at that end of the little house then, straining her ears for the sound of an approaching bicycle, tyre-noise and the rattle of the frame, an unfit cyclist's hard pumping breaths as he forced the thing along. As if by listening for it she might conjure it into being. Needing to — because it definitely was *not* just a matter of the peace of mind of Marie-Claude, it was the near-certainty — which one *had* previously envisaged — that if le Guen were arrested and tortured he'd tell them everything. The only way he might not would be if he died of fright before it started. Which regrettably one could hardly count on. There'd be a lot they'd want to know, and one of the things he would be able to tell them about was 'Zoé'.

So — if he didn't show up . . .

She sat at Jacques Perrot's stained and scarred kitchen table, put the pistol down in front of her, lit about her fifteenth cigarette and tried to think up any way that she might avoid having to run for it. Solid, immovable facts being one, he *would* be arrested and tortured, and two, he wouldn't find it possible to hold out for any length of time at all. He'd tell them everything he knew about her: and about 21B Place Saint-Matthieu, and those old people — who'd *try* not to tell the bastards anything, but — well, if their hearts didn't pack up quickly enough there'd be a straight line from them in their agony to Henri Peucat and his assistant Suzanne Tanguy — whom they'd inevitably recognize as 'Zoé'.

Incontrovertible — if François didn't show.

If he didn't, therefore — *what?*

See Marie-Claude on her way, would be the first thing. Maybe travel with her and Vannier up to Scrignac. That was in the right direction, anyway. Make for the coast, then, contact one of the *réseaux* who handled the Dartmouth motor-gunboats' secret landing and embarkation places. From this part of the country those were the obvious ways out: and with Peucat's house by then obviously unapproachable there'd be no way of getting to her radio to ask Baker Street for a Lysander pick-up — then hanging around somewhere or other waiting for an answer.

She rested her forehead on the gun's cold steel on the table. Thinking — well, the unthinkable, this nightmare scenario. If they had him already: had had him for an hour or two, say, had already broken him down, had the information gushing out of him — jerking out, spasms between screams — one tried *not* to visualize it . . . But he knew about Trevarez — at least that there was some unspecified action planned — and certainly about Kerongués. So Lannuzel and his friends — who at this moment would still be congregating on the broken-down farm near Laz . . .

She shut it out. Praying into the silent, odorous night: *François — get a bloody move on, please?*

Some time before eleven a truck of some kind passed. Something heavy and petrol-driven, more likely to be military than civilian. Hearing its approach she'd got up, moved to the door: the hinge side, where she'd be hidden if it was opened:

waiting with her hand on the pistol in her pocket. It might stop, turn in here — if they'd been working on le Guen already?

The pistol was a comfort anyway. Its main solace was as a guarantee that they would not get to work on *her*.

The truck had seemed to be slowing, but as it turned out she'd been mistaken, it was actually picking up speed as it approached and — now — thundered past.

She checked the time, slanting her watch again to the haze of moonlight in the doorway. Four minutes to eleven. About an hour now, was all le Guen had. Hour and a quarter maximum — by Lannuzel's projection. Lannuzel would be sending the Trevarez force on its way about now: then setting out himself in company with le Faisan and the others . . . But le Guen could still be coming — was still only an hour late, against the deadline she'd given him of ten o'clock; he *could* have been held up by — well, trouble with his bike, say. If it had buckled a wheel, for instance. Or been stolen: just not there when he'd gone for it, so he'd have had to set out on foot. It was entirely possible. Poor maligned François limping along, doing his best, still coming . . .

Otherwise — get out there just before midnight, stop them at the bridge?

It was warm in the kitchen and she was damp inside her clothes. Struggling to come to terms with the irrefutable logic in regard to her own position if he was *not* coming. Having to pull out with the job barely started but people already used to her, relying on her. Not least, old Henri . . .

She went out into the yard again. The remnant of a moon had drifted some distance across the sky since her last sight of it. Shadows had lengthened here, shortened there. She went over to the *gazo*, leant against it. An owl hooted: and another, further away. The sound took her back to Passenham in Buckinghamshire, her uncle's place: it was supposed to be haunted by a cavalier who on one night of the year was allegedly dragged screaming from the stirrup of a horse galloping along the river-bank and through a brick wall into the next-door rectory. When Rosie had been younger she'd wanted to sit up for it, but her stupid mother had never let her.

Car.

To the south — coming from the main road. She edged round into the space between the *gazo* and the wall of the house, in the shadow and shelter of the *gazo*'s bulk. She heard a gear-change: petrol engine revving-up then, another change of gear . . .

They used this lane because of the bridge up there, she reminded herself. That was all. It would pass as the others had — in a matter of seconds, now.

It was slowing, though. No mistake this time, definitely slowing. She crouched, with the gun in her right hand, left hand on the *gazo*'s right rear mudguard. The car was close now, and by the sound of it down to a crawl. Its driver — she felt certain — looking for the farm entrance. Coming from that direction the screen of poplars hid the opening until you were right on it: so anyone who didn't know the place would have to approach it slowly.

Might drive in, look around and drive out again. People did make mistakes . . .

Don't do anything damn silly, Rosie.

She wasn't going to be arrested, though. On *no* account was going to be arrested. Hearing it arrive — and now turn in — tyres scrunching in mud, stones, cowshit: low weakish beam of light from one masked headlamp, the flush of it brightening that corner of the barn, lighting the end of the house too . . . Then both headlamps in sight as it rounded the corner and weak light flooded the whole yard.

She'd left the kitchen door ajar. *Damn.* Door half open and the *gazo* standing here. They weren't likely to decide *No one at home . . .*

Not *they. He.*

Getting out. Bulky in a belted coat and wide-brimmed hat tilted slightly forward. Standard plain-clothes Gestapo outfit. Her brain took note of it, while her skin crackled and her heart began to pound as if it was trying to break out. She noted also as he rounded the bonnet of his car — he'd parked it slanting across the entrance to the yard — that it was a Citröen Light 15 saloon, probably just pre-war, front-wheel drive, top speed about 120 kph, paintwork dark grey or black. A Gestapo vehicle, beyond question.

He was clear of it, moving towards the half-open door, placing his feet carefully.

Look around inside, decide the bird's flown, climb back in, then beat it?

But he was bound to take a close look at this *gazo,* when he came out of there.

Get *under?* Might not look under it? Get down in the muck in preference to getting dead?

Although — thinking more positively — in the short term, one had the advantage here. Had him on toast: if the right tactic was to kill him. Not difficult: she was more than competent with this gun — and with him in the open, approaching the *gazo* as he would after he'd satisfied himself the house was empty . . . The question was, what might follow . . . Take his car, take *off?*

But then if le Guen turned up: or Lannuzel with the girl . . .

Le Guen wouldn't, though. They'd got le Guen. No other way this man would have known to come here.

He was at the kitchen door, had pushed it further open with his foot. A big man, Trilby-type hat, belted coat or raincoat. A torch flared in his hand, probing into the kitchen. He'd have a pistol in the other.

'Zoé?'

It was a shock — to hear her name called. But then puzzling, too. He'd spoken quietly — which was right out of character, for his kind. Either he had reason not to attract more attention than he had to, or — this didn't make sense, but — imagining he could con her into thinking he'd no hostile intentions?

Because he was on his own? They usually worked in pairs. One on his own wasn't normal: no more so than that quiet call had been. He was inside now: she saw flashes of the torch as he poked its beam around.

Her valise was on the floor beside the table.

She'd brought it in in order to get two chicken sandwiches and the spare clip of 9-millimetre out of it. Had been careful with cigarette stubs, and forgotten *that*. Now he'd know for certain. Confirmation of her identity, even, if they knew anything much about her. And there was only one other downstairs room and a wash-room-scullery to look in. A sort of stepladder led to two rooms upstairs which he might check.

'Zoé?' A pause, then again, louder: 'Zoé? If you're here, Zoé —'

In the doorway again: a dark swelling and the brim of the hat, and the torch-beam: the doorway itself partially hid him. It was the torch-beam she saw mostly: at this moment it was directed across the yard at the closed barn door. Swinging her way now — as he emerged — to spotlight the *gazo*. She was crouching, with her head down: not only not to be seen — in the dark or near-dark, eyes and facial skin reflected light — but also not to be blinded by the torch. He'd moved well out into the yard: the beam moving around a bit but coming back to her now. She rose — very slowly, and edging to her right — keeping the chimney of the burner between herself and him, stooping in its cover and with the gun up: she was aware of the importance of hitting and killing with her first shot. He'd stopped, half turned, the torch-beam swinging back to light the open kitchen door: hadn't looked into the loft, she guessed, had suddenly guessed she — someone — might have come down from there, behind him. In that second or two she'd have had him cold, but the light was back on her now — on the *gazo* . . .

'Zoé — hear me? It's Michel Prigent. Listen — we've got — probably only minutes. The whole thing's blown — I phoned Peucat, asked him to contact your — associates. Le Guen told me this was where he had to meet you — the SD have him now, had him since Thursday — you know what *that* means — Zoé?' She had the pistol in both hands, steady on the smudge of face below the hat brim. Safety-catch off . . . Actually on the point of killing him, brain as if in shock then, major effort to accept he *could* be who he said he was. Le Guen must have been arrested — so this *was* the disaster scenario — but the dentist might have been taken too. Although the voice was right — as she recalled it. She'd taken up the slack on the trigger . . .

'Don't move. *Don't.*' He'd visibly reacted — couldn't have known for sure she was here. Her voice croaked at him, 'Arms away from your sides. That pistol — *drop* it. Drop it! Now — shine the torch on your own face — push your hat back with it —'

Chapter 16

'So *where* — ?'

'Short of Plouescat.' He'd swung the car out in reverse, accelerated fast down to the T-junction on the main road and turned right — towards Quimper . . . Answering the question she hadn't finished: 'Plouescat's too near the coast. If by some miracle we make it that far we'll leave this car — well, it's a safe-house —'

'What if we're stopped?'

'You're my prisoner, I'm taking you to Morlaix. Anyway until we're a few miles short of the place. But — worst comes to the worst — we're both armed, make the best of it. Separate maybe — play it as it comes. D'you have a contact in Plouescat — if you were on your own?'

Crossfire of questions and answers: getting his answers and giving him hers, but still only scratching the surface, dozens more to come. Conclusions too — mostly sickening. That there'd be no admirals in the château when the RAF hit it, for instance: they'd have gone in the cars that had departed after dark last night — if they'd come at all, which they might well *not* have: le Guen had been in the SD's hands since Thursday, Prigent had told her. He — Prigent — had a profile like a Roman emperor's — high-bridged nose, heavy jowls. The most trivial question she'd asked him had been about this car — before they'd even got into it, when he'd been opening up the barn so she could drive the *gazo* in out of sight. He'd snapped, 'Tell you later — let's get away from here?'

Panicking a bit: but under the skin, who wasn't . . . Telling her then disjointedly later that it did belong to the Gestapo: 'No, *not* SD, Gestapo . . .' A French Gestapo driver who was — or had been — his own agent . . . Then about the call to Peucat, about which he'd begun to tell her and she'd interrupted with, 'Why Quimper, heaven's sake?'

'Because there's a lot going eastward, very little *into* town. As I say — unless your friend Peucat did have some way to get on to them . . . I *tried,* but if he doesn't — well, Christ —'

'One way he might.'

'*Would* have, then — wouldn't he?'

'Yes.' Brigitte, she was thinking of. Peucat could have phoned her: in fact she thought he would have. She wasn't likely to have the telephone number of the farm near Laz — Lannuzel in his obstinacy wouldn't have let her have it — but she *had* known the farm and that it was the rendezvous he'd been making for when he'd left; she'd mentioned it this evening when they'd been on their own. Rosie repeated — feeling sure that if Peucat had phoned Brigitte she'd have got there somehow — 'Yes. And I think he would.' Traffic flaring past: even some masked headlights could be dazzling. High vehicles, she supposed, the downward-slanting beams caught you just for a second. 'Which road *out* of Quimper?'

'Over the river and on to the Briec road. Once we're out and heading north —'

'Yes.' Might be less like Russian roulette, then. *Slightly* less . . . They'd be on the road on which a couple of hours ago she'd been unwilling to travel for even one kilometre. A risk that looked daunting in normal circumstances became quite acceptable when the stakes were suddenly jacked sky-high like this. But they'd also be on a route which the SD might not think it unlikely that he, Prigent, would take: if they knew he'd made a bolt for it. She didn't mention this: no point, really. In fact she was coming to see it his way now — After only minutes, and numerous changes of subject — with such a lot of ground to cover. And seconds counted: you couldn't sit around conferring. There might already be Boches at the Perrot place. Prigent's guess was they'd set up an ambush at the fork in Kerongués where there was that sign in French and German. They'd want to bag the lot or certainly all the leaders, and they'd do it quietly — lining hedgerows and ditches, showing no lights and leaving no transport visible.

So if Lannuzel had *not* had the tip-off from Henri . . .

Thinking of Henri's 'See you at breakfast.' Just a few hours ago. Breakfast, then Mass. 'We'll go together.' Christ . . .

'You said you phoned Peucat from the Berthomets. But how did you . . .' She tapped her own forehead: 'Oh. Le Guen, *he* —'

'Told me, yes. Well — the address, that's all.'

'All he knew. On Wednesday, you said that was?'

Three *Wehrmacht* troop-transports — head on, thundering past, out of the darkness and back into it: *whoosh* — *whoosh* — *whoosh* . . .

Gone. Faint glow of tail-lights already faded.

'Scraped up some more from somewhere. Out of the bars and brothels, maybe. Those'll turn up to the left at Coray, I suppose. Couldn't doubt le Guen's spilled it all now, could you?'

'They've had him since Thursday, you said.'

A grunt . . . 'Only heard last night.'

But *anyone* might have it spilled it all, by now. She changed the subject: 'Those trucks — there was a convoy of nine parked on the Châteauneuf-Briec road —'

'Really?' He'd interrupted her: 'Bridge ahead here now. Just praying it's not blocked. Doubt it would be — waste of their own time and manpower, this far from the action . . . About le Guen, though — yes, Wednesday — he came for one of our regular sessions and I grilled him. I'd had him followed, see.'

'Why?'

'Well.' He'd slowed a bit: they were approaching the bridge over the Odet: were on it now, humming over: moonlight glittering down there on black, fast-running water. 'Had my people keep eyes on him, anyway. One of 'em was with him when he made his drop in Place Saint-Matthieu. Saturday, that was . . .'

'*Why* have him tailed?'

'Because I smelt double-dealing. With you as chief suspect.'

'*Me?*'

A snort of humour. They were off the bridge now. 'Sound so surprised . . . My girl saw the two of you meet on Sunday, for God's sake. That was when you gave him the time and place for tonight's rendezvous — correct? Well, I *know* it, he told me. But heavens, why *wouldn't* I take an interest — fellow hates my guts — OK, he's entitled, I don't mind — comes twitching along saying he's thought better of it, where his duty lies, all that cock . . .' Braking, slowing in short pumping jerks: the junction was coming up, the Briec turn. 'I'm supposed to believe in this change of heart. I know it's possible he's working for the SD — there's one called Fischer who calls in at the *Kommandantur* quite often, and I remember wondering if our friend wasn't a touch cagey when the name was mentioned . . . But — I don't know, didn't credit him with the guts, somehow. Silly of me, I suppose: but it was *your* part in it that intrigued me. We've had little differences between us before this, haven't we — my outfit and yours?'

'One's heard of — friction. But I've worked for your people before this, I might mention.'

'I gathered so . . . Wouldn't light me a cigarette, would you?'

407

'Why not . . . Anyway, you faced le Guen with all this on Wednesday — at your surgery — and he told you about the message-drop on the previous Saturday.'

'Admitted it — I already *knew* about it. But he told me everything. Starting with an assertion that he was on my side — your side, my side, same thing, in his view — all right, it *is*, fundamentally — and only *pretending* to work for the SD because they had his daughter in Kerongués, so forth, and you were getting her out somehow, he'd be going *au vert* with her tonight.' Another snort: 'How you persuaded him into *that* — well, I take my hat off to you. But this was my first clear intimation that the SD were on to me.' He took the lighted cigarette from her. 'Thanks. And obviously I had to consider bailing out.' A long drag at the Gaullois. 'Got a message away — Wednesday night — and the answer came *last* night saying yes, pull out, and confirming they'd had a tip-off to the same effect — that I was blown — from SOE and originating with *you*. So now you tell *me*.'

'I will. But sticking to the subject for the moment — you went to Place Saint-Matthieu — ?'

'I'd like to clear my mind on *this* first. I'd been slow on it — on their having me under surveillance. I think it must have started after I'd recruited le Guen — and pressured him a bit much. That was — unwise. But you see I'd had reassuring inside information, I thought I knew I was considered to be OK. For one thing I'd informed on a so-called *Résistant* — about six months ago —'

'*You* did?'

'Double agent — a woman. Considerable threat to us. But the SD didn't know I knew that side of it, in fact they had reason to believe I couldn't have known. Wouldn't have expected me to — just a bloody dentist?'

'In their good books, anyway.'

'There were other reasons to believe so. The man whose job it is to drive this car is one source. A driver with sharp ears picks up a lot, you know.'

'What happens when the car's missed?'

'First thing tomorrow's the likely time. Yard broken into, chain on the gate cut through —'

'But if they're pulling out all the stops tonight?'

'Oh, it's possible. Anything is. But not probable.'

'Are we all right for petrol?'

'Yes. Tank's kept full.'

'Will he know it was you who took it?'

'Probably — but that doesn't matter. As long as his superiors don't guess he knows. *They*'ll put two and two together — once they know I'm on the run.' He cursed under his breath: easing the car over to the right, the narrow verge: the road was also narrow here and two other vehicles were coming around the long bend, the second of them swinging out wider than he should have: that had been a car like this one, and the leader a Mercedes: they'd bombed past, and Prigent had scraped this one's right side along a hedge that had sounded like it had barbed wire in it. Thorn, more likely. '*Salauds* . . .'

She began, 'If they already know you've taken off — and they do find it's gone —'

'Forget it. There's no obvious connection.' Shifting gear for the incline and the right fork that was coming up. 'And it'll be under cover by first light — God willing. What I was saying, Zoé — I learnt from le Guen on Wednesday that they were on to me — using *him*. But you were wise to it before that, weren't you. When did he tell you?'

'It was —' she put her mind back — 'Wednesday, I think. No — Tuesday.'

'Of *last* week.'

'Yes. I was in Quimper on the Tuesday and the Wednesday.'

'He told you this on the Tuesday — April second, that was. You notified London — when?'

'The next day — Wednesday. The soonest I could get a signal out.'

'Couldn't you have notified me directly?'

'No.' She knew what he was driving at: had seen it from the start — and thanked God she *had* decided to tell Baker Street when she had. Remembering that period of dilemma, and telling Prigent — as the offside wheels slammed jarringly through an exceptionally deep pothole — 'I'm sorry — couldn't. Knowing your line might be tapped — and already wishing I hadn't called you before, incidentally — using the name "Zoé" as I did — they might have been on to you *then*, for

410

all I knew — and if so, after that call they might well have been looking for me.'

'So what did you tell your people, that Wednesday?'

'As part of a longer message, as far as I remember it, *Micky reports Cyprien cover blown.*'

'You sent that ten days ago — and it came in this morning. Last night, actually, but to me this morning. Ten days after you'd told them!'

'I couldn't have contacted you direct. You *can* see that?'

'It's the ten-day gap that's the point. "F" Section hears from you that Wednesday, picks up a scrambler to my people within the hour — I'd have known by the morning of Thursday the fourth — nine days ago. We'll be passing through Moncouar in a minute. Could be — slightly crucial . . .'

Slightly. Grimacing to herself in the darkness, and touching the gun in her pocket . . . Moncouar being a point of access to the lanes leading down to and around the bridge and Kerongués and Lestonan. It was about as likely a spot for a road-block as could be imagined. Time now — she couldn't see it. Not less than eleven-thirty, anyway. She took a long pull at her cigarette, to get a glow of light from it, close to the dial. Eleven thirty-two.

Bombers in the air yet?

Ready for take-off, at least. Pathfinders first, of course. Perhaps thundering down the runway now, this moment.

Those Mercedes left in view at the château would be bait, nothing else. If the naval staff were meeting this weekend it wouldn't be at Trevarez. But to trap and annihilate a large force of Maquis — and perhaps as a by-blow get to their arms dumps, through torture of those captured — would be well worth the loss of a few old Mercs. The admirals might be glad to get new ones.

He'd eased the speed down a little, in preparation for Moncouar coming up. Taking the cigarette out of his mouth, clearing his throat . . . 'The puzzle of not hearing from London until last night — perhaps academic, here and now. Especially as I've known since Wednesday. It still intrigues me, rather. Why London would have sat on the information for so long. Eh?'

Because I asked them to . . .

She said, 'No doubt when we get to London —'

'*When!*'

'Has to be *some* explanation.' Crossing her fingers. There wouldn't be. Baker Street weren't going to open their files to SIS — not in one's own lifetime — or ever . . . She asked him, artlessly, 'What about your people or person here, however your signals come and go?'

'No. That's not the answer.' Cigarette between his lips again now, both hands on the wheel. 'But as you say — wash the dirty linen if and when we make it back . . . Here's Moncouar.'

It might have been better to have gone via Châteaulin, she thought, taken the left fork five kilometres back and steered slightly wider around the general area of all this. Slightly longer route, was all: but time *was* a somewhat vital factor.

Life and death factor. If this car wasn't missed until the morning, and practically every able-bodied Boche in Finisterre was concentrated around Trevarez, there might be some hope — *might* be — of getting clear: *if* one could make it to cover before daylight.

'When did you say you heard they'd arrested le Guen?'

'Friday night. I got Gabrielle away then.'

'Gabrielle?'

'My receptionist. Blonde, rather attractive?'

'Oh, yes. But I was going to ask — what about your wife?'

'Which one?'

'Oh. I thought — assumed, for some reason —'

'I have two ex-wives. Both a long way from here.'

'Both French?'

'No. Number Two is English. Well — Welsh. That's how I was over there — quite a lot, just before the war. Her uncle was — well, in the Foreign Office, in London.'

'How you got to be recruited, I suppose.'

A grunt, shrugging . . . 'As far as Moncouar's concerned, Zoé, seems we're in luck. And if we get through Briec as easily — oh, damn . . .'

A vehicle ahead — head-on, seemingly holding to the middle of the road. Prigent muttering, 'Get *over*, you Boche filth . . .'

It had a blunt, military look about it. And

413

wasn't large. Rosie thought suddenly of Lannuzel and his *bouc:* if Henri had got through to Brigitte, and Brigitte had got herself to the farmstead at Laz — by bike or maybe in the pickup — and Lannuzel knowing that she — 'Suzanne' — was sitting in Jacques Perrot's kitchen . . .

It had lurched aside, hurtled by: *was* some kind of military vehicle. Guy Lannuzel wouldn't have been on this road though, he'd have come the way she had, surely.

If he'd come at all. She hoped he wouldn't, but he might. Doubling-up his personal risk less out of *noblesse oblige* than simply because he wouldn't want her caught — exactly as she'd dreaded le Guen being caught.

'One way we're lucky.' Prigent delved in a coat pocket, fished out a pack of cigarettes and passed it to her. He'd flicked his stub out of the window a minute ago. 'In all this excitement, nobody can be sure who else is or should be on the road. And we don't look like fugitives in this little bus. Isn't going to occur to anyone, is it?'

She lit new cigarettes for both of them. Thinking of Henri Peucat, hoping to God he at least would have got clear. Then in the flare of the match seeing the time — fourteen minutes to midnight. Pathfinders and bombers would surely be on their way. If Brigitte *had* got to them at Laz — well, the Maquis would have scattered back into their forests, while Boche troops — several hundred at least, and other units might have moved in from the Carhaix direction too —

would be in position around and maybe inside the château. Le Guen hadn't known anything about an air attack. He'd guessed at an assault by Maquis; and she remembered that she'd neither confirmed nor denied it. Prigent, even, hadn't known the RAF were to be involved, he'd told her. The detail of 'Mincemeat' hadn't concerned him, only the provision of le Guen as informer.

The important thing, anyway, was that since le Guen hadn't known it, the enemy wouldn't either; current troop deployments would be aimed at catching the Maquis in the open and with their pants down, so to speak.

So there should be *some* benefits.

'In a way —' she passed Prigent his Gaullois — 'this may turn out rather well, as far as the bombing's concerned. With at least a few hundred concentrated there.'

In Briec not a soul was stirring.

She'd asked him — again — 'You went to the house in Place Saint-Matthieu because you knew it was where le Guen had dropped his message, so there'd be a line to me — to warn us —'

'Only way there was. Wasn't my business, exactly, but —'

'I know. And very much appreciate it — *however* this turns out.'

A principle in SOE training was that if you were in a spot and had a way out, you *got* out, didn't as it were throw good lives after lost ones. Prigent,

who not even being SOE had no shred of obligation towards her in any case, could have been out
and clear by now — straight out of Quimper, not
going anywhere near Lestonan . . . He was telling
her — about his going to the Berthomets' house
— 'Got a foot in the door, more or less. Hell of
a job convincing the old boy I wasn't Gestapo.
Want to know how I did it?'

'Yes — please . . .'

'I'd argued without getting anywhere. Suggested I'd go in another room and block my ears,
he'd get through and ask you or whoever it was
to ring him back — so I wouldn't know where or
who —'

'If you'd been Gestapo you could have told the
operator to identify the number.'

'I know. And he wouldn't play. So then I put
my Luger on the table, showed him there was a
round in the chamber and safety catch off, told
him, "Get through, then point this at me, if I do
anything but warn him they're all in danger, shoot
me." That did it, but only because the old girl
saw sense and persuaded him.'

'Hell of a risk. Shaky old hand?'

'I slipped the safety on again after the demon-
stration. As it happened he didn't touch it anyway. Not the killer type, eh?'

'I'm *very* grateful to you. For myself obviously
— but all of us. And old Henri in particular —
the one you spoke to. He's a splendid character.'

'I'm sure. Lots of 'em about. I hope he managed to pass it on, that's all.'

'I know who he'd have phoned, and she — well, as long as she *got* there . . .'

She paused. Looking out on her side across uneven, streakily moonlit countryside. Thinking of the bombers coming, and Trevarez being in that direction, roughly thirty kilometres away. It couldn't be far off midnight now. Thinking of Brigitte and her brother too, whether they'd have got away. He could have taken her into the Forêt de Laz with his Maquis friends to their farm — when the whole area would be crawling with Boche soldiery. There'd be the *bouc* to dispose of, too.

A spark, in the corner of her eye, out there in the east . . .

'Hey — I think —'

A grunt on her left: he'd seen it too. Like an expanding star, radiating whiteness: and another — two more, close together, opaque white blossoms floating in blue-black sky. She was winding the window down . . . 'Couldn't stop, could we?'

'Not here.'

Shifting gear, to cope with the incline. Not far ahead there'd be a crossing, side road to Gouézec, beautiful country down into the valley of the Aulne and to Châteauneuf — and Trevarez a bit to the right where a moon-coloured cupola of Pathfinder flares was throwing surrounding hills and forest into contrasting effects of light and darkness. The Citroën slowing, breasting a ridge, and the first bomb hit then — small and distant, a spark like the start of a match igniting, flame-

417

coloured, lasting only a split second but then others too — and the sound arriving now, at first individual thumps, single drumbeats becoming a long drum-roll: the last of the flares were falling into an upward-reaching orange-red glow. The château on fire, she guessed.

Bloody shame there were no admirals in there . . . She'd turned to make some such comment to Prigent, but he got in first: 'Seen enough?' And was taking it for granted that she had — shifting through the gears, picking up speed again, Rosie thinking that it would probably be no different at Kernével — where there'd been no ground action called for, just a straightforward bombing raid, and that it might have been better if this had been mounted the same way, irrespective of Resistance and Maquis politics and Count Jules' own ambitions. An air attack plus Maquis action such as Lannuzel had intended *might* have accounted for Messrs Doenitz and Bachmann, but only if they'd been there in the first place, and right from the start that had been a gamble.

Prigent broke into her thoughts . . . 'Looked good — if that was what was wanted?'

'But *I've* done no good at all. In fact more harm than good.'

'Well — the thing's gone wrong, sure —'

'Hasn't it, just. They didn't need me here to do *that*.' Gesturing back towards Trevarez. 'All I've helped to do is put good people on the run and — maybe worse. Hostages'll pay for it too.'

'They would have anyway. And the weak link

418

was le Guen, not you.'

'I brought him into it!'

'No — he was given to you. By *me*. I was asked whether I'd have any way of getting at least a few days' notice of the next weekend conference, he was the answer and London jumped at it. So I duly put you in touch with him. I'm not blaming *my*self, incidentally, I did what I was asked to do — as you've done, uh?'

'You're a much nicer man than I thought.'

'You *didn't* like me, did you? Thought I was unkind to our "Micky" . . . And I was. Actually I'm not *nice* at all . . . But listen — the people you mention, on the run and in danger, et cetera — they were taking their chances, weren't they? Name of the game — once you start monkeying around SOE-fashion, anyway. That's *my* grouse — I had a good set-up there, you know?'

'What I was saying — exactly —'

'As *I* said, Zoé — it was fouled up through le Guen. I'd probably have come to regret it sooner or later even if I'd had nothing to do with this business of yours — should have known better than to take him on in the first place. One can't afford weak links . . . Another point you might take into account is that operations *do* often go wrong. It's the nature of the business, has to be. OK, so there are the other kind too — for instance, weren't there some successful *parachutages* a week ago?'

'Where did you hear that?'

'My job, to hear things. Zoé, you'll live to fight

another day. It's not over yet — nothing like. All right, we aren't *out* yet —'

'Not quite, are we . . .'

Just short of Pleyben, they were stopped. Having crossed the Aulne at Pont-Coblant, three kilometres up the road the way to Pleyben was a right turn at what was effectively a T-junction; turning left would have taken them to Châteaulin. But a motorcycle combination was parked in the centre of their road — the Briec road — with one helmeted soldier straddling the bike and the other in the middle of the road signalling them to stop — moving a torch horizontally to and fro with its beam aimed at the car's windscreen.

'*Here* we go . . .'

Braking, with that pumping action. He'd been driving fast, hadn't planned on having to slow much for the turn.

Rosie's hand was on the pistol in her pocket, her thumb exercising the safety-catch; and Prigent, having brought the Citroën to a rocking halt, slid his right hand inside his unbuttoned coat. He had a Luger in there somewhere.

'Open the windows, d'you think?'

He grunted agreement: she was already winding hers down. Save delay or having to shoot through glass. After which you probably wouldn't get far — but still had to try. Obviously: like second nature, you'd try. The soldier who'd stopped them had turned his back, about five metres in front of the car, its masked headlights illuminating his boots and breeches. He was looking to the left, and the one on the motorbike — other side of the east-west road, on the grass verge — was looking back that way too, over his shoulder.

'Something coming from Châteaulin. Zoé — I'll do any talking.'

'How's your German?'

'Not bad. But I'm not pretending to be German.'

'No. OK . . .'

Prigent's later account of this incident ran as follows: *They were ambulances that passed, I think naval ones so they may have come from Brest — or some naval hospital in the coastal area. It would be pleasant to believe they were being rushed to Trevarez to help cope with casualties from the bombing, but if this is the case they'd have had to have been extremely quick off the mark. I do not know. They came into sight very suddenly, three of them, travelling at about 80 kph, and as soon as they had passed the soldier who had stopped us ran into the road and jumped into his side-car, the bike already moving off the verge by then and its rider waving at me to carry on. Which we did. It was less than half a kilometre into Pleyben: the ambulances and their escort had whisked on through eastward — on the Châteauneuf road — and I took it for granted that our intended route northward would be as clear and empty as all other roads had been up to this point. I therefore continued at a fair but not excessive speed through the centre and out on that leftward curve of the exit road, and there in front of me at very close range was a road-block — a truck on the left facing into the village, black-and-white pole across two trestles in the middle, three or four troopers dashing for cover as I came skidding round with the tyres screaming and not much hope of stopping short of the barrier. In fact I did not try — I saw there was a gap on the other side — the left, well beyond the parked truck by then — and dragged the wheel over, maintaining speed — i.e. no longer braking — and hit that end of the pole and sent it flying, but anyway we were through. In an attempt to confuse the issue I screamed out of the window in German, "Ich habe keine Geduld —" expressing exasperation at their having endangered us in this way. It might have worked — at any rate no shots were fired after us . . .*

He'd heard her laugh: at his shout, he supposed: that damn cheek. But any sense of fun was extremely brief. His account continues: *It seemed possible that the patrol manning that checkpoint might believe we were arrogant SD or somesuch, a type they would know well enough: that they would do nothing, therefore. It was conceivable. Alternatively, they might phone ahead — to Morlaix seemed the most likely — 45 or 50 k ahead of us, while my hope was to get within about 10 k of it before turning off west and northwest. It did not occur to me they might have colleagues in Brasparts, a middling-small village just up the road from where we were at that moment. But I think they must have: and a telephone link too. Either that, or what followed was just by chance.*

'Christ.'

Rosie had wriggled up on to the seat again: having ducked down out of sight when they'd looked like smashing into that barrier.

He glanced at her. 'You got a laugh out of it.'

'Well — better than screaming . . .'

'Oh — every time . . . Sorry, anyway. But if I'd stopped — we'd have hit it anyway, wouldn't then have been in exactly the most advantageous situation —'

'Damn right. Presence of mind — congratulations. I could use a smoke — could you?'

'*What* a good idea.'

'But d'you think we should divert now?'

'Maybe . . . But if we've got away with it — *might* have —' holding up a hand with fingers crossed — 'well, we'd be losing time — and anyway, divert where? Just plunging off into the lanes — when we're only a third of the way, so far?'

He was right, she thought — lighting both cigarettes at once, and thinking of that tangle of little lanes . . . This was home territory, more or less, with St Michel-du-Faou only a few kilometres eastward — via Quinquis-Yven, Marthe Peucat's village and allegedly safe house. She didn't mention it, didn't actually consider it for a moment as any possible solution to current problems; she'd imperilled those people enough already, she felt. She agreed: 'I think you're right. Let's stay on this road.'

'Great minds.' He took the cigarette from her. 'Thanks.'

From his account, again: *I was thinking we might have got away with it. Also what a splendid girl this was: so self-possessed, although she knew the score as well as I did — that we had at best a fifty-per cent chance, and what being stopped and arrested would mean. Anyway — about one cigarette later, I'd guess 6 or 7 kilometres north of Pleyben — there it was, our come-uppance: a truck in the middle of the road, its lights brighter than most and shining on yet another horizontal black-and-white pole — which could not have been smashed through or brushed aside, with the truck's bonnet practically in contact with it and soldiers in helmets both sides of the road. Zoé had been relaxing with her head back, maybe her eyes shut, and it was only my jamming the brakes on that woke her up to this. The thing was, I had just passed a road junction, a road leading off to the right, eastward. I slammed the car into reverse and had it whizzing back — oh, and I switched our lights off — telling her, 'There's a road off to the right back here —'*

'Yes — I know it.' She squirmed round on her seat, telling me — as calmly as ever — 'It goes to — Lannédern and Loqueffret —' Then: 'Oh. Lights behind us, Michel.'

She had seen them, I had not, I was looking for this side-road. Zoé added, 'Coming up quite fast.' We were where we needed to be, by this time: I spun us into the side-road — gears grating and engine screaming — all in just seconds, which was all we had. *I believe that crowd ahead could not have known there was a turning here. If any shots were fired at us while we were still on the main road, I neither saw nor heard them. And on the side road I was getting up speed, but still managing without lights, Zoé watching back for any sight of Boches and telling me from her local knowledge that if we could stay ahead of them for about 6 k to Loqueffret, a left turn after the village would take us north so we could then get back to our main route well up towards Morlaix. I thought it was too much to hope for: sooner or later I was going to need the lights — the moon was still helping a bit but not all that much because of the tall hedges — they would not be far behind us and if they realized we were aiming to return to the Morlaix road there would be others waiting for us up ahead. The point being that I felt I had to turn off before that — before they got on our tail, and as it happened I spotted a narrow turn-off coming up on the left, and at about the same moment Zoé saw lights behind us again. They would not have seen us though, at that range and with no lights, or seen us turn either. I shouted to Zoé to hold tight, yanked the wheel over, hit the verge with the left-hand wheels, jumped and careered around for a second or two but got hold of it again, at the same time seeing — vaguely — that for about the next hundred and fifty metres the lane snaked this way and that, then curved sharply right. I am not at all certain what happened — except I bungled it. We went into a slide, hit the bank again, bounced off skidding and rounding the bend more or less sideways. There may have been slurry or other* spillage on the road. Still did not have lights on. And what there definitely was was this stone wall, which we hit head-on before I even saw it. It was a hell of an impact and Zoé's head went through the windscreen. I got nothing but some cracked ribs and a lot of bruising. I suppose through being larger and a lot heavier. But I thought she was dead. In fact at that stage I had no doubt of it. In the faint haze of moonlight her entire upper body as well as her head was black with blood, her forehead felt squashy and I could detect no heartbeat. I got her back across the front seats and set about removing such items as it seemed to me were better not left for the Germans to find. I took her gun from her coat pocket, and a spare clip for it. Her papers too, which were in an inside pocket of the coat, and the valise which she had with her. It contained a jumble of stuff which I did not have time to examine: could have included codes, anything of that sort. (In fact when I did later on look through it, prior to disposing of it, I found a large sum of money in French banknotes — which of course I brought on with me.) As can be imagined, I had been working as fast as possible, but before leaving I tried again for pulse and heart and this time I found she was still alive, although the pulse was so faint that with a continuing loss of blood I guessed her chances of survival were very small indeed. In any case there was nothing I could do for her; I certainly could not have carried her with me, with something like 80 kilometres to go, and as a fugitive as well. My own chances did not seem to be very good, in fact, at that point.

I took Zoé's tip about the northward-leading road after Loqueffret. Headed eastward through fields parallel to the road from which we had turned off — having heard the Boche car belt on past soon after we had crashed and when I was preoccupied with poor Zoé, and not seen or heard it again. It was obviously essential to put distance behind me as fast as possible, as the wreck of the car would surely be found after daylight, if not before. Progress was slower than I would have liked, but after about 6 km — as she had estimated — and skirting around a second village which had to be Loqueffret — there was one before that, which she had mentioned — I followed this other road north until daybreak, spent a hungry and rather painful day lying-up in woodland — where I buried the valise — and pushed on again after sunset.

Chapter 17

Ben reached to the telephone, checking the time simultaneously, realizing the operator might have sugared off home by now. When she did pack up — at about this time — she connected the outside world to the Duty Officer's line. He himself didn't have the duty tonight, thank God.

'Yes, Commander?'

Still there. And that 'Commander' was what might be called greatly accelerated promotion. Saved her enunciating three syllables, anyway. He asked her, 'See if you can get Second Officer Stuart at "F" Section for me, Hilda?'

Waiting, he eyed the paperwork he'd dealt with this afternoon, and shifted a few stray items into the 'out' basket. Nothing had been left undone, he thought. The secret of getting rid of bumph as soon as it hit your desk was to hate it so profoundly that you couldn't stand seeing it lying around.

'Commander?'

'Yes, Hilda.'

'Second Officer Stuart's not in the building, they say.'

'You and I ought to get jobs there, Hilda. They don't even *come* to work.'

'Well — that'd be nice!'

'Anyway — I'm off now. Goodnight.'

It did seem that Marilyn never was in that bloody building. Not at any rate if she knew it was him calling: and it was impossible to get through without identifying oneself. It could have been paranoia that told him she was avoiding all communication with him, but if it was as it seemed, her consistency and obduracy suggested there'd have to be something more than just reluctance to tell him once again: 'No, Ben — sorry. Nothing . . .'

May 29 today — Monday. He'd been in the job a month exactly, and spoken to her only once, since the day he'd gone along to meet Hallowell. The last time had been about a fortnight ago — no, less than that — May 19, the day after the moonless period, the motor gunboats' last crossings. Between May 14 and 18 there'd been several deliveries on the Brittany coast and two pick-ups, one of some shot-down Americans from 'Bonaparte' beach and the other of three agents and a Spitfire pilot from Grac'h Zu. Both of which pinpoints were of still comparatively recent memory, to MGB 600's former navigator. 'Bonaparte' was the nearest, in the Bay of St Brieuc, more specifically l'Anse de Cochat, and Grac'h Zu was several stages further west, a little beach enclosed between jagged rock defences which made for a tricky navigational approach. He could still see it in all its threatening detail: the rock called Meau Nevez for instance which was an essential marker on the run in. Not easy, especially in the high white winter seas as it often had been, and of course pitch darkness — a *sine qua non,* with German coastal defence posts within spitting distance of any of those pinpoints. Anyway — of the three agents brought out on May 18 one had been categorized as SIS, male, and the other two as SOE, one male, one female, and Ben had had his crazy, short-lived dream — despite *knowing* it couldn't be her, not this soon. He'd asked Marilyn on May 19, 'Couldn't have been my girl, could it?' and she'd told him patiently, 'No, Ben. *Heavens,* no.' She'd added, 'If it had been, you'd have heard from me before this.'

'Heavens no', because otherwise it would have meant something had gone badly wrong, from SOE's point of view. And in any case when she did come out — touch wood — it was more likely to be by Lysander, he guessed, than by sea. Or over the Pyrenees, for that matter. One thought of the Brittany-coast route because it had been — and still was, though less directly — one's own business, but for all he knew she could be hundreds of miles from that coast. While another factor in his worrying — which he thought he might mention when or if he finally did get to talking to Marilyn, was that as she hadn't agreed to give him bad news as well as good, he couldn't ever rely on no news being good news.

News today incidentally — announced by Churchill in the Commons — was that 47 RAF officers had been shot by the Gestapo: having tunnelled out of a POW camp in Silesia and later been recaptured. If the report was accurate, it was cold-blooded murder. The Swiss government had been asked to investigate, Winston had told the House. But you could take it as read, Ben thought. It was how the Master Race displayed its superiority *über alles.*

And Rosie had been in those bastards' hands once. It amazed as well as appalled him that she could have been through such an experience and have suffered since in the way he knew she had — knowing it through the nightmares, fits of terror in the small hours, Rosie a small frightened animal clinging to him, soaking wet and whimpering — and still, by her own deliberate choice, gone back.

It had had a lot to do with the SOE work she'd been doing here, preparing other agents and packing them off to take *their* chances and asking herself *Why her, not me?* In her rare attempts to explain it to him, that had been most of it, and up to a point was understandable. The point — *his* — being that having done it twice already and both times got out only by a whisker she might have been satisfied to leave it at that. Although another element in it that he'd sensed — found hard to define but knew was there — was an assertion of her own Frenchness, combined with respect for the memory of her dead father.

As if it was something she owed *him.*

Ben checked that his safe was locked, locked the door of the office and took the key along to the colleague who had the night's duty, went down to the street and limped up to Piccadilly. Might have a drink in Hachette's, he thought, before getting on a bus. Thinking about Marilyn Stuart again, whether she was deliberately avoiding contact with him. SOE had several training establishments in different parts of the country, and as she was involved in the training programmes she obviously would be out of London much of the time. On the other hand, surely the message he'd left eight or nine days ago would have got to her and elicited some response? He'd told the girl he'd spoken to, 'I'd like her to give me a ring so we can fix a lunch date, tell her', and she'd said she would.

Leave it in her court, now? Bite on the bloody bullet?

Barrage balloons floated silver in the fading light. The last heavy raids had been three months ago — in February, when there'd been a week of it, the worst since May of '41. In reprisal, it was said, against RAF and USAF raids on German cities including Berlin, where the Allies had been getting some of their own back, of late. In that same month, extraordinarily enough — February, when Ben had been in hospital — there'd been protests in the House of Lords against the bombing offensive. It had astonished all of them in his ward: remembering the *Luftwaffe*'s onslaught in '40 and '41, the shattering of Coventry, Birmingham, Manchester, Hull, Liverpool, Sheffield, Portsmouth, Plymouth, Southampton, Belfast — and of course London. On one night in May of

'41 seven acres of the capital had gone up in flames, 1400 civilians had been killed. After those protests in the Lords, one of Ben's fellow patients had expressed the view that the Germans were lucky they weren't being carpet-bombed continually from frontier to frontier; and not even the nurses had disagreed.

Who'd started it all, anyway? Who'd set up the concentration camps and the gas chambers? Who'd voted the Nazis into power in the first place, screaming their *Sieg Heils* on cinema news-reels for the whole world to see and hear?

At the top of St James' Street he turned right and then crossed over. Piccadilly was already thronged with tarts. All in pursuit of the Yanky dollar; there were droves of Yanks on the pavements too. Overpaid, over here, et cetera. A lot of the girls were amateurs who worked in munitions factories and took steps to avoid being on late shifts, so as to get out of their overalls and into tight skirts and lipstick and come tripping up to town.

At Hachette's, in the bar off the curve of stairs leading down from street-level to the restaurant, there was a Coastal Forces book — as well as a Submarine book, and others — through which men on leave or in transit could contact any friends who might happen to be around. Ben glanced through it, saw a name or two but not of any particularly close mates. He drank one pint of the watery wartime beer — which cost him a shilling, but if they'd tried to sell it in Brisbane at *any* price might have provoked a riot — and then climbed back up, crossed the road and made his way towards the bus stop. The girls were out in force tonight, and he found himself repeating over and over, 'No, thank you', and 'Not this evening, thanks'. One of them, unwilling to accept the brush-off, joined him as he reached the bus queue, taking his arm and asking, 'Where we going, darling?' He gave it a moment's thought — others in the queue were agog to hear his answer — then stooped to whisper in her ear, 'You wouldn't want what *I* got, sweetheart.'

Conveniently, the bus arrived at that moment. But she was a nice-looking kid, as it happened, and after a shrewdly assessing look at him she'd laughed; he waved goodbye to her from the platform, and she waved back, mockingly. There was only standing-room inside, but that was OK — with straps to hold on to, and he wasn't going all that far. Swaying to the motion, he let his imagination wander: seeing that kid's boyfriend or fiancé as a young soldier in hard-worn khaki, dented tin hat, eyes slitted against the Italian sun and with the ruins of Monte Cassino as a backdrop: and an air-letter form — which *she*'d have written a couple of weeks ago, already sweat-stained and slightly crumpled in his hand: *Love you for ever, darling, keep yourself safe for me and please please come home soon . . .*

Cassino had been taken by British and Polish troops just twenty-four hours ago, after some of the fiercest fighting of the war.

Rocking from Knightsbridge, after ten minutes or so, into the Brompton Road . . . At the next stop after that a seat close to him was vacated, but with his stiff knee it would have taken a lot of getting into, and as there were only a couple of stops to go, he didn't bother. Instead he enabled a stout, grey-haired woman to squeeze past him and drop into it. She glanced up at him: 'Thanks, love.'

'You're welcome.' He moved his stick so she wouldn't see it.

The bus pulled in to a stop opposite Thurloe Place, then bore left — southward — and after only one more halt was in Fulham Road, where he got off — it was easy enough as long as they gave you time and a bit of room — and waited to cross the road into Pelham Crescent. Wondering where Rosie might be now, this moment. And how she was, how it was going, whether she was confident or frightened, lonely or with good people. It would make an enormous difference, he imagined. In fact that was one of the awesome aspects of the job as one envisaged it — that image of her as so utterly *alone*.

But he did have to stop this, he realized. Take a grip: evolve some formula in his thinking to reduce the level of anxiety. She was *there* — no amount of worrying would change that. And Christ's sake — if *she* could stand it . . .

Pelham Place now: and a short way up it on this side a terraced house, mellowed brick, faded blue shutters on the windows. Crumbly brick

435

steps: he paused at the door, found his key and let himself in. He paused again then, hearing voices — and while pushing the door shut behind him he noticed on the hall table a rather smart forage-cap that didn't belong here. Or anyway hadn't up to this morning. Visitor, presumably: and he didn't want to get caught up in anything — like sitting around making bloody conversation. He started quietly up the stairs. Left hand on the banister, stick assisting on the other side, his naval cap in that hand too. The stairs were awkward — two flights of them, steep and rather narrow.

'Good evening, Commander!'

Professor Mallinson, Ben's landlord: beaming up at him from the hall, having heard the front door, no doubt. He was a small man with bushy white hair, round face, thick glasses; he spoke seven languages fluently and worked at the BBC.

Ben had stopped — half turning, shifting the stick and cap hand to the banister. 'How're you doing, Prof?'

'Very well, thank you. But, Commander — we have a very special friend of my wife's here, and it transpires she's also a friend of yours!'

He needed a pee rather badly: another reason for not having wanted to hang around. And Mrs Mallinson was frankly a bit of an old cow, so whatever friend this might be . . . He temporized, 'If you'd give me a minute — get cleaned up —'

'Ben?'

She'd emerged from the living-room down

there. Joan Stack. In her MTC uniform. Gazing up at him: no smile, just that rather uncertain gaze.

'Joan . . .'

'Small world, Ben . . . And what's this "Commander" business?'

Chapter 18

A flash like an explosion woke her: in the contrastingly drab light that followed it she saw a hunchback with a camera stepping back from her bedside, and two other figures near the foot end of it, watching her. One of them growled in hideously German-accented French, 'The treatment our little friend needed, look!'

Because her eyes were open, she supposed. She'd seen and heard that one before — seen him sort of through her eyelashes when pretending to be asleep or half asleep. A day or two ago: or — God knew . . . But the French one — French voice now — no, he'd been here too. More recently, she thought. Asking her, 'Zoé? Is it all right, calling you Zoé?'

Stooping for a closer view: dark-haired and slim, almost boyish — less than thirty anyway, twenty-five, maybe. He had an Arab or Turkish look about him. The German was pale, wide-faced, with a bulge of neck over his collar. Both in civilian clothes. The Frenchman could be Gestapo too, she supposed. The German certainly was; the ward sister had told her he and others with him had been taking a close interest in her condition and progress, had talked initially of removing her to some other location, but had been dissuaded from this by the doctor. As an alternative they'd insisted on her isolation at this end of the ward, with guards stationed outside there on the landing, keeping an eye on her through the glass-topped doors.

Some pin-up, she thought, that snap would be. Maybe hideous enough to defeat what she guessed must be its purpose.

'Feeling stronger, are you?'

The Frenchman: leaning close so that she smelt the Gaullois on his breath. His expression was solicitous, even earnest. Fairly repulsive, therefore, in the circumstances; she turned her head away. As if *he'd* care how she was feeling: except in their own interests, of course, to move her. She'd never seen him at such close quarters as this. The Boche had the blunt, crude features that she remembered from another place and time. Well — Rouen. Not the same man but the same type. Himmler-type porcine features, matching the fat neck. He'd just told the photographer in his guttural French, 'Get it developed and deliver it to my office. If I'm not back there myself by then, see *Leutnant* Greber.'

'Very well . . .'

He left them. She had a brief sight of the uniformed guard on the landing as one swing door opened and clashed shut. The swarthy one — the Frenchman — addressed the German: 'I could take it to Paris, if you like?'

'No.' The German added, with his pale eyes on Rosie: 'Haven't finished with you here, yet.'

Then to her: 'You're lucky to be alive — d'you realize that — Zoé?'

It was their first use of that name. She realized, though — le Guen. Anything *he* knew: since evidently they *had* connected her with the Zoé he'd have told them about . . . She supposed she must have known they had . . .

'Is —' she licked dry lips — 'Zoé, is that my name?'

'Your code-name. You've also been calling yourself Suzanne Tanguy. Remember?'

She turned her head slowly, carefully on the pillow. It was morning, daylight out there, but gloomy, overcast. She muttered, 'No, I don't remember anything. Or hardly anything.' She was going to stick to that. She thought that so far they were accepting it: or at least not actually disbelieving . . . Looking around — eyes only moving now, keeping her head as still as possible — as if she'd only just arrived, didn't recognize any of her surroundings despite having been here for the past two or even three weeks, however long it was. This end of the ward had only her in it, but there were sounds from the other side of the drawn curtains separating her from the rest of it. She glanced back at these two: it was important to play the part well, not overplay it — for instance by asking questions of a kind which she'd obviously have asked of the doctor or the ward sister — so they'd know she was putting on an act.

Except she mightn't have remembered their

answers anyway. Play it naturally, she thought; there was quite a lot she truly did not remember very well. She asked the Frenchman, 'If I'm Zoé, what's my other name? And am I supposed to know who you are?'

'Your other name's Suzanne Tanguy — as this officer just mentioned. While we're at it, *my* name's Marchéval. André Marchéval.'

'What are you doing here?'

He smiled, shrugged . . . 'I am here — well, mostly to help *you*, Zoé.'

He had a quiet way of speaking, she thought perhaps in a deliberate effort to have his voice sound deeper than it might otherwise have done. There was something decidedly fishy about him, anyway. Deep, quiet voice matching the sympathetic smile: his eyes smiled too — crinkling up, impressing her with his sincerity. There could be very little in the world as loathsome as a French Nazi, she thought.

He pointed at the German with his head. 'You know *his* name, of course.'

Staring at him blankly . . . 'Do I?'

'Major Johan Hammerling?'

Of the *Geheime Staatspolitzei*. Gestapo for short. She asked Marchéval, 'Is today the thirtieth, or thirty-first? Sister did say, but —'

'Second of June. A Friday.' That smile again. 'Lost a few days, eh?'

'Do you remember the smash?'

The German had broken in with that. She let her eyes drift to him. 'Smash . . .'

441

'Car crash. How your face got to be the way it is. Have they let you see it in a mirror yet?'

'What?'

She knew how she looked. Hardly a square centimetre of her head, face and neck where skin hadn't been broken. They'd cut all her hair off, shaved a lot of her skull. Her head had taken the brunt of it; there'd been slivers and crumbs of glass to pick out of the abrasions, the sister had told her. Her face was covered in some yellow ointment, but there were no other dressings on it now. Her head was bandaged, eyes had been covered when she'd first come round. She'd smashed the car's windscreen with her head, the doctor had told her, appeared to have had her head right through it. She didn't remember the smash itself or events immediately preceding it; her last memory was of a distant view of bombs falling where she'd known the Château de Trevarez to have been, and Michel Prigent's voice telling her she'd live to fight another day. Another memory that seemed really no less recent was of being in hospital in Nice desperate with worry over how long it was taking her father to get there. Actually she'd been seven: she'd been knocked down by a cyclist who'd been travelling very fast and caught her on a downhill corner where she knew very well she should *not* have been running across the road; it hadn't been the fault of the boy on the bike at all. She'd given the matron her father's office telephone number in Monte Carlo because her mother had been away in England.

442

She'd been black and blue all over, she remembered, but only worrying about her father — in the Hispano-Suiza which even when he was in no great hurry he drove like the wind: she'd had a terrifying vision of the big car leaving that coast road at a bend, hurtling out over the sea . . .

Hadn't thought of it in years. But it was as clear as yesterday. She remembered bursting into tears when Papa had come dashing in.

The ward sister had told her she'd been found in the wreck of a car forty or fifty kilometres south of Morlaix — where she was now — and brought to the hospital by *Feldpolitzei* who'd then notified the Gestapo. As far as the hospital staff had known, she was just a road casualty — until the Gestapo had shown up. They'd been back several times, talked about taking her away and then settled for posting the twenty-four-hour guard on her. Nearly three weeks ago. The Frenchman, she thought, had only been here in the last day or two; earlier on they'd all been Germans and in uniform.

She'd wondered if the Frenchman might be 'Hector'. Had had some reason for this which for the moment she'd forgotten, but remembered having thought about when she'd woken during the night. Last night or the one before. Some link between Marchéval and whatever one had known about 'Hector'. Bob Hallowell hadn't mentioned his real name, she thought. *Wouldn't* have. But there'd been *some* reason . . . Beginning to get it then: suddenly *had* got it. A German voice —

could have been Hammerling's — asking in clumsy French, 'Are you *certain* you never saw her before? Even allowing for the state she's in?'

For the fact was she looked like something out of an Egyptian tomb. And this might have been several days ago, when she'd have looked even worse. It had sounded as if they'd brought him to look at her and maybe identify her. Conclusion therefore that he'd been an insider, in SOE himself, therefore possibly 'Hector'. But he'd said yes, he *was* sure. She'd been comatose most of the time, at that stage, genuinely so although with memory piecing itself together, and capable of both speech and fairly lucid thought — in exchanges with the sister, particularly — but definitely spending more time asleep than awake. It was coming back to her now — this theory about Marchéval: she'd heard him affirm that he'd never set eyes on her until that moment, and add something like, 'Of course, once she's fit enough to be moved —'

'Oh, yes.' German voice. '*She*'ll tell it all, then.'

Statement of fact. With which, in the light of her experiences in Rouen, she could not have argued.

Only *hoped* she might get away with the loss of memory. If she played it right. And — touch wood — if they'd swallowed it *this* far . . .

'All right, my child?'

The ward-sister. A little shrimp of a woman, in Holy Orders of some kind, with a sweet expression and alert, intelligent brown eyes. Like little monkey's eyes. Here now, attending to her: the German and his French collaborator must have left and she, Rosie, must have dropped off for a while. She was still sleeping quite a lot. Hadn't realized she'd dropped off, but must have. Aware now though of the sister's fingers very, very lightly touching her cheekbone and then that temple: light, cool fingers offering comfort, reassurance. Smoothing the pillow then . . .

'Thank you, Sister. You're so kind.'

'They've taken themselves off, anyway. Took your picture, eh?'

'To identify me, I suppose.'

'Will they have some way to do it?'

'May have. I don't know.' Actually it was frightening. Depending on whether there might be a matching photograph in existence, in some file in Rouen or Paris: Paris, probably, there'd been a reference to Paris, she thought. Yes, the Frenchman. But they might only be trawling, *hoping* to find a match.

'Sister — I may have asked this before — I meant to, perhaps I did . . . The clothes I was wearing when they brought me in —'

'Laundered and pressed. I did tell you — you asked, and —'

'May I see the blouse?'

'You may. But we had this conversation before, you know, and I told you then — if you were asking about those horrible capsules?'

She'd hoped she'd dreamt of that prior conversation. Obviously had not. *Had* been confusing

dreams and reality, at times . . . But the cyanide
— that was an option gone, an escape route
blocked off.

'What did you tell me then, Sister? I don't
remember —'

'Our pharmacist took them for analysis.' She
saw Rosie's lips move, to frame another question,
and anticipated it. 'He was instructed to dispose
of them. This is a place of *healing*, child!'

The doctor was three-quarters bald, with dark
bags under faded-looking eyes. He'd patiently answered questions which she'd almost certainly
asked before — on such subjects as the purple
bruise on her arm where they'd given her a trans-
fusion when she'd been first brought in, and his
near-certainty that her skull had not been frac-
tured. Concussion, yes, but not lasting brain
damage. The pains she'd had in her head would
have resulted partly from the impact and bruising
but might also have been a lingering after-effect
of the transfusions — transfusions plural, she'd
noted, that time. She shouldn't worry about her
face, he told her; there'd be very little scarring,
when it had all healed over. It wouldn't take long,
either. Even her scalp, where the lacerations had
been much more severe: by the time her hair had
grown again, none of it would show. Well —
perhaps a little, just here on the forehead, *this*
side . . .

He asked her, 'Were you disturbed by the
bombing, last night?'

She'd been distracted for a moment: thinking about Ben, and her forehead still scarred, maybe her face too, a little . . .

If he ever got to see it.

At least he wouldn't see her like *this*, thank heavens.

'Bombing? Here — Morlaix?'

'Everywhere, they say. Major cities all over France. In preparation for landings, they're saying.'

'Oh, may those come *soon!*'

So soon that they would get a chance to take her out of here, please God . . . Blinking at the doctor's anxious, tired face: imagining troops pouring ashore, investing coastal towns including this one, *British* soldiers taking over . . .

But — in the cold light of reality — not here. Daydreams and prayers notwithstanding. Not in Brittany, with the long sea-passage. Although after landings elsewhere there might well be a German pull-out — reinforcement of wherever the beachheads *were?* Then it would be only a matter of time with Free French paratroops maybe landing inland and taking the Maquis under their wing: that had been the generally anticipated scheme of things.

Foot of the rainbow, she remembered. Me and Ben. Oh, and Lise and Noally. *All* of us . . .

Could be weeks away yet, though. Even months.

'Doctor — if the Gestapo insisted on taking me —'

447

'There's no question of it. *I've* insisted, more than once, that you're in no condition to be moved. Any jar to your head, for instance, or further stress —'

'Although there's no fracture?'

'They don't know it. *I* can't be *certain*. Thanks to them, the paucity of our equipment here —'

'So they're waiting for me to get stronger, before they —'

'You need weeks of rest. Meanwhile, if there *should* be landings —'

'If it came to a crunch, though . . .'

'How d'you mean?'

'If they *really* insisted.'

'But they can't!'

'The Gestapo? Why, surely. Whatever pleases them. Whatever . . . But, doctor . . .'

He'd just checked his watch. Glancing back at her: 'H'm?'

'If they interrogate me while I'm still here — that one who was here this morning, for instance.'

'Difficult to prevent altogether, I'm afraid.' He'd shrugged. 'I can try to limit the time they spend with you, of course, but —'

'Better still, wouldn't you agree I've lost my memory? I *have* — and you must know it — don't you?'

'I know your memory was — impaired. And the period of concussion, period affected by the concussion — yes, those crucial hours —'

'Wouldn't you agree I've simply lost my memory? Give it as your opinion — professionally? *I* know it — it's a fact. I don't remember my own name — let alone anyone else's, or whatever I've been doing?'

He looked troubled. A hand up to his bald head, stroking it . . . 'One could say — after — well, *possible* fracture of the skull — the *fact* being only that we can't be entirely certain —'

'If I've lost my memory — as I *have* — don't you see, torturing me wouldn't get them anywhere?'

'*Torturing . . .*'

'We're talking about the Gestapo. They do use torture — didn't you know?'

'Yes. Yes, of course. But why would — ?'

'I was in their hands once before. One of them was on the point of using a pair of pliers on my nipples. They'd already half drowned me — and the scars on my knees you may have noticed, they did that with a shovel. My memory's good for all of that — you can imagine — but I want to say it isn't, that I don't remember *anything* — or maybe just bits here and there — childhood, so forth, but — nothing recent that makes any sense.' Her eyes were more challenging than pleading: 'You'd back me up on that, wouldn't you?'

'Yes. I suppose . . . Although a snag is that loss of memory from such injury could be expected to be only a temporary condition. Unless there *were* more serious injury . . . Another point occurs to me — Suzanne — you *have* remembered your name — eh? And told them? Haven't they been referring to you as Suzanne?'

'They told *me*. Mentioned a surname too — one I never heard of. Oh, and Zoé — that's another one. It's what *they* call me, that's all. Where it comes from, God knows — if they said I was Greta Garbo, I couldn't prove I wasn't!'

'Well.' He tried to smile, didn't get far with it. 'I'll — do my best, Suzanne. As a matter of fact, I *have* been — as far as I'm able . . .'

'But please, one other thing.'

He glanced at his watch again: 'I really *must* —'

'I had two capsules of potassium cyanide in special pockets in my blouse. Did the sister tell you?'

'I heard about it.' He'd nodded, frowning. 'I may say, with some degree of — shock. The pharmacist identified the poison and was told to put it down the drain.'

'You knew that, but you were surprised when I said I might be tortured? What did you think the capsules might be for?'

He spread his hands. 'One doesn't *want* to think about it — or know about it, possess information of a kind one might be — obligated to divulge . . . Suzanne — I haven't asked you about yourself, have I — for instance why the Gestapo *should* have such interest — ?'

'D'you want me to tell you — the little I do remember?'

'No. Please. That's what I'm saying . . . Suzanne — leave it like this. If we can keep you here, and the English and Americans land soon —'

'I'm praying for that too. And — thank you. But listen — isn't there a chance the pharmacist might have used only one capsule for analysis, and kept the other?'

'Why should he?'

'As a curiosity?'

'If he had, he wouldn't admit to it. Or surrender it. Nor would I ask for it — if that's what you were going to suggest. Look, I'm sorry, I *have* to leave you now . . .'

He was doing his best for her. He was also overworked and had to contend with dire shortages even of such basic things as bandages and aspirin tablets. Bandages were laundered and used over and over again. But he was a decent man, she knew it. In fact *needed* to know it, to have people — him and the ward sister — whom one could trust, regard as friends.

Because otherwise she was lost, here. That was how it felt. Barely knowing *herself:* knowing also very little of what was happening or might be about to happen, only that she was as much in the Gestapo's hands as she would have been in one of their prisons — which was where she would be in any case when eventually they took her out of here. The cyanide had been one hope, and making as much as possible of her loss of memory was another: but that was about as slender as a hope could be. All right for *now,* today, tomorrow maybe, but sooner or later she'd either give herself away or they'd simply lose patience.

Catching her mind slipping then *again.* Loss of

memory was the straw to cling to until Allied forces landed and the whole picture changed. That was the hope, the combination of those two things. Getting it straight in her thinking — as she had again now — made things a lot better. It made sense, truly *was* a viable hope, an answer to what at other times felt like a dead-end situation: you had to hold on to it, *and* say your prayers.

And talk to Ben, quite often. Promising to be with him soon. Or at least, eventually. She dreamt about him sometimes, actually tried to, tried to fall asleep with him in her mind.

It was three days before the one called Hammerling came back. That morning early she'd told the sister when she'd still been half asleep, 'Everything's going to be all right in the end, it really *is*.' This was part of her routine, waking-up procedure, searching her mind for that solution to her problems — loss of memory plus invasion soon — but she'd happened to say it aloud, and the little nun had taken one of her hands in her own two smaller ones, murmured, 'Of course it is. It *will* be. God does hear our prayers, Suzanne. Now, let me help you to sit up . . .'

Because moving still hurt her head and neck.

Hammerling came in mid-morning, and brought a younger Gestapo colleague with him, a lieutenant by name of Greber. She'd heard his name mentioned before but was fairly sure this was the first time she'd seen him. At a distance he looked quite normal — for a German — with close-cropped fair hair, regular features and a slim, athletic build — but in close-up any such impression was let down by his eyes. If she'd had to describe them she'd have said they were like a snake's: an absolute frigidity, reptilian, icy hardness. Nothing they saw would affect them or the brain behind them to any degree at all.

He was at the foot of the bed, with a notebook and pencil ready. Hammerling opening the interview — straddling a chair beside her — by asking her whether she knew what day it was, and she told him — with some effort of concentration — 'Yes. The fifth of June.'

'And what day of the week?'

'Is it — Monday?'

'Very good. Memory's on the mend, eh?'

'The sister told me — just before you came.'

Best to give a correct answer sometimes. Having no memory one might have no awareness of the extreme danger of recovering it. Therefore one would *want* to recover it. And it *had* been the ward sister who'd told her the day and date: she'd also whispered to her that Allied forces had taken Rome yesterday, and that during the night there'd been exceptionally heavy bombing of German coastal defences around Boulogne.

This fish-eyed bastard didn't know she knew *that*.

He'd just told her, 'Blowing a gale, outside. No attempt at invasion this week, eh?'

Blinking at him. It was a fact that the wind was

rattling the windows. The hospital was on high ground here, someone had told her, and particularly exposed to blows from the northwest. She glanced at the other German: and beyond him to where the head and shoulders of the soldier on duty on the landing were framed for a moment in the glass top of the swing doors, peering in at them. The guard was changed every two hours, she'd noted. She asked Hammerling, 'Was there reason to expect an invasion this week, then?'

'Oh, not necessarily. They'll try it some time soon, though. When they do, they'll be repulsed, we're more than ready for them. We have a few surprises in store for them, too. But I'm not here to gossip, I've some questions for you, that's all. First of all —' he was delving in a patch-pocket — 'tell me who this is, please.'

Photograph in a scuffed leather frame: Daniel Miossec. So they'd ransacked Peucat's house. Obviously they would have. A crucial point which might emerge now was whether they'd found her transceiver and codes.

She'd shut her eyes. 'His name was — Daniel. He was my fiancé.'

You had to remember *some* things. That was the right kind — she hoped. Fairly distant, and with emotional aspects, deeply embedded . . .

'Are you saying the engagement was broken off?'

'He was killed in a bombing attack on Brest. Long time ago.'

'How long?'

'I don't know. Remember. Years, though. Two, maybe.'

'And his surname?'

Eyes shut. Squeezing out a tear. The difficulty and pain she'd had in believing in her father's death. That frightful, irrevocable loss and emptiness, total finality: and her mother's immediate, even brisk preparations for their return to England. It had obviously been a contingency for which she'd been ready, despite Papa having been still quite young.

'Began with "M".' Sniffing. 'I'm sorry . . .'

'You've been working for a doctor by name of Henri Peucat — in the village of St Michel-du-Faou. Is that correct?'

Still damp-eyed, blinking. She sniffed again. 'Have I?'

'You're a British agent, employed by what they call Special Operations Executive, and you're a wireless operator or pianist. Where did you hide your radio apparatus?'

Good old Henri. If it had been under that attic floorboard still they'd have found it. She glanced — frowning — at the one with snake's eyes. Back at Hammerling.

'If I ever had such apparatus —'

'D'you take me for a fool?'

'But I don't *know!*'

He didn't either, she thought. That shout had been a symptom of frustration, baffled fury, the fact he *couldn't* be sure about her memory — whether or not she was lying, acting, whether he was being made a fool of.

The other one had made some notes. Hammerling let out a noisy sigh.

'Let's see what you do remember. And let me advise you that it's very much in your own interests to cooperate with us to the best of your ability. We have no wish to harm you, none whatsoever. In fact I'd prefer to leave you to make a full recovery before questioning you at all. It happens to be urgent, unfortunately, we need answers *now* . . . D'you understand me?'

'Not exactly. I hear what you're telling me, but —'

'How did you come to be working as an assistant to Dr Peucat?'

'I — I've no recollection of any such —'

'Oh, God *damn* it!'

'— of anyone of that name or — of working for him. Or with this — *any* of this —'

'You went by the name of Suzanne Tanguy, and a man whom you duped into working for you as an informer knew you as "Zoé". Remember *his* name?'

'I can't say I —'

'Never mind.' A glance at the lieutenant. 'What was it?'

'François le Guen.'

'But you don't remember him, eh?'

She shook her head. 'The doctor told me loss of memory should be only temporary. If I did know such a person — well, I don't *now*, that's all. *You* know more than —'

'How did you come to be in the car that crashed?'

She shut her eyes.

'The man driving it was an enemy agent — like you. Name of —'

'Michel Prigent.'

'Thank you, Lieutenant. Prigent met you at a farm outside Quimper, where you were expecting to meet this other person — le Guen. The background to your flight with Prigent however was that le Guen had told our colleagues in Quimper the whole story — your plot to arrange for the murder of very senior naval officers. That failed — *completely*, let me tell you. Although other lives were lost — thanks to you and to your accomplices — whose names you'll give us, by and by. Can you remember any of them now?'

She moved her head slowly from side to side. There was relief in their sticking to the Quimper scenario. Nothing about the photograph — as yet. Drawn blank in their researches, maybe. Please God, drawn blank . . .

'Lannuzel, for instance?'

Greber had asked that. She opened her eyes: 'None of it makes any sense. *Nothing* you've said.'

'The man driving the car — Prigent — he left you for dead. Ran away, saved his own skin. D'you think you owe him anything?'

'I don't think — or know — or — know *him*.'

'You knew where you and he were going, though. Where he would have made for when he left you there. That's another thing you'll tell me.

457

Where do you think you and he *might* have been heading for?'

She was limp. Eyes shut. Hammerling leant forward, shouted down at her: 'D'you hear me, damn you?'

'*Messieurs.*' The doctor's voice: quiet, but steady. 'This patient is still a long way from full possession of her mental faculties. If you want her to be able to help you with your investigations later — well, I appreciate that your enquiries may be urgent, but —'

'Extremely urgent, doctor!'

'Well, I'm sure . . . But — excuse me, Herr Major.' He was beside the bed, the other side from Hammerling. 'If I might show you — what I *suspect* is the case?'

Rosie felt his fingers close on her wrist and raise it, lifting the arm. She stayed limp, let its weight hang. Breathing lightly, evenly. The doctor let go, let the arm fall: like a dead person's might, a deadweight flopping down.

'D'you see?' He glanced up, at both of them. 'It's more a return to coma, than sleep. I'm frankly concerned . . .'

They were back next morning much earlier than they'd been before. Rosie had had her morning wash, assisted by one of the young trainee nurses, and was waiting for the ward sister to come and renew the dressings on her head. Head fairly spinning meanwhile: the girl had whispered to her that rumours were flying about intensive

Allied air activity over the whole northern coast during the night, also — if one could let oneself believe it — that there'd been parachute-drops in various places. Places all unspecified — of course . . . But seeing the Germans arrive then, so early, she had a sickening thought that there might be a connection, that they might have come to take her.

Although why they should — even if those rumours were true . . .

They were both in uniform — the sickening Gestapo black. Hammerling holding one of the pair of doors open, talking to the guard. Uniformed perhaps because it was so early: maybe they got up like that — for parade, or something?

He was coming on into the ward now. Greber following, catching the door as it swung back. Hammerling swaggering: felt more like his heroic self in uniform, no doubt. Boots. Swastika insignia. *Bastard* . . .

Staring at her with an air of triumph, as he halted beside the bed.

'We have more names for you now!'

Glancing down the ward — where the sister had poked her head between the curtains. She'd have heard them — the clash of the doors, and the men's boots loud on the wood floor, Hammerling's voice; she was approaching in her own entirely different manner, quick little steps in soft, almost soundless slippers. Like a little mouse . . . Hammerling turned as Greber arrived beside him, snatched a cardboard file from him and waved it at her . . .

'Suzanne, Zoé, Béatrice. Now we have her twin sister Jeanne-Marie Lefèvre, code-name "Angel". Want to tell me you don't remember her either — do you?'

She frowned, gazing up at him. There'd be no sense in seeming to remember anything. Although it was all up with her, she realized. Except for that whispered news — paradrops, and the entire coast under air bombardment. Remember *that,* believe in it . . . But if only to avoid torture, one should have no memory. Well — also to avoid being tortured to the point at which one might tell them whatever they wanted to know. In the Rouen area it would be about missile sites and the identities of Resistance leaders whom she'd recruited last summer as informants on that subject. They'd want those men's names anyway, simply as *Résistants;* but also, Intelligence reports in recent weeks had indicated that the deployment of the missiles or 'secret weapons' was imminent . . . Her head hurt: telling herself again to hold on to the memory loss — which was all she had. If they'd tied her to Rouen and identified her as 'Angel', therefore to the man who'd called himself 'César' — whom 'Angel' had killed . . .

'Here, now.' He'd put the file down on the bed and opened it. Glancing up at the Sister, who'd asked whether anything was wrong, he nodded. 'You could say so. Or more accurately, we've got it *right* now. Wait — I'll show you . . . Is the doctor here?'

'Probably in his office.'

'Get him.' Then a second thought: 'No — wait. Have a look here.'

'As you wish . . .'

He turned one photographic print for her to see.

'Taken here, four days ago. I sent a copy of it to Paris, for checking against records. And —' he flipped the other one around — '*Snap*. Hunh?'

She was studying them both. Shrugging then: 'There's a resemblance, but —'

'Not the least doubt — and you know it. All right — tell the doctor I want him here.'

Cool fingers stroked Rosie's hand. 'Don't worry. Whatever it is — put your trust — you know?'

'Get the doctor!'

Rosie smiled after her. *Brave* little mouse . . .

Wondering then whether landing-craft had touched-down on the beaches yet: and if so, where.

'Give me that chair.'

'Sir.' Greber slid it along, Hammerling reversed it and thumped himself down. Pointing a thick forefinger at her: 'Might as well stop the pretence now — eh, Angel?'

'I've no idea what —'

'Look at this, then!'

She moved her right hand over to take it from him. Her other one was inside the bedclothes: it was instinctive on this side of the bed to have it hidden, out of his sight and easy reach. Studying the print. She had no memory of having being photographed in Rouen, but she'd guessed they most likely would have, and here it was. It looked as if she'd flinched against the flash: might on the other hand have had her eyes shut, or tears in them that caught some reflection. Head back, mouth slightly open.

'Supposed to be *me?*'

'You know damn well it is!'

'I don't — at *all* . . .' She let it drop. 'When, where — ?'

'August — last year — in Rouen. From where you managed to escape by jumping out of a car, and subsequently knifed a German officer to death.'

'*I* did?'

A bark of mirth: 'Or this twin of yours!'

'I couldn't — couldn't *possibly* —'

'You're under sentence of death, anyway.' He looked pleased about it. 'Have been since August. And believe me, that's the only escape you'll ever make.' She blinked slowly, confused as to whether he was referring to the escape in Rouen or to the prospect of death, the *ultimate* escape. Ben came into it too, though — he was at the heart of her determination to stay alive if there was any way she could. Hammerling continuing meanwhile in his awful French — if she could believe her ears, wasn't misunderstanding — something about advantages to herself if she decided to cooperate. Advantages like avoidance of torture, perhaps.

It would be too. When one knew about the forms of torture: or some of them . . .

He'd asked whether she understood. He and Greber both staring at her, waiting for some response. She sighed, closed her eyes. Death would be by hanging, she supposed. Meaning — in Ravensbrück, anyway, as one had heard — strangulation, not the neck-breaking kind.

'Well?'

'I'm sorry. I couldn't quite follow . . .'

'Couldn't, eh? Well — doesn't matter. It'll be explained to you when you get to Paris.'

'Paris?'

He nodded to the younger man. 'Chain her up.'

He'd said it in German: she realized a minute later what it had meant. Greber on his way round to this side of the bed — and the doctor coming, she saw, shouldering through the curtain, an arm out behind him to hold it back for the Sister to come through behind him. Greber seized her right wrist, snapped the cold steel of handcuffs on it, locked the other cuff to the bedstead.

'Herr Major — what's happening, what's —' Aghast, pointing at the handcuff . . . 'What possible purpose — ?'

'Your patient, doctor, is a murderess, under sentence of death. Apart from more recent criminal activities, last August she killed a German officer!'

'Even if that were the case, Major —'

'It *is*. I just told you!'

'She's in no condition even to *try* to get away!'

'They may have thought so in Rouen when she made a run for it *that* time. Anyway — she'll be taken from here tomorrow morning. The guard will have a key, he'll release her at six, you'll have her dressed and ready by half-past. Clear?'

'But if she can't walk —'

'Then she'll be carried.' He looked down at her. 'Make the most of your last night in a bed.'

Chapter 19

Joan was in civies: and looked terrific, of course. Couldn't help it — she always *had*. In green again, this evening: in days of yore she'd known it was his favourite colour for her, and had tended to humour him in that way. A soft, mid-green, a suit made of some silky material, figure-hugging. He kissed her, out there on the pavement: 'Joan. Lovely. Really is.'

'Are you sure of that?' Laughing . . . 'Sure it's not some kind of penance?'

Big dark eyes inches from his: new arrivals pushing into the pub's entrance forcing them even closer together, when having kissed her cheek and practically inhaled a small jade ear-ring he'd been in the process of disengaging. And certainly not answering that question, was he sure: he wasn't, not in the least. He was worried out of his mind about Rosie, news of her he'd had from Marilyn Stuart. He'd set up this date with Joan before that, unfortunately, and the only way to have got out of it would have been to call her today, at such short notice that he'd felt he couldn't.

'This one of your regular haunts, Ben?'

'Not really. But convenient, I thought. Halfway house between you in your snooty neighbourhood and me in my doss-house . . . Look — eating takes place upstairs. More room up there, too.'

'OK.' A short, dark-oak staircase with a bend in it. Climbing it, saying over her shoulder, 'Amazing, you being at the Mallinsons!'

'Man I work with knew a guy who was moving out, that's all. Lucky timing. Amazed me *you* knew them, though.'

She'd explained the background to that, mostly when he'd telephoned her to make this date. Hermione, now Mrs Mallinson, as a young and penniless war widow in 1919 had been taken on by Joan's family as a sort of housekeeper. They'd got rid of her at some time around 1930, as one of a number of then essential economies, but Joan, aged about seventeen at the time, had been fond of her and kept in touch. They'd swapped Christmas cards and occasional letters, mainly changes of address from Hermione and from Joan's side any special news of herself or of her brother. Hermione had had a series of comparatively short-lived jobs, all of a domestic nature and usually described as housekeeping, but she'd finally landed up with Professor Mallinson, a widower, and married him.

'I gather the Mallinsons don't know you and Bob are getting divorced?'

'Yes. I mean they don't. Bob being in the Med's enough to be going on with.'

'Except sooner or later — why wouldn't you want them to know, anyway?'

'Because Hermione's very stern on such sub-

jects. Used to lecture me — no end of pi-jaw . . .
Anyway — when it's a *fait accompli* —'

A young but heavyweight waitress intervened:
'That table all right for you, sir?'

'I'd say so. OK, Joan?'

'Fine — backs to the wall . . . Ben, this *is*
nice . . .'

Actually, pretty awful. With nothing in his
mind but Rosie. He pulled the end of the table
out so she could get in behind it, and she chose
that moment, as she swung her shapely hips in,
brushing against him quite deliberately, to make
it worse: 'Am I right in suspecting that you and
little what's her name aren't seeing all that much
of each other, these days?'

He hesitated: on the point of manoeuvring himself in beside her . . . Staring down for a moment
at her wide, bright smile. The bitch *was* sensa-
tionally attractive. Just about every other man in
the room who had a view of her seemed to be
thinking the same thing. He asked her — quietly,
politely, suppressing that flare of anger — easing
himself in, then moving the stick over to the
outside to be out of her way — better than hitting
her with it — 'Joan — a favour, please. Any *other*
subject. Tonight especially. OK?'

'But *why*, my darling? I mean all right, but —'

'Here — menu. No — hell, drink, first. Gin,
or — what, Horse's Neck?'

'*Lovely* idea!'

He'd felt he had to ask her out, after he'd met
her at his digs, and guessing it was likely he'd see

her there again. In any case he'd wanted a chance to make her understand that there was no prospect whatsoever of their resuming any kind of close relationship: having a lasting if somewhat confused memory of that evening six weeks earlier. But not in any negative, censorious attitude to her break-up with Bob — water under the bridge now, didn't have to be his business anyway — but positively and emphatically because Rosie was and henceforth always would be the one woman in his life. So he'd rung Joan at her brother's flat and dated her; three or four days ago. Four — last Thursday, aiming to fix something up for the weekend, which hadn't been possible because she'd been going out of town. And then at the weekend — this was Monday now, June 12, D-day plus six — on Saturday, Marilyn Stuart had rung him in his office in St James', asking him to meet her that evening — when as it happened she'd be on *her* way out of town, to one of the SOE country-house establishments where she'd be spending the weekend. Yes, she'd said, she did have news. She'd added, 'It's not good, Ben. Don't expect it to be: it just isn't. Only not quite as bad as it would have been if I'd had to update you a few weeks ago.'

Puzzle *that* one out, he'd thought: putting the phone down with a sudden hollow in his gut.

She'd met him in the Gay Nineties, which for him was an easy hobble up from St James'. He'd given himself a couple of stiff ones before she arrived: he'd known she'd be there on the dot —

Rosie had told him he wouldn't believe how punctilious she was — so he'd got there at six, climbed on to a bar stool and lit his first cigarette by two minutes past. Dreading whatever it was she was going to tell him: something that would have been worse if she'd responded to any of the messages he'd left a few weeks ago. He'd been in the 'F' Section building a couple of times on official business since then too, seeing Hallowell about passengers and munitions cargoes for Brittany, and had manfully resisted the temptation to ask whether she was around: she knew damn well he and Hallowell had to meet quite often, could have left a message of her own with *him* if she'd been so inclined.

But OK. Maybe it had been a kindness — if it was going to be better now than it would have been earlier on.

She'd arrived in uniform. He'd been drinking gin and water and she'd asked for a Horse's Neck. They'd moved to a small table in the anteroom to the eating area, which was quiet and empty this early in the evening. She'd opened straight away with, 'Ben, I wish to God I didn't have to tell you any of this. It's only because of your own insistence — and the fact you're practically one of the family.'

The SOE family, she'd meant. He nodded. 'Thanks.'

'You *won't* thank me. *Nobody*'d want this kind of news.'

She was preparing him for it, he'd realized.

Putting him on his mettle. No doubt she'd had to impart bad news before. And she was very fond of Rosie, he knew that. On the other hand — reminding himself *again* — it couldn't be all *that* bad because she'd already said it might have been worse.

'So — let's hear it?'

A nod. 'First thing is — brace yourself, Ben — if I'd seen you more than a week or three weeks ago I'd have had to have told you Rosie was in a car-smash in northwestern France on May fourteenth and had been left virtually for dead.'

He hadn't flinched. Hand white-knuckled around his gin-glass.

'But that's *not* so?'

'No. What we know now is she was alive on June seventh, day after the landings. She *had* been in that car smash, but she spent the next three weeks in a hospital — in Morlaix. You'd know where that is?'

'Head of a long estuary between the Beg-an-Fry and Grac'h Zu pinpoints.'

She went on: 'The source of the first information — that she'd been killed — was the man who was driving the car. An SIS agent. He was brought out in one of your MGBs from the Grac'h Zu pinpoint on May seventeenth. I've spoken to him at length, also seen his written report. He'd got Rosie out of an extremely tricky situation, I must tell you, can't go into detail, but —'

'Cigarette?'

'I don't — thanks . . . Ben — I must emphasize this — the man I'm talking about took a huge risk, getting her out of the spot she was in earlier that night — May thirteenth. Bearing in mind that we and SIS are poles apart, functionally — well, he risked his life for her: in fact if it hadn't been for the crash —'

'She'd have come out with him?'

Imagining it. Inhaling hard. That last embarkation from the Grac'h Zu pinpoint: she'd have been one of them.

Instead of which . . .

Marilyn took a gulp of her drink, checked the time.

'I'm emphasizing that point because when it happened — well, she'd gone through the windscreen, and there was a lot of blood, at first he thought she was dead, then detected a very faint pulse. He doubted she'd last: but even at that, he was in a very crucial situation, there wasn't anything he could have done for her.' She'd glanced round, and lowered her voice still further. 'It was in the middle of the night, they were being chased by some Hun patrol — having already broken through one road-block. He'd switched his lights off and swung into a small lane — at high speed, hit a wall, and — that was that. This was miles and miles from where they had to get to, to contact the escape *réseau* — he couldn't possibly have carried her, for instance. All he could do was leave her there, and get away himself across-country. Which he did. He's in no way to be blamed, Ben.'

471

'All right.' Swallowing more smoke. 'She wasn't dead, and they — someone — got her to the hospital.'

'German military police.' Marilyn nodded. 'And what we know now is she was taken out of the hospital five days ago — on the seventh. We've heard this from SIS — who got it from some agent of theirs in Morlaix — and they say she was transferred by prison van from there to Paris, that day. She was seen being brought out to the van, and a nurse from the hospital confirmed that one, it was a young female patient who'd gone by the name of Suzanne Tanguy — which *was* her cover name — and two, that the Gestapo —'

'Gestapo?'

'Yes. They'd assumed charge of her during her three weeks in the hospital, apparently, then suddenly ordered her transfer to Paris. Ben — I'm sorry, I'm *sorry,* and I *hate* this, but — look, with the way things are going for us now —'

'Gestapo had her before, didn't they?' Shaking a new cigarette out of the packet. 'Christ Almighty . . .'

'Ben — the way it's going now, they *must* know the writing's on the wall, they're surely going to pay *some* regard to —'

'The niceties?'

'Well — not *quite* the word . . .'

The Normandy battle *was* going well, Marilyn had been right, he thought, that the Boches would at least suspect by now that they were going to lose. Once they lost Caen — which insiders were saying would enable Allied forces to break through between the German 15th and 7th Armies — they'd *have* to. The beachheads were all joined up, and in these first six days the Allies had put ashore more than 300,000 men, 50,000 vehicles and 100,000 tons of stores. It wasn't any walk-over. Twelve German divisions were in action, including four of Panzers. But Allied air had destroyed every bridge across the Seine below Paris, and most across the Loire, so the enemy could only move through the eighty-mile gap between Paris and Orléans, and the airforces were hammering them hard there.

That was the background — some of it — as of tonight. To Ben, it was *all* background. In the foreground and his own focus was just Rosie.

Joan asked him — having talked about her brother Gareth, who was in Italy and had been all right when he'd written her an air-letter card about a fortnight ago — 'Has the invasion changed your job much, Ben?'

Small-talk. They'd both had fish pie, she'd eaten hers and he'd had some of his, then offered her a pudding which she hadn't wanted, so ordered coffee and brandy . . . Convivial evening and small-talk with one's former bedmate. With Rosie in some Gestapo cell?

You needed a shutter on your mind.

'Ben?'

'Yeah — sorry. My job, you asked about — started me thinking . . . No — the answer's no, not much different. Hardly at all, really.'

The flotilla was being worked harder, that was about all, but his own work related only — or primarily — to their activities in the moonless periods. In the one that was coming very shortly, for instance, there were the usual crossings scheduled, agents and supplies to be landed and others — shot-down airmen too — to be brought out. One rather special commando-type operation — an SAS team who'd be conducting a reconnaissance in collaboration with a Free French paratroop mission, linked to a possible landing in strength on the west coast of Brittany — was to be conducted by MGB 600, Ben's old ship. There was plenty going on. Brittany was still full of Germans. It also had — according to latest estimates — thirty thousand *Résistants* under starter's orders, as it were.

He told her, 'Goes on much the same. How's the MTC?'

She shrugged. 'Oh, *us*. Wouldn't think *I* worked at all, would you?' She picked up her glass. 'I do, actually. In fact that's what I was doing all weekend — *and* back to it tomorrow. Here's to you, Ben.'

'And to you. But — if you could bear it, Joannie — I'd like to explain something very personal and — well, important.'

'If you absolutely *must* . . .'

'Yes. Sorry, but — I know I shut you up, just then —'

'I hit a raw spot. Not another word until it's

better — or worse, whichever.'

'It's not what you think. Nothing even remotely like you're guessing. And this is *very* serious, Joannie. What I want to say first is — well, just that I'd like it if you and I could stay friends. You know how I've felt about you and Bob, but that's not the point. Point is that I love Rosie and there's nothing short-term about it, as soon as I can I'm going to marry her. You've got to realize that — it won't change.'

Toying with her glass . . . 'So how come you're on your own now, day in and night out?'

'Rosie's in France. That's how come.'

'In France.' Gazing at him: frowning. 'Since when?'

'*This* time — well, the night we bumped into each other in the Wellington — I was drowning my sorrows, she and I'd have been together that weekend, and —'

He tossed back his brandy. Nobody would have given it any stars. 'I'd tried to persuade her not to go back, but . . .' He shook his head. 'I know it won't do us any good in the long run, but we'd better have some more of this. If you can stand it?'

'Oh — you know *me* . . . This France thing — your Rosie — nothing to do with the invasion — no, obviously —'

'No.' Signalling to the waitress. 'Nothing at all. And this isn't the first time she's been — over there. But as it happens, just at this moment it's — particularly *fucking* awful. If you'll excuse my French.'

475

'I think — broadly speaking — I'm *beginning* to catch on.'

'Not a thing one's supposed to talk about. Only for you to understand — well, what I was saying then. But it's creasing me up, Joannie.'

'It would. If I'm guessing correctly. Well — God, wouldn't it . . . SOE — right? Oh, you poor darling . . . But why now suddenly — is it some crisis, or — ?'

'No. I mean yes. But — as I said, subject's *verboten*. In any case — oh . . .'

'Get you something, sir?'

The waitress: he nodded, touched his brandy glass. 'Two more — large ones again, please?'

Joan murmured as the girl left them, 'If there's one bunch of people I really do quite desperately admire —'

'Me too. So desperately, it hurts. Here — smoke . . .'

He walked her to her brother's flat, kissed her goodnight in a brotherly manner and set off limping back to Pelham Place. A long haul — on one engine, as it were — but it was a fine night with a magnificent display of stars, and he was in no hurry to go to bed and for a third night running not sleep until it was about time to turn out again. Dreams were bad too, when you did drop off — including the happy ones, waking up then to reality. What you needed — and he was having to fight hard to hold on to — was fundamental hope — *faith*, might be the word. In which connection

— this hit him suddenly, as he was crossing Sloane Square — unaware as yet, of course, that most of the spoiling of his sleep tonight would be due to the first flying bombs landing in south London, in the early hours — might do worse, he told himself, than recall to mind a lecture given him by Bob Stack, Joan's husband — soon to be ex-husband. Talking about Rosie and her intention of returning to the field, and Ben's fretting about it, Bob had jeered at him: 'Scares *you* witless, Ben? How about *her?* How about bloody thousands of 'em — wives of bomber crews for instance, d'you think *they're* not bloody terrified?'

Well — OK. Not that the circumstances as they were now had been foreseeable then, in the context of that pep-talk. They'd been — envisageable, certainly. But — leaving Sloane Square behind now, heading for Draycott Avenue — he told old Bob in his mind, Easy to *talk* like that, old mate . . .

Chapter 20

On the night of June 23, in the Gestapo-run prison at Fresnes where she'd been for about a fortnight, she thought for a second she'd seen Lise.

Weak in the head as well as body. Hallucinating: telling herself so in the *next* second — by which time she was down on her hands and knees, in pitch darkness. The stout and viciously unpleasant wardress had flung her in sideways and she'd cannoned off the door-jamb, glimpsed that bewildering image in the brief flood of lamplight from outside before the door had clanged shut again, the clang of its steel like a physical impact inside her skull, and pain flaring in her back, her bruised spine; her entire back and shoulders and right-side ribs could as well have been on fire. Crouching — then subsiding: her head on her palms-down hands and her left hip on the concrete floor; she'd subsided into that position and had for the moment neither the strength nor any urgent reason to move further. Wondering whether there hadn't been a second figure beyond the one that might vaguely have resembled Lise. The mind did play tricks — was entitled to, after a day such as this had been — although it was still working after a fashion, alert for instance to the fact they did use stool-pigeons and informers inside the prison, even inside its cells, and that they'd give a lot for evidence that she had *not* lost her memory.

From somewhere outside a wailing protest rose to a scream, then tailed away. Echoes then: another cell door slammed. She'd got up on to her hands and knees again, somehow: asking into total darkness, 'Is there any bed-space?'

She could hear movement. As they no doubt would be listening for hers. She wasn't approaching them, though: it took all sorts to fill a place like this, and she wasn't asking to have her eyes scratched out.

A whisper, then: 'Might make room, I suppose . . .'

It had been a question, maybe, addressed to a third occupant of the cell. She heard a mutter of, '*You* might!' Then the first one again: 'Not big, are you?'

She'd have seen her in that same instant: black against the light from outside, with that ape-like creature propelling her in. She admitted, 'Not big. No.'

'You hurt? Where've you sprung from, what's your name?'

'Rue des Saussaies, *numero onze*. But I was here this morning — cell I've been in — don't know how long. Weeks . . .'

That afternoon, they'd whipped her.

She'd been woken at about dawn, told to wash

— cold water, as always, and no soap — and had been given breakfast of so-called coffee and a piece of bread, then led out to a van like the one that had brought her from Morlaix and locked into one of its individual compartments. The vans had separate compartments so that prisoners could be isolated from each other. From Fresnes into the centre of Paris was only about seven kilometres, and there couldn't have been much traffic on the roads. In Rue des Saussaies she'd been ordered out, and pushed into the swastika-draped entrance of number 11, which before the Gestapo took it over in 1941 had been the head-quarters of the Sureté Nationale. It must have been about eight a.m. They'd man-handled her down into the basement — winding stone stairs, into a stink of damp concrete — and one uni-formed thug had just about crippled her, jabbing the butt of his rifle hard into the base of her spine. Because she'd paused for a moment at the sight of a barred door ahead of her. Then they'd left her in a filthy cell all morning, allowing her a piece of bread and a tin mug of lukewarm, un-identifiable fluid as a midday meal before drag-ging her up to the top floor for interrogation.

As it had turned out, for a wait of another hour and a half *before* interrogation: with her wrists and elbows strapped to the armrests of a heavy timber chair, a desk in front of her with a more comfortable-looking chair behind it, and portraits on the wall of Adolf Hitler and Heinrich Himmler. She'd been left alone in here, but with the door ajar. Outside it she could see half a metre of corridor, its wall painted in two shades of brown. Voices were audible, from some distance, and some perhaps through other closed doors: it was mostly French, occasionally a burst of louder German. Other sounds came and went: doors opening or shutting, boots on the wood floor.

On the desk in front of her were two buff-coloured files, and a dog-whip.

Better than pliers, anyway.

Loss of memory was still the answer. The *only* answer: and it would only help her if she could make it stick, convince them of it, and if they needed whatever they thought she'd be able to tell them badly enough to have the patience to wait for it. Patience and of course time: the invasion and Allied advance inland from the beach-heads must surely affect the issue, impart some sense of urgency. To expect them to show much patience, in fact, might be to expect too much. If what they wanted was identification of Resistance leaders in the area she'd been concerned with last summer — effectively from Seine-Maritime into the Pas de Calais — they'd want it *now*.

Whatever they wanted, they'd want now.

Her back pained her: the base of her spine, where that bastard had cracked her with his rifle. Hitting her would have been his way of encouraging her to keep going. She'd staggered forward and collapsed against the door, hanging on to it for a moment so as not to fall. She'd been having

481

giddy fits in any case, wasn't too steady. Hadn't looked round at the guard partly because she wouldn't have been able to control her facial expression — hatred — and it might have prompted another blow. In any case why look at any of them, when they were all the same. She'd only thought — for her own relief — *Ben would kill you:* then in a follow-up thought that so would she — given a chance.

The truth was she'd barely have had the strength to kill a fly. But dreams helped. You could find ways of convincing yourself that things would change, that this couldn't conceivably be the end — or the beginning of the end. It *was,* but she didn't know it. If God's idea of justice or mercy or all those virtues he was supposed to be so hot on was to allow *this* —

The thing was, to survive. Think of Ben, not God. Of getting back to him. In other respects to deaden the mind, just try to hang on.

She'd been in the women's wing at Fresnes for the past sixteen days. In a cell ten feet by five which she'd been sharing with two Frenchwomen who'd stolen food from a military ration truck. The cell had a lavatory in one corner, with cold water you got from a push-button tap above it; food was 'soup', a small ration of dry grey bread and about every second day a slice of cheese or sausage. Starvation rations: certainly not calculated to build one up. Whereas here in Rue des Saussaies the cell she'd been in this morning was larger but a lot dirtier, really foul. It had a similarly high, barred window — into some basement area, presumably — and an iron bedstead with a straw mattress that stank. To get to the lavatory you rang a bell and a woman Gestapo guard who looked like a Lesbian weight-lifter would in theory escort you to it. But would not do so, the one who'd locked her in there had warned her, between eight p.m. and eight a.m. Which might have accounted for the state of the mattress. But the inference from that warning had been that she'd be returning to her cell here for the night. If that had been the intention, they must have changed their minds.

She'd first heard of Number 11 Rue des Saussaies during her SOE training, notably at Beaulieu in Hampshire where amongst other skills one had been taught resistance to interrogation. And since then it had frequently come into conversations in Baker Street and elsewhere. The other place — where one would have been just as likely to wind up — was SD headquarters in the Avenue Foch. The main difference, she'd gathered, was that in the Avenue Foch they tended not to use torture as an aid to interrogation, whereas here they did. In Avenue Foch the threat was simply of death — or transportation to Ravensbrück, which would amount to the same thing. Here in Rue des Saussaies you had that *and* torture.

She looked again at the dog-whip. They really were a bit bloody obvious, she thought. Several hours in that squalid basement, then a couple more up here, in solitary again and with *that* to feast one's eyes on. Subtle as anything . . . At interrogation, though, they *were* quite expert; it wasn't going to be easy, pretending to have no memory when in fact she had it all back now. The doctor in Morlaix had been right, it *had* been a temporary condition. Of which these bastards would no doubt be well aware.

If they were, could they be persuaded that she truly did have no memory at this time, might decide to wait until she did have?

Give them a fragment or two, let them believe it was coming back?

Side-thought, though — looking at the dog-whip: who'd want to whip a dog?

Steps approaching . . .

She turned her head to face the half-open door, and a figure appeared in the gap: extraordinarily, humming to itself. Male, in civilian clothes, shouldering in: she recognized him at once — the one with the carefully calculated friendly charm. Marchéval, he'd said his name was. French, but a Gestapo crony, and possibly — perhaps this was too imaginative, had only jumped into her mind because 'Hector' 's possible defection had been in and out of her mind a lot at that time — *possibly* SOE's former Air Movements Officer.

'Zoé . . .'

He'd spoken the name as if it was somehow precious to him. Shutting the door quietly . . . He was dressed as he had been in Morlaix — light beige jacket, blue shirt, patterned tie, brown trousers. Dark-eyed and swarthy. 'I *heard* they'd brought you here!'

As if commiserating. Old friend, startled to see her in this predicament. She asked him, 'Do I know you?'

'Yes — of course you do!'

'Do you work here?'

He looked hurt.

'I'm not Gestapo, if that's what you're implying. I'm like you — French through and through!'

'There are such things as French Gestapo. And you seem to be at home here. Anyway, *I've* never been here before, so —'

'Zoé — or Suzanne . . . Or is it Angel?'

'What are you talking about?'

'Those are all names you've used. Don't you remember?'

'Are you my interrogator here?'

'Zoé, please — I sneaked a look at your file, in Morlaix —'

'Morlaix?'

'You were in hospital there, remember?'

'A hospital somewhere . . . Vaguely. Morlaix, perhaps . . . You were there, were you?'

'Yes. My name's André Marchéval. Zoé, listen — you won't think much of me for it, I dare say, I admit I'm making the best of a bad job —'

'What d'you mean?'

'What do I mean . . . Well, I was arrested, and they made me certain offers — also threats. The stick-and-carrot treatment. One either went along with it, or —'

'If I'm supposed to have a notion what you're talking about —'

'One has — family responsibilities, Zoé. People other than oneself — if one refused to co-operate —'

'What had you done to be arrested?'

'I think it's more than likely you know that. In fact, almost certain. Huh?'

'I've no idea at all. I *assure* you — who or whatever you are —'

'In any case, my personal situation is no concern of yours, it's irrelevant. The fact is simply this, Zoé — if you defy them, you've no hope at all. Truly — *none.* But if you tell them what they want to know, you could have the sort of deal I have. You're not well yet, you know — you should still be in hospital. Frankly, I'm *appalled* —'

'What did you say your name is?'

'André Marchéval. But I do beg you —'

'Some sort of deal?'

'Interested? Well, thank heaven. But there's another thing too. I'll make a guess you're thinking because the British and Yanks have a toe-hold in Normandy it's all over bar the shouting, you've only to hang on. But it's not so. They're being held, and before long they'll be driven back into the sea — or just rounded up. Incidentally, for the past few days there's been a terrific gale blowing, they haven't landed a damn thing and the front's static, exactly where it was ten days ago. And on top of that, it won't be long before England has to sue for peace anyway. D'you know about the secret weapons — flying bombs?'

'No —'

'Small pilotless aircraft, more or less, full of explosive, launched at England from ramps in the Pas de Calais and in Holland. The first of them hit London ten nights ago, and since then day and night they've been raining down, killing *thousands!*'

'I'm supposed to believe this?'

'It's what's happening, anyway. At this moment. And there's even more to come — believe me —'

'By "sue for peace", you mean surrender?'

'Think it out for yourself. That huge invasion force bogged down on the coast, towns, ports and harbours being smashed, civilian population demoralized . . . Zoé, the point is — for *you* — no one's coming to your rescue. I'm sorry, that's how it is.'

'Why should you be sorry? What are you — French, or German?'

Spreading his hands: 'I'm *human* — and you're young, attractive, your whole life before you —'

'What's that whip for?'

'My whole *point*, Zoé —'

'I'm to be beaten with it? Or just to scare me?'

She *knew* he was Hector. Doing a first-class job for a heck of a long time, that man Hallowell had said. A traitor, serving the Gestapo now for how long? Some relations as hostages — allegedly. Father with an engineering business, mother

Scottish: Hallowell again. But he'd have been turned long before Baker Street had decided the allegations had to be looked into, she guessed. How many fellow agents — including quite probably some *she*'d have known — would he have caused to be arrested, tortured and killed, by this time?

So close she could smell his breath. Names, they'd want. And still send her to Ravensbrück when they'd got them. She couldn't even look at him. And trying not to breathe . . . Footsteps were coming loudly along the corridor, anyway: he'd heard it too, and straightened.

'At least *think* about it?'

'You are — *contemptible!*'

The door banged open: a tall, uniformed Gestapo major barked at him, 'You — get out!'

'*Jawohl*, Herr Major . . .'

Out like a rabbit. The tall man standing with his booted legs apart, fists on his hips: lean, hard-faced, more soldierly-looking than most of them.

'Friend of yours, is that?'

'I've met him before, apparently. He says when I was in a hospital.'

'Ah, yes.' Moving to his chair. 'You're the one with no memory.' Still standing, he poked at the files with a forefinger. 'Yes, I read these. This one Rouen, July–August last year, SOE agent "Angel", alias Jeanne-Marie Lefèvre, and the other more recent. Quimper, Châteauneuf-du-Faou, Suzanne Tanguy or Zoé. Angel to Zoé — A to

Z, was that the idea? Whose — Colonel Buck-master's?'

'I don't know what — or who —'

'You look like a cat that's been in a lot of fights.' He still hadn't sat down. Looking at the portraits of his leaders: then moving towards them. A hand to each, lifting them carefully from their hooks.

'There, now.' He brought the framed prints to the desk, slid them into a drawer. Where they'd hung, on that end wall, she saw iron rings which they'd covered — a couple of feet apart and six or seven feet up. He heeled his chair back and sat down, studying her.

'Those straps —' he pointed — 'transferred to the rings you see behind me — huh?' Reaching up: 'Like so?' He picked up the dog-whip then: 'Get the idea? I see you do. It's up to you, though. My job's to get the answers to certain questions, and one way or another I *will* get them.' He slapped the whip down on the desk-top. 'Under-stand me? My French good enough?'

'It's very good.'

'It's important we understand each other . . . I have a list of questions here — relating to both areas, both of your — deployments. I'll read through them, or some of them, and you may stop me in order to — to answer, clarify, or com-ment. But it's all straightforward. After this re-connaissance of the terrain we'll take it question by question, and according to the readiness and quality of your replies you'll either remain in that chair or go on the rings. Understand?'

'Yes — but I have no memory. I truly have *not*. You could whip me to shreds —'

'If necessary. But let's hope memory returns so fast you'll surprise yourself. Here we go, now. One — in August last year you murdered an officer of the *Sicherheitsdienst* on a train somewhere this side of Brest. You were on your way to an escape *réseau* that handled a clandestine sea-route to England. I want every detail of that escape-route, personnel, safe-houses, place of embarkation, et cetera.'

'Are you saying I went to England?'

'Are you telling me you didn't?'

'Not as far as I know — or remember —'

'I'll skip, in that case —' he'd turned a page — 'to question number — thirteen. You arrived in France from England approximately eight weeks ago — most likely by a Lysander aircraft touching down on a field near Soucelles, in the district of Angers. How did you get from there to St Michel-du-Faou, and whom did you contact *en route*, especially in Rennes?'

She was looking at the dog-whip. Shaking her head. 'As far as I know I've never been up in an aeroplane of any kind.'

'Are you asking me to believe that after murdering that officer you remained in France?'

'*I* can't believe I'd have murdered anyone!'

'Perhaps we're wasting time . . . But I'll try a few more. Back to July of last year . . . You arranged for some *parachutages*. One, anyway, within easy travelling distance of Rouen, and

there were others later. In making the arrangements you obviously also made the acquaintance
of certain leading *Résistants*. And then again, you
met others in order to have them pass back information on the location of secret-weapon sites.
I want the names and places of residence of everyone you met in the course of that work.'

She'd begun to shake her head even before he'd
finished. 'I couldn't give you *one* name. Don't
even remember being in Rouen!'

'Tell me.' He'd put that list down on the file.
'This is my own question, not listed there. Do
you anticipate that if you stall long enough it'll
all end happily for you with victorious British or
Americans storming into Paris?'

'I'm *not* stalling! Can't tell you what I don't
remember, that's all!'

'Well — I recommend that you think again,
and *make* yourself remember. You'll either answer all of it — and in the course of the next few
days, at that — or you'll die of —' he inclined his
head towards the whip — 'that kind of thing —
or you'll be written-off as hopeless and put on a
train for Germany. That would mean — well, I'm
sure you know. But believe me, it's policy.'

She wondered when the whipping would start.
She knew it would: so that when the next session
started she'd be in no doubt that whatever worse
things he might threaten were no bluff.

'*Do* you believe me?'

'I don't know. Suppose so . . .'

'Do you really think we'd want people like

yourself left here — left *anywhere?* Be realistic, use your head. You'd have tales to tell, wouldn't you?'

'No. Well — I mean —'

'Of course — you would. Foolish to pretend otherwise.'

He picked up the typed list again. 'A few more sample questions. If your memory starts working — go right ahead, interrupt me. Then you could enjoy a cup of tea and a cigarette, we'd talk things over quietly, I could hang the pictures back on the wall there and put this away.' The whip: his fingers touched it while his eyes watched for her reaction. She remembered that in Rouen the one with the pliers had offered her a cup of tea — before things had reached that stage . . . He sighed, shrugged slightly: 'All right. Question number — eight. Who is the mastermind of the Résistance in Finistère? No? Well — question nine: you came to join this Dr Peucat with references from some French source. From whom, who set it up? Ten: you arranged a *parachutage* to Maquis forces in the *Montagnes Noires.* We know about that one, but there was another on the same night — where, and with which Résistance leader were you working?'

It sounded as if Jaillon and Count Jules — and his girlfriend — were in the clear. As they should have been: they'd had nothing to do with 'Mincemeat'. She had no idea what might have happened to the letters between Peucat and the former actress. She'd kept them with her other papers, but she'd never been called upon to show them.

Didn't know what had happened to the other papers, for that matter.

'No answers, eh?'

'I've said — over and over —'

'Very well.' There must have been a bell-push under the edge of his desk: his hand had moved, and a buzzer sounded somewhere outside. There was a shout — a name in German and some answer . . .

'You either don't have any memory, young woman — in which case it's just your bad luck — or you're very stupid.' There was a rap on the door, and it opened. 'Herr Major?'

He nodded, and gestured towards her — a chopping motion, then that hand's thumb pointing at the rings behind him: 'String her up.'

In her dreams in the cell at Fresnes she was in Ben's arms, whispering it to him. How while the underling had been securing her wrists to the iron rings her interrogator had lit a cigarette and remained in his chair at the table leafing slowly through the contents of the files, and had continued doing so even when the other man had left the room — finishing the cigarette, as absorbed and silent as if he'd forgotten she was there. Rosie leaning with her weight against the wall and the pain throbbing in her spine. He might have been doing this deliberately for its effect on her, racking up the tension on her nerves, or giving her time to change her mind and give in — perhaps less out of cruelty than in the hope of not having to go through with it. He must have at least suspected that she was in a frail state of health, that it wouldn't take a lot to kill her. She'd looked round at him only once — a major physical effort that hurt, left her wishing she hadn't.

I just thought about you, then, kept picturing you in my mind, how you might look when I got back to you and where it would be, what time of day and whether it might still be summer: hearing him move, then, pushing his chair back and I suppose stubbing out the cigarette, and I think he took off his jacket — tunic, whatever you'd call it. Oh, Ben, I love you so: those were dreadful minutes but if I'd had a cyanide pill and could have got to it I think I wouldn't have taken it even then, because while there might still be any chance of getting back to you —

'I'll give you the first question again. Answer it, and the beating will stop. Answer it *now*, it won't even start. You listening? Right. After you killed the SD officer, where did you go to contact the escape *réseau?* I'll count to five now.'

She tightened her arms round Ben, tightened her whole being against the recollection of that first indescribably frightful slash of the whip across her shoulders. She'd thought this might be how she was going to die. He'd repeated the question, struck again, she'd had a sensation and mental vision of splitting open, an image of her spine and right-side ribs visible through parting flesh. She'd screamed, and through it heard his bellow close into her ear! '*Answer!* Answer the question, *damn* you!'

'Hey — what the hell —'

Girl's, woman's voice, in sharp protest. The warm bulk which in her dream had represented Ben wriggling and pushing her off, disengaging her arms and shoving her away. She felt the edge of the bed as she went over it, landing on the concrete on her side. Hurting everywhere, hellish pain in her spine and head, back and shoulders burning as if she'd been skinned and rubbed in salt. Same female voice — above her somewhere, and a tone of concern now — 'Hell, *sorry,* but what —'

'What's going on?'

'It's all right, Irène. Nightmare — I don't know . . . Hey, you OK?'

'A dream I was being whipped. *Was,* yesterday. Oh, Christ . . .'

'Really *am* sorry — I was asleep too, didn't — here . . .'

'Oh God, it's — morning?'

Greyish light was seeping from the small, high window. She knew where she was, remembered being thrown in, last night. Telling this girl who was helping her up, 'I *was* whipped — in Rue des Saussaies, yesterday. Must have passed out. I came to in the van on the way back. So they'll start again today — *expect* they will . . .'

'I don't *believe* this!'

A whisper: the girl was stooping, peering into her face, hands gentle under Rosie's jaw-bones, turning her face up to such light as there was.

'Suzanne?'

The hands were on her shoulders now: partially holding her up. 'Suzanne. Is it *possible?*'

She didn't know. Seemed it was, though. Weak and hurting: but it *seemed* real. Trying a smile: '*Lise?*'

'Christ, it *is!*'

Fingers — Lise's — were feeling the scarred abrasions on her face and forehead. As light as the ward sister's had been. Rosie whispering, 'I'd forgotten — I thought last night — decided it *couldn't* be — just someone like you, but any case I wasn't — wasn't entirely *compos mentis* . . .'

'Wait.' Lips close to her ear. 'Want to make sure this one's asleep. Wouldn't trust her a centimetre. Hang on.' She'd pulled away, was bending over the body that was curled against the wall . . . 'Irène?' Very quiet, low whisper. 'You asleep?'

It had seemed to be part of a dream to start with, but it was real, all right. Feeling gingerly where her filthy blouse had stuck to her. Carefully — if she'd pulled it off the crusted blood it would have started the bleeding again. Real as that: and, astonishingly, that this *was* Lise. Although — in the long run, what difference? All right, a tiny interlude *now,* but then back to the Rue des Saussaies — with the knowledge that Lise was in the same boat not exactly comforting. In fact the opposite. And what about Noally?

'Suzanne —'

'No, *Christ!*'

She'd been on the point of putting an arm round her: had caught on quickly as Rosie pulled back . . . 'Sorry!' A laugh like a couple of short breaths, then another quick apology — 'Not funny, is it? Not in the least. Only — don't know about you, I'm — *dazed* . . . Listen, though — they'll be turning us out, any minute now, probably separate us, but —'

'What about Noally — Alain —'

'They killed him. Several others too. He went to a meeting, an informer had leaked it and the SD had the place surrounded. Alain and some others tried to break out, there was a lot of shooting, and — that was that.'

'Lise. I'm so sorry. It's too *awful!*'

'It still *doesn't* seem possible. *Is,* though.'

They were holding each other's hands . . . 'They'd have known who he was and where you lived, so . . .'

'Yes. Actually I bolted, but they still caught me. What happened with you?'

'Long story. One thing, I'm saying I've lost my memory. I think they don't know whether to believe it or not. But I won't know *you,* if —'

'Better not anyway. Vice versa.'

'Yes. They asked me yesterday who I saw in Rennes. I didn't tell them — not *anything.*'

'Good for you. Nor have I, as it happens. They beat *me* — God, *didn't* they!'

'Here?'

'In St Brieuc. What happened was a friend telephoned, told me about Alain, I made a break

497

for it — to a safe-house, so-called, at Fougères. Weren't you going to Fougères when you left us?'

'No. I went west. But your safe-house —'

'They had it staked out, a *souricière*. I walked right into it, like a bloody fool! But I'm denying any connection with SOE. I was Alain's help and artistic disciple, and we fell in love. God knows *that's* true. but if he had other business I didn't know it. I'm just me — Elise Krilov, aspiring artist, Paris-born and educated, never been in England and they've no proof I have. OK?'

'But they're not swallowing it?'

'Associating with an agent's worth a death sentence, isn't it? I can't prove I didn't know — wasn't a pianist, et cetera. They want to know where I'd stashed my radios, of course. Oh, hell, here we go . . .'

Shouts, cell doors crashing open . . .

'Wakey-wakey time. Listen, if you get back and I don't, tell them what happened to Alain?'

'Yes — not that it's likely.'

'And that I didn't tell them anything, and I have no fingernails on this hand.'

'*Lise!*'

'I fainted. Before that I shut my eyes, screamed blue murder, thought about being in Pont Aven with Alain. That would have been such fun. Suzanne —'

'Better not use names?'

'No — you're right . . .'

The light came on: one bare bulb, high up. They were face to face, still holding hands. Shock in Lise's expression at the way Rosie looked, until she'd got it under control. But she herself — Lise — wasn't much changed: a year or two older, maybe — after just a few weeks — and starved, that desperate look they all had. Rosie whispered quickly, 'One thing — in case *you* get back and *I* don't — tell them "Hector" *is* working for the Gestapo, any radio he was using before is likely to be Boche-controlled.'

'I remember — I told you he'd been arrested, you told *us* it could have been faked. But you *will* get back —'

'I know. So will you. Only *in case* —'

'Frankly I wouldn't care all that much. But let's — let's make a point of it?'

'What is it with you two then?'

Irène was sitting up, drawing her legs up too, as into a yoga position. Black accusing eyes, dyed-blonde hair, forty-ish. Staring at Rosie: 'Jesus — *you're* a sight for sore eyes!'

'Thanks.'

'Rats been at you?' She laughed. She had some front teeth missing. Asking Lise, 'Taken to her, have you?'

'Poor kid was flogged yesterday.' She asked Rosie, 'What did this to your face?'

'I'm told I went through a car windscreen. Don't remember it, but —'

The cell door was thrown open. Lise's hands tightened: 'Good luck today. God bless you.' A wardress — not the one who'd dumped Rosie in here last night — checked items on her clipboard, and pointed at Irène. 'You're for release. Second floor, first. You two, queue for breakfast, then *you* —' she meant Rosie — 'back to your old cell.'

Not Rue des Saussaies?

Two days later she saw Lise in the exercise yard. There'd been no recall to Rue des Saussaies. Allowing her time to get her memory back, she guessed. That, or they'd given up on her. No point in thrashing someone who passes out as soon as it starts. That could be it: she didn't know what had happened except that she *had* lost consciousness and before that must have been hit seven or eight times. But if they'd given her up as useless, why waste cell-space, why not get rid of her?

Not a happy thought. More than anything, because of Ben; exactly as in Lise's case it *would* have been because of Noally. Otherwise the fear was less of *whether* it happened than of *how*.

In the exercise yard, Lise had been one of a group just finishing their parading round, Rosie and her two cell-mates — the women who'd stolen Army rations — just arriving. She and Lise had looked at each other with no sign of recognition or mutual interest. That had been June 26, a Monday. One of the less unpleasant wardresses was prepared to confirm dates, days of the week, what the weather was like outside, and so forth. She'd also told them that morning, with apparent relish, that London's civilian population was being evacuated, as a result of the constant and heavy bombardment by 'reprisal weapons'. The Allied invasion, she gave them to understand, wasn't getting anywhere.

Could be that 'Hector' — Marchéval — hadn't been so wide of the mark about that?

Every morning she'd been expecting to be called to another session in Rue des Saussaies, and when on the thirtieth she was ordered out she assumed this was what was happening. The summons came earlier than on the last occasion, before the general réveillé; while she was getting her 'coffee' and piece of bread she'd heard a few other cell doors slamming, but on her way out with a wardress's meaty hand on her arm hadn't thought of others being called out too. Torture was one's own affair, no one else's. Emerging into the courtyard, however, she saw that instead of the prison van it was a military truck waiting — tail-flap down, armed soldiers standing around and three women prisoners already on board, perched in a row on one of the side benches. A guard pointed, gestured with his submachine-gun, and another reached from inside to haul her up. One of the three women on the bench she immediately recognized: a girl by name of Maureen Dennison — round-faced, with brown hair like a bird's nest — who at the age of nineteen or twenty had left on her first deployment when Rosie had been working in Baker Street, earlier in the year. She smiled at her, murmured, 'Hello, Maureen', and saw first the start of surprise, then that all three were in chains. Leg irons, shackles on their ankles with a short chain linking them, and handcuffs. The guard pushed Rosie on to the bench facing these three, and crouched to equip her in the same way. Rosie said, in English — the bastards obviously knew they were all SOE, there couldn't be much to lose — 'This is really a bit much, isn't it?' and a pretty but battered-looking redhead sitting between Maureen and an older woman nodded agreement, told the German haughtily, 'I should warn you, my good man, I have every intention of writing to my MP!' He didn't even know he was being addressed: he was checking Rosie's cuffs — that they were tight enough, she wouldn't be able to pull her rather small hands out of them — and now moved to the rear end, to haul Lise up.

She flopped down, sat expressionlessly watching him fitting her with leg-irons. Commenting in French then with a glance at Rosie, 'He's terrified of me. Hands shaking so much he can't get the key in.' She asked her, 'Where have you been, the last few days?'

'Oh — you know. Around.'

'Busy, eh?'

'Madly.'

'It's a whirl, isn't it?'

'What *I'd* like to know —' the exhausted-looking woman with grey-streaked hair, this was — 'is where are we being whirled off to *now?*'

'Yes. In all this finery.' Maureen jingled her chains. 'Wouldn't be Ascot — d'you think?'

The redhead smiled. '*Wouldn't* we wow 'em!'

Laughter: looking at each other, imagining it, and the guards — two inside with them now and two outside, slamming the tail-gate up and bolting it — glancing round at them in surprise. Lise murmured into Rosie's ear, 'To be boringly serious, I'd say it might be Germany. Clearing us out before the troops get here?'

Chapter 21

At Gare d'Est, they were roughly helped out, Lise murmuring, 'Guessed right, eh?' The two guards who'd come with them had lowered the canvas flap at the rear before they'd started, but even travelling blind it had been obvious they'd been heading into and through Paris. The grey-haired woman, who'd told them her name was Edna and that in her pre-SOE life she'd taught French and German at a particularly famous girls' school, supplemented Lise's remark with: 'Destination Fürstenberg, what's the betting?'

'Fürstenberg?'

A guard shouted, *'Silence!'*

'Rail terminus for Ravensbrück. Fifty miles north of Berlin.' Edna looked scornfully at that guard: 'All right, keep your wool on.'

Rosie whispered, 'Careful . . .'

'What else can they do to us?'

She thought, *They'll think of something . . .*

They were an inventive people, in their own spheres of expertise. At Ravensbrück for instance they either worked you until you dropped or killed you out of hand; either way you ended up in the incinerator. One report had come out, from a Dane who'd had the luck to be extricated by the Swedish Red Cross, of a group of eight English-speaking women prisoners who on the morning after their late-night arrival had been taken out to a gravelled yard, made to kneel in pairs — they'd been allowed to hold hands — and shot in the backs of their heads. And you could say they'd had it easy, at that. Compared to the strangulations, bludgeonings, injections of Phenol in the spine, all of which one had heard of. But now, Rosie told herself — getting the hang of the shuffle-step, the constriction and drag of the chain on her ankles — one's hope had to be to stay alive long enough for liberating forces to arrive.

OK — fat chance, maybe. Recalling the rhetorical question her interrogator had put to her: *'Do you really think we'd want people like yourself left here — left anywhere?'*

A new guard had taken over from the Fresnes lot: neither Gestapo nor SS, ordinary soldiers in drab, greenish uniforms; a corporal signed for them and was given the keys to their chains. Two went ahead, clearing the way — the station was quite crowded — then the five women in single file with guards on both sides and the corporal behind. Shuffling, chains clanking and scraping on stone. Steam hissing deafeningly from an engine. Scared, shocked faces of civilians pausing to let the cortège pass by. As if they could read the placard which in Rosie's grim imagination those in front might have been carrying: *EN ROUTE TO SLAUGHTERHOUSE*. A railwayman surreptitiously gave them the 'V' sign: Rosie smiled at him. Thinking, with the tune suddenly in her head, *The last time I'll see Paris* . . . What a way to leave: and what a shame not to be here to see these savages with their hands up, whining their surrender. It would come, mightn't even be long in coming, unfortunately one wouldn't be around to see it. This had to be their destined departure platform now: up ahead the only view she had was of cattle-trucks, one with its doors open, the rest maybe already loaded. So that one awaited *this* little party. Until this moment she hadn't thought about it, but she did now: envisaging the kind of journey one had heard about, long-distance transportation in a space designed for forty men or eight horses but into which they'd cram a couple of hundred deportees, usually Jews, in the certain knowledge that a number of them would be dead on arrival.

You knew the risks, Rosie, nobody pushed you into it.

Then Ben's voice, urgent in the night: *Pete's sake, WHY do you bloody have to?*

A female English voice cut in then, pitched high over surrounding noise: 'Crikey — proper carriage!'

Daphne — the redhead, who was next-ahead of Lise. Amazingly, it seemed she was right — they were being halted here, opposite what might be the only passenger carriage in the train. Having had her focus mostly on the still open cattle-truck, that dark rectangle through which she'd been steeling herself shortly to file into the truck's gloomy, cavernous and probably foul-smelling interior, she hadn't looked to her right, where in any case one guard had been keeping level with her. She did now, though, facing a carriage of the sort that had separate compartments in it and no corridor. And an SS officer up on the step of this nearest one, watching some activity on the other side of the platform; looking that way over her shoulder Rosie saw a surge of movement, a herd of people flowing by. All women, some clutching children. Long curve of platform, men's shouts, steam blasting: silent, frightened women thronging past.

Heading for that cattle-truck, she realised. Suppressing an urge to scream: steadying herself, feeling dizzy and almost staggering: for a second or two she'd seen herself as in that crowd, with a small child's hand in hers . . .

'Suzanne!'

She came to: closed up towards Lise. Thinking that no scream would help unless it was loud enough to reach heaven. Even if it did — who'd hear it? Two of the soldiers were standing by to help them into the train: in the leg-irons it would otherwise have been impossible. Daphne was pushed up first: Lise followed, then it was her own turn. Then Maureen, finally Edna. The seats were wooden, slatted, hard enough for what promised to be a very long journey but a lot better than the floor of a cattle-truck. She wondered vaguely, *Why us?* Presumably because they were *active* enemies of the Reich. Adding to that thought: *And proud to be. How could one* not *be?*

One of the soldiers climbed in after them and pushed through to check that the door on the other side was locked.

'What do we do for a pee — or anything?'

'Perhaps there'll be stops?'

'Wouldn't count on it. Even though it *is* a heck of a long haul.' You could imagine Edna at a blackboard, chalk in hand. Not looking quite as she did here and now, of course, but with the same glint in those small blue eyes. Smiling at Daphne: 'One benefit of not being over-fed, eh?'

Rosie sat beside Lise. 'Better than it might have been. Favoured-nation treatment?'

'They'd call it Special Category. Anyway, my nation's France, Suzanne.'

'So's mine, really. My real name's Rosie, by the way.'

'Rosie . . .'

'Rosalie, I was christened.'

'Pretty name . . . Listen — if it *is* Ravensbrück we're going to — have to face this, Rosie.'

'They'll kill us when we get there. I know.' It was the fact one *did* have to face. You could resolve to hang on, grit the teeth, cling to life at all costs, but when the time came you couldn't argue with a bullet. She told Lise what the Gestapo interrogator had said, and concluded, 'It must be what they've been doing all the time, but in present circumstances they surely *would* want to sweep us under the carpet — don't you think?'

'I don't know.'

'He actually said, *It's policy.*'

'I was going to say, we have to face that as — well, not at all improbable, but — for instance, with our troops from the west, and the Russians from the east — they *might* — mend their ways? Depends how they look at it. Get rid of us, as you say, or — well, sort of start trying to ingratiate themselves. Like — you know how some dogs learn to smile — like pretending to be human beings?' She'd relapsed into French. Her English was good enough but it was still a foreign tongue to her, an effort. Insisting, 'I think it's very important *some* of us should survive, Rosie. If only so there'll be some who can tell what happened to the ones who *don't*.'

Precisely what the Boches would be determined to prevent, Rosie thought. But there was an interruption at this stage: the SS officer she'd seen earlier — a heavy-set, white-faced creature with a Luger holstered on his belt and what looked very much like a dog-whip in his hand — climbing in with another SS man behind him. A sergeant: a machine-pistol hung loosely in his left hand.

'Attention!'

Glaring round at them as if he loathed them. Rosie thought he probably did. She certainly loathed him. He began to read out a statement in gutturally accented French, from a typed half-sheet of paper. Rations, if they arrived before the departure of the train, would be distributed. If they did not, a meal would be provided at destination. If time allowed, when the train stopped for other purposes, prisoners would be given an

opportunity to alight for 'natural functions'. Any
prisoner attempting to escape would be shot: the
escort under his command had orders to open
fire even on suspicion of any such attempt. Heil
Hitler.

He jumped down to the platform, with the
sergeant following at his heels. Lise observed:
'Won't be doing without *his* rations, the fat swine
. . . Rosie, listen — on that subject —'

The subject of survival, getting back to tell the
tale: suggesting they should fill in some of the
hours that lay ahead of them by telling each other
everything that might interest Baker Street. Like
'Hector', for instance.

It was about an hour before the train pulled out.
Ten a.m., maybe. Nobody had a watch: watches
were gaolers' or arresting officers' perks. Towards
the end of the waiting period two other prisoners
were dumped in with them: a comparatively well-
dressed French-speaking Belgian woman of about
forty and her daughter of about fifteen. They
looked too well fed to be anything but collaborators, Rosie thought. Or black-marketeers. They
wore no chains or handcuffs; were pushed in by
the SS sergeant, and within minutes the train
started — as if it might have been waiting just for
them. The daughter was obviously terrified,
looked as if she'd been crying for a week, sat
huddled against her mother. Occasionally they
whispered to each other. On arrival the woman
had stared around at the prisoners with a look of

shock and obvious distaste, then she was taking care not to look at them at all, concentrating rather unnaturally on the view from the window as the train pulled out.

Lise asked the mother, 'Are you prisoners, Madame?'

A sharp, unfriendly glance: 'Would we be here, if we were not?'

'Perhaps not. But by the look of you, you haven't been long in Boche hands.'

'I prefer not to discuss it. And my daughter is — unwell — so if you don't mind —'

'Not in the least.'

Lise shrugged, met Rosie's eyes and raised her eyebrows. The train was picking up speed. Edna was telling Daphne, 'The direct route, I suppose, would be through Reims and Luxembourg. As well as I can visualize the map, that is. Then I suppose Frankfurt and either Hannover or Leipzig. But with the amount of bombing that's going on — or *was* going on —'

'Might be diversions.'

'Indeed. Might go a long way round to stay clear of it.'

'Crikey — could take bloody *ages!*'

Rosie murmured, 'Lise . . .'

'Huh?'

'I want to say — haven't had much of a chance until now — I'm *desperately* sorry about Noally — Alain.'

'Yes. Yes, thank you.' She shook her dark head. 'But —'

'Sooner not talk about it.'
'Yes. Please.'

She told Lise later, in the course of swapping information for Baker Street — and having reverted to English, because of the strangers in their midst — 'Where I went badly wrong was with this François le Guen. I should have told Baker Street the Trevarez operation wasn't on. Just to let the RAF have a crack at it, if they liked. But le Guen, when the Boches were already taking an interest in him — that was insane, really. How it came about was that Count Jules proposed it — partly for the obvious reasons, the hope of killing Doenitz and company and at least discomforting the U-boat people, and partly to enhance his own standing with communist elements in the Maquis. Baker Street then looked into it, realized it would depend on getting a tip-off well in advance, and asked SIS whether they had any ideas — which was a bit rash, really.'

'Very unusual, surely.'

'One reason was I'd done a job for them, last year, and it had turned out quite well. And I was in line for this deployment.'

'Crafty old Buck!'

'Well . . . SIS referred the question to their man on the spot, who produced le Guen. It looked like a gift, and we jumped at it. Then when I was there and the complications set in — the ball was rolling by that time, my reaction was to find a way around the problem. Not to pull out.

In fact I *should* have pulled out. Count Jules even suggested it, in one conversation we had. I didn't take it seriously; there's a certain amount of rivalry between him and the other man I mentioned, Lannuzel — who was confident we *could* make a go of it.'

'So you went ahead.' Lise nodded. 'I would have, too.'

'Well — if I'd taken the hint from Count Jules —'

'You'd still be there, organizing *parachutages* and flirting with your old doctor. But that's hindsight, Rosie.'

'I did *not* flirt with him!' She smiled. 'Nice old man though he is. Please God, still *is*. I think he must have got away, all right. Either to the Maquis — who knew him, would have welcomed him I'm sure — or he could have done a bunk through the good offices of his sister Marthe.'

'Who operated an escape line.'

'Safe-house as part of an escape-line. I'm fairly sure she was also connected to the man I told you I saw being arrested. Timo Achard. I'm pretty sure he was hand-in-glove with both the Peucats. Well, I've told you all that — a lot of it's speculation, but there were a lot of wheels within wheels, in that community. Incidentally, Henri Peucat would have taken my Mark III transceiver with him — he knew where I'd hidden it, I'm sure he would. That's the point, really — he certainly merits "F" Section's thanks.'

'All right.' Lise had her eyes shut. 'I'll remem-

513

ber. If I have to, which please God I won't. The important thing's "Hector", of course. But the Trevarez business, I really don't think you should blame yourself for it. I'm sure *they* wouldn't. If you *had* called it off, they'd have said, "Oh, Rosie's got cold feet." We've all taken chances, haven't we — wouldn't have got anywhere if we hadn't. Sometimes they pay off, sometimes they don't.'

'Let's have *your* story.'

'All right. There's not much of it, though. It was all in signals, Baker Street know everything except for the very end. The two things that matter are the safe-house in Fougères that's blown — at least, if I could get that news to them *now* it might save a life or two — and about that shit of an informer. One, some detail so they can pin it on him — he deserves to hang — and two, to have them know it wasn't any blunder of Alain's. I'll start with that . . .'

The train's first stop came after about four hours — or three, or five — at a station in a sizeable town which wasn't identifiable. No name-boards on the platform, and on the signal boxes it had been painted over. Bomb-damage had been visible, apparently, during the approach, but Rosie didn't see it. Edna thought the place wasn't big enough to be Reims; she thought earlier that they'd been on a more easterly or south-easterly route than the Reims direction, which would be north of east. Rosie had been dozing when the train was pulling in, only came properly awake when the Belgian woman began shouting and banging on tne window to get the attention of soldiers on the platform. They'd swarmed out almost before the train had stopped; it seemed they were travelling in the other compartments of this carriage, and some had been sent forward at the double to patrol around the cattle-trucks up front. The Belgian woman was yelling through the quarter-open window — there was a stop preventing it from opening any further — that her daughter had to get to a *toilette*, the poor child was in agony. Rosie murmured to Lise, 'Does she think the SS care if their prisoners suffer agonies?' Surprisingly, the SS sergeant did come along, heard what she wanted and went away again. Mother and daughter were both in tears then, but he came back, unlocked the compartment door and detailed two soldiers to escort them to the lavatory. Others who wanted to go too were told to shut up. Edna grumbled, 'One law for the rich . . .' Rosie sat back and shut her eyes: she'd been having a dream in which Ben had featured, and wanted to get back into it. She heard Daphne saying how dreadful it must be for the women in the cattle-trucks — no one was escorting *them* to any damn *toilette*. Edna commented, 'You're quite right. We should count our blessings,' and added, 'count our blessings and just let rip!' There was some laughter, then Maureen's tearful-sounding, 'But it'd be so *uncomfortable* . . .' Muttering under her breath,

'Please, *please* come and take *me?*'

Compared to being made to kneel and then shot in the back of the head, it seemed a small thing to worry about, Rosie thought. But she'd always had excellent control in that department. What concerned her much more was hunger. Thirst too, but mainly hunger. Partly through awareness of how weak she was already: so it was partly psychological, easier therefore if one could keep the mind off it. Sleep was the best thing: if one *could* get back into it.

'Must say, they're taking their time about it!'

That had been Daphne. Then Lise was nudging Rosie. 'Some commotion out there. Rosie — look . . .'

A mêlée of soldiers: some kind of disturbance. The SS sergeant appeared suddenly amongst them — with a gun — machine-pistol — in his fist, other arm waving men back towards the train, and the scene resolved itself into the Belgian woman being frog-marched back to the compartment with one soldier behind her and one on each side with an arm each, and the daughter following with another trooper holding her by the scruff of her neck.

'Must have tried to get away.'

'Maybe. Crazy . . .'

'There go *our* chances of a pee!'

The sergeant wrenched the door open, his men shoved the mother up and the one with the child lifted her in too. The sergeant still held the door: he was holstering his pistol. His officer arrived

516

then, pink with anger. He climbed in, stood glaring down at the panting, weeping woman, told her in his laboured French: 'You are fortunate not to have been shot!'

Glancing around: a hard look at each of them in turn. Rosie, who was opposite the Belgians and therefore behind him, was the last to be inspected. She'd seen it coming and by that time was looking down, at her handcuffed wrists.

Try never to look them in the face. A stare returned can be taken as a challenge . . .

'Here.' He handed the sergeant a bunch of keys. 'Take the leg-irons off this one, and —' gesturing towards Edna — 'that pair of handcuffs. Put them on this stupid bitch.'

Leg-irons from Rosie, handcuffs from Edna. Rosie blessed that SOE lecturer for his advice on looking weak and inoffensive.

'Excuse me, sir . . .'

Lise. The SS captain paused, scowled at her. 'Well?'

'We would all — please — like to visit the *toilette*.'

'*Would* you?' He edged to the door around the sergeant, who was crouching, trying different keys in Rosie's ankle-cuffs.

They were stopped for about an hour, and each in turn was escorted to the *toilette*. Rosie had a suspicion that in Maureen's case it might have been too late. Edna had said to Lise, 'Pity you didn't tell him we'd like a meal too, while you were at it.' The Belgian woman had gone into a daze, and the child was having trembling fits. Edna had tried to talk to her, but the mother had snapped at her to leave them in peace.

Rosie thought, Some *peace* . . . She couldn't get back to sleep; sat watching the passing scenery and thinking about Ben. Wondering whether Marilyn Stuart would have told him she'd come to grief. They'd have no detail of what had happened — unless of course Prigent had managed to get out — but they'd know she was in trouble; having had no responses to signals, and no report on 'Mincemeat', or further requests for paradrops. Except possibly phoney ones, if either of her transceivers had fallen into Boche hands. In fact the radio left *chez* Peucat would be safe enough, in *his* hands, only the one they'd dropped with the 'S' phone and which she'd left in that weapons cache might be less so — if the cache was unearthed, as so many had been.

She hoped — not for the first time — that Lannuzel and Brigitte had come through all right. If they had it would be thanks entirely to Messieurs Prigent and Peucat. But one wouldn't know until it was all over, or at least until the Boches were cleared out, and she could go back and visit them. Taking Ben with her: showing him off to Sara de Seyssons, finding Henri Peucat then — please God. And touching wood, knowing that even *dreaming* of such things was purely wishful, never-never land. Except you couldn't say it was *totally* impossible: who could know *anything* with total certainty, in this kind of situation? She glanced at Lise, who was dozing: getting back to that dream then, recognizing that even if some magic wand did wave and make any of it possible one would definitely not be visiting Pont Aven. It would have been the peak of everything, but it would be out of bounds now. Unless Lise decided otherwise: which she wouldn't, surely. She was marvellous, Rosie thought. Stricken by her deprivation, but keeping it resolutely to herself. One saw that stricken devastated look from time to time — when she was lost in her own thoughts and unaware of being observed — but she didn't *let* it show.

'That's a great story.'

She'd been telling Lise about her first meeting with Ben and the highlights of their subsequent relationship including the fact that after that first alcoholic and tempestuous night she'd hidden herself from him for about a year, only met him again by chance when she'd been leaving for France in the Dartmouth gunboat of which he'd been navigating officer. And something that hadn't been mentioned before — that Lise must at least have seen him, on that beach on Guenioc Island. To her he'd have been just one of about a dozen dark figures busy around the dinghies in that boil of surf: and she, Rosie, an unknown, faceless fellow-agent who'd approached her and wished her luck.

'And I was so stand-offish, eh?'

519

The train's whistle had shrieked: now there was the roar of a goods train thundering past. All closed trucks. Gone, then: doubtless full of munitions for the front in Normandy. Its passing left a contrasting quiet, only this train's pounding rhythm . . . The Belgian woman had her head back and eyes shut, but wasn't sleeping. Her daughter hadn't woken though, was still folded against her, fast asleep with her tousled head on Mama's shoulder.

Lise sighed. 'Must be — what, eight, eight-thirty?'

'Nearer nine, I'd have thought. Oh, we're slowing . . .'

For another stop? The surroundings had become suburban and industrial: she hadn't noticed until now. Light beginning to fade, too. Estimates of time had been the subject of general discussion an hour or so ago, each of them giving her own notion of it, and arriving at an average of the guesses. There might be a check of sorts, before long, based on Edna's estimate that sunset would be at about nine-fifteen.

This was a large town coming up.

'Where are we, Edna?'

'I was wondering.' Blinking at rows of houses without gardens, and beyond them the rectangular bulk of factories. 'Could be *anywhere.*'

'Wouldn't it be nice if we could be.' Daphne, smiling at her. 'Anywhere, I mean. With a free choice, where would one choose? London? Tunbridge Wells?'

The Belgian had her eyes open, but her daughter still slept. Squinting down at her, having to move both linked hands, using a forefinger to told her collar down. Then meeting Rosie's eyes, and glancing quickly away, her expression tightening. The train's rhythm was slowing even more.

'I don't think we are going to stop.'

Maureen, peering out as a signal-box swam by on that side. Then on *this* side a platform, station buildings, unreadable notices in French and German, a group of *Veldpolitzei* and a scattering of waiting passengers.

'*Aren't* stopping. Big place, though. Come on, Edna, make a guess!'

The rhythm in Rosie's brain spelt out *Ra*-vens-brück, *Ra*-vens-brück, *Ra*-vens-brück. Places *en route* didn't seem to have much to do with anything.

L'enfer des femmes. Which had been a nightmarish concept in her more sombre thinking throughout three deployments now . . . Looking round at the others, she was struck by how weirdly minds could, for at any rate brief periods, shut out reality. A disparate bunch of women, some in chains, chatting together like a bunch of tourists discussing their itinerary.

Notionally, were they so to speak holding hands? An ostensibly crazy reflex with a purpose, therefore?

Edna called out suddenly — in French pronunciation — '*Nancy!*'

'What?'

'The town is Nancy! I saw it — on that signal-box, they've painted it over but the paint's worn thin!'

'So what does that tell us?'

The Belgian met Rosie's glance, and for the first time held it. 'Did she say that was Nancy?'

'Yes.' She smiled at her: and saw the girl's eyes were open. 'Your daughter's awake now.' To the child: 'Nice sleep, you had.' The rhythm was changing again — shorter, faster: *Ra*vensbrück, *Ra*vensbrück . . . Edna telling them — estimating how long it might be before they crossed the frontier into Germany — 'I suppose — if it's nine o'clock now, say — which going by the light it might be — well, depends where we're aiming for. Strasbourg, Karlsruhe — that would be more in the right direction.'

'*Right* direction?'

Daphne — shaking her head, 'Honestly . . .'

Dozing, half remembering and half dreaming. She was in the naval hospital at Haslar, the first time she'd been allowed to visit him since he'd brought his gunboat back from the French coast smashed up and near-sinking, full of dead and wounded, the wounded including himself. He'd been encased in bandages and plaster and had been due to have a second operation on his knee next morning. When she'd first had the news it had sounded as if things were touch-and-go, whether he'd survive or not; she'd had to wait four days before they'd let her see him, and they'd been about the worst four days of her life. She'd told him so, he'd pointed at her with the arm that didn't have a drip-feed connected to it, and rasped, 'Liar!'

'Ben, I am *not* —'

'How about when the bastard Gestapo had you?'

'Oh.' Relaxing, shrugging. Pervaded through all of this by a feeling of huge relief because half an hour earlier a doctor had told her Ben was going to be OK; he was extremely lucky that the damage to that knee was repairable and that he wouldn't have to lose the leg. Smiling at him. 'That was different.'

'I bet it was!'

'Anyway, I've been through it, it can't happen again.'

'Can't?'

'Odds heavily against. Ben, you take your chances — right, and end up like this? Well, I take mine.'

'*Hell* of a bloody difference!'

Laughing: reaching to hold that hand. 'I love you, Benjamin.'

'Bloody better. Same here, though. Couldn't do without you, Rosie. Don't know how I ever did.'

'You won't have to again.'

'Huh? Changed your mind? God's truth, Rosie?'

'No — *that's* not what I'm saying. I mean long-term — the rest of our lives. No, Ben, I've got to

— I've *told* them, I can't back out.'

'Wish to God you would.'

'I'll see this one through, then I'll be back and that'll be it. I swear.'

'I love you. Listen, soon as I get out of here —'

Howl of the train's whistle: juddering of brakes or wheels, that rhythm breaking up. She was awake — or coming awake: seeing the others' faces, expressions of alarm, the whole compartment shaking and the screech of iron braking on iron. Fading light out there: a wide river on the right, open pasture this near side. In front of her the Belgian girl was bolt-upright, clutching her mother's arm.

'Breakdown?'

'Something on the line ahead, more like.'

As it turned out, that was it. The train was sliding to a jerky stop, and there was a roar of escaping steam. Rosie, on her feet then at the window — thanks to not having leg-irons on now — saw soldiers jumping down on to the track and running up towards the engine. The SS captain was out there too, shouting after the sergeant as he too trotted off in that direction.

Edna's voice behind her: 'What's cooking, Rosie?'

She described it, as much as she could see. The SS man had posted riflemen to watch these doors — or this door — and strutted off after the rest of them. Maureen said wishfully, 'Perhaps we'll be stuck here for the night.'

'Big deal. With not a damn thing to eat?'

'Oh, don't remind me . . .'

'Anyway, it's a lovely evening for it!'

Jocular: on the count-your-blessings principle. But it *was* a lovely evening. Pinkish sunset glow, deep-green meadowland with a wood beyond it, and on the train's other side a placid stretch of river curving away southward. Definitely southward because the line behind them pointed near enough into the sunset: the direction of travel at this point had been just north of east.

Soldiers led by the SS officer were coming back now.

'Our lord and master's returning to us.'

Returning without his sergeant, she noted. Trying to understand what was going on. The window was as far open as it would go, and she'd been hearing what she now guessed must have been cattle-trucks' doors crashing open.

The Belgian woman asked her, 'What is there to see?'

'Nothing much. But the officer's on his way back, might condescend to tell us something.'

He was issuing orders — which seemed to amount to leaving some men here and sending the rest up front where he'd just been. Taking his cue from the grand old Duke of York, maybe . . . Glaring round then, seeing Rosie standing at the window watching him, he pointed at her with his stick, bawled in crude French, 'Sit down! Sit, wait!'

She sat. Lise had seen some of it from where she was sitting. Rosie told the others, 'He said sit and wait. I *think* they're disembarking the people from the trucks. Sounded like it — and he's sent most of the soldiers up that way.'

Maureen murmured, 'Beautiful light, out there.'

'Quite soon be dark, though.' Daphne, that had been. She was right; the landscape had the depth of colour that invariably precedes summer dusk. Lise murmured very quietly, 'You don't think it could be —' She'd paused, glancing round; finished cryptically, 'What it *might* be?'

'Hardly think so. Why bring us *here* for it?'

'Another question might be why all the way to Ravensbrück?'

'Because that's one of the places where they do such things. Unseen and unheard-of by the outside world, they hope.'

She looked out to the other side, at the luminous glow on the river's surface. 'Would you like to paint that, Lise?'

'No. It's too pretty. For *me*, that is. Maybe your man — Ben, is it?'

'Good memory.' She hadn't mentioned him since the night she'd spent in Rennes, in Noally's house. 'But I doubt it. He goes for — more dramatic scenes. Movement —'

'Drama.'

'Right.'

Edna, Maureen and Daphne all had their eyes on the river. Edna admitted she didn't know the names of any in this part of the country except for the Moselle, which couldn't be far from here but she thought would be a lot wider.

'Moselle.' Daphne sighed. 'Evocative, eh?'

'Germans call it *Mosel.*'

'Germans don't know their arses from their elbows.'

The door in Rosie's side was unlocked, pulled open: a soldier of some kind — corporal, maybe — shouted, *'Raus!'*

Edna translated, 'They want us to get out. I wonder why.'

Lise glanced at Rosie with an eyebrow cocked, asking the same question.

'Well . . .'

The Belgian was on her feet, pulling her daughter up with her. Edna had begun to move too, but no one else had. As if the compartment had become some sort of refuge, safe haven?

The soldier shouted again, more angrily. Two others were standing back with their rifles more or less levelled; the one who'd shouted, and another, their own weapons still slung, seemed to be waiting to help the women down. The chained ones anyway. She went out first, slightly handicapped by the handcuffs, and one of them grabbed her arm to steady her: before she could stop herself she'd muttered, *'Merci . . .'*

'Attention!'

The captain. Pistol still in its holster, she noted. Stick in hand — it was more swagger-stick than whip, but you could bet he'd use it for hitting people when he felt so inclined. Soldiers faced them, and the train was at their backs: she met

Lise's glance again and slightly shook her head: whatever they were going to do they'd hardly do it here, in the open and right beside the tracks. The German began: 'A train is — how to say this —'

'Captain,' Edna broke in, in German, offering to translate.

He'd glared at her, angry at being interrupted, but now nodded. 'Good.' Edna, Rosie thought, *might* survive Ravensbrück, making herself useful as an interpreter. Unless they already had as many as they needed. She was looking to her right, seeing the tail-end of the column of people from the cattle-trucks diminishing in that direction, with the blaze of sunset at their backs.

It truly did *not* look propitious. Except that logic suggested they'd hardly slaughter them in open countryside.

'He says —' Edna, interpreting — 'the line's blocked and we've got to transfer to another train. Something's happened to a train ahead of this one and they've brought another that's waiting up there beyond it. Sounds like it might have been bombed. Blocking both lines, apparently. Bombing *might* spread it around a bit, I suppose. Anyway, we've got to hoof it — pronto, while it's still light.'

Rosie put the gist of it into French for the Belgians. The German pointed his stick at Edna and told her something else: she translated, 'Anyone attempting escape, he says, will be shot dead.'

Rosie translated that too. The woman queried

peevishly, 'Escape, like *this?*' She clanked off, shrugging, in the wake of the SS man and with her daughter hanging on to her. In the irons you couldn't cover the ground easily even when you'd got used to them, and the German wasn't waiting, was leaving it to the soldiers to bring them along. It must have been at about this moment, in a very quick assessment of the situation in which this left them all that Rosie made her decision. Lise saw her standing absolutely still — noticeably so, as the others began to straggle off — gazing out across darkening grassland at the belt of trees — or a wood, it might have been, an edge of forest. Lise called to her — quietly, no note of urgency or concern, not wanting to draw the Germans' attention to what seemed like a show of independence, knowing the Boche tendency in such circumstances to use rifle-butts — and Rosie looked round at her — hesitantly, was Lise's impression — before moving to join her. The nearer of two soldiers on the field side of the prisoners did look round for her — may have counted the others first — saw she was on her way to tag on beside Lise — also that another guard was not far behind and catching up — and was satisfied with that. The formation as they all moved off was thus the Belgian and her child leading, Edna close behind them, Maureen and Daphne together behind Edna, then Lise with Rosie closing in on her left. The SS captain was well ahead, passing the now empty cattle-trucks whose doors some recently detached *soldaten* had been slamming shut, and here there were four left guarding them — two on the outside, more or less abreast of the Belgians and Edna, one on the inside — ahead, frequently looking back over his shoulder — and the fourth now only a few paces behind Lise. Behind Rosie's right shoulder, therefore.

'Lise.'

She turned her head. 'Huh?'

'Don't faint or scream, but — I'm going to make a break for it.'

A hiss: 'You'd be *crazy* —'

'— going to run for those trees —'

'Two hundred metres —' a glance that way, then back at her — 'at *least* —'

'I'll dodge like mad. I'm up to it, been resting all day. No — hush . . . When they start after me — well, shooting — the one behind us now'll rush out to the left — there. Only way he *can* go — get a clear field of fire. That'll leave you on your own, and they'll *all* be looking that way, Lise —'

'You won't get ten metres — not a *chance* —'

'There's a *good* chance — for *you*. Only way it can be — they took *my* chains off, not yours, so I do the running. Lise dear — under the train — crawl under — and into the river. Stay till it's dark and they've gone. They'll have to go on — *have* to. God knows what then — get to a house, farm, offer them money. Tell them fifty thousand francs, Baker Street'll pay. Lise, this *is* a chance, Ravensbrück's *no* chance, you know it. Good luck, God bless . . .'

'*Rosie* —'

She'd ducked away, was sprinting, manacled hands up against her body. The man behind Lise shouted, started after her. As she'd known he would. In front the nearer one whipped round, lifting the rifle to his shoulder, swivelling back then to bring his sights on her. Daphne's voice in a scream — 'Oh, *Christ!*' And bedlam. Lise heard the first shot as she hit the ground, crawled and rolled into darkness under the train, jacking herself over the rails with her forearms in the clinker, knees drawn up, toppling herself over: there was a lot of shooting, German shouts, women's screams. She was out from under the train then, off the clinker under a wire-and-timber barrier into grass with a down-gradient towards the river. Gasping, sobbing, still telling Rosie no, *no*, Rosie — hearing a shout like an echo of her own plea, Edna's shriek of, 'Oh, God, *no-o-o!*' One single shot, then. She was rolling: legs together, forearms together too, pressed close to her chest: the shine of water darkened by the train's shadow gleamed close sooner than she'd expected, with a drop of three or four feet into its shallow muddy edge.

Chapter 22

Ben had his elbows on the table, face in his hands and a cigarette between his fingers. August 1, close on noon. The US 1st Army, the BBC had said this morning, had broken through at or near St-Lô. Marilyn Stuart had telephoned him at his digs when he'd been listening to that early bulletin and asked him if he'd meet her here in the SOE building in Baker Street at eleven. She had no *good* news for him at all, she'd warned, only confirmation of what had been guessable since June 10 when she'd given him the last update.

Progress of the war in France had seemed slow, in these weeks. Around the beachheads the weather hadn't helped, while the doodlebugs had been bumbling across the Channel from launch sites in the Pas de Calais and Belgium to kill women and children in the streets and in their homes. It might not be long — please God — before those launch sites were over-run. The Germans' retreat had been cut off now in Normandy: roads were jammed with their retreating columns and Allied air forces were giving them no peace. Avranches had fallen: Canadians and British were attacking down the Falaise road. From Avranches, some divisions of General Patton's 3rd Army had swung west into Brittany. It was the U-boat bases the enemy would be most desperate to hang on to: U-boats with their new homing torpedoes were still taking a heavy toll of Atlantic shipping. Those bases would be the Yanks' targets — Brest, St Nazaire, Lorient, La Rochelle. While throughout Brittany 30,000 *Résistants* had come out of the shadows now, were fighting in the open.

Rosie, who according to Marilyn Stuart had helped to arm them, seeing none of it.

He took his hands away from his face, in the process fingering moisture from his eyes. Flicking a length of ash from the cigarette, inhaling smoke. He'd known it: had known it with increasing, sickening certainty for the past — what, six, eight weeks . . . Telling himself there still was hope — because there'd *had* to be. He'd seen Marilyn once, in that time — met her by chance in this building, and seen in her face that she had no illusions either: they'd said hello Ben, hello Marilyn — nothing else.

Nothing else *to* say.

Until now. Forcing himself to it, the words shaping themselves darkly in his brain: *Rosie's dead.*

No point kidding oneself any more. The loss was total and permanent. He took another drag at his cigarette; looking across the table at Elise. Elise Krilov: she had a name now, this hitherto shadowy, almost mythical creature. An hour ago when Marilyn had introduced them, before starting to read a transcript of some of her de-briefing, it hadn't been easy to merge her into his image of the girl on the Guenioc beach of whom Rosie had said once, 'That girl's *me*, Ben' — when she'd been trying to explain the dichotomy of a compulsion to re-

533

turn to the field and a clear recognition — and horror — of what was entailed in doing so.

Not Elise, though — Lise. She'd told him this, after Marilyn had introduced her as Elise. She was tall, slim, with short dark hair and wide, rather slanted eyes. They were green, he thought. Marilyn hadn't turned any lights on; after all, it was mid-summer and near-enough midday — but this briefing room wasn't well lit and there was a grey sky out there. Earlier there'd been some drizzle.

He cleared his throat. 'I'm very sorry about — not sure I got the name, was it Noally?'

'Alain Noally, yes.'

Looking down at her hands, frowning. Then a shrug . . . 'You and he would have got on well. Rosie thought you would. She liked him very much. The four of us were going to be great friends — so she and I both hoped.'

'That's it, then. We would've. But —' he looked at Marilyn — 'going back to this escape — if you have the time to hear about it —'

'You'd like to. Well —'

'What river did you say it was?'

'The Meurthe.'

Lise had put that in, saving Marilyn from having to look it up in the transcript. Ben hadn't ever heard of it. He said, 'From there to getting signals out via your bloke in Nancy — sounds easy the way you have it there, but —'

'With one bound.' Lise smiled. Her French accent was attractive. Asking Marilyn, 'Like me to tell him?'

'Well, why not.' Checking her watch. 'I *must* look back into my own office — return a call or two, and —'

'Never returned mine, far as I remember?'

'Well, Ben —'

'I know. Don't worry. Forgave you long ago.'

'You're a kind man, Ben.' She was gathering the stuff into her briefcase. Having read the story somewhat selectively to this point, he'd realized — skipping the odd line or paragraph, doubtless to spare his feelings. She hadn't been exactly unmoved herself; she and Rosie had been close colleagues for quite a long time. But bare facts as transcribed from recordings in any case reduced the emotional content, to which either or both of them might have succumbed. He *had,* to some extent. And she'd left out the bit he wanted now because all that directly concerned him was the fact and manner of Rosie's death, and the circumstances leading to it: so from there she'd skipped to Lise having somehow established contact with the SOE's *chef de réseau* in Nancy and through him passed to London vital information which Rosie had confided to her. In other words, Rosie had been doing her job right up to the last minute — had effectively passed the ball to Lise, before giving her a chance of running with it.

Then there'd been a pick-up arranged — a Hudson of the Special Duties Squadron from Tempsford in Hertfordshire.

The door closed behind Marilyn. Ben prompted Lise: 'You went into the river, with chains on your wrists and ankles — and obviously not in exactly tip-top condition?'

'That was even more so in Rosie's case. How she made that run . . . She'd said earlier she felt as weak as a rat. Those were her words. I even had to laugh. Some little rat — eh?'

He nodded. Looking down again, fiddling with his lighter. Lise went on, 'Anyway — I lay there for maybe an hour. I knew if I moved I might be seen — ripples in the water reflecting light, you know . . .'

He offered her a cigarette, and lit it for her. Seeing it all happen, then, as she described it. Lights flashing around for some while up where the train still stood: she'd guessed they'd have been expecting to find her under it. The river was as still as glass and she was invisible to them in the lee of the low bank; from up there it would have looked as if the water just lapped the grass slope, with no vertical bank at all. A trick of the light, maybe, but she hadn't known there was a bank until she'd rolled over it. She'd been pre-pared to drown herself, she said, if it had looked like they were going to find her. The chain's weight anchored her legs to the mud, and she'd reckoned she'd be able to pass the handcuffs over her head so that the chain linking them would rest across the back of her neck and hold her face down in the water. She didn't experiment with it because she didn't want to make a ripple or any sound, after the disturbance of her splashing in had settled.

'After some time the train backed away. It would have had to go all the way to Nancy, I think, to get to — is it called points?'

'Right.'

'And the guards must have all have gone on with the prisoners . . . You don't — wouldn't understand if I told this in French, I suppose?'

'Not very well. But maybe — if you spoke slowly —'

'No, it's OK. Just I'm lazy.'

'Hell, it's *me* that's —'

'I heard the other train go. Rosie had been right, they couldn't stay for ever. My poor friends, I thought of, maybe in a cattle truck now instead of a carriage . . . Two things then — no, three. One, I'm weak, hungry, cold, didn't have much strength to waste. Two, must all the same get away from there as far as possible while it's dark. Three, with the chains on me, and resembling a — well, a *drowned* rat — I better try to be out of sight before daylight. OK, four — I must have shelter and food, or I'm — *kaput*. You understand, Ben — Rosie did not do what she did just for me — although I am sure she would have — it was also so the truth would get back about some other things. I was thinking about that, a lot. And in the first light, the dawn, I am just sort of trudging along the river bank — I think wandering in my mind a bit — I hear a sound that is coming closer, and it is oars. And these fishermen show up. Little boat, two old men. I mean, quite old. I call, splash in, it is not deep, I can wade out to them. They are scared, and when they see the chains one of them starts shouting, even tries to hit me with the oar — it's crazy for a minute, but thank God the other one shut him up. I tell you about them — what I learn in the following hours. The one who owns the boat does go fishing, but this trip they are really scavenging, with the friend along to help, he's going to where he's heard is the wrecked train. His name is Patrice, he grows vegetables for market and catches fish, not much else. The other one, who is related to him some way, is a builder — you say handyman? From the wrecked train perhaps they find materials, they think — seats, anything. But it's not legal, they should not be there, he's scared and after that one's calmed down I'm not getting any trouble from them.'

'Took you into the boat, did they?'

'Some luck, eh? I call it Fate. Not always so kind, unfortunately . . . Anyway — I lay in the bottom of their boat, and they rowed back to the home of the one who owns it. I promise them a a lot of money — and this persuaded his wife too, when we get there — his wife and a daughter-in-law, their son's in Germany on forced labour. They have almost no money, twenty thousand francs sounds like a fortune to them. Five thousand for his friend, twenty for them if they hide me in their house and feed me, and to make contact for me with local Resistance. It's what happened — easier than it might have been of course because they all know the Boches are going

538

to lose, it's only a matter of time — only dangerous for them for a short time, therefore. The old
man and the daughter-in-law filed off the handcuffs, then left it to me to file the leg-irons. Very
hard work — but OK, I have nothing else to do,
except eat and sleep. The mother meanwhile goes
into Blâmont — it's a town not far away — and
talks to some person they know, a *Résistant* — a
railwayman, as it happens — and that's the ball
rolling, after only two, three days the SOE *chef
de réseau* in Nancy has been in touch with — here,
Baker Street, and my identity is confirmed, from
then on I am safe. Any doubt of it, they'd have
killed me, but it's OK. They send the other information for me then, and — oh, just a few more
days, they send an airplane from Tempsford to
pick up me and some others from a place between
Nancy and Metz. SOE have agreed, by the way,
they will pay those people what I promised. I think
there are many such debts, for payment soon.'

'You still make it sound easy, Lise.'

'Made it *short* — you don't want to listen to
me all day, eh?'

'Well — might listen to you over lunch — if
you'd care to join me?'

'Oh — I'm sorry —'

'Some other time, then.'

'It's sweet of you, Ben. I'd like it, too — please,
some other time — if you want to ask me —'

'No *if* about it. But — you've been in England
— about three weeks?'

'Just over two weeks. There's been de-briefing

— a lot happened in Rennes before any of this, you see — a *lot* of de-briefing . . . Also letting my hair grow — long way to go yet, of course —'

'Grow it long, will you?'

'Longer than it is now, sure!'

'And what else? I mean the future, what —'

'There's still work. Maybe trials of persons named in my report and Rosie's — one especially, I can testify to what she told me . . . And a man who betrayed Alain. Could become complicated soon, with Gaullists taking over — well, please God —'

'D'you have any family?'

'My father and mother are in Switzerland — since the war started. Before that we lived in Paris. I will see them, some time, but — no hurry. Well — *can't* hurry.'

Her eyes *were* green. An almost oriental slant to them. Very calm in her manner, very — composed, he thought. After what she'd been through — what *they'd* been through . . . He asked her — giving himself another cigarette — 'You don't mind being asked all these questions, I hope?'

'By you, Ben, not at all.'

'Well — thanks —'

She showed him her left hand. 'Very different kind of questioning was going on when they pulled those nails out.'

'*Christ!* Oh, the *bastards!*'

Reaching over — to hold that hand for a moment. On the point — almost — of kissing it: complete impulse, and the thought of Rosie —

as if it were *her* hand . . . '*Heard* of such things, but —' He checked as another thought hit him: 'They do anything like this to *her?*'

'No. No, Ben, they didn't. Nothing . . . But — I want to tell you — Alain was a sculptor — you maybe never heard of him, but in France he was well known. And I paint, that's how we got together. Then we fell in love: they don't realize it here — here in SOE, I don't think they do, we were just pianist and *chef de réseau,* is all they know. But — Rosie said you paint too?'

'Haven't touched a brush in years. Dabbled, that's all. You're good, I dare say?'

'I'd like to be. I will be one day — I hope.'

'Your name, Krilov. Are your parents Russian?'

'My father, yes. Mama is French. Papa came out of Russia at the time of the revolution.' She smiled. 'I don't have to ask *you* so many questions, Ben, I know quite a lot. Your parents in Australia in the timber business, and before that your father was a sailor?'

'Rosie telling tales . . .'

'But you don't feel sure you'll go into the business with your father as he wants?'

'Do have mixed feelings on that. But the war's got a long way to go yet, hasn't it . . . One idea, mind you — pipe-dream maybe — look, I don't want to bore you —'

'Don't worry, you won't.'

'Want to bet?'

'Please . . .'

'Well — mate of mine at Australia House here

tells me they're hatching a scheme to get more land into productive use. Idea is they'll *give* you a grant of land — bush — long as you clear it and fence it inside a certain time-limit. Big tracts of land — he was saying maybe two and a half thousand acres to kick off with, then if you do it in the time you're allowed you can go for another slice. It's all in the air, they're still chewing it over, but — hell, be room to bloody *breathe*, you know?'

'Very hard work?'

'Yeah, but —'

'With your knee?'

'Knee's better every day. In fact I'm trying to get back to sea. Wasn't trying all that hard until now. You know, to be here, if — well, what *won't* happen, now —'

Marilyn came in, looking flustered . . . 'Finished? Impressed, Ben?'

'He should be.' Lise told her, 'I made myself out a real heroine — didn't I, Ben?'

'Reminds me.' Marilyn wasn't rejoining them, by the looks of it; anyway she wasn't sitting down. 'Ben — speaking of heroines — Colonel Buck's putting Rosie up for a posthumous George Cross. He thinks there's a good chance she'll get it.'

He was silent: looking down at his hands on the table, thinking about it. Rosie, GC. And why the hell *not* . . . Nodding at Marilyn: 'Good. *Good.* In fact — stupendous . . .'

He was suppressing emotion *now*, all right. Helped slightly by his own next thought of how much more stupendous it would have been to have had her here now, totally undecorated, un-adorned, just neat, live Rosie . . . Marilyn saying to Lise, meanwhile — he suddenly woke up to this — that she was sorry, she'd had to change some lunch arrangement: it was a thing she couldn't argue with, Colonel Buck and some Air Chief Marshal . . .

'Listen,' Ben cut in. 'I was going to ask you both to have a snack with *me*. But if Lise's on her own now —'

'Ben, that's an excellent idea!'

He met Lise's calm, thoughtful gaze.

'Will you?'

'It's very kind of you —'

'Not kind at all. Except to myself.'

'Oh, but — Lise . . .' Marilyn, having started to leave them, turned back, her fingertips on the back of the chair she'd sat in earlier. 'Did you mention — you know, the straw we — well, *tried* to clutch at?'

'No.' Lise looked troubled. 'Because I don't believe in it, and it could be hurtful, only — prolong the hurt.' A shake of the head. '*I* think.'

'But it is *possible*.' Looking at Ben now. 'I don't think we can totally ignore it, Ben. Probably isn't any more than — wishing for the moon, but —'

'What isn't? If Lise doesn't mind, what —'

'When she made her run for it — under the train and down that slope — embankment, what-ever — she heard shots and screams — and one final shot, that's the worst, perhaps: but the point is, Ben, we don't know, not for *certain* —'

'Because I didn't see her killed. It's true — I did not, but —'

'You heard it.'

'Yes, Ben. I heard it. I truly did. When I think back to what I heard, I *see* it.'

Downstairs, then, passing through the narrow hallway in which he'd first met Rosie: literally bumped into her . . .

He pulled the door open: 'Where I first set eyes on her. Right here.'

'She told me. Your first date.'

'Wasn't a date, exactly. We both needed a few stiff ones, that's all. She was drowning sorrows, I had reason to celebrate, so —'

'So there you were. Yes. She told me the whole story.' They were outside, on the pavement, now. 'I'm so sorry, Ben. So very, *very* sorry.'

'It's the finality of it, isn't it? Doesn't go away, won't ever. Same with your — Noally, I'm sure. *I*'m sorry . . . Listen, I thought we'd go to a club called the Gay Nineties. D'you know it?'

'I don't know London at all well.'

'Used to take Rosie there quite often. She liked it.' He went to the kerb, stood looking up and down the street. Rosie in his mind: and that merciless irrevocability . . . Muttering a curse — looking back at the French girl, shrugging: 'Going to get a bit damp —'

'Oh, how *terrible!*' Smiling, and turning up her collar. It had begun to rain, and naturally there weren't any bloody taxis.